Let Her Go

Dawn Barker is a psychiatrist and author. She grew up in Scotland, then in 2001 she moved to Australia, completed her psychiatric training and began writing. Her first novel, Fractured, was selected for the 2010 Hachette/Queensland Writers Centre manuscript development programme, was one of Australia's bestselling debut fiction titles for 2013, and was shortlisted for the 2014 WA Premier's Book Awards. Her second novel is *Let Her Go*. Dawn lives in Perth with her husband and three young children.

Also by

Let Her Go
More Than Us

let her go

DAWN BARKER

First published in Australia and New Zealand in 2014 by Hachette Australia

This edition published in the United Kingdom in 2021 by

Canelo Digital Publishing Limited
31 Helen Road
Oxford OX2 0DF
United Kingdom

A CIP catalogue record for this book is available from the British Library.

Print ISBN 978 1 78863 817 3
Ebook ISBN 978 1 911591 70 2

Quotes on pages 56 and 141 are from 'The Rime of the Ancient Mariner' by Samuel Taylor Coleridge. Quote on page 140 is from 'Mirror-role of Mother and Family in Child Development' in *Playing and Reality* by Donald Winnicott, Tavistock Publications (1971).

Printed and bound in Great Britain by Clays Ltd, Elcograf S.p.A.

To Isobel, Isla and Olivia

Prologue

Zoe turned to look out to sea. She hunched over so that her chin covered the head of the baby held against her chest, as if they were one being, as if she could make enough room for the child to simply melt into the space in front of her heart, where no one could ever take her away. Is that how it would have felt to have borne her? She wanted to lock Louise in a place where she could stay exactly as she was now, a baby, oblivious to the world around her, where she would know that Zoe would never let her go. It didn't matter about Zoe's sister, or even her husband, not when it was just the two of them.

She pulled her long grey woollen cardigan around Louise, huddled in the baby carrier. Zoe's hair whipped around her face, wet strands writhing in the blustering sea wind and clinging to her damp cheeks. She held the cardigan closed with one hand; with the other, she raked back her hair, twisted it and tucked it into the back of her collar. She knew she should take Louise inside, out of the wind, but here on the deck she could at least stare at the horizon and hope her nausea would settle. She didn't want to vomit. There was no one to hold the baby while she bent over and retched. Besides, she hadn't thought to pack spare clothes in her carry-on bag, and even the suitcase in the crate on the back of the ferry held only the few things she had quickly thrown in.

The ferry was lifted by a wave, then seemed to pause in the air for a moment. Zoe looked over the edge at the trough in front of them, deep and black. The boat began to tip forward. She grabbed the handrail as her stomach lurched; the boat rolled and slammed into the ocean's surface, the impact reverberating through Zoe's bones and teeth. She breathed through her mouth, trying not to smell the noxious engine fumes. Leaning her head back, she tried to breathe the fresher air above her, but the nausea rolled around her head and throat, threatening to spill over. The last time she had taken this ferry, years ago now, she'd thrown up all the way back to Perth into white paper bags, with Lachlan rubbing her back. The gagging had been tolerable then: it was proof, proof that the baby was there, inside her. The day the nausea had stopped should have been a relief, but she had known it was too soon, too sudden. Just one of her many failures to hold onto a child.

She focused on the horizon again, waiting for Rottnest to come into view. On a clear day, she could see it peeking over the edge of the Indian Ocean as she drove home from the city, travelling parallel to the long stretch of white beaches towards Fremantle. Some days, if the conditions were right, the island would shimmer, multiplying into two, sometimes three islands perched on top of each other, wavering in the blue sky. When they were kids, Nadia used to tell her that the mirage was a trick played by the spirits of all the prisoners who had died on the island over the years, frozen, starved, ravaged by diseases alone in their damp cells, or those who'd been eaten by the great white sharks when they tried to escape. Nadia would say it was the spirits' bait, their siren song to lure boats in and smash them on the coral reefs. She said that the prisoners' voices were trapped in the shells scattered on the island's beaches, and that if Zoe held one to her ear too long, she'd be cursed. Zoe used to lie awake on the bottom bunk of their holiday rental, sure she could hear them singing, chanting above the whispering of the waves lapping on the sand: hush, hush, hush. She'd cross her fingers, hoping that the skippers of all the boats out on the ocean would see the lighthouse, that they wouldn't end up wrecked in the bay.

The ferry pitched; Zoe grabbed the rail again. The metal was cold, slippery with spray. She moved her feet into a wider stance, trying to let her knees bend and sway with the boat, keeping her torso – and the baby – still. Holding the rail with one hand, she pulled Louise's pink knitted hat down more securely over her head. The ocean in front, behind, all around, seethed and churned. Even in summer, when the water was turquoise and calm, Zoe had never liked swimming too deep. She needed to be able to plant her feet on the bottom, on sand. Not in weeds that swayed with the tide, not on rocks that hid poisonous spines of fish and stinging tendrils of jellyfish.

She wiped her eyes with the back of her free hand; it came away damp, her tears lost in the drops of salty, sticky brine that coated her stinging cheeks. She looked behind her, through the glass doors, streaked with salt water, to the interior of the boat. There were only a few others there: a tall, thin man wearing headphones and a fluoro jacket, slouched in his seat staring out the window, nodding his head ever so slightly to the music in his ears; a middle-aged couple trying to take pictures through the window while the boat lurched; a woman with dark curly hair pulled tightly off her ruddy face, chatting to the ferry attendant near the bar.

Zoe stumbled again as the ferry reeled to the right. Was that port or starboard? Lachlan would know. She corrected herself: Lachlan *would* have known. It had been so long now since he'd gone out to fish or to pull the craypots.

Facing ahead, she watched the island come closer: the white beaches, the jetty, the lighthouse. Patchy sand swirled in the wind and was strewn over rocks jutting out from the shore. Zoe wanted to cry out for someone to help her. She didn't want to be here on her own. But what else could she do? She took a deep, shuddering breath. Anyway, she wasn't alone, she reminded herself, she was with Louise. Her daughter. *Her* daughter.

The ferry slowed and manoeuvred towards the jetty. Zoe staggered back inside, holding her breath against the musty smell of permanently damp seats, then teetered down the steep steps to the ferry door. She waited behind the tourists as the attendant let down the ramp, then walked carefully down the slippery gangplank with one hand on Louise's back. The wind roared; Zoe shivered. To her left, the beer garden of the wharfside pub was empty, the plastic chairs turned upside down and tilted against the tables. She looked back towards the ferry and watched the staff unloading a bundle of newspapers and magazines, the corner of a paper cover flapping against the plastic cord holding the sheaf together. They unloaded crates of beer and wine, bottled water, bread. Bicycles.

Zoe swallowed and looked towards the mainland. On the skyline she could see the colossal red cranes at the port of Fremantle and the Norfolk pines of Cottesloe Beach, where she'd stood so many times in summer to watch thousands of swimmers leap into the water to swim the twenty kilometres that the ferry had just travelled. Lachlan had done it once, one of a team of four. She thought back to his face yesterday: the hatred in his eyes, his clenched jaw as he stood over her. Did he even know she was gone? Probably not; he'd assume she was still at her parents' house. What would *they* think when they realised? And Nadia? Would they try to bring her back? Zoe tried to quell her fear, reminding herself that they didn't know where she was.

She took her phone from the back pocket of her jeans and glanced at the screen. Lachlan hadn't called. She told herself that she was relieved, but what she really felt was disappointment. She clenched her fists, feeling her nails dig into her palms. She was not going to be one of *those* women, making excuses for their husbands. He had ruined everything: now Nadia had what she needed.

Zoe hoisted the nappy bag over her shoulder, and for a moment rested her cheek on the top of Louise's head, feeling the scratch of her woollen hat. Darling Louise. Nadia was not going to take her away, not now, not after everything they'd been through.

She watched the luggage being loaded into a van, one of the few vehicles on the island; they'd deliver the bags later. Zoe started up the slope towards the visitor centre to collect the keys for her rental. She squeezed her eyes shut, hoping they weren't too swollen or red. *Oh yes*, the staff would say when someone came looking, *there was a woman with a baby, on her own. She'd been crying*. Taking a deep breath, she increased her stride. No one would think to look for them here. She just needed some space, some time to work out what she was going to do. About Lachlan. About Nadia.

About Louise.

Chapter One

Three years earlier

Zoe stood on the front step of her parents' house, staring at the two floating helium-filled balloons tied to the door handle. Inside, she could hear the rhythmic beating of music pierced by laughter and the clinking of glasses. They were late.

'You OK?' Standing beside her, Lachlan squeezed her hand slightly.

She clutched him tighter, but didn't move. 'I don't think I can do this.'

'We don't need to stay long, we'll just show our faces, then we'll go home again. I promise.' He let go of her hand and put his arm around her.

Zoe nodded, then closed her eyes for a moment. If she didn't go in, there would be too many questions later. She opened her eyes again, looked up into Lachlan's face, then tried to smile. He smiled back, then pushed open the door. Inside, the narrow hallway was lined with even more balloons, distorted *60*s stretched on the taut blue metallic skin, each string weighed down by a book. Her mother must have gotten the idea from a magazine. Zoe stepped in, swatting at the balloons as they drifted towards her face. Lachlan followed her and closed the door behind them.

The music was Paul Simon, of course, her stepfather's favourite. With each thump of the deep bass, her body vibrated. The noise seemed to rattle through the hollow of her pelvis, as if it was something more solid than sound. She wanted to turn around and run, but instead she shuffled down the hallway towards the party.

When they emerged into the kitchen, Zoe forced herself to smile and wave at her mum. Rosemary had been to the hairdresser: her ash-blonde hair barely moved as she put a tray of sausage rolls down on the kitchen bench. She spotted Zoe and Lachlan, and raised her hand and smiled back. Zoe had an urge to run to her and tell her what had happened, but her mother had already turned away and was gesticulating to the two teenage waitresses. Besides, this wasn't the right time.

Lachlan's hand was in the small of her back; she kept walking through the open-plan kitchen to the lounge room. All the furniture had been pushed to the edges of the room, and the patio doors were open onto the timber deck, which was thick with people.

Lachlan leaned down towards her ear. 'Do you want a drink?'

Zoe nodded, then stood still as he went to find one, not trusting herself to be able to walk without Lachlan by her side. One drink wouldn't hurt, not tonight.

People pushed past her, a few saying hello. She heard herself responding, as instinctual as breathing. Lachlan came back, a beer in one hand, a glass of champagne – of all things – in the other. She took a sip, then a gulp, grimacing at the bubbles popping in her mouth. She drank another mouthful, then followed Lachlan out onto the deck.

Her stepfather, Martin, stood by the barbecue, holding long tongs. His nose was red and shiny in the glare of the deck lights, and his cheeks were flushed. Someone spoke to him and he threw back his head and roared with laughter. Zoe smiled, genuinely this time. He was wearing the apron with the image of a bodybuilder's torso on it that she and Nadia had given him one Father's Day. He was sixty now. Zoe couldn't imagine herself at sixty. She mightn't make it that long; if she did, who would come to her party? Her parents would be dead, probably, in another twenty-four years. She would have no children. No grandchildren.

Shaking off her maudlin thoughts, she gulped down her drink. Tonight was about Martin. She put down her empty glass, laced her fingers through Lachlan's, walked towards Martin and touched his arm.

'Happy birthday.' She stood on tiptoe and kissed his cheek, then took the shiny silver parcel from her handbag and handed it to him.

'Hi!' Martin cried. 'How long have you been here? Thanks!' He put down the tongs and started to open the parcel.

'We just got here. I hope they're OK, I didn't know...'

Martin grinned and moved the open box from side to side so that the cufflinks caught the light. 'Zoe, they're great!'

She smiled. 'Are you sure, I—'

He put his arm around her and kissed her forehead. 'They're perfect.' He looked at Lachlan, then clasped his shoulder. 'Lachie! Great to see you! When did you get back from Kalgoorlie?'

'Happy birthday, mate,' Lachlan said. 'I just got in last night, I'm back for a couple of weeks.'

'That's good timing! I'm glad you could make it. You got a beer?'

Lachlan held his up. 'Got one here!' He looked around the garden. 'Good turnout.'

As Martin and Lachlan chatted, Zoe let the noise around her fade out. Lachlan didn't have great timing at all. Yes, he'd made it back in time for the appointment with Dr Patel this morning, but he'd been away so many other times in the past few years when she had needed him. What about the times she'd woken up barely able to move because of her joints burning, her face swollen, a livid rash scalding her cheeks, and knowing that it meant the lupus had flared up again? Or the times when an ache in her abdomen had sent her running to the bathroom, praying that she wouldn't see streaks of blood on the toilet paper, but knowing that she would? While grief had torn through her body, he hadn't been there. Yes, he'd offered to come back early, but in the next breath told her that he didn't want to tell the guys on the mines what was going on, and that someone else would have to cut short their own time with their wife and kids to take his place. So, the last time, Zoe had told him not to come back; after all, it wasn't like she hadn't been through it before, she'd be OK. But she hadn't meant it.

'Glad you like them,' Zoe said to Martin, even though he wasn't listening any more, busy talking to Lachlan. She took the box from him. 'I'll put these inside.'

She walked back into the house, taking another drink from a waiter's tray as she went through the kitchen and down the hall to her parents' bedroom. She opened the door and slipped inside. The room hadn't changed in years, and standing there, on the edge of the dark red Persian rug, looking at the grey floral bedspread that she remembered from when she was a kid, she felt uneasy. Her parents' bedroom had always been off-limits when she and Nadia were children. The door was kept closed; it had been her mother's space. Martin always had work at the bank to escape to, or golf, or the pub, while her mum had tried to gather the pieces of two broken families and hold them together. It couldn't have been easy for her, marrying a widower and raising another woman's child as her own, especially when Nadia's mother's photograph still sat on the mantelpiece. And then later, when Zoe was diagnosed with lupus at the age of fifteen, her mother had been the one who dragged her to appointments, who slept by her bed, who forced her to take her medication when she refused because it made her fat and gave her acne. Zoe blushed at the memory of how she'd treated her mother back then, and took a deep breath. There was no point thinking about that now. That was the past. She put the present on Martin's bedside table, next to a pile of thrillers, then left the room.

In the hallway, she closed the door and took another gulp of her drink. Her cheeks were warm; the champagne had gone to her head already. Suddenly, she felt completely adrift. She needed to find Lachlan. Her breath quickened. She should never have left his side, not for a moment. He loved her, she knew that, but would he still want her now? There was nothing wrong with *him*. He could have children with someone else if he wanted to.

She started to hurry back towards the party, but stumbled in her heels. 'Shit!' Her shoulder banged into the wall and her drink splashed out of the glass. She wanted to let herself fall, curl up in the corner and wail.

A small voice said, 'Are you OK, Aunty Zoe?'

Zoe looked down. 'Oh, hi, Charlotte. Silly me, I almost fell! How are you?'

'Good.'

Zoe kneeled down so she was at eye level with her seven-year-old niece. 'You've got a pretty dress on.'

Charlotte looked coy but smiled and held out the skirt of her green dress. Nadia always dressed her children beautifully. Zoe wanted to reach out and give the little girl a cuddle, stroke her wavy brown hair, but she didn't trust herself not to break down.

'Where are your brother and sister?'

Charlotte shrugged.

Zoe put her hands on her knees and stood up again, then held onto the wall to steady herself. She shook each of her legs to get the blood flowing again. 'I'll come and play with you later, OK?'

Charlotte nodded then ran back towards the two other bedrooms, where Violet and Harry must be playing. Zoe wished she could just sit in the doorway, unobserved, and watch them. But she knew she couldn't bear it.

When she reached the living room, Zoe couldn't see Lachlan through the crowds on the deck and couldn't face trying to push through everyone. She walked back into the kitchen and poured some white wine into her empty champagne glass; to look busy, she started tidying up the bench. She wouldn't stay much longer. There would be a cake, and a speech, then she could go.

She felt a tap on her shoulder and slowly turned round. She knew exactly who it was by the scent of her perfume. 'Nadia. How are you?'

Her stepsister wore a navy-blue dress, silk or something, tied at the waist. Her face looked smooth, with perfectly straight eyeliner and shiny lip gloss. Her light brown hair was sharply cut in a bob, with fair streaks framing her face. Zoe shifted her shoulders back and brushed at a grease spot she suddenly noticed on her top. People used to say that she and Nadia looked alike – although that was unlikely given that they didn't share any genes. But no one would think they were related any more. Yes, Zoe's medication had made her gain weight, drained the colour from her skin and darkened her eyes with shadows, but she knew the cause of her worn appearance was more than physical. Grief had spilled out into her bloodstream and left its mark on the outside. She drank some of her wine and stood up straighter.

'I'm great,' said Nadia. 'How are you? Is Lachlan here?'

'Yes, he flew in last night. He's out the back having a drink with your dad.'

'Is he back for long?'

Zoe shrugged. 'The usual. Two weeks on, two weeks off.'

Nadia wrinkled her nose in sympathy.

'Where's Eddie?'

Nadia gestured around her in a vague way. 'Don't know, he's here somewhere. Probably on the phone; he came straight from work. Sometimes I think of Lachlan's job and wish Eddie did fly in, fly out, too. It must be hard when he's away, but at least when he's back he's at home all the time, you know? Eddie seems to work constantly, every day, then he's out to dinners or on the phone all night, or emailing…'

'Must be hard,' Zoe said curtly.

Nadia frowned.

Zoe shook her head a little, then sighed. 'Sorry. I've just had a shit day. Do you want a drink?'

'I'd love one, but I'll have to drive so I better not. I don't know how long the kids will last, and we've got a birthday party tomorrow morning, one of Violet's little friends…'

Zoe let her go on a bit longer about how busy she was. There had been a time when she had loved to listen to Nadia talk about everything to do with being a mother, a time when she'd dreamed of experiencing it too. But now, she didn't want to hear about how exhausted Nadia was. God, what Zoe wouldn't give to experience that, to be part of that world. But what could she say?

She knew she was going to cry. She put her hand on Nadia's arm, interrupting her mid-sentence. 'Sorry, I need to go to the loo. I'll see you later.' Before her stepsister could say anything more, Zoe spun around and walked away.

–

A couple of hours later, Zoe watched her mum rummaging in the kitchen drawer. The cake was iced in white, and sat on a chopping board covered with aluminium foil. There was a blue plastic *6* and *o* on the top, with a miniature decoration of a golf bag. Thin blue candles were arranged evenly around the outside, though Zoe could see one that leaned slightly towards the edge of the cake. A bit of heat from the flames, just enough to soften the icing, and it would fall off. She realised she had laughed aloud; her mother looked up at her and frowned, then beckoned her over.

'I can't find the matches, God knows what Martin's done with them. Does Lachlan have his lighter?'

'Thought you didn't approve?' Zoe didn't approve either, not when they'd had so many problems. But now, what did it matter?

'Zoe! I'm not approving of him smoking, I'm just trying to light these damn candles!' Rosemary's cheeks were red, her lips tight.

'It's in my bag. Hold on.'

Zoe came back with a lighter and handed it to her mum. Rosemary flicked her thumb against the metal wheel, did it again, then rubbed her thumb with her forefinger and shook her head. Zoe leaned against the fridge, waiting for her to ask. Rosemary tried again, then glared at Zoe.

'Do you want me to help you, Mum?'

'Of course I do! Don't just stand there and watch!'

Zoe took the lighter; in one movement, the flame appeared. 'Would you like me to light them too?'

Rosemary narrowed her eyes. 'Yes. Please. How much have you had to drink?'

Zoe raised her eyebrows, then lit each of the candles, trying to keep her hands steady.

'Thank you,' said Rosemary. 'Now, could you turn out the lights?'

'Certainly.' Zoe walked to the light switches in the hallway and turned them all off. Someone turned the music off. There were a few squeals and shouts, then the chatter died down as Rosemary began to sing: 'Happy birthday to you…'

The room filled with singing: booming male voices, simpering old lady voices, tuneless, high-pitched kids' voices. Zoe just listened, and her eyes filled with tears. She blinked and watched the blur of the candlelight as her mother carried the cake from the kitchen towards the back of the house, then outside, where Martin was still manning the barbecue. An image popped into her head of her mum tripping, of the cake falling, the icing and sponge splattering all over the floor, the flames teasing and licking their way across the floor to the fringes of the beige rug and climbing up the skirt of the sofa. She shook her head and focused her vision again. Martin was blowing out the candles. The singing had stopped; the *hip-hip-hoorays* had started. Someone put the lights back on, and Martin started to speak. Zoe wished she could run over to him, and that he'd pick her up like he used to when she was a little girl, and make it all better. She was drawn towards the patio.

Nadia was there, beaming up at her dad with three-year-old Harry in her arms, his blond head resting on her shoulder and his tiny arm around the back of her neck. His dark eyes were wide open, though rimmed with red. Zoe swallowed and turned her attention back to Martin. Seeing her, he gestured with a flick of his head for her to come over, then kept on talking. '… and my beautiful daughters…'

As Zoe reached him, he put one arm around her, and the other around Nadia, still holding Harry. Rosemary stood just to the side of them, with one hand on the head of each of Nadia's little girls. *What a perfect picture*, Zoe thought, as a flash went off in her eyes. But of course it wasn't perfect. Zoe saw, as if it was a solid mass, the vast, gaping space where her own children should be. Her arms ached and her neck muscles strained with the weight of emptiness. If she saw the photo that had just been taken, she was sure there would be a ghostly white outline in the shape of a child below her knees, like an old Victorian daguerreotype, or perhaps three tiny dark shadows over her heart. The babies she'd lost. *Lost.* As if she'd misplaced them, been careless. If she could have clutched onto them any more tightly, held them inside until they were strong enough to survive, she would have given up anything.

She turned her attention back to Martin, who was finishing his speech. The crowd clapped and whistled, then returned to their drinks and conversations as the music came back on. Zoe slipped away.

Her feet ached; she sat on the limestone wall of the raised garden beds around the perimeter of the garden. The lawn was littered with the crimson petals of the flame tree in the corner of the garden, in full flower. A plant tickled the back of her neck, and the spicy tang of basil wafted around her. She let her head loll back and looked up at the sky, at the stars of the Milky Way pulsating behind the high, smoky clouds. She felt a wave of nausea and tasted sour champagne in the back of her throat. Her eyes went out of focus. Covering her face with her hands, she bent forward, putting her head on her knees, wishing the dizziness would stop.

'You OK?'

Zoe slowly sat up. She cleared her throat and peered to her right: Nadia again.

'Yeah.' Zoe looked back down at her knees, pursed her lips and exhaled slowly.

'A bit too much to drink?' Nadia asked, sitting down beside her.

'No. I'm just hot.'

Nadia nodded as she stretched her legs out straight. 'Dad seems to be having a good time.'

'Mmm.'

'So, how've you been?'

'You know, the same.' How could she tell her sister? It would break her heart too. They'd always talked about how their children would be close, imagined long afternoons drinking tea in the garden while the cousins played together at their feet. Now, it would never happen. 'How are you, Nadia?'

'Yeah, you know, I'm OK.' Nadia sighed. 'I'm tired. Really, I feel a bit stuck. Eddie's so busy with work, it's like I'm running an army camp, getting everyone ready and out the door in the mornings...'

Zoe gripped the stem of her wine glass. Nadia put out a hand and touched Zoe's arm. 'Sorry, that was insensitive of me.'

Yes, it bloody was insensitive. But Zoe reminded herself that Nadia didn't know what Dr Patel had said this morning. No one did, except Lachlan. Zoe's mouth was dry; she needed some water. 'It's OK.'

Nadia tilted her head to the side and spoke softly. 'Any more luck on that front?'

'No.' Zoe's cheeks burned. *Not now, Nadia*, she wanted to say. *Leave it alone.*

'Well, there's plenty of time – you're young, you've been pregnant before, there's no reason why it can't happen again. And I guess with Lachlan away it might be hard to get the timing right, if you know what I mean.' Nadia smiled and raised her eyebrows.

Zoe glared at her sister. This wasn't the time for jokes, innuendo. The pressure of the day, of the weeks and months that had built up to this moment, to nothing, grew and grew until she was sure she would scream. 'Do you know what, Nadia? Not everyone wants to be like you! You're so boring, so fucking boring, all you talk about are your perfect kids and your wonderful husband and how damn busy you are running around after them all. What happened to you? What do you actually do? Is this what you wanted for yourself, what you dreamed of when you went to university?'

'Jesus, Zoe! I was trying to help!'

'Oh, here we go, that's your excuse for everything, you were just trying to help!'

'I was just asking how you were, I didn't mean anything! Forget I asked.' Nadia stood up, looking hurt and confused.

Zoe stood too, but she had jumped up too quickly; her head reeled. As she took a step to steady herself, she stumbled over a handbag on the ground. Her wine glass dropped onto the wall and smashed into jagged shards around her as she fell to her knees. She looked around: eyes glinted through the dim light, as though there was a pack of nocturnal animals, watching her, waiting. The world was still spinning; her lip began to quiver. 'Sorry,' she whispered. 'It's just... Sorry...'

The music still played. Nadia's face was red; Zoe knew that her sister was about to cry. She saw Eddie striding towards them in his work pants and shirt, holding Harry, who was reaching for his mother. Zoe squeezed her eyes shut and opened them, letting her own tears spill out, then stood up. The tops of her feet were sticky with drops of wine. What was she doing here? She should never have come out tonight. She let her arms hang, her body drained, then sat heavily on the wall again. Rosemary had appeared with a dustpan and brush and was crouched over the broken glass on the ground.

Zoe looked up at Nadia and spoke quietly. 'I'm sorry. I didn't mean to take it out on you. But... we've tried. We've done everything we can. We can't – well, *I* can't – ever have kids.'

Nadia's mouth opened. Eddie was hovering by her side; she waved him away. 'What do you mean?'

Zoe laughed, ignoring her runny nose and the tears dripping down her cheeks. She hadn't planned to talk about this, not tonight, but now she wanted to tell Nadia everything. They used to share so much, but Zoe had pulled away from her over the past few years and the distance between them had grown. But now, she needed someone to know how she felt, so she could stop pretending; someone to prop her up. 'I've lost three babies. Pregnancies. Two more after the one you know about. The last one almost a year ago. We've had all the tests. We went to see the obstetrician today, but there's nothing else we can do.'

Nadia sat down next to her, and clasped Zoe's hands in hers. 'Why? What did he say?'

'They can't do anything. It doesn't even matter why I kept miscarrying, because the investigations show now that I'm in early menopause, so there's no way I can get pregnant again. He said it's probably because of one of the medications I took when I was younger for the lupus, but it might just be a coincidence and I have the worst luck in the world. Anyway, my rheumatologist said my kidney function is worsening, so even if I could get pregnant, it would be too risky for my health to carry a child. So it's over. That's it.'

'Oh, Zoe. I'm so sorry.'

Zoe couldn't look at Nadia. She knew Nadia would be crying too; when they were children, they were always so sensitive to each other's feelings. Zoe hated to think that she had upset Nadia, but she was glad she'd said it out loud. She took a few deep breaths while Nadia held her hand. She was calmer now. She wanted to go home.

'You OK?' said a male voice.

Zoe looked up: Lachlan was in front of her. He smiled sadly at Nadia, then crouched down and spoke quietly, tenderly to Zoe. 'Let's go, yeah? Why don't we go home? I'll run you a bath, and we can have an early night.'

Zoe could only nod. He gently helped her to her feet. Then he put his arm around her waist, and led her through the crowd to the front door, supporting her all the way.

Chapter Two

Nadia woke to the sound of Harry calling from his bedroom. 'Mummy,' he wailed. 'Mummy!' She sighed and picked up her phone from her bedside table: it wasn't even six yet. She propped herself up on one elbow and lifted the blind above the headboard. The sun was already up and the summer heat was beginning to build. She let the blind clatter down and lay on her back in her knickers and an old, soft singlet. She had kicked off the sheet during the night. Turning her head to the right, she looked at Eddie, his puffy jowls, his doughy belly, the thick dark hair creeping down his neck towards his shoulders. He was lying on his back, head turned away from her, pretending he hadn't heard Harry. God, she used to think he was so sexy. But he had thought the same of her once, and look at her now. She tried: she went to the gym, had her hair cut at nice salons, dressed well, but Nadia knew she looked like a mother of three, not the young woman she was when they had met. She saw the mothers of the kids' schoolmates at the gym, the hair salon, the shopping centre, and was always shocked to see how middle-aged they looked, as she knew she looked just like them. In a way, she cared more about impressing them than Eddie.

She closed her eyes, hoping Harry would drop off to sleep, but he called out again. She sighed loudly. Eddie rolled away from her, onto his side; clearly he had no intention of getting up. At least he wasn't hungover; they hadn't stayed at the party much longer after Zoe and Lachlan had left. Nadia had tried to pretend that everything was OK, for her dad's sake, but she couldn't just switch off after being told such awful news. She'd told her parents what Zoe had said, of course; they'd seen all the commotion. Nadia's eyes filled with tears. Poor Zoe. It wasn't fair: she'd been through enough. But the world didn't work like that, did it? There was no one up there distributing good and bad luck, deciding when one person had had enough to bear. Zoe would have made a great mother. And Lachlan would have been a brilliant dad.

Zoe had been right last night: Nadia had been insensitive to carry on about her own problems when she didn't have any, not really. Perhaps her life was getting stale, boring even, but she wasn't unhappy. Life couldn't be everything you dreamed of, could it? She glanced at Eddie again. He was just a man, a person – like her – with his own faults, but so many wonderful qualities too. He loved the kids, and her, and he provided for them. What more did she expect?

'Eddie?' She touched him lightly on the shoulder.

'Hmm?'

'Are you awake?'

'Yes,' he mumbled, without moving.

'What would you have done, if it had been me?'

He sighed and rolled towards her. 'What? If what had been you?'

'If it had been me who couldn't have children. What would you have done?'

He reluctantly opened his eyes and blinked hard. 'I don't know. I've never thought about it.'

Nadia's voice wavered. 'Would you have stayed with me?'

He draped his arm over her. 'Don't be silly. Of course I would have.'

Nadia nodded, then inched closer to Eddie until her head was touching his shoulder. What if *he* had been infertile? She couldn't imagine her life without the children. She remembered how it had felt when the desire to be pregnant flooded her, when she envied every expectant woman she saw, when she thought about nothing else but having a baby. Would she have made an excuse to leave Eddie, acted terribly so she could pretend that it was the relationship that was flawed rather than him? Or secretly found another man who *could* give her children? She and Eddie had been married for ten years now, and all they seemed to talk about was Charlotte, Violet and Harry. What happened when the edges of a relationship frayed and there were no children to stitch it back together? What would her life be like now if it was just her and Eddie?

Empty.

Harry cried out again from his bedroom. Feeling a flush of guilt, Nadia forced back her irritation and sat up. At least he could call for her. Yes, she was sleep-deprived, but she was also incredibly lucky. She jumped out of bed and hurried towards Harry's room.

-

Zoe woke to the screeching of rainbow lorikeets from the grevillea tree in the front yard. The noise scraped through her head as if the birds themselves were clawing at her brain and pecking the back of her eyes. It was too hot; her skin was clammy, her heart was beating too fast, and each pulse brought with it a wave of pressure. Her stomach churned and her mouth filled with saliva. Beneath the nausea, her abdomen was painfully empty. She considered getting up for some paracetamol and fresh water, but the thought of standing and walking to the bathroom was unfathomable. She hated her body for failing her, for being so frail. Trying not to move her head too quickly, she reached slowly for the glass on her bedside table. She brought it towards her lips: it was empty. She could have wept.

Lachlan wasn't in bed. Zoe heard the faint sounds of music videos coming from the television in the living room. He was always up early when he came back from the mines, still conditioned to the rigid shifts that controlled when he slept, ate, worked. She wanted to call out to him, ask him to bring her some water, to lie next to her, to cry with her, instead of carrying on as though this was just another Saturday, but didn't want to ask for his help. He should know that she needed him. She was sick of this life, of being on her own all the time. What kind of relationship was it when her husband was six hundred kilometres away from her for half the year? Yes, when he was away, they talked every day on the phone, but over time the calls had become briefer, more practical, less emotional. She would open his mail, and ask him what bills he wanted her to pay. She'd tell him what she was having for dinner, or that the washing machine was leaking, and he'd tell her to call a repairman. But so much of a relationship was about the things unsaid –

the looks, the gestures, the sensing of a mood. The little things: bringing your husband a cup of tea; interrupting each other on a Saturday morning to read out pieces from the weekend papers. When all that was reduced to a five-minute phone call each day, in snatched moments between Lachlan's shifts and her work at the hospital, what kind of marriage was it?

She moved her head slowly and propped herself up on her elbows. She hadn't drunk that much last night, had she? But then she hadn't eaten. Or slept. Her face burned as she remembered blurting everything out to Nadia, smashing a glass, crying. She had made an idiot of herself. A hot, clammy sweat came over her. She nodded her chin to her chest and closed her eyes, and let the tears fall as she lay back down on the pillow.

She must have dozed off. Some time later, she woke to the sound of one of the wooden drawers grating as Lachlan pulled it open. 'What are you doing?' she croaked.

'Sorry,' Lachlan whispered. 'I thought I'd go for a run.'

'A run. Now?'

'Yeah, I won't be long.'

Zoe sat up, ignoring the pounding in her head. Lachlan pulled his running top over his head then put his phone into his armband. She didn't want him to leave. 'But it's too hot to run.'

Lachlan sat on the end of the bed and pulled on his socks. 'I'll be OK. I thought you could do with a sleep-in.'

'I'm awake now. Don't go.'

He stood up and ground one foot into a running shoe. 'I won't be long, then we'll go out to breakfast.'

'Aren't you going to say anything? About last night?'

He sighed, then looked at her. His shoulders slumped. 'I don't know what to say.'

'Was it that bad?' she whispered.

He walked over and sat next to her on the edge of the bed, then gently swept her hair off her forehead. 'It wasn't bad at all.'

'Do you think everyone's talking about me?'

'No, of course not. No one even noticed – the music was so loud you could barely hear people when they yelled in your ear!' He smiled, then leaned down and kissed her forehead. 'Don't worry about last night. You did nothing wrong. The only person who heard what you said was Nadia. She'll understand. Anyway, who gives a shit what people think? We've got nothing to be ashamed of.'

She couldn't help but smile. Dear Lachlan. He always knew how to make her feel better. It wasn't his fault he had to go away so much. 'OK. Go for your run. But could you do one thing for me before you go?'

He frowned. 'Of course.'

'Can you get me some water and painkillers?'

He smiled again, hugged her tight and murmured into her ear, 'Of course. I love you. Everything will be fine, I promise.'

–

They went to a local cafe in the back streets of Fremantle, away from the tourists. Zoe wasn't hungry, but managed to stomach some toast and two flat whites. She tried, during breakfast, to be pleasant. Lachlan talked the whole time, about anything and everything: property prices, the other people in the cafe, the weather. She knew he was trying to make her feel better, to make jokes and laugh and smile, but she didn't want to pretend this wasn't happening to them. She wanted to talk about it, to dissect every detail, to make him open up and tell her exactly how he felt about it, about her.

She didn't want to go straight back home afterwards. Lachlan drove north along the coast road, along stretches of white beach fringed by the Indian Ocean. Zoe stared out of the passenger window at the towering dunes covered with ugly plants with tentative footholds in the shifting sand. Across the road, in front of the showy houses, were parched verges, with shrivelled grass, crisp from weeks without rain. She hated the Western Australian summers, the relentless heat and the hot wind that whipped bare legs with stinging sand. Sweat dripped down her thighs beneath her baggy shorts; she turned up the air-conditioning and slumped down in her seat so that the cold air blew on her.

'You OK?' Lachlan said.

'I'm so bloody hot.'

'Is the vent open properly?' Lachlan leaned towards her and began to fiddle with the air-conditioning.

'Yes!' Zoe said, swatting his hand out of the way. 'I'm not stupid, I know how to work it!'

Lachlan put his hand back on the steering wheel. Zoe looked at him and saw him raise his eyebrows.

'What, Lachlan?'

'Nothing.' He looked straight ahead.

'Just say it!'

'Say what? I'm fine!' He shook his head.

'I don't need you to be angry with me!' Zoe's eyes filled with tears.

'I'm not the one who's angry.' Lachlan indicated right and slowed down as the traffic lights turned red. He looked over to her, then groaned. 'Oh, Zoe, don't cry…'

She shook her head and turned away from him, feeling pathetic. 'I just feel like… like it's all my fault.'

Lachlan put his hand on her leg. 'Babe, don't be silly.' The lights turned green; he put his hand back on the steering wheel.

'You don't sound very convincing.'

'Jesus, Zoe, what do you want me to say? I'm upset too!'

'Well, why don't you say anything, why are you just driving the car like nothing's happened? You never talk about anything important, then you disappear back to work. It's all right for you: you can go up there and forget about me for two weeks. I've been through hell, all on my own!'

'You're not on your own—'

'Yes I am! You're not here for me, who else is there?' Zoe was sitting upright now, spitting the words at Lachlan. She knew she was hurting him, she knew she was being hysterical, but she wanted him to feel as bad as she did. A part of her wanted to push him until he stopped being so nice and admitted that he blamed her.

'You have so many people who love you. Your friends, your parents, Nadia…'

'She can't understand. No one can.' Zoe slumped back in her seat, exhausted. Tears fell down her face; she didn't bother to wipe them away. She could see Lachlan reflected in her passenger-side window. He was staring straight ahead, but his eyes flicked towards her every few seconds.

'We'll be OK, Zoe,' he said softly. 'It's not the end of the world. We'll get through this.'

She spoke quietly. 'How? How can we get through this? I've pictured it for so long: our baby, us as a family. Haven't you? All our friends have kids. How can I look at them without hating them for what they have? Everything has changed now, every single plan I had for us, for the future.'

'We've still got each other, Zoe! It's you I love. Let's just give it some time, then see how we feel. As Dr Patel said, there are other options. There's adoption—'

'I want my own baby. Our baby.' She turned away again. Lachlan just didn't get it. He hadn't felt the thrill of knowing there was a tiny life starting to grow inside him. He couldn't understand her despair at knowing she'd never give birth, never go to mothers' groups and swimming lessons and school coffee mornings. He said it wasn't the end of the world, but he didn't understand: it was.

–

They drove in silence for the next half hour, then turned around and drove south again. Lachlan parked the car in the street outside their house. He was silent for a moment, then he turned off the engine, sighed and opened the door gently. Zoe swallowed and climbed out too, then walked towards their home.

She had loved this place when she'd first seen it: an old dockworker's weatherboard cottage, the cladding white-washed except for the chequered exposed brick around the sash windows and the dark green door. But today it looked tired, faded in the harsh midday sun. Zoe looked up at the blue sky, squinting despite her sunglasses. She longed to hear the clatter of rain on the tin roof again. She wiped her forehead with the back of her hand and pushed her sunglasses back up her nose.

Leaning over the iron gate, she lifted the latch and pushed it open. Lachlan followed close behind her. The gate creaked as it swung closed, then shut with a clang. She walked up the steps to the wooden verandah and waited for Lachlan to unlock the door. When they had bought this house, she had imagined herself sitting out here, with a drink, at the white wrought-iron table on warm summer evenings, but the whining mosquitoes and the acrid stench of sheep urine from the animals packed on the ships in the harbour had driven her inside. The grevillea tree screened them a little from the people who walked along the pavement to the cappuccino strip, but it also littered the ground with old red flowers that gave her a rash when she touched them.

Zoe swatted away a blowfly that buzzed around her face, and followed Lachlan inside. She closed the door quickly behind her and immediately switched on the air conditioning.

As she walked along the dull, scratched jarrah floorboards of the hallway, past the two bedrooms and the tiny bathroom towards the small living room and kitchen at the back of the house, she reminded herself that they didn't have room for a child anyway. The spare room was full of clothes, surfboards, junk that they had nowhere else to store. She put her handbag down on the beige laminate benchtop of the kitchen, a previous owner's ugly renovation from the eighties. When she and Lachlan bought the house, they had laughed at the decor and vowed to do it up. But three years later, they had done nothing. There had always been something more important to worry about. And now she was used to it. You can get used to anything, she knew that. You habituate, no longer notice the things that were once so important.

She collapsed into a chair at the small wooden table squeezed into the centre of the kitchen where she'd imagined making pancakes with her son or daughter one day. Despair welled up in her chest. She clutched her head in her hands.

Lachlan put his hand gently on her shoulder. 'Do you want some lunch?'

'We just ate.'

'Oh. Yes.'

She knew that he was trying to do something, anything, to make her feel better. 'I'd love some tea,' she said, trying to smile at him.

Lachlan sighed. 'Zoe. I'm so sorry.'

She looked down. 'You've got nothing to be sorry for.'

'I'm sorry that I haven't been here, that you've had to deal with so much of this on your own.'

'It's not your fault.'

'I'll look for a different job. One that's based here.'

'No. Don't be silly. We need the money.'

'We can manage.'

Zoe shook her head. They both knew there weren't many jobs for mining engineers in the city. Although now they wouldn't be having a baby, now she didn't have to give up nursing, maybe they could survive without the extra money he got from working fly in, fly out.

Lachlan walked over to the bench and stood near the fridge, staring at the kettle as if he didn't know what it was, his arms hanging by his side. His face was red, but as he looked down from the kettle to the floor, Zoe could see the pale skin on the back of his neck where the desert sun didn't reach. She walked over to him, stretched her arms around him and they held each other.

After a few moments, Zoe helped him make the tea, then they went through to the living room together and sat on the couch, staring at a chat show on the television, a story about a woman addicted to plastic surgery, who had spent thousands fixing her non-existent problems. If only it was that easy to go into hospital and come out with what you really wanted.

Lachlan put his mug on the coffee table, then leaned back and put his feet up. Would they be doing this exact same thing, sitting here – just the two of them – with cups of tea in front of the television for the rest of their lives? Zoe picked up her own cup, walked back along the hallway to their bedroom, and closed the door.

The bed hadn't been made, as usual, but today she couldn't stand it. The quilt lay in a lumpy heap at the end of the bed, and the sheet that they had slept under was tangled and knotted, probably still damp from the sweaty night. She started to straighten the sheet, then pulled it off, bundled it up and threw it into the corner of the room. Every single drawer of the chest was pulled open, like a skewed staircase. She slammed them closed.

She sat down on the bare mattress, then, keeping her feet on the floor, lay back and covered her face with her hands. All that she could remember from her teens was being the sick girl who was treated differently by everyone. Over the years, she'd learned to live with it, but now to know that it had also taken any chance that she had of being a mother…

Zoe sighed. What could she do, except get used to this too?

Chapter Three

Lou giggled as she turned back to look at the car. Her laugh seemed to echo through the quiet street; she clasped her hand over her mouth, and glanced around, but saw nothing to worry about. The engine and headlights were off, but she could just hear the muffled laughter of the others from inside. She dangled the bunch of keys in the air, and heard her friends cheer. She brought her index finger up to her lips, hunched over theatrically, then tiptoed to the front door of the surgery. Nobody would be there, she knew: it was after eleven on a Saturday night; they wouldn't be back until Monday. And even then, she doubted anyone would notice. They never had before.

She hesitated, holding the key millimetres from the lock, then glanced back at the car again. It belonged to Theo's mum – he was in the driver's seat. The passenger seat, where Lou had been sitting, was empty. For a moment she wanted to run back over and jump in, swig some red wine and have a drag of the joint to take this edge off. How many pills had they taken? She laughed at herself – was it out loud? Not enough, that was the answer. Astrid and Ben were sitting forward in the back seat, their hands waving wildly as they chattered at Theo. Lou took a deep breath, unlocked the door and walked inside.

The alarm began to beep, quietly. She knew she had thirty seconds to switch it off before it would escalate and alert the security company. Her fingers trembled as she moved them towards the display; dexies always gave her the shakes. She wasn't nervous, not really. She knew the code: it hadn't changed since her mum had started working here, years ago. Lou typed it in, pressed enter, and the beeping stopped. She let out a breath, grinned, then poked her head back out of the doorway and gave her friends the thumbs-up. She heard them all cheer inside the car again; she wanted to run over and hug them all. They understood each other so well, they were like her family – no, *better* than her family.

She turned back inside, stuffing her mother's key ring into the back pocket of her skinny jeans. She wouldn't put the light on; she knew where she was going. In the doctor's office, dimly lit by the streetlight outside, she opened the top drawer of the desk and found the small key for the filing cabinet. It unlocked easily. She pulled open the filing cabinet drawer, screwing up her face at the grinding noise and clunk as it stopped at full extension, then paused for a moment in case anyone came running to investigate. No one did. She took another deep breath. She should have made Astrid come in with her. Her stomach knotted and her pulse quickened; she wanted to get out of here, get back in the car with the others. She thought about her bedroom at home, her own bed, her parents asleep in the next room, thinking she was safe, at Astrid's place. Maybe she could just go back outside and say she couldn't find anything, that the drugs must have been used up or moved; then they could just go home and tomorrow they could go to the movies or something.

She thought of Theo again, waiting outside in the car, waiting to spend a few more hours – the night – with her. She was just being paranoid. The drugs did that sometimes, gave her this feeling, this edginess as she started to sober up. She was here now, and she knew that soon it'd all be better. Lou reached into the open drawer and riffled through the cardboard sample boxes. She knew what she was looking for. Not the antidepressants – they'd tried those and they did nothing except make them dizzy. Here they were: the ADHD drugs. There were six boxes, each with four pills in them. She couldn't take them all. Two boxes were enough: one for her and Theo to share; one for Ben and Astrid. Before she could change her mind she grabbed them, slammed the drawer shut and locked it again.

Then she stopped.

The sallow glow cast by the streetlamp outside had been replaced by red and blue lights that rotated silently around the room. Lou closed her eyes for a moment, hoping it was a hallucination, but she could still see the lights pulsing through her eyelids. She heard a car start and the screech of its tyres as it sped away, a car door opening, then closing, and footsteps clip-clopping across the car park to the front door of the building where she was now trapped. Voices yelled. The lights went on; Lou couldn't move, but saw herself as if she was the officer about to walk through the doorway: a thin, bedraggled teenager, too much make-up, drunk, high. Stealing amphetamines. Her hands began to shake as she desperately tried to think of what she could say to get out of this. When she heard the voices at the doorway to the office – one male, one female – she knew it was all over and there was nothing she could do. She hadn't even had the sense to drop the boxes of tablets into the bin or kick them under the desk. Lou suddenly felt very sober. Sick. She sank down to the floor and waited.

–

Lou sniffed as her dad drove up the driveway. He hadn't said a word on the journey home from the police station; her mum hadn't even come with him. All Lou wanted to do was to go to sleep and wake up somewhere else, in someone else's life. Or take off. Her parents wouldn't understand, they never had. In between her bouts of tears, she kept thinking about how Theo and her so-called friends had abandoned her to save themselves, leaving her to look like a junkie when she was doing it all for them. She hoped they were hiding somewhere, terrified in case she had told the police about them. She should have, but she wasn't like them: she stood up for her mates.

As the car stopped under the carport, she tried to open her door, but the child lock was on. She tried the handle again, letting it whack back against the door, then again.

'Lou! For God's sake, just wait!'

She glared at her father, then slumped back in the seat and waited for him to walk around and open the door from the outside. He held it open, waited for her to get out, then slammed it shut. She walked about a metre behind him to their front door, then followed him inside. She thought about turning around and running; maybe then he'd do something, say something. Or maybe he wouldn't. Maybe he'd just let her go and lock the door behind her.

She followed him down the hallway to the kitchen. In the doorway, she hesitated. Their golden retriever, Sandy, bounded over to her, wagging his tail; Lou bent down and tangled her fingers in Sandy's thick coat as she watched her dad walk towards the sink and fill the kettle. Her mum, in her dressing-gown, was sitting at the kitchen table. She looked up at Lou, shook her head a little, then dabbed at her eyes with a damp tissue. No one said anything. Then her mum gripped the edge of the table, pushed herself up and stared at Lou. Lou's face got hotter and hotter. She wanted to run over to her and lean into the fluffy gown, while her mum kissed her head and stroked her hair. Instead, she stood still while her mum pushed past her, out of the room and along the hallway. Her dad leaned on the grey granite kitchen bench with his back to her as the kettle started to boil.

'Sorry, Dad,' Lou mumbled, trying to keep her voice steady.

He nodded but didn't look up.

'Is Mum OK?'

She saw the muscles in his jaw tense. 'What do you think?'

'Dad?'

'Just go. Go to bed. I can't talk to you right now.'

Lou pressed her lips together, trying to stop her bottom lip from quivering. She wanted him to make her a Milo and let her drink it beside him on the couch while he watched TV, like they often did when she and her mum had fought. But he only took one mug out of the cupboard, and one tea bag. Lou hung her head and walked out of the kitchen and along the hallway towards her room with Sandy padding after her.

In her bedroom, she closed the door behind her. The room was as she had left it before she went out. Clothes were piled on her unmade bed, and shoes lay on the floor in front of the mirrors of her built-ins along the wall opposite the door. Her desk, underneath the window, was piled with books and folders, homework that she had to finish tomorrow. After a few minutes, she heard her parents talking in harsh whispers. Her mum must have gone back to the kitchen. The kettle slammed into its base, spoons clattered on the benchtop, the fridge door thudded. Lou sat cross-legged on her bed; she patted the space next to her and her dog jumped up beside her. Lou wiped her face, and her hands came away smudged with black eye make-up. *Be quiet!* she wanted to shout. *Stop fighting, go to bed, please, sleep.* Because she couldn't sleep until they did, couldn't shut them out; all she could think about was what they were saying about her, and why they didn't shout at her instead of each other.

She turned on her iPad – no doubt it would be confiscated tomorrow when they remembered – and started streaming a music video. She wanted to turn it up loud to drown out their bickering, but she also needed to know when they stopped. They were forgetting to whisper now: her mum's voice was getting higher, her father's deeper, though their words were still unclear. Lou brought her hand to her mouth and started to scrape off dark red nail polish with her front teeth, spitting out the little chewed-up balls onto her bed. Then she bit her nails until they were down to the quick, and started gnawing on the skin around them. She told herself to stop but couldn't pull her hands away. Tears fell quickly now, and her head hurt. She needed a drink of water. How did they expect her to sleep like this? With all this noise? Her skin was so itchy; she began to scratch at her neck, her arms. Her jeans were too tight: she couldn't get at her legs. She put her hand down the neck of her t-shirt and scratched at her chest and under her arms. But she'd bitten her nails too short; there was no relief from the itching. She rubbed at her face as the noise around her continued: music, shouting, slamming, crashing, pounding in her head. She squeezed her hands into fists as hard as she could, but it wasn't enough. Her whole body was agitated now. She knew what she needed to do.

She got off the bed, went to her bookshelf and took out the big hardback dictionary that her grandparents had given her for her last birthday, two months ago. Opening it at C, she took out the thin, sharp razor blade that she kept there for emergencies, for times exactly like this. As she looked at it her breath quickened in anticipation. The tension inside her body, her muscles, her head, was building, building, peaking, but she knew that in only a few moments she would release it, let it all out, and sink down, down, down…

Chapter Four

Zoe ran down the escalators to the ground floor of the shopping centre. She could see Rosemary sitting at a cafe table on the floor of the mall. Zoe would rather they sat inside where she didn't have to watch all the mums pushing their babies in strollers with toddlers running alongside. The centre was new, all silver and white and glass and metal, high ceilings and touch-screen maps, but the shops were the same old high-street chains that you found everywhere. Zoe reached the bottom of the escalator and hurried past a nail salon where Vietnamese girls scurried around the silk-scarved middle-aged women having pedicures.

Just before she reached the cafe, Zoe paused and looked in the window of a luggage shop. Her face looked OK in the reflection, but it would probably still be blotchy in the daylight. Her mother would certainly notice. She reached into her bag and pulled out a lip gloss that she'd got free with a magazine. The colour wasn't right, but she put it on anyway. Moving into her mother's line of sight, she waved. Rosemary smiled and waved back.

'Hi, Mum. Sorry I'm late.' Zoe leaned down and kissed Rosemary's cheek, then put her bag on the floor and sat down.

'I haven't been here long, it's fine.' Rosemary waved her hand dismissively, her plum-coloured nails catching the light.

Zoe smiled and sighed. She knew her mother would have been here for at least ten minutes, and probably longer.

Rosemary picked up the cardboard menu and scanned it. 'Do you want anything to eat?'

Zoe shook her head. 'Just a coffee.'

'You look like you need it.'

Zoe shrugged. 'I didn't sleep very well last night. Where's the waitress?' She looked over her shoulder to break her mother's stare, and caught the eye of a young, red-cheeked girl, who smiled and came over to their table.

Once they had ordered, Zoe turned back to her mum and said quietly, 'I'm sorry about the other night. The party.'

'Oh, love, there's nothing to be sorry about. *I'm* sorry we were all so preoccupied and didn't realise what was going on. How are you feeling?'

Zoe's face heated up and her eyes prickled with tears again. She blinked hard and looked away. 'I'm OK. Anyway, I hope I didn't ruin it.'

'Of course not. No one even noticed!'

'Did the rest of the night go well?'

Rosemary smiled. 'Well, Martin and Uncle Mark ended up drinking whiskey and singing a duet at two in the morning, so I'd say so!'

Zoe smiled as she pictured her stepfather. She hated to think that she might have ruined his special night. Martin never seemed to let anything worry him, although Zoe knew that it must be a veneer. He had lost his first wife, Hilary, to cancer when Nadia was only an infant. Zoe had always wondered how Rosemary had managed to deal with the emotional repercussions of taking on a traumatised widower and his young daughter. Of course, Martin had taken *them* on too: Rosemary, scarred from divorce; and Zoe, a toddler who missed her father. That was different, though – her dad was estranged, but still alive, living in Sydney and full of flaws. But Hilary's memory was held sacred.

The waitress returned with their coffees. Rosemary smiled and shifted the menu and sugar bowl to the side to make room for their drinks. When the waitress had gone, Rosemary shook her head and tutted. 'Half my coffee is in the saucer.'

Zoe sighed. 'Well, you should have said something.'

'What's the point? The prices they charge for some coffee beans and milk, they should employ someone who knows what they're doing.'

'She's probably studying law or medicine, and doing this on the side in the holidays. Maybe she recognised you from university and has a grudge against you…' Zoe tried to joke, aware as she said it that neither of them was in a jovial mood. Rosemary worked in the university library, and there were still a few weeks before the new semester started.

'It doesn't matter if this isn't her career. She should still take pride in her work.'

Zoe sipped her coffee, stopping herself from reacting to the phrase she'd heard so many times before. Even when Zoe had been sick, Rosemary had always made her try her best, reminded her that she must always be proud of herself and everything she did. Zoe knew it had been her mother's attempt to prop up Zoe's self-esteem. What Rosemary had never said aloud, though, was that there had never been much for Zoe to be proud of. Nadia was the one whom everybody admired: clever, pretty. Healthy.

Rosemary wiped her saucer and the bottom of her cup with a napkin, then took a sip. She cleared her throat. 'Zoe, I'm so sorry to hear about… well, you know…'

Why didn't she say it? 'About not being able to have a baby?'

Rosemary nodded, then reached across the table for Zoe's hand. 'I was so shocked, we all were. It breaks my heart.' Her eyes filled with tears and she took another napkin from the metal dispenser on the table.

Zoe pressed her lips together. She had barely been able to contain her tears for the past few days. At home, she had let herself go: she cried, she shouted, she screamed. What did it matter if she wallowed in it? She had taken sick leave from work, and let herself lie on the couch all day and watch television while poor Lachlan begged her to talk to him. But she had hoped that being out, doing something normal, might make her feel better. She needed to hold it all together here. She shook her head quickly, then pressed her fingers to her temples. 'I can't talk about it now, Mum, sorry.'

'I know, darling. It's OK.'

Zoe drank her coffee just for something to do. It wasn't OK though, and that was what was so awful. She had never understood how much she wanted children until the doctor had told her that she couldn't have them. Perhaps it was only because she *couldn't* that she now felt so desperate. She'd spent her life having to relinquish control to other people, to her illness. Not a week went by without hearing about someone who'd beaten the odds: run a marathon after shattering their spine; swum the Channel after having limbs amputated; been cured of an incurable cancer. But this wasn't a case of showing determination; there was no miracle waiting for her around the corner if she only fought harder. If only. It was luck, bad luck. Fate.

People would always wonder why she had no children. She had done the same in the past when she'd met childless couples. She'd pitied them, imagined their distress at miscarriages or failed fertility treatments. She supposed some couples were childless by choice, but couldn't really imagine that now. After all, who doesn't really want to have children? What would people think of her? What would she tell them?

She breathed out. 'Sorry, it's just hard for me to talk about.'

'So there's nothing they can do, nothing at all?'

Zoe shook her head. 'No. Nothing.'

'What about adoption… ?'

'I don't want someone else's child. And…' Her voice dropped into a whisper. 'I want a baby, Mum. I want my *own* child. I wanted Lachlan and me to have a baby of our own, one that looked like us, that was made of parts of us.'

Rosemary leaned forward. 'But you'd soon think of an adopted baby as your own.'

Zoe's voice rose. 'I wouldn't. Every time I looked at the child I'd know that its mother was crying somewhere, wondering where her son or daughter was. You'd have to be desperate to give up your baby, or a terrible mother.

And I don't want a child who's scarred by that loss, who has something missing. Even an infant knows his mother, and that would never be me. It's like our family: you must feel the difference between me and Nadia, don't you?'

Rosemary paled, but she said nothing.

'Oh, Mum, I'm sorry, I didn't mean to put you on the spot.' Zoe had overheard Rosemary telling Nadia many times that she was as much her daughter as Zoe, but Zoe had always assumed that it wasn't true.

'It's OK. What about surrogacy? You hear about it all the time now. Didn't that actress, what's her name—'

Zoe shook her head again. 'It still wouldn't be my child – my body isn't making eggs any more.'

'People donate their eggs – I've been reading about it. Or you can buy them overseas.'

'Mum, we're talking about a baby. I can't just… buy one from China or Thailand or wherever, like a cheap handbag.'

'I'm just saying it's an option, darling. At least the baby would be Lachlan's.'

'Lachlan's and someone else's! That would be worse.' Zoe had thought about it, but feared that she might never be able to love a child who reminded her of her failings every time she looked at it.

'Just give it some time. You might change your mind. You do come to think of children as your own, even when you didn't give birth to them, I promise.'

Zoe nodded. Her mum was right: in the midst of this thick, cloying grief it was impossible to clear her eyes and her head and her heart; she couldn't rule anything out. But how could she and Lachlan adopt a child, with him away all the time? Zoe would need Lachlan's support to care for a child who'd been torn from its mother, and that support was part-time and distant even now. And if he was a part-time and distant husband, then it was better that he didn't become the same type of father. But it was too hard to explain all these things to other people. There was no point in talking about it, not even with her mother.

'Thanks, Mum.' She had finished her coffee now, and took it as an opportunity to change the subject. 'Hey, I might go and see a movie this afternoon, do you want to come?'

'Sounds great. Something funny, yes?'

Zoe smiled. 'Definitely.'

–

'Here you are.' Nadia handed a glass of white wine to Rosemary. 'Dad, you still OK for beer?'

'Yeah, I'm good thanks,' Martin said, smiling.

Nadia poured herself a glass then sat down on the wooden garden chair next to Eddie. She sipped her drink and reached for an olive from the tub on the table. The girls were inside playing dress-up, and Harry was right next to the adults, in the plastic clamshell sandpit. She leaned back and let out an exaggerated sigh. 'That's better,' she said. 'It's good to see you both here. I know it's a long drive.'

'Part of the attraction of living in the hills, eh?' Martin said, smiling.

'Yes, for me, but Eddie gets a bit fed up with commuting an hour to work every day, don't you?' Nadia nudged Eddie.

'Yeah,' he said. 'It's a bit tiring.'

'I think he likes the peace and quiet of the drive, a good excuse to stay away from the kids.' Nadia winked at her dad, then leaned into Eddie. 'Only joking.'

Eddie raised his eyebrows.

'I texted Zoe in case she wanted to come over too, but she didn't reply,' Nadia said.

'How is she, Rosemary?' Eddie said.

'Oh, I don't know. I had a coffee with her today, then we went to a movie. She's putting on a brave face, but she's not good.' Rosemary shrugged. 'You know what she's like. She doesn't like to talk about things.'

'Did you get any more details from her?' Nadia was frowning. 'Is there definitely nothing that the doctors can do?'

Rosemary shook her head. 'I called Lachlan too this afternoon, just in case... well, sometimes you don't take in all the information at medical appointments when you're upset. But he said the doctor was definite. They can adopt, or use a surrogate. That's it.'

'Shit,' Eddie said. 'Do you think they will?'

Rosemary sighed. 'I don't know. Zoe's adamant that she wants her own baby. She kept saying that adopted kids would have problems.'

'She's probably right,' Nadia said. She'd worked with enough disturbed kids – before she had her own children – who'd been through the child protection system to know that it wasn't easy for them, or for the families who took them on.

'But she'd cope, she's a kids' nurse!' said Martin. 'What better person is there to adopt?'

'Yeah, but Dad, it's not easy. By the time a child's been fostered in dozens of families, not to mention the abuse or neglect that got them there in the first place, they've often got issues.'

Martin moved his chair back into the shade, which had shifted as the sun dropped lower. 'But not all kids up for adoption have been abused or neglected, love. Maybe their parents have died or something.'

'That's still a huge trauma for a kid, Dad.'

Martin nodded, then looked down at his feet. Nadia watched him out of the corner of her eye. He never spoke about her mum. But she knew he still thought about her, particularly at moments such as this. She knew he wasn't looking at his shoes, the tiny green shoots of onion grass sprouting up between the patio bricks, the trail of ants tramping across the ground. He was seeing Hilary. Did he see Hilary as his young wife, happy, vibrant, laughing? Or did he see her in her final days, fading in a hospital bed? Nadia wished she could remember her mother. She glanced at Rosemary and her face flushed with guilt. Rosemary had always been there, trying to fill the space left by Hilary's death, but despite her best efforts, had never quite succeeded.

'Martin. Could you pass me the chips, please?' Rosemary's voice was a little too loud, her smile strained.

Martin looked up, startled, then slid the bowl over the table towards Rosemary.

Rosemary took a chip, ate half of it, then spoke. 'Anyway, Zoe won't hear of it right now, but I think surrogacy might be her best option.'

'Surely the process would be just as complicated as adoption – more, even,' Eddie said, frowning.

Rosemary shrugged. 'It happens all the time these days. I was reading about it in a magazine last week, a gay man bought eggs from Thailand and then used two different surrogates in India and got twins!' Nadia noticed Rosemary glance at her before she continued in a casual tone. 'The problem is, it's illegal to pay someone to act as a surrogate here, so she'd need to find someone who'd do it for altruistic reasons, or else go overseas, which is very expensive.'

'I can't imagine many people would volunteer to do it,' Martin said.

Rosemary glared at him. 'I'd do it in a heartbeat if I could.'

Nadia shifted uncomfortably. 'Well, there's not much point in us talking about this. It's her decision, hers and Lachlan's. And, to be honest, it sounded to me like she was pretty final. I can't imagine them wanting to go through the stress of all that anytime soon.'

Rosemary wiped a drop of wine from the side of her glass with her finger. 'But just imagine, Nadia. Imagine that you never got to experience having Charlotte, or Violet, or Harry. How would that feel?'

Nadia flinched. She *had* imagined how it would feel, over and over. She didn't need to be reminded. She had spent her adolescence being told how lucky she was to be the healthy one who didn't have to be in and out of hospital or take medications with terrible side effects as her sister did. Nadia looked over at Harry, pottering around in the sandpit, and her face burned as she felt unmistakable relief that she wasn't Zoe.

'I can't imagine,' she mumbled. 'Oh, Harry, don't eat the sand!' She stood up and hurried over to her son so she didn't have to look at her stepmother and consider what she was suggesting.

–

'Daddy!'

Nadia looked up from folding the washing as Charlotte ran out of the room towards the front door. She saw the pink netting of her daughter's fairy dress disappear down the hallway, then heard her squeal and laugh as Eddie greeted her. Nadia picked up the piles of folded clothes from the couch, put them in the basket and balanced it on her hip as she opened the laundry door, then shoved it inside. She closed the door behind her, quickly untied her ponytail and combed her fingers through her hair, then surveyed the house. To her left, the kitchen wasn't too bad: an open carton of milk; coloured plastic plates with half-eaten muffins; the girls' lunchboxes next to the sink waiting to be emptied. In front of her, the ash dining table was covered with colouring books and pencils. The girls' schoolbags were abandoned on the floor, and Harry's toys were strewn around the room.

Eddie walked down the hallway carrying Harry in one arm, the other holding Charlotte's hand. Violet skipped along behind him waving her magic wand. Nadia couldn't help but smile at the joy on the children's faces at being with their father.

In the first few days after she and Eddie had heard about Zoe and Lachlan's infertility, they had felt a renewed closeness to each other, both consciously cherishing their relationship and the children. Their affection towards each other had seemed less cursory, more spontaneous, but as the weeks had passed, they had drifted back to routine. It wasn't just Eddie – Nadia was aware that she too had slipped back into the tangle of her children, her home, wishing each day would end so that she could have some peace, some time to herself. But she kept catching herself, reminding herself that this knot of children and chores that she was entwined in was what life was. And that no matter how tired she was, Charlotte, Violet and Harry made her laugh every day, and when their skinny, smooth little arms hugged her at bedtime, she knew that this life she had chosen, as a mother, was more important than anything else. And then she would think of Zoe.

Nadia had meant to call Zoe today, but had run out of time – again. In the first few weeks after the party, she and Zoe had talked every day, met for lunch, gone for long walks together while Nadia did what she could to support her. But more recently, Zoe seemed to be coping better, and Nadia had stopped making the effort. Her face flushed with guilt; she would definitely call Zoe tomorrow. She knew her sister would still be struggling.

'You're home early!' she said, as Eddie put Harry down.

Eddie nodded. 'I thought you'd be happy.'

'I didn't say I wasn't.'

'I thought I'd come back first. Dinner's not until eight.'

'Dinner?'

'Remember, I told you? I'm going out tonight. The guys are over from Singapore.'

'You didn't tell me. I wish—'

'Yes I did! I told you last week.'

He hadn't, she was sure. She didn't forget things like that. She spoke slowly, trying to stay calm. 'Well, I don't remember you telling me.' She pointed to the whiteboard on the kitchen wall, where she updated the week's activities every Sunday night. 'Maybe next time you could write it on the timetable.'

He raised his eyebrows, smiling a little.

Nadia shook her head and smiled back. 'Fine. I was going to get takeaway for us anyway. Take the kids outside on the trampoline for a while so I can get their dinner on.'

'OK, I'll just get changed.'

Nadia started cleaning up while Eddie marshalled the kids. What would happen if Eddie came home one night and she told him without warning that she was off to have dinner with friends? Why did he think that he could just make plans without discussing them with her? He assumed she had nothing better to do, that of course she would look after the children while he did whatever he wanted. It was his job: that was always his trump card. What could she say to that? He was the earner, he had to work, and that involved going out to dinner, making overseas phone calls late at night and early in the morning, and travelling around the world.

Eddie rarely said it out loud, but they both knew that Nadia had wanted to give up her job when they had children, so she had also given up the right to complain. She'd always planned to go back to work when Charlotte was six months old. But when the days and weeks rushed by and Charlotte grew before her eyes, the thought of leaving her in a daycare centre to compete with other babies for attention filled Nadia with fear. She was a psychologist; she knew how important that first year was, and having grown up without her own mother, she wanted to make sure that she and Charlotte had the relationship that she and Hilary had never been able to have. Eddie had been happy when she extended her leave: he liked her being at home, and they didn't need her income, not really. She'd planned to take another six months off, and then she'd go back, when Charlotte would at least be able to play a bit more independently, move around. But instead of enjoying the extra time with her daughter, Nadia had started to count down the months then weeks before she'd have to leave Charlotte with someone else. Anyway, she had wanted another child, so the best plan was to stop breastfeeding and fall pregnant again quickly, the perfect excuse to stay home longer. When she felt that familiar shift in gravity, that queasiness when she stood up, she had told her manager that instead of returning from maternity leave, she was leaving the workforce to look after her children. She hadn't wanted to be a working mum; being a mum was more than enough.

It *had* been what she wanted – still was – but sometimes she wished it was her who was rushing out the door to a morning meeting or a dinner, leaving someone else to deal with the chaos of the children. No, not someone else: Eddie. So that he understood what it was really like; so he wouldn't glance around the kitchen when he got home, and wonder what she'd done all day. How did other mothers manage to work *and* do all this – keep their house running and still spend enough time with their husbands, their children? It was more than that, though: how did they find enough energy to enjoy the time with their family, rather than resenting the moments children stole from their own need for space?

She closed her eyes for a second. What a bloody cliché she'd become – *they'd* become. But, she reminded herself, there was plenty of time for her to go back to work. And she had no right to complain: Eddie was a good dad.

She opened the fridge, took out the Pyrex bowl of marinated chicken pieces, and started to make the children's dinner.

When the children were finally in bed, Nadia cooked herself some pasta, ate it quickly in front of the TV, then tidied away all the dishes and made the girls' lunches for tomorrow. It was almost nine by the time she sat down again. Eddie would be halfway through dinner now, in some swanky restaurant with expensive wine. The kind of restaurants that they used to eat in together. Before children. She wondered who these clients from Singapore were. Were they women? Women who didn't have children yet, young women full of drive and energy and fun, women who drank and flirted and had something interesting to talk about with her husband? Nadia could picture him smiling in that way he did with his head tilted to the side and his dimples winking, looking coy, the way he used to look at her. In her imagination, though, he was putting his hand on someone else's shoulder, telling them that yes, he was married, but they had fallen out of love a long time ago. Nadia bit her lip. Was that the truth, the issue that she was skirting around, that they really had fallen out of love? But they hadn't fallen – they had trudged and stumbled and slowed to a halt.

She shook off the thoughts. God, what was wrong with her? When did she start losing the trust she'd had in their marriage for so long? No, she was losing trust in herself, in the identity that was drifting away, getting lost in the doldrums, *a painted ship on a painted ocean*. She used to be proud of herself, to love what she was doing, raising the children. But now they were growing up: Harry would be in kindy in a little over a year. Then what would she do?

She pushed herself off the couch and walked into the kitchen to make a cup of tea. She filled the kettle, switched it on, then off again. Opening the pantry, she looked at the case of wine – a fancy pinot, Eddie's favourite – on the floor, under the shelves. She stuck a steak knife into the tape that held the box closed and dragged it towards her. She pulled out a bottle, smiled as she twisted the top off, then filled a glass to the brim.

She checked the time on the oven clock, and then picked up the cordless phone and took her wine over to the couch before dialling Zoe's home number. It rang three times, and then the answering machine clicked on. Nadia sighed, then sipped her wine, swilling the taste of blackberries around her mouth as she listened to the automated recording telling her to leave a message.

'Zoe,' she began, 'It's me—'

'Nadia.'

Nadia jumped as Zoe answered. 'Oh, hi, sorry, did I wake you?'

'No, of course not. Just watching a renovation show.'

'Lachlan's still away?' Nadia asked, though she knew he was.

'Yeah. Another week to go. What are you doing?'

Nadia sighed. 'Oh, just the usual.' She recalled Zoe's accusations at the party. No, she wouldn't tell Zoe her own problems tonight. They were insignificant. 'Eddie's out so I'm just having a glass of wine by myself.'

'First sign, eh?'

Nadia smiled, picturing Zoe smiling too. 'How are you, Zoe? I'm sorry I haven't called you for a while, things just… well, I'm sorry.'

'Don't be silly. Mum's been making sure I have absolutely no time alone. Suddenly, she seems to be *in the area* an awful lot more than she ever was!'

Nadia laughed. 'I can imagine! But seriously, how are you holding up?'

'I'm fine, honestly. It's a bit harder with Lachlan away but in some ways it's easier, you know? Sometimes I don't know what to say to him. He's trying so hard to be positive. I know he's upset too but neither of us seems able to talk about it properly to each other. I know he's afraid he'll upset me.'

Nadia leaned back on the cushions, resting her glass on the arm of the sofa. 'It'll get easier.'

'I know. I just need to get back to some sort of routine, find something else to focus on.'

'But Zoe, don't be too hard on yourself. You're allowed to be sad, and angry. It's not fair. You're allowed to grieve, no one expects you to just shrug it off.'

Zoe's voice was thick and nasal. 'Thanks, Nadia. Good job I've got a psychologist for a sister!' She laughed and sniffed. 'See, there I go again, crying. But seriously, I'm doing OK, I promise. Thank you for checking in on me. I appreciate it, I really do.'

Nadia wiped away a tear of her own. Zoe always had to just cope with everything thrown at her, and she always succeeded. 'I wish I could do more. I'm here if you need me, you know that, yeah?'

'Of course. Thanks, Nadia.'

'Take care, and we'll talk soon. Maybe I'll take the kids over to see you on the weekend or something. They miss their Aunty Zoe.'

'That would be great.'

Nadia ended the call, then drained her glass and stared at the black flecks in the dregs of the red wine. She ran her tongue around her mouth and scraped her bottom lip with her top teeth. She pictured Zoe getting into bed in her empty house, Lachlan's side cold and empty, and knew that she'd probably cry a little, before falling into a fitful sleep.

Returning to the kitchen, Nadia refilled the glass, then put it down again and switched the kettle back on. She was lucky. Maybe her own marriage to Eddie wasn't the fairytale, but their story wasn't a tragedy either.

–

It was Friday again. Weeks had passed, each night much the same as every other, but Nadia hadn't been able to stop thinking about Zoe. She put on her yellow rubber gloves and squirted some dishwashing liquid into the sink, then swirled the water around. She leaned close to the sink as Eddie squeezed past her to fill the kettle. While he took out two mugs, she began scrubbing the baking tray. She stared at the bubbles. How many times had they done this exact same thing? Once he'd made the tea and she'd finished the dishes, they'd sit on opposite ends of the couch, drink their tea and stare at the screen. Eddie would choose what to watch; Nadia would get bored and go to their room to read until he came to bed.

But this evening, she needed to talk to him. Not just the usual executive summary of the day – the kids, the bills, the problems – but a proper discussion. She breathed out slowly through her mouth to calm her nerves. It wasn't that she was having second thoughts: she was sure she wanted to do this.

She took the clean tray out of the sink, rinsed it, then stacked it on the drainer. She turned around; Eddie was wiping down the benchtop. She cleared her throat. 'Eddie.'

'Mmm?'

'I need to talk to you.'

'OK.' He turned to the fridge, opened it and took out a carton of milk.

She took off the gloves and reached for his arm, speaking gently. 'Can you stop that for a minute?'

'Just a second.' He poured milk into each of the mugs, put the carton back in the fridge, then looked at her. 'Are you OK?'

She steered him towards the dining table and they both sat down. 'I've been thinking about something. We're so lucky, you know. We love each other…' Nadia smiled at him. He smiled back, though his brow was furrowed. 'We're happy, we've got three beautiful, healthy kids. Everything we could ever want, really.'

'Yes…'

Nadia made herself continue in the same even tone. 'I've been thinking about Zoe and Lachlan. You know, nothing seems to go right for them. She's been ill for years, Lachlan's always away, and now they can't have kids.'

'Yeah, it's a shame—'

Nadia held up her hand. 'Wait, let me finish.'

Eddie frowned. 'Go on.'

Nadia's heart was thumping now. Was she really going to say this? Do this? 'Well, she's my sister. And so I've been thinking, we're so lucky. I thought maybe I could do it for them.'

Eddie cocked his head to the side, then his eyes widened. 'Do what? Nadia—'

'Be her surrogate. Have a baby for her.' Nadia's mouth was dry. She had said it, and even to her own ears, it sounded outrageous.

Eddie opened his mouth but said nothing.

She hurried on. 'I've thought it all through, Eddie. I just have to carry the pregnancy, the baby, then we'll get back to normal. The pregnancy is the easy part, isn't it? It's the newborn stage that's hard, and that won't be something we have to deal with. It's just like babysitting, really – I'm just letting the baby grow in me, that's all. I promise it won't affect us.' She made herself stop, then watched him, her eyes wide, waiting for a reply.

He sighed; as he exhaled, his chin dropped to his chest as if he was deflating. 'Nadia… I don't know where to start. It's not that simple. My God, it would be so much more complicated… Think about the effect it'd have on you!'

'I'd be fine.'

'Being pregnant again? You hated being pregnant!'

'No I didn't! I loved it, I loved every moment of it.'

'No, you were exhausted all the time, sick for months. We've got three other kids to look after now…'

'Well, you can help, and I'm certain Zoe and Rosemary would babysit all the time if I did this! Is *that* what this is about? How it will affect you? That you'll have to help out more, be here in the evenings and spend time with me and the kids?' Nadia's eyes filled with angry tears.

'Of course it's not, but we're just starting to get our lives back to normal – you've been saying that too! The girls are at school, Harry'll be at kindy next year, and then you'll have some time back for yourself, to start working again, we can go on holidays…'

'Don't be so selfish! Who cares about going on holidays? Anyway, who says I want to go back to work?' Nadia grasped his hands, pleading with him. 'It just doesn't seem… *important* to me any more. I'm better at this, Eddie, at being a mum – surely that's more important than working! I can do this for Zoe, it's an amazing thing! Yes, things are getting easier now with our kids getting older, but Zoe can *never* have that! Never. Not unless I do this. Think about our life, about the kids, and how gorgeous they are, how funny, how amazing. There's plenty of time to go on holiday, but not for having children. This is her only chance.'

'Nadia,' he said patiently, still holding her hands. 'I think you're amazing for even thinking about it, I really do. But you're almost forty, we've got three kids of our own, and I just don't think it's as easy as you make it sound. Aren't there risks? Could you really give birth to a child, then hand it over? What about the children, how would we explain it to them?' He swallowed, then spoke softly. 'Nadia, this isn't your responsibility. You don't have to be the one to try and fix Zoe's life. They can adopt, or foster, or use someone from India or wherever. You don't have to do this.'

'I do, Eddie.'

Nadia thought back to what Rosemary had said, that she would do it for Zoe in a heartbeat if she could. Eddie was wrong: this *was* her responsibility.

–

'Don't push Harry so high, Charlotte!' Nadia shouted across the playground. Charlotte turned to look at her, laughing, her dark, defiant eyes flashing. The same eyes as her father. Nadia smiled and shook her head, then turned to Eddie, sitting next to her at the wooden picnic table. Charlotte went back to pushing the swing. Harry was laughing and holding his head back so the wind flew through his fair hair.

'Who do you think she gets that from?' Nadia asked.

Eddie smiled. 'I don't know what you're talking about. I was a good child.' He put his arm around her shoulders and squeezed. 'You OK? You didn't sleep well.'

She rubbed her eyes. 'I've got a lot on my mind.'

He nodded, but Nadia knew he wasn't going to bring it up again if she didn't. After their discussion last night, they had both retreated into their thoughts. Eddie had agreed to think about it; Nadia had thought she had made her decision, but hearing Eddie voice the fears she'd been pushing away had confused her. She could counter every argument he put up, but she knew his concerns were legitimate.

Last night, while Eddie had slept deeply next to her, Nadia had lain awake. After about an hour, she had got up and tiptoed into the children's rooms to watch them sleeping. She had thought again of Zoe, sleeping restlessly alone at home, with her husband away and no child to keep her company.

Now Nadia sipped at her takeaway cup. 'Where's Violet?'

Eddie pointed towards the climbing frame. 'There.'

Nadia nodded as she watched Violet clamber up a ladder in her bare feet. Always the quiet one, off by herself.

Such a serious little thing. As Nadia herself had been. She must spend more time with her. It was so easy to leave Violet alone to read or draw or dress her dolls, so easy to forget to ask if she was OK. Nadia looked down at her sandy toes peeping out of her tan leather sandals. 'Do you remember when Harry was born?'

Eddie turned towards her on the bench. 'Of course.'

'Do you remember how relieved we were to have three kids, all healthy? I remember turning to you and smiling and just sort of knowing that we were done. Our family was complete.'

'Yeah, of course. And not just them – my relief was about you too. You were healthy, safe. When each of the kids was born, I used to have this fear at seeing you there on the hospital bed, with all the monitors, in such pain. In case you didn't make it.'

Nadia thought about her mother. Hilary never got the chance to see her baby, Nadia, grow into a toddler, a teenager, an adult; to watch her sleep, to push her on the swing. She wished she could remember her. Sometimes she thought she did, but she was only an infant when Hilary had died, so she knew it was her mind trying to fulfil her wish, integrating photos she had seen with stories she'd heard. But though she knew it was impossible to remember her mother physically – her face, her voice, her touch – she also knew that memories weren't always visceral. They could be implicit, formed from intense experiences – like the fierce love of a mother – and held in the cells of our deepest brain structures. Nadia knew that Hilary was merged with her, the good and the bad – and it must have been bad, near the end. No matter how much love there was in that hospital room, there must also have been terror, a wrenching sorrow and regret. Nadia glanced at Eddie. How would he have coped with a little baby if Nadia had died like her mother had? Her eyes filled with tears at the thought of her father as a young man, left alone with only grief and an infant daughter.

Eddie put his hand on hers, drawing her back to him. 'You've forgotten how hard it was on you.'

'It wasn't that hard.'

'I just don't think you've thought this through.'

Nadia shook her head. 'You're wrong. I *have* thought it through. She's my sister, Eddie. What if it was us?' She raised her hand with the coffee cup towards the children. 'Can you imagine life without them? Why shouldn't Zoe get a chance to be a mum too?'

'Of course I can't imagine being without them.'

'Where would *we* be without them?'

'What do you mean?'

'Well, do you think we'd still be a couple?' To her frustration, Nadia heard her voice waver, and her eyes began to water.

'What?' Eddie frowned. 'Of course we would.'

'What keeps people together, Eddie?'

He cocked his head to the side. 'What are you talking about? Are Zoe and Lachlan in trouble? If so, that's even more reason not to go through with this—'

Zoe grimaced. 'No. Never mind. I just mean that kids are what makes a family, you know. And she's my sister, I just want her to have the same thing I do.'

Eddie stretched out his legs in the sun, splaying his toes. 'But maybe the fact that you're her sister makes it even harder. Wouldn't it be easier if she used a stranger, someone from overseas? That's what usually happens, isn't it?'

'She can't afford it – it costs a fortune. Zoe isn't some movie star who's left it too late to have kids. It's different. She deserves a child – not that those other people don't, but… Anyway, even if she did have the money, how can that be better than using me? We're not talking about a business transaction. This is a child. I hate the thought of her having to pay to rent someone's body part. How can that be good for the baby, or her? If someone is only in it for the money, how desperate must they be? They wouldn't have decent hygiene or nutrition if they have to resort to surrogacy to feed their own children!'

'I don't think it's that bad, love.'

'Well, who would carry a stranger's child if they didn't have to? What kind of motives would they have? It can only be about money. I don't trust anyone who'd want to make a profit from this. I want to give her a child because I'm family, and because she'd do it for me.'

'Would she?'

'Of course she would.' Nadia knew it was the truth.

Eddie rubbed his face. 'She hasn't got eggs, what—'

'We'd use my eggs, I'd go to the clinic and be inseminated. It's easier, cheaper, less invasive than donor eggs and IVF.'

'But then the child would be yours! It'd look like you, like our kids! What if when you saw the baby, you—'

Nadia put up her hand to stop him. 'I've told you, Eddie. I'm happy with three kids. I'm done, finished. It'd be her baby – and Lachlan's, not mine. I would know that from the start. People donate eggs and sperm all the time and know that their genetic child is walking around out there, but they know it's not theirs, not in an emotional way. I'd just carry it for her. I'd be the baby's aunt, that's all.'

Eddie lifted his coffee cup to his mouth and tipped it up. 'You're just telling yourself what you want to hear. What about me, seeing you pregnant with someone else's baby?'

'Oh, for God's sake. It's not like I'd have to have sex with Lachlan!'

'Jesus, Nadia! The kids then, what would you tell them?'

'The truth! I'm proud of this. It's a good thing to do.'

Eddie gripped her hand and looked straight at her. 'I know that. I don't doubt that it's a good thing to do. But I'm worried about you.'

'Don't you think I'm strong enough?'

Eddie raked his fingers through his hair, then leaned closer to her. 'Nadia, it's not that I don't think you're strong, it's just that I know how much you love being a mum, and I know how much you loved the kids from the minute you were pregnant. This will be too hard for you...'

Nadia blinked back tears, and nodded. 'It will be hard. I know that, Eddie. But it's what I want to do. It's just forty weeks of pregnancy, then it's over. What's a year out of our life? It's nothing, it'll go so quickly, but then Zoe will have a child forever.'

'But it's not just a year, is it?'

Nadia finished her coffee to give herself time to think. How would it feel to have a baby inside her again, kicking and prodding her? She would be sick, she would be tired, and of course she knew it would be difficult emotionally.

But Zoe had been sick, still was, and she hadn't asked for that. Even if they weren't biologically related, Zoe was her little sister. Family bonds weren't forged from blood, they were welded by shared moments, from intimacy, from vulnerability. She sniffed and took a deep breath. 'Let's go.'

Eddie sighed and picked up their empty cardboard cups. 'Let me think about it, OK?'

Nadia nodded as she collected her bag and three pairs of kids' shoes, then walked towards the swings. They could talk about it some more, but she knew what the right thing to do was. Some siblings gave each other a kidney, or their bone marrow; how was this any different?

Chapter Five

Zoe gave the driver a ten-dollar tip then slammed the taxi door behind her and hurried towards her house, grinning. She had almost called Lachlan from the pub, but resisted; this was something she needed to tell him in person. It was almost like telling him she was pregnant: it should be special. She laughed to herself – this *was* like telling him she was pregnant. She unlatched the gate and ran up the path to the front door. Her hand shook as she held the key up to the lock. Could this really work?

Zoe had been surprised when Nadia had called her and asked her to go for a drink tonight; they had been spending much more time together lately, and Zoe had enjoyed feeling close to her sister again, but Nadia rarely socialised in the evenings because of the kids and the long drive to the city. When Zoe had arrived, Nadia was already there, compulsively sipping her drink and drumming her fingers on the pockmarked wooden table.

'Zoe,' Nadia had begun in a hesitant voice. 'There's something I want to talk about.'

Zoe sat down and waited, a stab of anxiety going through her. But then Nadia spoke the words that changed everything.

'I'll do it.'

'Do what?' Zoe said, frowning.

'I've thought about it and done lots of research and considered all the risks and everything, and I've talked to Eddie about it. I'll have a baby for you.'

Zoe sat up straight and stared at Nadia. She shook her head quickly, and looked down, tears already springing to her eyes. 'No, don't be—'

'I want to, Zoe.'

Zoe fumbled in her bag for a tissue and dabbed at her eyes. 'No. We've talked about it, it's too hard. I'm just not meant to be a mother. I've accepted that now.'

Nadia reached out and took Zoe's hands. 'It's the perfect solution. I mean, we have to sort out all the medical and legal stuff, but I want to do this for you.'

Zoe lifted her hands out of Nadia's and covered her face, her whole body shaking. She couldn't take it in. Was Nadia serious? She slowly took her hands away from her face and looked at her sister, who smiled, then jumped up, walked around to Zoe and hugged her hard.

It had been one of the most amazing evenings of Zoe's life, in the bar, surrounded by music and laughter, seeing the earnest look on Nadia's face as they drank and talked about how, together, they would make this happen. But now, standing on the doorstep of her little house, in the dark, it almost felt as if it had been a dream. No, it *had* happened. Nadia really had offered to be a surrogate for them.

Zoe took a deep breath, turned the key in the lock and pushed open the door. 'Lachlan? Lachlan!'

She had a sudden fear that he wasn't home from soccer training yet and that she'd have to wait, but then she saw his kit bag in the bedroom doorway and heard the TV. She dropped her bag on the floor of the hallway and hurried to the back of the house.

Lachlan was sitting on the couch with his bare feet propped up on the coffee table, a bottle of beer in his hand. He wore an old, soft grey t-shirt and blue tartan boxer shorts. His dark hair was damp, springing up into curls, and she could smell the fruity scent of her shampoo. She gazed at him for a moment, and felt a wave of pity. He looked worn out. She'd been so self-absorbed, demanding that he support her, when he was also dealing with the knowledge that he'd never be a father. She recalled her accusations that he would leave her, and blushed; she'd been terrified about the inevitable day when he'd decide that he wanted children more than he wanted her, and angry at him for having the option to find someone else and have a baby. In some ways she had been pushing him, giving him an excuse to leave her now while she felt so low that another blow almost wouldn't matter. She had wanted him to voice the hatred she felt for herself. But she saw now that he was trying his best too, and she had pushed him away. He was kind, he was patient. He was her husband. He had told her again and again that he loved her long before they had thought of children, and that if it was a choice between her and a child, she won. But now, because of Nadia, he'd never have to make that choice.

Zoe walked to the sofa and squeezed in next to him, snuggling into his chest and breathing in the scent of his clean skin. She wrapped an arm around him.

Lachlan kissed the top of her head. 'You look happy! How was it?'

She pulled away a little, and grinned at him.

He smiled back at her, looking curious. 'Zoe? You're shaking! What's going on?'

Zoe opened her mouth to explain, but instead of the carefully crafted speech she had practised on the way home, the words just tumbled out. 'Nadia… she… she's going to do it, Lach, she'll have the baby!' She grabbed his hands.

'What?'

'She said she's been thinking about it, and she's talked to Eddie, and obviously we'll have to go to the doctor and do tests and see a lawyer and all that, but she'll be a surrogate for us! Can you believe it, babe, it's going—'

'Whoa!' Lachlan took his feet off the table and sat up straight. 'Hold on, hold on…'

'I can't believe it!' Zoe grinned, clutching his hands tighter, willing him to share her excitement.

But Lachlan was no longer smiling. 'Zoe! Calm down! We've already talked about this. We decided it was too complicated, too risky.'

'But that's the best part, babe. I didn't ask her – she just offered, out of the blue! She's thought about all the pros and cons, and she knows that she wants to do this for us. It's the perfect solution!'

He stood up, then paced around the room. 'Just wait! This has come out of nowhere! I just don't know… It's one thing for a stranger to do it, someone we'll never see again, but your sister…'

'It's better this way!' Zoe insisted. 'We can be part of it all, we're not paying someone, she's doing it because she wants to help us have a child. Her family is complete, she's healthy, and it means we don't have to go through all the stress and expense of doing it overseas. She can use her own eggs too, so the baby won't look like a stranger.' Why didn't he understand that this was the only way? She felt her excitement of the past few hours drain away, replaced by despair. Was this a ridiculous fantasy? She couldn't bear to lose this – her last – hope.

'But it'll look like Nadia, Zoe, not you,' Lachlan said softly. 'How will that make you feel?'

She shook her head. 'Don't, Lachlan – don't spoil this. The baby will look like *you*. And looking like her aunt is better than looking like someone random. I'd always wonder if an egg donor was going to knock on our door one day, looking for her child. This way, everything's kept in the family, everyone knows where they stand. Please, Lachie, please...' Zoe made herself breathe deeply. She had to stay strong here, to prove to him that she could cope with this. She knew it wouldn't be easy to watch Nadia carry a child for them. The image of a child with Nadia's fair colouring instead of her own dark hair and eyes had already gone through her mind, but she had pushed it away. 'Look, I know it will be hard. Our journey to being parents will be different from other people's. I know that, but this is the only way. What choice do we have? Nothing is ideal. What would be ideal is if somehow I didn't have this bloody illness and could have a baby myself.'

Lachlan sighed, shook his head uneasily. 'I want it as much as you, Zoe. It's just such a shock...'

Zoe tried not to sob. She knew now that this was what she wanted. Knew it utterly and completely. 'Please, Lachlan, think about it... We can trust her, be part of it all from day one, from now...'

Lachlan pursed his lips and exhaled. 'It's just the last thing I expected to hear. Just... don't get too excited, don't get your hopes up too much, please. We need to look into this properly. I need some time—'

'Time?' Zoe grabbed his arm, suddenly furious. 'Jesus, Lachlan, we've wasted so much time already! The time we've spent trying to get pregnant, the time we've spent hoping that I wouldn't lose a baby – again – the time I've spent crying and tearing myself up with anger and guilt. You weren't here the last time. You have no idea how it felt when I sobbed into the brick-hard pillow in the hospital, nurses barging in at all hours with their torches and needles and plastic gloves to examine me. I can't bear it, Lachlan, I can't imagine a life without children, being here on my own while you work away and all my friends have kids. This is my only chance, the only way for me to ever have a baby!' She stood up, glaring at him. What was there to think about? 'You haven't been here, Lachlan.'

'Oh, don't start that!' He gritted his teeth. 'That's always what it's going to come back to, it's my fault for not being here. It's my *job*, Zoe. I was in the middle of the bloody desert stuck in a donga. I said I'd come back, but you—'

'Alright, forget I ever mentioned the surrogacy idea, then.' Zoe let go of him, her cheeks burning.

Lachlan spoke quietly. 'Zoe, please don't be like that. I'm just saying that I need to think about it.'

'No, Lachlan, just forget I said anything. It's all right for you. *You* have a choice. *You* have time.' As soon as she said the words, she regretted them, but it was too late to take them back.

He looked at her, then looked down at the ground and shook his head.

'I'm sorry, I didn't mean that.' Zoe tried to keep her voice steady. This was not a time to fall to pieces, even if all her new hope was crumbling. 'It's just that this was meant to be the moment when our life got better. I thought you'd be thrilled.'

'Come here, please...' Lachlan stepped towards her.

Zoe shook her head, turned around, and walked out before she broke down in tears.

–

In the morning, Zoe was already awake when her alarm went off at five o'clock. She was on an early shift. Her eyes stung with the grit of fatigue. She stiffened when Lachlan patted her shoulder; she knew that he had slept as badly as she had.

He touched her shoulder again.

'What?' she mumbled, keeping her eyes closed.

'Can you switch that off?'

Zoe clenched her teeth. Flinging off the sheet, she sat up, then slapped the top of the alarm clock with the palm of her hand to silence it.

'What was that for?' Lachlan said, propping himself up on his elbows.

Zoe stared at him for a few seconds, then shook her head.

'Are you still angry at me?' he said.

'I'm not angry.'

'Really?' Lachlan raised his eyebrows, smiled a little. He relaxed back, put his hands under his head and sighed.

This was what he always did: smiled at her that way, then she'd smile back and they'd forget the argument, and things would carry on the way they always did. But not this time.

'Aren't you going to mention it again? Discussion over? So you get to decide and I have no say?'

He groaned. 'Zoe…'

'You're going away this afternoon, again. And then we can't talk, can we? And by the time you come back in two weeks, you're hoping I'll have forgotten about it. But I won't. This is not just your decision—'

'Or yours,' Lachlan said quietly.

Zoe stopped, nodded. He was right. 'OK. But it's not over. I want you to think about this. Properly.'

He turned onto his side, reached up and swept the hair off her forehead. 'I will. I promise. I'm sorry I have to go away at a time like this.'

Zoe's eyes filled with tears. 'Lachlan, I'm sorry if you think I've made my mind up. I was just so excited that maybe, finally, we could have our baby. I thought you'd be pleased too.'

'I know.' He kissed her cheek, wiped away the tears. 'I'm not saying no. I'm just saying that we need to slow down.'

Zoe reached out and put her hand on his chest. 'I know you're worried about me.'

'Zoe, so much could go wrong. I don't know if you – if we – can cope with any more disappointment. What's in this for Nadia? I can almost see why people would do it for money, but why would she put herself through all this?'

Zoe answered quickly, although she had wondered the same thing too. But she'd convinced herself of the answer. 'Because she's family, and she knows how much this means to me. And she'll be the – our baby's aunty, so it's perfect. She'll look after herself when she's pregnant, and she'll love the baby too.' Nadia did well at everything she did; she'd succeed at being a surrogate too.

'But maybe it'd be easier with a stranger, less complicated.'

Zoe shook her head. 'We've talked about this before! It's virtually impossible. We'd have to go overseas, it costs tens, hundreds of thousands…'

Lachlan closed his eyes for a moment. 'OK. Can you email me some stuff about it? I'll read it at work.'

Zoe gave a little smile. 'Of course. Just think about it, babe. Please. It's just nine months, and then we have our baby. So many couples can only dream of this happening to them. We *have* to say we've tried everything. Otherwise I'll always wonder what might have been…' She wriggled over and nestled her head into Lachlan's shoulder, then wrapped her leg over his hip. She inhaled deeply and began to kiss his chest. 'I love you,' she murmured. She kept kissing him, firmer and firmer, moving her lips up to meet his, until he pressed his body closer to hers and she knew that she could convince him.

Chapter Six

Zoe put down the phone, then forced herself to sit down and think. She pressed her palms on the kitchen table, but her fingers still trembled. More than three years had passed since they'd agreed that Nadia would be a surrogate mother for Zoe and Lachlan, and finally the baby was coming. Today.

It wasn't meant to happen yet; the baby wasn't due for another four weeks. Nadia had gone to a routine check-up with the obstetrician, but her blood pressure was too high, and she was on her way to the hospital. They needed to get the baby out. Today. But Zoe wasn't ready, and Lachlan wasn't due home for almost two weeks. Then the shock subsided a little, and a swell of excitement took its place. It made no difference whether she was prepared or if Lachlan was away: her baby was coming.

Zoe picked up the phone again and called Lachlan's mobile, but it went straight to voicemail. She scrolled through her contacts and found the site office number. It rang and rang, but no one answered. Zoe tried the mobile again, left a message, then sent a text message. She stood up, twisting her long dark hair into a bun and securing it with the hair elastic from around her wrist. She couldn't afford to wait for Lachlan to ring back; she had to get to the hospital. At least she had the overnight bag ready.

They had already agreed that she would stay with Nadia in her room after the birth so she could bond with the baby while Nadia breastfed to establish her milk supply; in preparation, Zoe had packed toiletries and clothes for herself, and pink outfits for the baby.

She thought back to the day of the scan when they'd found out the baby's sex. Eddie hadn't come; it was just Zoe, Nadia and Lachlan. Nadia lay quietly on the bed in the scanning room with her top hiked up while the sonographer ran the probe over her pregnant belly. She had wiped away a tear as the grainy images appeared on the screen on the wall, then turned her head away. Zoe had squeezed her hand, but Nadia had brushed her off, then sat up, wiped the jelly off her abdomen and pulled down her top. The sonographer had printed out the strip of black-and-white ultrasound images, then held them out to Nadia. They had all paused, and the sonographer blushed, mumbling that she'd print out a second set. Nadia had nodded, reached out her hand for the photos and stared at them; Zoe's heart had pounded as she waited for her copies. That was how she had felt for the whole pregnancy: like an outsider hovering over her sister, waiting to be invited into the experience. She took a deep breath; it didn't matter now. Her baby girl was coming, and this would be behind them.

–

Half an hour later, Zoe was driving to the hospital, grateful for the quiet midday traffic. She knew exactly where to park, thanks to the hospital tour she'd taken with Nadia, just like any other expectant mother. She knew there was no rush – Eddie had promised on the phone that they would wait for her – but she didn't want to miss a moment. When she was a few minutes away from the hospital, her phone rang. She answered it, holding the mobile between her left shoulder and ear as she drove.

'Lachlan, thank God! I've been trying to call you for ages. I told you, you *have* to be contactable all the time at the moment!'

'Sorry, I just got the message. So the baby's coming already? Where are you?' His voice sounded strange: flat and distant.

'I'm almost at the hospital. Nadia went for her check-up and her blood pressure's too high and her legs are swollen and they say she has pre-eclampsia so they're admitting her now. Eddie said the doctor wants to do the caesarean today!'

'Shit. Are you OK? I'm—'

'You have to come back, *now*! I'll ask them to wait – you might just make it. When's the next flight? Or can you get a car and drive? It might be quicker, although that's, what, six hours? I just don't know yet how serious it is and if they can do it at night or wait until tomorrow.'

Lachlan's voice shook. 'I won't make it.'

'What do you mean? Just try.' Zoe paused as Lachlan sniffed. 'Are you crying? Oh, Lachlan, it's OK, you might make it. Don't be upset, please... Just go straight to the airport and get on the next flight. They'll make room for you if you tell them you're about to be a dad!'

'What about the baby? Will she be OK?'

'Oh God, I hope so. I think so...' Zoe had been so caught up with contacting Lachlan and getting to the hospital that she hadn't really considered that her baby girl might not be OK. Until now.

She indicated left and pulled over. Eddie and Nadia were together at the hospital now, making plans without her, while Lachlan was six hundred kilometres away in the desert. She could picture him sitting in the site office that teetered on the edge of the super pit, the open-cut gold mine carved deep into the rust-coloured earth, terraced edges of rock descending deep into the ground, while giant trucks hauled tonnes of minerals up the winding road around the edge of the mine. Zoe had gone there with him once. She'd wanted to see where he spent half his life. They had driven east from Perth, past road trains caked with thick red dust heading to the city, past the villages of the hills, over the Darling Scarp to the wide open spaces of the desert. They'd followed the golden pipeline that pumped water from the Mundaring Weir to the towns of the goldfields, hundreds of kilometres away. As they drove, Lachlan had told her the story of C.Y. O'Connor, the pipeline's engineer, who never lived to see the water flow, instead only ever hearing the attacks and criticisms of those who were convinced he'd fail. Thinking back to that long, hot drive, Zoe realised how far they were from each other now. She began to cry.

Lachlan spoke more steadily. 'Zoe, it's OK, it's not that early.'

'It's four weeks!'

'The doctors know what they're doing. Don't cry, it's good news, our baby is coming.'

She could barely breathe. 'But you're not here, and you're going to miss it.'

'Zoe, stop. Stop!'

She held the phone away, slowing her breathing, then wiped her eyes and nose. Lachlan was right; she had to calm down. 'Sorry. I'm just… scared. I need you here with me…'

'Listen to me. Just get to the hospital. I'll get there as soon as I can, even if I have to walk.'

Zoe laughed through her tears. 'Don't you dare. The last thing I need is you running off into the desert and getting lost. Just… just hurry, Lachlan. Please.'

His voice was thick. 'I will. I'll try… I just have to sort out a few things here.'

'I know, but—'

'I said I'll try!' he shouted.

Zoe froze, startled. Lachlan rarely raised his voice to her. He was usually the one who calmed her down, but then again, he must feel so powerless, knowing he was so far away. 'That's OK, babe, I know you'll try. I'm just worried. It's our baby, Lach.'

'I'm doing my best!' His voice cracked; it sounded like he was crying.

'I know, I know, sorry… I love you, Lachlan. I just don't want you to miss this.' She spoke gently, trying to soothe him.

'No, I'm sorry. It's just crazy here at the moment. I love you too. I'll let you know as soon as I've sorted something out.'

Zoe ended the call and stared at the phone. Despair welled up in her at the realisation that she was going into this, the birth, on her own, but she breathed deeply until she felt in control again. She wasn't alone; Nadia and Eddie were there, and they were all in this together. There was no need to be frightened; she should be excited. Her baby was coming. Everything else was insignificant.

–

Nadia gazed down at the little red face of the baby lying against her bare chest, at her swollen lips, still a little blue, and the sticky dark strands of hair on her head. But rather than having Eddie's dark eyes, as Charlotte and Violet and Harry all had when they were born, this baby's eyes were blue, like Lachlan's – and her own. And the baby looked like her in other ways: her fair skin, and her strawberry-blonde eyelashes. But she was the aunt, not the mother. She had to remember that.

Nadia started to shiver; suddenly she was freezing. Her jaw trembled, her teeth chattered, her legs shook. Eddie pulled the blanket up around her shoulders. She held the baby closer to her, breathing her in. She wished she could have stayed pregnant and kept the baby all to herself for a few weeks longer, even a day; any time longer than now, when she had to let her go. Nadia couldn't take her eyes off the child, but she could hear Zoe sniffling at the end of the bed, and she knew that her sister was desperate to hold the baby. Her baby. But Nadia needed a moment longer.

The infant opened her eyes, just a little, and squinted at Nadia, looking puzzled. She remembered that gaze from birthing her other children, that moment when a mother and child were bonded forever by something other than a physical connection. Nadia knew she had to hand her over now, before it was too late. She cradled the baby in her arms, then, as her tears began to fall, she closed her eyes and held out the little bundle.

'Take her,' she whispered.

'Are you—?' Zoe said.

'Just take her.'

Nadia kept her eyes closed and felt the infant being lifted from her arms. She let her arms hover in the air for a moment, crossed at the wrists, holding nothing but the weight of air. She heard Zoe's footsteps retreat to the far corner of the room, her whispered greetings to the child, her sobs of relief. The baby snuffled, mewled. Nadia could practically feel the oxytocin surging through her body in response, rushing to her womb, her breasts, her heart, the messenger of the most basic human instinct, to feed your newborn and hold her close.

She opened her eyes and looked at her arms, still held aloft, then let them slowly drop. She gripped the sheets, to ground herself and prevent herself from leaping off the bed. She couldn't look over at Zoe, who was laughing and crying with the baby, so she turned her head towards Eddie. He was pale, and his eyes darted around the room. She could see how confused he was, how wrong it felt to have watched your wife give birth to a child, then watch her give that child away. She reached out for his hand; he squeezed it. They looked at each other, eyes wild, but neither of them said a word. Nadia put her other hand on top of her abdomen, just under her breasts, far away from the caesarean stitches; here, less than an hour before, her baby had slept and grown and kicked and tumbled. Already, it felt soft, doughy.

Empty.

–

'Hello, baby!' Zoe whispered through her tears. She laughed as her newborn daughter screwed up her face. She stroked the fine, downy blonde hair on her cheeks, traced her finger up the baby's jaw to her papery ears, then back down to her chin. She had called Lachlan from the bedside as the baby was being born, narrated the scene for him so he could picture the obstetrician lifting the tiny creature from Nadia's abdomen. He'd heard the baby's first cry through the phone, and he had cried too, and then he'd had to go.

They'd all agreed in the plan, drawn up with counsellors and lawyers, that Nadia would hold the child first, as soon as she was born. They'd done their research: skin-to-skin contact was good for the baby. And Zoe had wanted to do that for Nadia; it seemed cruel to leave her lying on the bed as if it was an organ being removed and whipped away from her sight. But when she had seen Nadia open the neck of her hospital gown and lay the tiny infant face down on her chest, watched her gently pat the child's back and murmur into her ear, she desperately wanted it to be her own heartbeat pounding through the baby's body, soothing her. And when Nadia had gazed at the baby, and the child had stared back, Zoe had wanted to grab the baby so that it was *her* face imprinted on her visual memory. She knew that babies could recognise their mother's voice from being in the womb; would Nadia's voice be embedded in the baby's memory forever? How could Zoe compete? But it wasn't a competition, she reminded herself.

When did a child learn who its mother was? Was it at the moment the cells met and merged and multiplied, when a mother's blood started to flow through the umbilical cord, or when the baby's body reacted to its mother's hormones when she felt fear, or shed a tear? Or was it the moment when a baby was born and looked into her mother's eyes, then nursed from her breast? Zoe's eyes filled with tears. No, a child was yours when she was made up of part of you, not just your genes but your love, your utter devotion to her. That's what Zoe had, that's what she could give this baby.

And now that she was holding the child, her child, Lachlan's child, she didn't ever want to put her down. She sat on a chair in the corner and just held her new daughter close as the nurses bustled around the room, writing, counting instruments, bundling laundry into a basket. They kept their eyes expertly averted as Nadia and Eddie hugged silently.

After a while, minutes maybe, the baby began to squirm, turn her head from side to side, licking her lips, opening and closing her mouth. *Not yet, baby, not yet.* This had been in their plan too: Nadia would breastfeed, just for a week, and then she would express milk. Just to give the baby the best start. But Zoe didn't want to give her back now. She glanced over; Nadia was looking at them. Zoe smiled at her but dropped her eyes when Nadia smiled sadly in return.

Zoe swallowed, then stood up and walked to the bed. 'I think she's hungry,' she whispered.

Nadia nodded. 'Shall I try to feed her?'

And although it terrified Zoe to let Nadia and the baby connect again, she smiled at her sister, who had done so much for her, nodded, and handed the baby to her.

-

While Nadia started to feed the baby, Zoe left the room, went down in the lift, then walked through the hospital lobby, past the gift shop full of teddy bears and shiny balloons on sticks, and out of the sliding doors to get some fresh air. The sun was low in the sky. She rubbed at the goosebumps on her arms, then sat on a wooden bench and called Lachlan.

He answered straight away. 'Hi, how's the baby?'

Zoe let out a sigh, leaned back on the bench and looked up to the sky, smiling. It was so nice to be able to be excited without feeling guilty about Nadia seeing her happiness. 'Oh, Lach, she's perfect. I held her for ages, but then she needed a feed, so I've left her in the room with Nadia and Eddie. How are you? Any word on when you can leave?'

'Yeah. I'm on the seven-twenty flight tonight, so I'll get in by nine.' He sounded tired.

'Oh, thank God! That's brilliant. Can you come straight here from the airport?'

'Of course.' His voice broke. 'All I want to do is be there with you and the baby. It's been a horrible day...'

Zoe couldn't imagine how hard it had been for him, being stuck out in Kalgoorlie, unable to get back to see his daughter being born. 'Oh, babe, it's OK. You'll be here in a few hours and then we'll all be together. In a week's time it'll just be the three of us, at last.'

'Are we still going to go to Nadia's?'

Zoe hesitated. 'Yeah. We agreed, just for a few days after they're discharged. I wish we could just go home straight away, but we owe it to Nadia. Just to give her some time, and to get the feeding all sorted. It's best for the baby.'

'OK. As long as you're sure.'

Zoe laughed. 'I'm not. Not really. But Nadia can't drive for weeks, and she needs time to say goodbye. Anyway, no point worrying about it – it's in the plan, best to stick to it. Hey, look, I better go. I'm going to call Mum so she can bring in Nadia's kids to meet their… cousin.'

'OK, I'll let you know when I get on the flight.'

'Lachlan?'

'Yes?'

'We should give her a name. Our daughter. Do you want to wait until you get here, or are you still happy with…'

'Louise,' he said firmly.

Zoe laughed. 'Louise. It's perfect.'

Chapter Seven

'Jesus Christ, Lou! What have you done?'

The voice wrenched Lou from a restless sleep. She jumped up, heart racing, then fell back on the pillow again. She screwed her eyes shut as her head pounded. 'Turn off the light, Mum!'

'No, I will not! Look at the state of you!'

Lou opened her eyes slightly to peer at her mum. She was standing next to Lou's single bed in pyjamas that were meant for someone Lou's age, not an adult: multi-coloured polka dots on the baggy white pants, a black velvet chicken on the grey top. Her hair, usually blow-dried into a straight bob, was unbrushed, matted on one side where she'd slept on it, and her eyes were puffy.

Lou followed the line of her mum's horrified gaze, then gasped and hugged her arms defensively against her chest. 'I've told you not to come in here without knocking!'

'I do *not* need to knock when my teenage daughter was arrested last night for breaking into my work and stealing amphetamines! And I certainly don't need to knock when my daughter has cut herself all over her arm! My God, Lou! When did you do this?'

Lou shrugged, face burning. She rolled onto her side, away from her mum, and wriggled down lower in the bed. As she pulled the white sheet up to her shoulders, she noticed dark brown spots of blood on the cotton. Usually she bandaged up her cuts, but she'd been too wasted last night. Tears welled up behind her closed eyes, but she set her jaw firmly.

'I thought you'd stopped doing this to yourself. What were you trying to do? Look at me!'

'Mum...' Lou's mouth was dry and rough; the words scraped through her throat. She slowly rolled back and opened her eyes.

'Jesus, Lou, when will this end?' Her mum pressed the bridge of her nose with her finger and thumb, then rubbed her eyes and blinked rapidly. Lou didn't want to see her mum cry. That's not what parents were meant to do; they were meant to be strong enough to take everything hurled at them. They were meant to be in control, but right now, her mum was flailing. But so was she; Lou needed someone to keep her afloat.

She didn't want to think about the sadness in her mum's body, the way she had let her shoulders slump, her chin drop, her arms hang limp. Instead, she thought about Theo, how they'd laugh together later when she impersonated her mother's shrill voice. They'd only been together for a few months, a few exhilarating months when finally someone understood her, cared about her, made her feel special. He was in his final year too, at the boys' school along the highway from her own girls' school. She bit the inside of her cheek as she remembered the sound of him driving off last night with Astrid and Ben. Surely one of them could have warned her when they saw the police car? Beeped the horn, called out, run inside to get her?

'Are you listening to me?'

Lou blinked and looked at her mum. *No*, she thought, *I'm not, because I've heard it all before.* 'Yes.'

'Stop bloody smiling, Lou, this isn't funny!'

Her mum's chest rose and fell rapidly underneath the velvet chicken. She sat down on the edge of Lou's bed and took her hand, and Lou relaxed: it was the same old pattern, every time. Her mum yelled and got upset, then the fear took over, the fear that if she pushed too much, she'd lose her daughter – maybe Lou would kill herself next time, or maybe she'd run away to whatever horrors her mother imagined were out there. It was just the dance they did, the game they played. They both knew how it worked, and they were both too afraid to change it.

'Darling, you need to understand how serious this is. I have to go and call Matthew and tell him that my own daughter broke into his surgery and stole sample packs of amphetamines, with *my* keys, and that she knew the alarm code. I could lose my job, Lou, do you understand that?' Her mum was blinking away tears now, her voice trembling. 'The police want to charge you, and I'm sure Matthew will too. Do you know what that means? To be seventeen, charged with breaking and entering, stealing prohibited drugs? What that'll mean to your future? For school, university, jobs? A criminal record?'

'Sorry, Mum,' she said in a monotone.

'Are you?'

'Yes.'

'I just don't know what to think any more, Lou. Your dad and I love you so much, but you do these things... Why don't you talk to me? Why don't you tell me what's going on? We're here to help you!'

Lou's face began to tingle; she knew her cheeks were turning red. Her mother was the last person she would talk to about her feelings. Her mum knew nothing about her. She didn't really care how Lou felt anyway; this was about her getting in trouble at work, having to admit to her friends that her daughter wasn't perfect, and that maybe she wasn't going to finish year twelve and go to university and have a wonderful career. Lou drew up her knees; her stomach churned.

'I need to go to the toilet.'

Her mother sighed, then rubbed her face with her hands. 'What do you want us to do, darling? What is it? What's wrong?'

'Nothing. Why does something have to be wrong?'

'Are you joking? Louise, you are stealing drugs, you are cutting yourself – do you think that's normal?'

'Lots of kids do it. It's not a big deal.'

'For God's sake, of course it's a big deal! I don't get why you don't understand this!' Her mother stood up, her face livid. 'I can't talk to you right now. Get up, get yourself cleaned up and come straight through for breakfast. I'm going to call work and tell them what happened, then the police to find out what they are going to do, and I am going to discuss the consequences of this with your father. When you come down, we will let you know what is going to happen, but be very clear, Louise, this is extremely serious.'

Lou watched her mother stomp in bare feet over the carpet and out of the room, then pull the door closed behind her. Lou's eyes prickled with tears. She wanted to call Astrid, but her dad had taken her phone off her last night on the way back from the police station. She wondered if Astrid had called her, or Theo or Ben. For all they knew, she was locked up in a police cell with rapists and murderers. They acted like they were her friends, but she was the one who'd taken all the risk, and look what had happened. They were just as guilty as her, but instead of being in trouble, they were sleeping off their hangovers while their parents sat downstairs reading the Sunday papers, eating croissants and drinking pots of tea. Lou's eyes filled with tears. What had she done? She felt like shit.

She let the tears fall, and looked at the smudges of dried blood bridging the ladder of cuts on her left forearm. Some of the lacerations were deeper than usual. Her arm stung. What a mess she was. Maybe they'd scar this time and then they'd be etched on her forever, a lifelong reminder of last night. Was her mum serious? Would the police charge her? Would she have to go to juvie? And what about school? She hated so much about it – the rules, the snobbery and hypocrisy – but she didn't want to be expelled either. Maybe she could get a job; but if her mum was right, perhaps no one would hire a seventeen-year-old with a criminal record. A sweat came over her; she smelled the alcohol oozing from her pores.

She sat up and swung her legs over the side of the bed, waited for the pounding in her head to stop, then shuffled towards the door. As she opened it, she could hear her mum and dad talking in low voices from the kitchen, but she didn't want to hear what they were saying. She headed for her bathroom.

Chapter Eight

Zoe stood on one side of the patio doors and looked through her own hazy reflection at Nadia, sitting on a frayed wicker chair, leaning back on a faded blue cushion with her bare feet resting on another cushion on top of a wooden garden table. Her fair hair framed her pale face as she gazed down at Louise, asleep in the crook of her arm. It would have looked like any other picture of a contented mother and her infant, if it wasn't for the tear running down Nadia's face from beneath her sunglasses. Zoe felt a pang of something, something unpleasant that made her feel like they were little kids again: jealousy, the part of her that wanted to run over and lay claim to Louise, to take her from Nadia like a toy that she didn't want to share. Zoe pushed the feeling away. Why should she be jealous of Nadia now that she had what she'd always wanted? Or perhaps the sensation was guilt, but really, what did she have to feel guilty about? They had all gone into this knowing it wouldn't be easy. Zoe closed her eyes for a moment; it was almost over.

Nadia hadn't seen her yet, and Zoe didn't move. She wished she knew what her sister was thinking. She could breeze over there and act like there was nothing unusual about this situation, sink back into the other chair, put her feet up too and chat away. But there was no protocol for this, no book to read to tell you what to do, what to feel, how to act. She would give Nadia a few more minutes, she decided. Zoe had the rest of her life with Louise; Nadia had no time at all.

Nadia suddenly sat up and raised her eyes to look at Zoe. They stared at each other, just for a moment, through the glass, speckled with streaks of dust and children's fingerprints. Zoe tensed, then Nadia smiled, and Zoe's face flushed. She reminded herself that Nadia had offered to do this for her; she was amazing. Smiling back, she slid open the glass door, then walked over to her sister and put her hand on her shoulder. 'She's asleep,' she said quietly.

Nadia nodded, silent, not taking her eyes off Louise.

Zoe wanted to reach down and take Louise, but she forced herself to wait, to be patient. Soon she, Lachlan and Louise would be driving away, back down the long highway from the hills, through the suburbs, through the city, and back to Fremantle, leaving Nadia far behind them.

She lifted her hand off Nadia's shoulder and sat down. The back of the chair creaked as she leaned back, trying to look relaxed. Eddie and Lachlan were kicking a footy on the green, even lawn with Charlotte, Violet and Harry. They were using the posts of the swing set as one goal, and the poles of the large round trampoline as the other. The lawn was framed by garden beds with neat rows of plants and flowers. Zoe thought about her own courtyard at home. The brick pavers there were unsteady, the sand beneath them eroded by the thousands of frantic ants that scurried around each summer, excavating their nests and biting her feet and ankles. But she would change that; it mattered, now that she had a daughter.

She looked down at her feet, her old brown thongs, and stretched out her toes, looking at her chipped red nail polish. She looked up at Nadia. 'You've got great kids.'

Nadia nodded, swaying her upper body ever so slightly from side to side, rocking Louise as she slept. Zoe wanted to say it again, louder, to remind her to look up at her own children, not down at Louise. Was Nadia regretting this? Did she wish that Louise was hers, that four children would jump on that trampoline every day? She'd said that she was happy with three children, but that was before all this. Before Louise.

Zoe's heart began to pound. She looked at Nadia and Louise again, the way Nadia had both arms wrapped tightly around the baby, her baby, and her mouth went dry. She turned and stared at Lachlan, hoping he would look over and see what was going on, but he hadn't even noticed she was there. Since Louise's birth, he'd seemed preoccupied, distant. Zoe's hands started to tremble; they needed to go.

She fixed a grin on her face, then faked a yawn. 'Well, I'd better go upstairs and make sure we're packed.' She stood up and walked back into the house before Nadia had a chance to reply.

Upstairs, Zoe zipped up her suitcase and looked around the room for the last time. She had already stripped the bed; the sheets were bundled up in the far corner of the room. The grey carpet was flecked with threads, crumbs and tiny bits of tissues. She should have vacuumed: Nadia still wasn't meant to do any lifting. She glanced at the clock on the wall. They needed to get going so they could be home in time for Louise's next feed. There wasn't enough time for a conversation, for a change of mind. There was only enough time for her, Lachlan and Louise to get in the car and drive away.

Zoe couldn't wait to be able to care for Louise without Nadia watching her, commenting on how she might feed or settle or change her differently. Zoe was a new mum, and like every other first-time mother, she'd find her way. She knew how hard it must be for Nadia to watch Louise's dependence shift away from her to Zoe. Still, it had been hard not to let her resentment grow; there was something about living with Nadia again that made her revert to their old dynamics, to letting her big sister take charge. But no, it was more than that. Zoe's submission was not just to do with their history. It was the knowledge that she was not the one with the power; Nadia was. Zoe would forever need to fall at Nadia's feet in gratitude. Because really, what she had done, what she was doing today in watching her flesh and blood be carried out of her home, was selfless. Zoe owed her so much and couldn't risk upsetting her. Would it have been easier if they had taken Louise home straight from the hospital? Beforehand, it had seemed cruel to break the bond so abruptly, but maybe it would have been better after all. Had they prolonged the pain, cultivated the confusion for all of them? For Louise?

Zoe scooped up a toppled pile of coins that trailed across the bedside cabinet, then picked up two glasses with dregs of cloudy water and put them by the door. She bent down for a ball of scrunched-up wrapping paper from one of the few gifts they'd received, then pulled Lachlan's damp towel from the top of the door and threw it into the corner, on top of the sheets. The bassinette, adjacent to her side of the bed, had been stripped too, and those sheets were folded up in her suitcase. Nadia had insisted that Zoe take them, saying that she had no more use for them. But if she was so sure she didn't want more children, why hadn't she thrown them out after Harry was born? Why had she kept them all this time? Anyway, it didn't matter. When Nadia insisted that she take the sheets, Zoe had smiled and thanked her, even though she had three brand-new sets at home. She would give these old ones to an op shop.

Lachlan's work holdall was on top of the bed, filthy with the film of red dust that always stained his clothes and hair when he came home. It took days to wash it off his skin; as the rust-coloured water drained away, it took with it the harshness of his life in the goldfields. But since returning this time, the ruddy dirt still clung to every line on his face, and had buried itself deep in his knuckles and around his fingernails. The old Lachlan hadn't emerged yet. He'd been quiet since they'd arrived at Nadia and Eddie's place, but then again, they were all pretty overwhelmed by the situation. He hadn't been sleeping well; she'd felt him moving around in the bed next to her as she lay awake listening to Louise breathing. She'd heard Nadia at night too, creeping about downstairs, hesitating outside their bedroom door when Louise cried. But Louise took milk from the bottle easily: any breast milk that Nadia managed to pump, and top-ups of formula when there wasn't enough. Nadia had nursed Louise almost constantly for the first few days, and had then withdrawn to her room with the electric pump every few hours. Zoe loved the feeling of holding Louise close while she drank from her bottle, her little fist clutching Zoe's finger. She'd seen

Nadia glare at the tin of powdered milk as if it was poison. Zoe sighed. It was hard for them all, and things would be much easier for everyone once she, Lachlan and Louise were gone.

Zoe stacked Lachlan's bag on top of her own suitcase near the door. He could carry them down. She zipped up the nappy bag, slung it over her shoulder along with her handbag, then picked up the dirty glasses and walked out into the hallway.

Louise's cries drifted up the stairs. Smiling, Zoe stood still and let the sound lap over her like warm water. She walked slowly down the stairs, forcing herself to stay calm, to resist the urge to run down, grab Louise and flee with her. She didn't want Nadia to think she was rushing her; Zoe knew how sad she was by the way she had been laughing too loudly all day, chattering constantly yet not really saying anything at all.

At the bottom of the stairs, she walked back through the open-plan kitchen towards the patio doors. Nadia hadn't moved from her chair. She now held Louise upright, over her shoulder, and patted the whimpering baby's back while whispering in her ear. Zoe's hands began to shake and her eyes filled with tears; she leaned on the kitchen table and took a few deep breaths. This would be the hardest part, taking Louise from her sister.

But Louise was hers to take.

Chapter Nine

Zoe sat at a wooden picnic table in the shade of a peppermint tree and sipped her coffee, listening to the clanging masts of the boats moored in the harbour. Across the park, the ocean was still. The sea breeze tiptoed around her and hissed through the canopy above, the branches heavy with dark green leaves and frosted with tiny white flowers. Zoe picked up a leaf that had fallen onto the table, and bent it in half until it snapped; holding it under her nose, she breathed in the warm, peppery scent of spring.

Louise was asleep in the stroller. Zoe rocked it back and forth with her left hand while she stared in awe at her. She hadn't been able to stop looking at their daughter since they'd taken her home. It had only been three weeks since they'd left Nadia and Eddie's, but she could barely remember how life had been before they had Louise. It was miraculous that she was really here, that she really existed. Zoe wanted to make up for every moment that she had missed out on by not carrying Louise in her own body: she responded instantly to every whimper and cry; she carried her all day in a sling across her chest, until their bodies seemed to be one and the same; she spoke quietly to her so that she knew who her mother was. Zoe was tired, more tired than she'd ever been in her life, but she refused to even think about complaining. She would embrace every moment of being a mother, moments that she almost never had.

But despite her joy and amazement, Zoe hadn't been able to fully relax: Louise wasn't hers yet. It was still Nadia's and Eddie's names on the birth certificate. Twenty-eight days – that was when she and Lachlan could lodge their application with the family court to finalise the transfer of parental rights. Of course, before they'd even started they'd had legal approval to go ahead with the surrogacy, after months of meeting with lawyers and psychologists and each other to decide what they'd do if the baby was disabled, or if one of them died or changed their mind, but all of that meant nothing until the court issued a new birth certificate that said *they* – she and Lachlan – were Louise's parents. Nadia could still say no. She had assured Zoe time and time again that she wouldn't, but until she had that piece of paper, Zoe wasn't Louise's legal mother. While every day she felt more comfortable in believing that she finally had a daughter, she did need that document to be at peace.

A crow cawed; Zoe blinked and looked around. In the middle of the park was a children's playground. A slide, two swings and a wooden boat all sat in a bed of sand. The older local kids would be at school, but there were a few tourists with their children, waiting for the Ferris wheel at the harbour's edge to open. Two toddlers waddled around in the sand while their mothers sat cross-legged on the grass watching them and chatting. Zoe sipped her coffee again. Excitement rushed through her and she wanted to run over to join them instead of avoiding them as she'd always done before; she was now one of them.

She stood up and pushed the stroller over the uneven grass towards them. As she passed the two mothers, she saw that one of them was pregnant; the woman looked up and caught Zoe's eye then smiled.

Zoe smiled back. 'You're going to have your hands full!'

The woman laughed and put a hand on her stomach. 'Yeah, don't know what I was thinking!'

Zoe laughed back.

The woman struggled to her feet. 'Oh, she's adorable! How old is she?'

Zoe's heart started to flutter. 'She's almost four weeks now.'

'Wow! So little. And look at you! You're so skinny! It took me ages to lose the baby weight. What's her name?'

Zoe shrugged and tried to push out her stomach. 'It's Louise.' She took the brake off the stroller with her foot.

The woman continued. 'Our friend, she's got a little boy, about the same age – he'd be five... no, six weeks?' She looked to the other mother, who nodded. 'Where did you have Louise? You were probably in the hospital at the same time!'

Zoe's mouth went dry. 'St John's.'

'Oh, I think she was in Murdoch. Did the midwife hook you up with a mothers' group? That's how we met.'

'Oh... yeah, she did, thanks.' Zoe could feel her face reddening. She gave a final smile, mumbled her goodbyes, then started quickly walking away. Once she was out of sight of the women, she stopped again and breathed deeply. Why did she feel like such a fraud? What was she frightened of? Why couldn't she say that she was infertile and her sister had carried her child? Zoe felt her face blazing inexplicably with shame.

Louise was stirring. Zoe walked to the front of the stroller and squatted down. She clasped Louise's little fist in her hand then leaned in and kissed her forehead. 'Are you hungry? Let's go somewhere quiet…'

She pushed the stroller past the convict-built limestone buildings of the university, across the railway line and alongside Arthur Head with the Roundhouse towering above them. Louise was starting to cry; Zoe walked more quickly. She hesitated at the entrance to the old whaling tunnel, where three empty beer bottles lay on the ground, but there was no sign of the homeless men who usually drank there. She took a deep breath and hurried through the tunnel, her footsteps reverberating around the cool walls, merging with the echoes of the whalers' footsteps from almost two hundred years before. As they emerged into the sunlight she exhaled deeply.

She sat on a bench in the shade of a patch of tea-trees and wattles as the waves lapped over the sand, over the remains of the whalers' hearths where they had rendered blubber into oil to light the settlers' fires. She held out her right hand, palm up, as she had been taught as a child, and looked at the silhouettes of islands on the horizon. Her thumb pointed at Rottnest; her index finger to Stragglers Rock; her middle finger to Carnac Island, where Lachlan fished, returning with stories of sea lions and tiger snakes; her ring finger to Garden Island; and her pinky to Penguin Island. The palm of her hand, right here where she lived and where her daughter now lived, was Fremantle. She smiled and curled her palm tightly closed, holding onto home, onto family.

She took her bag from beneath the stroller and prepared Louise's bottle. Twenty-seven days had passed. Tomorrow their lawyer was submitting the documents, and in a matter of weeks this would be over, and she could finally relax.

–

Nadia poured six glasses of champagne from the bottle she'd kept in her fridge, just for today, then held her glass in the air. 'To Louise!'

'To Louise!' replied the others in synchrony, all grinning.

Nadia clinked her glass with Zoe's first, laughing at the joy on her sister's face, then with Lachlan, Eddie, her dad and finally, Rosemary. The men were still in their suits and ties. Rosemary wore a black dress, and Zoe a skirt suit. Nadia hadn't been able to fit into hers; her belly and thighs were still carrying the weight of the pregnancy, and she couldn't have anything tight over her caesarean scar.

They had all gathered at Zoe and Lachlan's house to celebrate after the Family Court hearing. The parentage order had been officially approved, and a new birth certificate had been issued in Zoe and Lachlan's names. Nadia had known there would be no problems; from the moment she had offered to be Zoe's surrogate, Nadia had made sure that everything went to plan. She kept a ring binder of information, divided into colour-coded sections with copies of the legislation, reports, a timeline, a flow chart of the steps they each had to take. She couldn't have coped with any complications, any reason to give up. The process had taken more of an emotional toll than she'd prepared herself for. It all took so long, and as she,

Eddie, Zoe and Lachlan went back and forth to lawyers and clinics and counsellors, she watched her own children grow older. Harry was almost six now, Violet eight and Charlotte ten. By the time Louise was Charlotte's age, Harry would be practically finished high school, following his big sisters to university, to his own life, and leaving Nadia to hers. Nadia had kept thinking, as she lay in the obstetrician's clinic under a sheet while they inseminated her, what if this baby was mine? She felt the pull of having another child at home, one who'd need her for years after her own children had left.

Last week, her court-appointed counsellor had told her how other women in her situation felt when they handed over a child, then asked her if she was still sure about the decision. Nadia had dropped her eyes and answered *yes.* After all, she was different to the other surrogates. She was family, and she would still have a relationship with Louise. She'd always be part of her life; she would see her grow into a young woman. Nadia knew that she wasn't being very convincing, to either the counsellor or herself. It was enough to satisfy her lawyer, and the court. But the truth was that in the month between Louise's birth and today, Nadia had been surprised at how much she'd struggled to separate herself from Louise. Her head told her that her role had ended and that Zoe was now Louise's mother, but her body, her physical core, didn't understand where the baby she had borne had gone.

There was a hand on her shoulder; Nadia looked up.

'Are you OK?' Zoe said quietly. The others had moved, chattering excitedly, into the living room, leaving Nadia and Zoe alone in the kitchen.

Nadia nodded. 'Yes. You know, I am OK. I was worried I wouldn't be, but I really am. I'm just so happy for you.'

'Thank you, again. I wish there—'

Nadia waved her free hand in the air. 'Don't be silly, there's no need to thank me.'

'Yes, there is. You've done an amazing thing for me, for us.' Zoe's voice was wavering.

Nadia felt her own eyes fill with tears, but she knew it wasn't from regret. She could see that Zoe's life was complete now, and Nadia was so happy for her sister, and proud that she had been the one to help her.

'You're going to make me cry,' she laughed, through her tears. 'Please don't ever thank me again. Just enjoy being a mum, OK? And you…' She looked up at Lachlan, who was now standing beside them. 'Enjoy being a dad.'

Lachlan's eyes were wet too, though he was smiling. 'I certainly will. Th—'

'No!' Nadia held her hand up to stop him. 'Don't thank me. It's over now. But I'm still allowed to spoil my niece!'

'Oh, Nadia…' Zoe put her arms around Nadia and the sisters clung to each other. Now that her legal bonds to Louise were cut, Nadia knew that she could finally move on with her own life, something that she had put on hold for three years.

-

Back at home that night, Nadia tucked Harry into bed, kissed his forehead, then turned out the light and walked towards the girls' room. Sighing, she leaned down and picked up a pair of shoes from the hallway. Eddie had gone to pick up some takeaway curries; the kids had eaten some horrible fast food for dinner. Tonight, Nadia didn't care.

Charlotte and Violet were sitting on the floor of their room in their pyjamas, hair still wet and tangled from the bath, playing with Barbie dolls. Nadia rubbed her eyes and forced herself to smile. 'OK, girls, tidy-up time. Let's get this all cleared up and get into bed for your story.'

'OK, Mum!' Charlotte said, grinning up at her. Nadia smiled back and tilted her head to the side. The girls flung the toys back into the basket in the corner of the room, then clambered into their beds.

Nadia took a book of fairy stories from the shelf and settled herself down in the white rocking chair between the beds. She leaned back with the book on her lap, feeling the thin cushion on the seat slip forward and the wooden slats dig into her spine. She had nursed all the children in this creaky old chair. Eddie had bought it from an antiques shop when Nadia was pregnant with Charlotte, and she still loved it. Once the children had stopped breastfeeding, she'd rock them on her lap and sing them to sleep. Maybe one day she would sing to Louise in this chair too, if she was babysitting. Her eyes filled with tears. Her milk had dried up after a few weeks of pumping, the plastic cup and mechanical sucking and whirring no substitute for a baby's mouth and cries. She had wanted to do at least that for Louise. It hadn't worked out as she had hoped, but what could she do? She had tried.

Nadia blinked quickly. She pulled a splinter from the arm of the chair, then looked to either side of her at her two beautiful daughters, lying on their sides gazing at her. She could imagine how they felt, because she remembered being their age and lying next to Zoe while Rosemary read to them. Poetry had been Rosemary's favourite thing to read; Nadia still recalled her stepmother's voice as she recounted 'The Rime of the Ancient Mariner', and her own anxiety at the plight of the sailor with an albatross hanging around his neck.

Nadia smiled again, remembering Zoe's elation after the court today, joy that she had rarely seen on her sister's face before. It had all turned out so well. Nadia was so fortunate, and now Zoe was too. Nadia was being too hard on herself; this confusion, this conflict of emotion was what having babies was all about. She had felt guilty about so many things with her other three, and still did – too much television, too few vegetables, too many after-school activities, too few after-school activities. Guilt came with being a mother. Who hadn't had a child and thought, *What have I done?* She knew from experience that those thoughts were fleeting, that they'd soon be overpowered by the joys of Louise. Anyway, there was no use in dwelling on second thoughts, because it was too late to go back.

Chapter Ten

Lou went into the kitchen for breakfast, and frowned: her dad was standing at the coffee machine steaming some milk. Usually he would have already left for his work in the city by the time she got up for school. He was dressed in the casual work clothes that all his business colleagues seemed to wear – dark blue jeans and a pale blue checked shirt, unbuttoned at the collar – but he was still in his socks, threadbare at the big toes. Her mum was wearing her work clothes too, her hair blow-dried and her face made up, but instead of rushing around, she sat at the kitchen table staring at the newspaper. She looked up when Lou walked past her to the pantry, and smiled a little.

'Morning,' Lou said. If they weren't going to mention the fact that something was up, then neither was she.

'Good morning. Did you sleep well?'

Lou shrugged, then took out a bowl from the cupboard and poured some cereal. She opened the fridge for the milk, then remembered that her dad was using it. She closed the fridge door again, walked towards him and picked up the carton. Feeling him watching her, she sighed.

'OK. What's going on?' she said, trying to sound casual but not meeting his eye.

Her dad poured the hot milk into his mug, wiped the metal steamer with a cloth, then cleared his throat. 'Well, Louise, today we're all going to a meeting.'

'Yes,' her mum said. 'We've both taken the morning off so we can go together. It's very important.'

Lou's pulse quickened. Was she being expelled? The police had only cautioned her for the drugs, after her mum's boss told them that he didn't want her to be charged. She'd thought it was all under control: she was grounded, she'd promised to stop cutting herself, she was studying hard. 'What kind of meeting?'

Her parents looked at each other, then her dad walked over to the table and sat next to her mum. 'Sit down, Louise,' he said.

Lou shook her head. Despite herself, tears sprang to her eyes. 'What kind of meeting, I said?'

'Don't get upset,' he said. 'You're not in trouble. We're going to see a therapist who works with young people and families; he wants to see all three of us. We know that this is not just about you, Lou – your behaviour is about all of us, so we're taking responsibility for this too.'

Lou sniggered. Clearly her dad had already been talking about her with this therapist; those weren't his own words. He'd never seen her behaviour as anything other than her own responsibility, and he'd told her that, many times. Her mum used that lingo all the time, but with her it was superficial, nothing but sounds coming from her mouth.

'What do you think, Lou?' Her mum was biting her lip.

'Does it matter?'

'Well, yes, of course it matters.'

Lou narrowed her eyes. 'If I say no then we won't go, is that what you mean?'

'Well, no... I—'

'What your mother is saying,' her dad said, 'is that we *do* have to go. It was one of the conditions for the police letting you off, and for school not expelling you. You don't have to say anything, but you do need to come along and at least be polite.'

Her mum nodded, eyes darting between Lou and her dad. 'Just give it a chance, darling.'

'Well,' Lou said. 'We've started off brilliantly, making the decision together as a family. Bodes well, doesn't it?' She picked up her bowl and stormed out of the room.

–

Lou sat in the back of the car while her dad drove. Her mum, in the passenger seat, looked out of the window, nibbling at her nails. Lou was surprised they hadn't put the child locks on the doors, or that her mum hadn't sat in the back with her to make sure she didn't jump out and run off. They were obviously trying to show that they *trusted* her.

They didn't travel far: just five minutes along the highway, past the turnoff to Lou's school. They stopped outside a Californian-style bungalow with a bronze plaque on the limestone wall bordering the paved front yard: *Seaview Therapy Centre.* A flock of sulphur-crested cockatoos pecked at the verge out the front, in the shade of a tall pine tree. Lou's mum's repeated sighs merged with the crashing of waves on the beach at the bottom of the road. Lou's stomach was churning, but she said nothing as she followed her parents inside.

The waiting room was clearly the converted lounge room of the original house: scratched floorboards, a dusty fireplace with a decorative basket of logs, a pressed tin ceiling with patterns of entwined roses. A receptionist sat behind a modern black desk in the far corner of the room. Lou waited, shifting from foot to foot, while her mum checked in, then they all sat on white plastic chairs while her mum filled in some forms on a clipboard.

A few minutes later, a bearded man wearing jeans and a polo shirt came out and called them through to his office. Lou took a deep breath; her dad put his arm around her shoulders and ushered her through, with her mum following behind.

Inside the small room, four mismatched chairs were arranged around a circular coffee table that Lou recognised from Ikea. There were rustles and creaks as everyone settled into their seats.

'Good morning,' the bearded man said. 'I'm Ross Pettit. Thank you all for coming along today.' He smiled at her parents. 'We've spoken on the phone, obviously.' He turned to Lou. 'Louise, is it?'

She nodded, then looked down at her feet. Of course, they'd been talking about her behind her back.

'So, Louise, my name is Ross.'

You said that, she wanted to say, but instead she stared at the scuffed toes of her black school shoes.

'I'm a therapist. I see families and young people who are having some difficulties with their relationships, feelings or behaviours. Does that make sense?'

Lou shrugged.

'And I know from Mum and Dad that your family has been having some difficulties lately. Do you think that's fair to say?'

She shrugged again.

'Well, what I'm going to do is start out by finding out a little bit about you and your family, and then we'll talk about the problems you have at the moment, and hopefully we'll come up with a plan. I'd like to talk as a family first, and then I'll spend some time with each of you alone, so if there's anything that you find difficult to say in front of each other, save it up and tell me later.' Ross leaned forward. 'Now, Louise, it's important that you know that anything you tell me is in complete confidence, and I won't say anything to your parents unless I have your permission. There are exceptions to that, though: if I think that you or someone else is in danger of being hurt, then I have to break your confidence by law. OK?'

Lou nodded. She noticed her mum and dad glance at each other, and almost smiled at their discomfort as they realised that she could say whatever she wanted to Ross and he couldn't tell them: she bet that wasn't part of their plan. She pressed her lips together. Did they really think that this would make her open up and tell them what she was thinking, when that had never been how their family worked? Her mum and aunt were polite to each other, but distant. She saw her mum's parents quite a lot, but her dad's father had died, his mother was in a nursing home and his sister lived in South Australia. Harry, Violet and Charlotte lived interstate now, and besides, they were all so much older than her that even if they lived closer, there was too much of an age gap for her to have much of a relationship with them. So she could hardly be blamed for not *communicating*, could she?

Ross began asking the basics: how old everyone was, what did they do, if they had any pets. Lou stared at him and raised her eyebrows at the ludicrous questions. She knew he was trying to put them at their ease, lull them with the simple things and make them believe he was a friend, and then hit them with the tough questions.

'And so,' he said finally, 'I'd like to talk about what brought you here today to see me. Who would like to go first?'

After another round of uncomfortable glances, her mum cleared her throat. 'OK, I will. Unless you want to, sweetheart?' She aimed a tense smile at Lou.

'No thanks.'

Her mum let out a big breath and clasped one crossed knee. 'OK. Well, as Louise knows, we love her very much, more than anything.'

Lou looked up at the ceiling, at a discoloured patch that was probably possum piss, or maybe rat. She didn't want to see her mum cry again, though she wasn't sure whether it was because she was embarrassed for her, or because she knew that she'd cry too.

Her mother went on. 'But things have been very difficult with her for a while now. Probably for a year or so, don't you think?'

Her dad nodded. 'About that.'

Her mum counted out Louise's issues on the fingers of her left hand. 'She has been withdrawing from us, cutting herself, her teachers say she's doing much worse academically at school—'

'I still get Bs! I'm hardly failing.'

'No, sweetheart, but you used to get As.'

'So? The work is harder! It doesn't mean you had to drag me here!' Lou shouted.

Lou's mum kept her eyes and smile fixed on Ross, as if to say, *See what I mean?* 'Well, of course we're not here because Louise is getting Bs. Lou knows very well what's been happening. The crisis that brought us here today is that she's been using drugs – hard drugs – and two weeks ago, she broke into the medical practice where I work, and stole amphetamines from the doctor's office, then got herself arrested.'

'I didn't break in. I had your keys.'

'Louise!' Her dad glared at her. 'Don't be a smart arse.'

Lou leaned back in her seat as they all looked at Ross; she raised her eyebrows. Was he going to let her dad swear at her like that?

'Louise, is there anything you'd like to say about what your mum just said?' Ross asked.

'I don't use hard drugs.'

'What drugs *do* you use?'

'No more than any other teenager. Mum has this idea in her head that I should be the perfect daughter all of the time, but she doesn't understand that every single kid in my class does the same things that I do.'

'That's rubbish,' her mum said.

Lou swivelled in her chair. 'How would you know?' She spat the words at her mother, tears filling her eyes. 'How the hell would you know, Mum?'

Her mum looked at Ross, her face flushed. He leaned back in his chair and crossed his legs at the ankles. Lou could see his stripy socks and pale, thin shins covered with wiry dark hair. He made a steeple with his fingers.

'Perhaps now is a good time for us to split up so I can hear from each of you in turn. Louise, would you like to talk to me first, or would you like me to talk to your parents?'

'Don't care,' said Lou, then, 'Them.' She indicated with her head.

'Well, if you wouldn't mind taking a seat outside, I'll just talk to your folks for twenty minutes or so. I'm just going to ask them some questions about your childhood, themselves, and what their worries are, and then we'll swap, OK?'

Lou nodded, then stood up and left the room.

–

The receptionist was playing the radio softly. Lou flicked through a magazine, wishing she'd turn the radio off so she could make out what her parents were saying behind the closed door. Every so often, she'd hear the low tones of her father, or a high-pitched cry or giggle from her mother. This was the way it had been for so long now; Lou felt like she'd spent the last year or two hovering around closed doors straining to overhear conversations, trying to make sense of whispers. But a closed door couldn't hold back the tension that seeped through the house. And now there were sobs coming from Ross's office. Lou's pulse began to quicken and she tapped her foot on the ground, wanting to listen, yet wishing that she wasn't here, that if her parents had to get upset, they would have the decency to wait until she wasn't around so she didn't have to hear them.

'Can I get you anything? A cup of tea?'

Startled, Lou looked up at the receptionist, who had spoken loudly, as if trying to distract her. Lou shook her head.

'Some of those magazines are a bit grown up for you, eh? We should get some more for the young ones. What do you like to read?'

Lou frowned. 'These are fine.'

The woman kept talking, asking Lou about school, her friends, persisting in spite of Lou's monosyllabic responses. Finally, the door opened. Lou looked up, biting her lip. Her mum smiled, though her eyes and nose were red. She walked quickly towards Lou and hugged her. Lou sat stiffly in the embrace. Her mother so rarely hugged her these days that Lou didn't know what to do, so she patted her on the back and waited until she let go.

'Your turn now, Lou.' Her dad smiled.

She nodded, glanced again at her mother, then walked into Ross's office.

Chapter Eleven

Nadia dropped the children at the school gates, then glanced at the clock on the dashboard. She'd still make the gym class if she hurried. She'd been putting it off for weeks. She'd been for her six-week check-up with her obstetrician last week, and he'd given her the all clear to start exercising again. It had been three weeks since Louise's parentage order had been made and it seemed like everyone else had settled back into a semblance of normal life. Nadia knew that she had to try to do the same. Remnants of the pregnancy with Louise still clung to her, and she needed to shift them. She wanted her old body back; she needed to sweat out all the reminders of what she'd been through, to get back to the capable, confident mother of three that she'd been before all this.

Nadia checked over her shoulder, pulled out into the road and drove to the local shopping centre. After parking in the rooftop car park, Nadia took her sports bag from the boot, then walked quickly towards her gym. She scanned her membership card at the door, hurried to the changing room then walked quickly out into the gym with her towel and water bottle. The musty, damp, sweaty smell hit her. To her left, three rows of running machines, cross trainers and exercise bikes faced a wall of TV screens. About half the machines were occupied, mainly by women, though one elderly man strolled on a treadmill. The women were all about Nadia's age, school mums. Who else had time to go to the gym on a weekday morning? She recognised a few of them; they all had the same routine. She saw them at the school gates, at the supermarket, at the park; like cliques of teenage girls, there was an unspoken hierarchy, a tacit competition – to have the cleverest children, or the nicest car, or the fittest body.

She jogged towards the group fitness room, skirting a few men on the weights equipment, then pushed open the glass doors. The warm-up was just finishing. Nadia breathed out; she hadn't missed too much. The instructor was on a stage at the front of the room, and the uneven rows of women bobbing up and down on their step platforms were reflected in the mirrored wall in front of them, briefly disorientating Nadia. She put her water bottle and towel down against the wall, picked up a step platform and risers, then negotiated her way to a space near the front of the room. She picked up the rhythm, beginning to clap her hands from corner to corner as she kicked and curled along with the loud music, the stress dripping out of her.

When the class was over, Nadia put her step away, thanked the instructor and went back through the doors into the main part of the gym. Two women whom she'd known from when their kids went to playgroup together were chatting just outside the door to the creche. Nadia looked at the floor, but they saw her and waved. She looked up, feigning surprise.

'Hi, Kate, sorry, I was in a world of my own there,' she said.

'Hey, Nadia, how are you?' Kate said as Ankita's eyes flicked down briefly towards Nadia's stomach. Nadia sucked it in.

'Yeah, good. Hard class, wasn't it? I was late as usual…'

'Haven't seen you for ages,' said Ankita. 'How are the kids?'

'They're good, thanks. They're all at school, which is great, gives me some time to myself, you know?'

'And… the baby?' Kate blushed and looked at Ankita, who smiled, then looked at the ground.

Nadia fixed a smile on her face. Why were they tiptoeing around the subject, blushing and whispering? She had never kept it a secret; she'd been proud of being a surrogate, even though it clearly made everyone else feel uncomfortable.

'Louise? That's her name. She's seven weeks now.' Her voice cracked; she took a swig of water from her bottle. 'Zoe and her husband are thrilled.'

Kate and Ankita both smiled, and Kate raised her eyebrows. 'Wow, Nadia. That's amazing. Good on you.'

'Was it hard?' asked Ankita. 'You know, giving birth then giving her away? I don't know if I could do that.'

Nadia blinked rapidly. 'No – well, yes, a bit, but I knew from the start. The baby – Louise – I was just carrying her. So I didn't let myself get attached.' She looked up at the clock on the wall of the gym. 'Sorry, ladies, I'd better go, I've got to do the grocery shopping. Good to see you…' She raised her hand in a wave and started walking towards the door before she started crying.

–

Nadia didn't make it to the supermarket. She was too shaken by the encounter with her old friends. She sat in the car and tried to compose herself. She turned the radio on to a loud pop song, then switched the air-conditioning on full and aimed it at her face as she took deep, slow breaths. She gripped the steering wheel tightly to try to stop the trembling in her hands. She was shocked at how she'd responded to Ankita and Kate's questions; she'd thought she was in control, that she was coping with the aftermath of the surrogacy. And she was, generally, but she also knew that not far below the surface, she was shattered by the experience.

Nadia knew that throughout the entire pregnancy, she'd only been pretending that she was OK, pretending to everyone: Eddie, Zoe, the clinic, the lawyers, and herself. When the pregnancy test first came back as positive, on their second cycle of trying, she'd been thrilled for Zoe and Lachlan, and flushed with a feeling of success, of achievement, as though she'd proven herself. And for as long as the pregnancy had just been a hormone level on a computer screen, she had almost succeeded in detaching herself from the baby. Then the morning sickness had hit.

One morning, when she was about eight weeks pregnant, she'd woken at the peak of her unrelenting nausea. She wasn't sure what had woken her: the girls squabbling in their bedroom, or her pounding headache. She didn't want to open her eyes. Eddie was snoring gently. Slowly, she rolled her head on the pillow to face him, waiting for the dizziness to hit her. Then she smelled a sour, chemical odour, old aftershave or deodorant; she turned back, breathing through her mouth. She knew what was coming. As her stomach spasmed, she clasped her hand over her mouth. She gagged, then it passed. She lay still, a cold sweat trickling across her upper lip.

Eddie opened his eyes. 'You OK?'

'Mmm.' Nadia nodded her head in a tiny movement, hoping it was enough to convince him but not enough to trigger the hammering in her head. She'd been trying to hide the nausea from him and, until now, thought she'd succeeded. The last thing she needed to hear from him was, *I told you so.*

'Are you sick?'

She tried to smile. 'Oh, a little. Not too bad, it's OK.' She turned away and reached for her glass of water, then took a sip. It felt lukewarm and gritty, as though it was full of dust.

Eddie frowned.

'I'm just going to the toilet, be right back.'

She sat up and stepped out of bed, knowing she had only moments to reach the bathroom. She wanted to go to the toilet out in the hall, but that would have looked suspicious, and besides, she wasn't sure she'd make it in time. She took two big strides across the carpet to the ensuite and closed the door behind her.

After turning on the tap to hide the noise, she kneeled in front of the toilet and tucked her hair behind her ears. Even though the cleaner had been the previous day, the foul smell of drains turned her stomach, and once she started retching, she couldn't stop. She coughed to try to disguise the sound. When it was finally over, she flushed the toilet and curled up on her side on the bathroom tiles. Her forehead was clammy and the roots of her hair were damp with sweat. This was the worst of it, she had told herself. But she had been wrong: perhaps it was the worst time physically, but emotionally, every single day since then had been more and more difficult.

Breathing slowly, she had gotten to her feet again, splashed her face with the water still gushing from the tap, then patted her skin dry with the towel. She brushed her teeth, swilled mouthwash, then went back out into the bedroom.

Eddie had placed her pillow on top of his own to prop himself up, and was reading something on his phone. He looked up as she collapsed into bed. 'I told you this wouldn't be easy.'

Nadia closed her eyes. 'I'm fine, Eddie.'

'I'm not an idiot. I know what morning sickness is, I've seen you go through it three times. You can tell me, you know, you don't have to pretend.'

'I'm not pretending anything. I feel a bit nauseous but I'm OK.'

'Really?'

'Leave me alone! What are you saying it like that for?'

'Because I don't know what you're trying to prove.'

'Please. Just let me rest for a few minutes.' He was right: what was she trying to prove, and who was she trying to prove it to?

He sighed. 'Sorry. Come here…' He lifted up the blanket for her to come closer.

Nadia shuffled her body towards him, then turned so her back was against his chest. He dropped his arm and the blanket around her. She put her hand on his broad arm, soft with hair. As she began to relax, her eyes filled with tears. It was so hard not to think about the tiny baby inside her. With her own children, she had welcomed the nausea, knowing it was a sign that the pregnancy was strong, that hormones were flooding her body and making sure she knew to be careful, to watch what she ate, because her babies were growing. But this pregnancy – Zoe and Lachlan's – was different. She didn't want to think like that about the child she was carrying, to be reminded of it every moment of the day, every time she breathed; she didn't want to think about the child at all. She knew then that when she felt the quickening in a few months, the tiny flutters and twitches of the growing baby, it would be impossible to keep herself and the child separate. Closing her eyes, she let a tear drip down her cheek as she heard Harry cry and the girls laugh. She had promised that the children wouldn't suffer because of the pregnancy; she had promised that nothing would change. How could she have thought that was possible? With a sigh, Nadia had forced herself to get up and start the day, wishing that it was already over and they could go back to normal.

But the pregnancy *was* over now, and yet things were far from normal. The fact that she couldn't talk about it without breaking down attested to that.

–

Zoe slid open the screen door to the back garden, wincing as it screeched. She froze, listening, with her white washing basket balanced on her hip, one bare foot poised to step outside. Louise was only now starting to get into a routine, and Zoe had finally managed to rock her to sleep. But, thankfully, there was no noise from her room.

Zoe tiptoed outside. She loved spending all her time with Louise, but it was harder work than she'd anticipated, especially when Lachlan was away, as he was now, so she needed the time when Louise napped to get things done.

Although – not that she'd ever admit it to Lachlan – in many other ways, things were easier when he was away: his moods had become difficult to predict, and often he was so distant towards her and Louise that it made little difference whether he was there or not. Zoe understood how tiring it was for him to work away, and that he'd want some solitude when he came back home, but he needed to make up for the time he spent on the mines so that he and Louise had a good relationship.

They'd gone to Kings Park on the weekend, just before Lachlan left for Kalgoorlie again. After weeks of spring rain, it had been a clear sunny day, warm and still. They walked past colourful wildflowers to a shady spot under a sugar gum tree, overlooking the Swan River; behind the river, on the horizon, were the hills of the Darling Range. Zoe put a sunhat on Louise, then laid her on her back on the picnic blanket. A breeze blew in off the river, swishing through the leaves above them, and dappling their faces with sunlight. After they'd eaten the sandwiches she'd made, Zoe sat with her legs bent to the side, leaning on her right hand, looking down at her own freckled arm next to Louise's pale, smooth skin. Lachlan lay on his back, his thongs discarded near their bags. Every so often, he raised his head just enough to sip from a can of lemonade, then relaxed back down again and closed his eyes. Louise rolled her head on the rug, eyes wide, watching a butterfly flap around her face. Zoe smiled to herself as she looked at her little family.

Then a shadow passed over them. Zoe looked up, shielding her eyes with her hand.

'Hi, guys!'

'Pete, mate, how are you?' Lachlan smiled, stood up. He slapped Pete on the back and grinned. 'You remember my wife, Zoe?'

'Hi!' Zoe picked up Louise and stood up too. Pete was an old workmate of Lachlan's. He was heavier than she remembered, with a solid paunch. His face was lined by years in the sun. He was walking a panting black labrador on a lead.

'Of course!' said Pete. 'It's been a while – probably haven't seen you since that Christmas party, what, three years ago?'

Zoe laughed. 'Yeah, probably. God, that was a big night! Are you still working up north?'

'Nah, got sick of the travelling. I've got a job here now, a boring nine to five. Money's not so good, but better for the wife, you know. And who's this little one?' Pete leaned forward and stroked Louise's cheek; she smiled, then turned her head into Zoe's shoulder.

'This is our little girl, Louise,' Zoe said.

Pete turned to Lachlan. 'I didn't know you had a baby! Congratulations! You kept that one quiet.'

Zoe looked at Lachlan; he shrugged, then put his hand on Louise's shoulder. 'Yeah, she's two months old now.'

'Seven weeks,' Zoe said, making sure she kept smiling as Lachlan shifted from foot to foot. 'Have you got kids yet, Pete? Lachlan never tells me anything…'

'Yeah, yeah, an eighteen-month-old, and another on the way.'

Lachlan laughed. 'See, I didn't know you were having another one either, you're as bad as me.'

Louise squirmed; Zoe shifted her into her other arm and bounced up and down at the knees while the men talked about work, but she wasn't really listening. Lachlan and Pete didn't work together any more, but they had many mutual friends. How could Pete not have heard that they had a baby? Especially given how Louise was born – people didn't forget that in a hurry. She held Louise tightly to her until they said their goodbyes and Pete walked away with his dog waddling beside him.

As soon as he left, Zoe handed Louise to Lachlan. 'Here, take her.' She collected the sandwich crusts, scrunched them up with the used cling wrap and threw them in the esky, then wrapped up the cheese and chucked that in too. Her face burned.

Lachlan strapped Louise into her stroller, then looked up. 'What's wrong now?'

Zoe shook her head. 'Forget it.' She moved the esky onto the grass, grabbed the picnic blanket and shook it out.

'Careful!' Lachlan flapped his hand in front of his face. 'Forget what?'

'You really don't know?'

'No!'

'Fine. Why didn't Pete know you had a baby? Why didn't you tell him?'

'Jesus, Zoe. I didn't *not* tell him, I haven't seen him for ages. I was hardly going to call everyone I've ever known. I don't go round making a big deal of it.'

'A big deal? You don't think having a baby is a big deal? I don't understand why you haven't told people!' Zoe looked at him with wide eyes. 'Why aren't you shouting it out? We haven't done anything wrong, Lachie!'

'Of course we haven't done anything wrong.' He rubbed the back of his neck. 'But people haven't seen you pregnant, so they don't expect to see us with Louise, and I just don't want to have to explain all the gory details every time. Everybody wants to know how it happened, whose kid she really is.'

'She's *our* kid!'

'Yeah, but they assume that we've paid some poor bloody Indian woman to take all the risks while we lounge around, and then when they hear about Nadia they make jokes about me making babies with your sister, or—'

'That's ridiculous! Who says that about you and Nadia? People don't think that! Maybe that's what *you* think about, but no one else does!' Zoe realised as she said it that she was finally voicing a long-buried fear, the fear that her sister and husband shared such an intimate connection.

Lachlan shook his head, his face grim, then started to push the stroller away.

'That's right, just walk away, as usual!' Zoe picked up the nappy bag and picnic blanket, then stormed after him. 'I'm sorry I couldn't carry our child. I'm sorry that you have to put up with questions about where our daughter came from and that you're ashamed of her.' Zoe wished she could stop the words, but she couldn't. She wanted to hurt Lachlan, to make him feel rejected in the same way she thought he was rejecting her – and Louise.

Lachlan stopped, then spun around, eyes blazing. 'Stop it! That's a horrible thing to say. I'm not ashamed, I'm not blaming you – you are! Just give it a rest.' Lachlan grabbed the esky in his left hand then pushed the stroller towards Zoe, the muscles in his forearms rigid.

Zoe took a tiny step back, blinking away the tears that stung her eyes. She'd never seen him look so furious; now, she regretted pushing him so far. 'Lachlan, calm down, just look at you—'

'Look at *me*?' he said quietly, his jaw bulging, as he stopped just in front of her.

Zoe took a deep breath and lowered her eyes to look down at Louise, who was watching two dogs playing at the other end of the park. Louise shouldn't have to hear this; the surrogacy had made her life confusing enough. Zoe had started this; why had she ruined such a nice day, their last day together for a fortnight? Lachlan was constantly on edge at the moment, and he'd never been like that before, but was he really the problem, or was he merely reacting to her own self-doubt and anger? 'Sorry, my fault. Let's go,' Zoe mumbled.

'No—'

'People are watching! I want to go home!' She had taken off towards the car, listening to the squeak of Louise's stroller and the rhythmic clunking of the esky as Lachlan had followed her.

Now, Zoe sighed and walked across her courtyard carrying the washing basket. The bricks were cool under her feet. She hadn't slept well last night; she'd dreamed that there was a heavy blanket on her face and woken several times gasping for air, paralysed and confused in that hypnopompic moment between dreaming and waking.

A breeze wafted through the garden and scattered the dry gum leaves across the pavers. She reached the washing line, strung between a branch of the gum tree in the back corner of the yard and the drainpipe on the wall, and put the basket down at her feet. She shuddered as a sticky thread brushed her forehead. A huge web glinted silver in the sun, extending between the clothesline and a branch of the tree. She let her heart settle: just a garden spider. Glancing back at the wall, she saw a messy redback nest tangled behind the drainpipe. She must call someone to spray it before Louise learned to crawl. She began hanging out the clothes on the section of line adjacent to the web.

The doorbell rang inside the house. She jumped, then dropped the damp towel she was holding and hurried towards the back door. She didn't stop to wipe the grit from the soles of her feet, but ran past Louise's room, hoping to get to the front door before the bell rang again. Louise cried out. Zoe swore under her breath.

'It's only me!' Nadia called from outside.

Zoe tried to slide the chain open without scraping the metal, but Louise cried again. Too late. She let it fall with a clatter, then wrenched open the door.

Nadia stood on the doorstep, smiling. She was wearing workout pants, running shoes and a tight pink lycra top. She had a big black bag slung over her shoulder and in her other hand, she held a white cardboard box.

'Hi! I thought you might be in. I've just been to the gym so thought I'd pop in to see Louise – and you!' Nadia frowned and raised her eyebrows as Louise cried. 'Oh, sorry! Did I wake Louise?'

Zoe forced herself to smile back. 'Oh no, it was about time she woke up anyway, she'd been asleep for a while. I was just hanging out the washing before lunch…' She gestured vaguely towards the back of the house and moved aside as Nadia stepped through the door.

Zoe closed the door behind her sister. What was she doing here? Nadia never just dropped in; she lived almost an hour away. Then Zoe reminded herself of what Nadia had done for her, and how close they'd become again throughout the surrogacy. Louise shouldn't change that.

Nadia was halfway down the hall already; she turned back to Zoe. 'Go and finish hanging your washing, I'll get Louise up.'

'No, that's OK.' Zoe stepped in front of Nadia and opened Louise's door, then walked towards the cot.

'Look,' Nadia said, peering over Zoe's shoulder. 'She's getting so big!'

'Yes, she is.' Zoe smiled, picked Louise up and turned around.

'She looks so much like Lachlan, look at those blue eyes!' Nadia reached out and stroked Louise's arm.

Zoe's face burned as her smile faded away. Why did Nadia have to say that? To emphasise that Louise didn't look like her, Zoe? 'Do you want to go and see Aunty Nadia?' she said to Louise, in a high-pitched voice that she knew sounded silly and strained. She held Louise out towards Nadia, who took her as if it was the most natural thing in the world. Louise's face wrinkled and her mouth opened. She looked back at Zoe then coughed out a cry.

'Aw, bit tired still?' Zoe said and stepped closer, hoping her relief didn't show on her face.

'She's fine,' Nadia said. 'Aren't you, Lou-Lou? Yes!' She made a stupid face and nuzzled her head into Louise's chest. Louise stopped crying, frowned, then tilted her head to the side and smiled. 'Aw, look. That's the first smile she's given me!'

'Yeah. I wasn't sure at first if she was just practising, but she's definitely smiling at people now.' Zoe cleared her throat. 'Well, I'll go and finish hanging that washing, be right back.'

Back outside, she pursed her lips and let out a long, slow breath. She quickly shook out the damp towels in the basket and pegged them up, not wanting to leave Louise alone with Nadia for too long. She closed her eyes; she was being ridiculous.

Returning inside, Zoe forced herself not to rush to Louise, but instead took the kettle, tipped the old water down the sink, then refilled it. While it boiled, she took down her red teapot and spooned tea leaves from a floral caddy into the strainer. She opened the cupboard above the sink to get the mugs, then changed her mind and reached onto the top shelf for the pale duck-egg blue cups and saucers that she and Lachlan had been given as a wedding present. After wiping the dust from the insides of the cups with some paper towel, she placed them on the saucers. She opened the lid of the box that Nadia had brought with her, now sitting on the kitchen bench; it held two chocolate éclairs. She put them on a plate, then filled the teapot with boiling water.

'Nadia, tea's ready.'

Nadia appeared in the kitchen, Louise in her arms. 'Thanks! I can't believe how much Lou has grown in the past couple of weeks. She looks... well, not like a newborn any more. She's a proper baby now.'

Zoe nodded and smiled. 'I know. It's amazing to see.'

'Shame Lachlan isn't here to watch her grow. When's he back?'

'Another week yet. It goes quickly, though, and at least he'll be back for Christmas this year. How's life up in the hills?'

'Yeah, it's good. Oh, I don't know, sometimes it feels like it's so far away from everyone, but we like the space...'

Nadia sighed, and looked towards the teapot. 'The tea will be ready now, do you think?'

'I like it strong.' Zoe reached for a chocolate éclair and took a big bite. 'Mmm.' She picked up the plate and held it out to Nadia.

Nadia shook her head. 'I couldn't eat a whole one! Go and cut a bit off for me, would you?'

Zoe blushed and licked cream from the corner of her mouth, putting down her own pastry. She took a knife from the top drawer and cut off about a third of the éclair, then held the plate out to Nadia again. 'I'll take Louise.'

Nadia took the piece. 'No, don't worry. I'm an expert at eating one-handed, you'll get used to it.' She sat down at the table, held the éclair out of the baby's reach and took a nibble. 'So, how are you coping with Louise?'

Zoe sat opposite her. 'Oh, well, you know, it's tiring, but we're doing OK.' She tilted her head and smiled at Louise, still in Nadia's arms.

Nadia frowned at Zoe. 'You look like you've lost weight. Are you eating OK?'

Zoe looked down at her legs. Her pants *were* a little loose on her. 'Yeah, maybe I have. Not that I'm complaining!' she laughed. 'Sometimes when Lachlan's away it's easier for me just to eat some cereal for dinner, or eggs on toast.'

'You know I'm here if you ever need anything. I've been through it three times so I've learned a few things along the way. Or if you ever need me to pick you up some groceries or anything, just ask. I can even bring you meals.'

Zoe reached her hand across the table to Nadia. 'Thanks, Nadia. I really appreciate it, but we're fine, honestly!' Zoe knew that she could do with some help, but she didn't feel she could admit it to her sister. She didn't want to do anything to let Nadia down, to make her think that she wasn't looking after Louise properly, not after everything Nadia had done for her. 'I'm going to Mum's for dinner tomorrow night so she'll feed me up.'

'In the meantime, eat some more cake. Go on, I remember what it was like. Babies are hard work, there's no shame in admitting that!'

Zoe laughed, but blushed. She *was* ashamed to admit things were hard on her own with a baby, especially with Lachlan being so preoccupied when he was home. She didn't want to acknowledge that life with Louise was anything but perfect, and especially not to her sister.

Nadia shifted Louise to her other arm. 'That tea will be strong enough for me now, do you mind… ?'

'Oh, sure, sorry.'

She poured the tea into the mugs, started to look in the cupboard for the milk jug, then took out the plastic container from the fridge and plonked it on the bench. She reached for the baby, and this time, Nadia handed her over. Zoe cuddled her, and felt her heart start to settle. She kissed Louise's head, and wrinkled her nose at the smell of Nadia's perfume. At least she could wash out that remnant of her sister later.

Chapter Twelve

Zoe woke to the sound of Louise starting to whimper from her room. For a moment she willed her back to sleep, then remembered. It was Christmas Day, Louise's first Christmas, and Lachlan was home. She smiled, pushed herself up on her elbows and turned to Lachlan, who was turned away from her. 'Merry Christmas!'

'What time is it?' he muttered.

'It's almost six. The sun's up!' She leaned over and kissed his shoulder. 'Try to be happy just for one day, please.' She threw back the covers and walked towards Louise's room.

Louise was crying now, kicking her legs inside her thin sleeping bag. But when she saw Zoe, she stilled and quietened. Zoe paused, savouring the beautiful knowledge that Louise was soothed by her. Finally, she felt the bond between them strengthening; she'd always been strongly attached to Louise, but she'd feared it might never be reciprocated. That fear was ebbing away. She reached into the cot and lifted her up.

'Merry Christmas, sweet pea!' She kissed Louise's chubby cheek and laughed as Louise opened her mouth and shook her head from side to side. 'Let's get your bottle, yes? And then we'll see what Santa brought!' Zoe pointed to the red felt stocking that she'd hung from the end of the cot after feeding Louise at three am. She thought back to her own happy childhood Christmases. Although at three months old, Louise was too young to know what was going on, Zoe still wanted to re-create that feeling for her. She had wanted to stay at home this Christmas, cook lunch herself, just the three of them, but last year they'd been to Lachlan's parents' place for lunch, and this year it was her mum's turn. Nadia would be there too. Zoe pushed away the flutter of nerves; she still felt as though she had to continually show her gratitude whenever she saw Nadia, or that she was doing something wrong with Louise, revealing her inexperience. But it was Christmas, a time for family. They would have lunch, and then go to Lachlan's parents' in the afternoon. It was only a few hours, and then it would just be the three of them again.

She took Louise back through for Lachlan to hold while she microwaved water in a bottle then added spoonfuls of formula. She shook it up while she went back through to the bedroom. 'Do you want to give this to her?'

Lachlan smiled and reached for the bottle. 'Sure.'

In the living room, Zoe switched on the television and found a music channel playing Christmas pop songs. She turned it up loud and hummed along as she made a pot of coffee, poured two glasses of fresh orange juice and switched on the oven to heat the chocolate croissants she'd bought yesterday. The day was warm already; although the breeze wasn't in yet, she opened the front and back doors, leaving the flyscreens closed.

Lachlan came through to the kitchen carrying Louise. He smiled at Zoe, but his eyes were bloodshot.

'You didn't sleep well?' she said.

He shrugged. 'It was hot.'

She nodded. 'I tried to be quiet when I fed Louise.'

'I know. It wasn't you.'

Zoe took a step towards him. 'Here, give me the baby, I'll go and get her changed. I said we'd be at Mum's at about eleven so there's plenty of time if you want to go for a swim down the beach?'

'Yeah, I might do that.'

'After breakfast and presents, OK? I got champagne so we can make buck's fizz...'

'That sounds great.' His cheeks flushed; for a moment, Zoe thought he was going to cry. He blinked, then smiled at her.

She smiled back. She was imagining it; he was just tired. After changing and dressing Louise, she took their camera out of her bedside table. She snapped a few pictures of Louise in her new red and green Christmas dress, then went through to the living room and put her in a bouncy chair.

Zoe chattered to Lachlan over breakfast; afterwards, they sat on the rug in the living room, next to Louise. Zoe took one of Louise's parcels out of the felt stocking, partially ripped open the paper, and jiggled it in front of her until she grabbed a piece of the paper and put her fist to her mouth.

Zoe laughed. 'Take a picture, Lachlan!' She opened the present herself – a little padded book with pictures of farm animals – and then did the same for the rest of Louise's presents.

She had bought Lachlan some clothes, and a mug with a photo of Louise on it. She blushed when he frowned at it. 'I thought you could take it up to work with you...'

He laughed, but it sounded hollow. He handed her two presents: a new red diary, the same one that he bought her every year, and a voucher for a spa treatment. Zoe leaned over and hugged him. 'Thank you. Now, I'm going to put Louise down for a nap – go have a swim while I tidy up and get dressed.'

–

Zoe closed her eyes and took a deep breath, trying to stop her stomach churning as Lachlan parked on the verge out the front of her parents' house. She sighed deeply, but didn't open the door.

'It'll be fine,' he said.

'I know. I know that, but I still feel... Never mind. I'm just being silly.' She wanted him for once to acknowledge how difficult this whole situation was for her. Life *was* wonderful now, but Nadia was a constant reminder of the part of Louise that Zoe had missed out on. Every time she saw her sister, Zoe wondered if it would have been easier to have hired a surrogate overseas: the break would have been cleaner, the truth more quickly forgotten. But, she reminded herself, Nadia was Louise's aunt. That was all. Families were built on relationships, not genes. Weren't they?

Lachlan squeezed her thigh, then took the keys out of the ignition and opened the door.

Zoe bit her lip, sniffed, and wiped her eyes. She quickly got out and opened the back door to unstrap Louise.

Rosemary and Martin answered the door together, and everyone kissed and hugged and wished each other a merry Christmas. 'Come in!' Martin said. 'Nadia and Eddie are out the back with the kids – they brought their new bikes and scooters and God knows what else from Santa!'

'Great!' Zoe said.

'Merry Christmas, Louise!' Rosemary said, taking her from Zoe. 'Isn't it wonderful? Her first Christmas!'

Rosemary had draped strings of silver tinsel around the picture frames on the wall, the vases and lamps, and a gold, shiny banner hung above the patio doors. The tree in the corner of the living room was the same one they had brought down from the loft every Christmas for as long as Zoe could remember, though the plastic needles had gradually dropped off. Red and green baubles dangled from the branches, and foil-wrapped chocolates hung by loops of thread. Zoe smiled when she saw the angel that she had made in junior school, with its ping-pong ball head and a cone of felt for a dress. Under the tree were piles of presents, and a plastic Santa that Zoe knew sang 'Rocking Around the Christmas Tree' and danced when it was turned on, as it inevitably would be after lunch. Zoe put her own plastic bag of presents under the tree with the others; they always waited until after lunch to open them.

She heard Louise start to cry behind her. Somewhere in her gut, her muscles contracted, and she involuntarily turned towards the sound. Everyone was outside on the deck. Her mum was bouncing the baby over her shoulder; Nadia was patting her back. That wouldn't work, that wasn't what Louise liked. She was tired; she needed to lie down somewhere quiet and suck her dummy, not have everyone fuss over her and jiggle her around. But if Zoe ran over there, she would look insecure. Louise was fine; it was all fine. She cleared her throat then rearranged the presents under the tree.

Louise cried again. This time, Zoe would go; she'd given them a chance to settle her, but Louise needed *her*, her mum. She walked towards the door, then saw Nadia take Louise from Rosemary. Louise stopped crying. Nadia held her in the crook of her arm and rocked her from side to side. As she did so, she gazed into Louise's eyes, and Zoe could see from the way her lips moved that she was singing. Louise's little fists relaxed. Zoe's heart almost stopped. Louise's eyes were open and bright and she stared into Nadia's eyes with a tiny smile on her little red lips, hypnotised. Nadia looked down at her with her head tilted. *The precursor of the mirror is the mother's face.* Zoe now understood what that line meant; it was from a book about mother and infant attachment she'd read when she was watching Nadia's abdomen grow, with a mixture of excitement and envy about what she was missing out on. Zoe knew Louise could see her own image in Nadia's face. Nadia had gathered up Louise's anxiety, held it until it burned away, then reflected the security back to her. She could almost hear Louise's heart rate settle and feel her blood pressure falling. Zoe almost cried out. Lachlan was chatting to Eddie; neither of them had noticed. She hurried over to Nadia. 'Is she OK?'

'She's perfect!' said Nadia, not taking her eyes off Louise. 'She's just gorgeous, Zoe!'

Zoe swallowed, wishing she could take credit for that. 'Thanks. Do you want me to take her?'

Nadia shook her head. 'No, we're fine, aren't we, Louise? Don't worry, go and sit down, have a drink. I know what it's like with a little baby, you never get a minute to yourself – go and relax. It's been a long time since mine were babies…'

'I don't mind, when she's tired, she—'

'Zoe, honestly, we're fine. Go and have a drink!'

Zoe smiled, but her eyes began to blur. She nodded, turning away. What she really wanted to do was grab Louise and go home. She walked into the kitchen and poured herself a glass of water. As she sipped it, her mum came back through to the kitchen and took out two punnets of strawberries from the fridge. She took a chopping board out of a cupboard, then reached for a knife from the block.

'You want a hand, Mum?'

'No, no, it's OK, go and relax.'

'You sure?' Zoe said quietly.

'Yes, I've got everything under control.' Rosemary bustled past Zoe and started chopping the fruit. 'Go and sit down, Zoe, you're in my way.'

'Sorry.' Zoe picked up her glass and walked back towards the patio doors. Lachlan and Eddie leaned on the wooden garden table drinking beer; Martin was basting the turkey in the Weber. The children were on the lawn, paddling in a blue plastic clamshell filled with water. Nadia was sitting in a garden chair, humming to Louise. Zoe brushed away a tear. Why wasn't she happy? She had everything she wanted. Why did she feel as if she was intruding on a painted scene, her body daubed in the corner as an afterthought?

A painted ship on a painted ocean.

–

There was far too much food, as usual. The turkey, wrapped in foil, was resting on top of the oven, and a huge glazed ham, scored and dotted with cloves, sat on a platter. The dining table was covered with a dark green tablecloth, set with the best cutlery, sparkling glasses, and Christmas crackers. In the centre, next to a small wooden reindeer and a ceramic angel, was a big plate of barbecued prawns, marinated in coriander and chilli, with segments of lemon wedged around the edges, as well as a bowl of cold, unshelled prawns. An unopened bottle of Marie Rose sauce was next to it. The six adults were seated at the dining table.

Next to the adults' table, Rosemary had covered a smaller table with a crepe-paper tablecloth with pictures of Santa. Charlotte, Violet and Harry sat around it, already eating their bread rolls while they waited for lunch. Louise was in the spare room, asleep in a travel cot.

Rosemary put a tray of vegetables in the oven then wiped a strand of hair off her forehead as she walked back to the table. 'Get started, everyone, don't let it get cold,' she said. 'Oh, Martin, put on the air-con, would you?'

'Eddie, these look amazing, thanks for bringing them,' Zoe said.

Eddie grinned. 'Thanks! Hope they taste as good!'

Zoe reached for a prawn, smiling at Martin as he did the same.

'Ah, hold on.' Martin stood up and licked his fingers, then wiped them on his napkin. 'Drinks!'

They all waited while he went outside to the fridge on the deck, and came back with a bottle of champagne. He popped the cork, and everyone laughed as the bubbles foamed up and trickled down the outside of the bottle.

'Quick!' Nadia squealed, holding out her glass to be filled.

Martin filled all their glasses, while Rosemary poured the kids tumblers of lemonade, then Martin stood up again. 'Merry Christmas, everyone!'

'And especially to our newest granddaughter on her very first Christmas!' Rosemary added.

Zoe smiled, overwhelmed with tenderness towards her family. She had to stop worrying so much; she was so lucky. They all raised their glasses and clinked them together. Nadia went over to the kids' table and did the same with her giggling children, then gave each of them a kiss. Zoe watched her, and smiled. It was nice to see her, after all.

After the entree, the table was laden with the turkey, ham, potatoes, trays of roasted vegetables, jars of cranberry sauce, pots of mustard. Everyone ate and drank, and Zoe felt herself relaxing. When Louise woke up, she didn't jump up to get her immediately; she let Nadia go to her and instead helped Rosemary clear the table. She reminded herself that she had done the same thing herself when her sister's children were young; there was nothing sinister in wanting to hold a baby, it was a natural instinct. She filled the sink with hot water and detergent and chatted to her mother while Rosemary whipped the cream for the pavlova.

When they had all sat down for dessert, the children wriggling in their seats with excitement, Nadia picked up her spoon and tapped it against her wine glass. She cleared her throat.

'Just before we start eating even more food, I've got something I want to say. First of all, thank you, Rosemary, Dad, for all this.' She held out her arms over the table. 'And I want to say an especially happy first Christmas to baby Louise.' She inclined her head and smiled at Lachlan, who was feeding Louise her bottle.

Zoe kept smiling, but she felt a flutter of anxiety in her stomach. She glanced at Lachlan, but he was smiling back at Nadia.

Nadia licked her lips, then took a sip of her wine, clearly not finished her speech. She put the glass down, slowly, and glanced at her children, then Eddie. 'I also have some news – well, *we* have some news.'

Zoe held her breath, trying to ignore the building dread. What news? Nadia couldn't be pregnant again, could she? A jolt of jealousy shot through Zoe; why was it so damn easy for her? No, she told herself, Nadia was drinking; she couldn't be pregnant.

'Gosh,' Nadia laughed. 'You all look so serious! Well, I've been thinking about this for a while, but since Louise was born, I've realised how important family is to me, and so we're moving back to Perth!'

'But you only live an hour away!' Zoe said, before she could stop herself.

'I know, but Eddie's spending so much time travelling to and from the city for work every day, and the kids are getting older and I want them to go to better schools. And anyway, an hour is too far now that the kids have a new cousin!'

'That's great,' Martin said. 'It'll be fantastic to have you a bit closer. You won't miss the space you have?'

Eddie shrugged. 'A bit, but it means I can spend more time at home with the kids, make it easier for Nadia. At the moment I barely see them, they're often in bed by the time I get home.'

'That'll be so nice for them,' Martin said, smiling over at Charlotte, Violet and Harry.

Zoe kept the smile fixed on her face, but it felt like the room was spinning. She didn't want Nadia any closer. 'Where will you move to?'

'Somewhere around here, close to all of you. We'll rent our house out for now and keep it as an investment property, then we'll just find a rental near here to get us started,' said Nadia. 'I've enrolled all the kids in school here from the start of next term.'

'Wow, that soon? That's only a month away.'

'Yeah, well, I thought it was better to start them there at the beginning of the year so there's no more disruption to their lives.'

'Makes sense. Well, congratulations, it's a big decision but it sounds like it's the right one for your family.' Zoe tried to make her voice sound light-hearted.

'Well, that's great news, we look forward to it!' Rosemary said.

Nadia started to chatter about rental property prices. Zoe picked at a serving of trifle, then took Louise from Lachlan and went to sit outside in the shade. She hoped that Lachlan would notice and come to sit with them, but he opened another beer with Eddie and Martin, and kept on drinking.

–

Zoe held it together through the rest of lunch. She drank a big glass of water, already feeling hungover from the alcohol, then made herself a coffee, pulled crackers with the children, put on a red paper hat and read out the lame jokes.

After the meal, Martin disappeared into his bedroom, then came out wearing a fake white beard and a Santa hat. 'Ho ho ho,' he said in a deep voice.

'Santa!' the children squealed and ran towards him.

'It's Grandad!' shouted Charlotte.

'Shh!' Zoe said, forcing herself to laugh.

She sat on the floor with the children, Louise propped up in the space between her crossed legs. Martin – as Santa – handed out the presents. He and Rosemary gave Louise a toy piano that played nursery rhymes. Thanking her mum, Zoe gave her a hug, and the smell of Rosemary's hairspray and perfume almost made her weep. She wanted to tell her mum how she felt, how Nadia's news had left her with a pit of anxiety in her stomach, but she couldn't spoil the day. She knew what Rosemary would say: that she was overreacting, and misjudging Nadia. Maybe she was.

Violet handed Zoe a small parcel, beautifully wrapped in shiny silver paper with a white ribbon and bow. 'For Louise,' she said.

Zoe smiled and smoothed Violet's hair back from her face. 'Oh, Louise says thank you very much!'

'Open it, open it!' Violet squealed.

'OK!' Zoe squealed back, laughing. Her hands trembled as she began to untie the bow. She handed the ribbon to Louise to play with while she turned the box over and began to peel back the corner of the sticky tape with her short fingernails. As she gently took off the paper she stared at the cream-coloured box inside, the name of a jeweller etched in black on the lid. She didn't want to open it; she wanted to hand it back straight away. She knew it was something expensive, when all she had bought for

Nadia's children were sticker books and selection boxes. Charlotte, Violet and Harry were watching her with wide eyes, bouncing up and down.

Lachlan nudged her. 'Go on, open it.'

She lifted the hinged lid of the box. Inside was a solid silver charm bracelet, with a single charm attached. A stork, carrying a baby in a sling from its mouth. Zoe's heart pounded.

'I hope you like it,' Nadia said. 'I thought I'd get her something nice, you know, for her first Christmas.'

'It's beautiful, thank you,' Zoe managed to say. 'Look, Lachlan.'

He took the box from her. 'Wow, thanks!'

Didn't he see what she saw? But Lachlan had put the box down and was opening his own gifts now, as if there was nothing amiss. Zoe lifted Louise up against her chest. 'I'm just going to change her nappy. Then we should go. We're due at Lachlan's folks.'

'OK,' Lachlan said. Zoe began to push herself up off the floor with one hand.

'Here, I'll take Louise,' said Nadia, leaning over the arm of the couch.

'No! I'm fine, just a bit stiff…' Zoe struggled to her feet then looked at her sister. Nadia's eyes were so sad; Zoe remembered again exactly what her sister had done for her.

'Sorry,' Zoe mumbled. 'She's just a bit clingy at the moment. I'll be right back.'

After changing Louise, Zoe bundled up all their presents into a bag. As she, Lachlan and Louise were leaving, she noticed that Nadia didn't come to the door to say goodbye.

-

Zoe walked ahead of Lachlan to the car, shielding Louise's face from the sun with her hand. She strapped Louise into her baby capsule; she cried and protested, but settled as soon as Lachlan started the engine. As they drove away, Lachlan said nothing. Zoe switched on the radio, then looked out of the window at the quiet streets. The heat shimmered off the tarmac. She tilted the air-conditioning vent towards her, then fanned her face with her hand. Shifting in the seat, she glanced sideways at Lachlan; he kept looking straight ahead. She cleared her throat. 'So, what do you think about Nadia and Eddie moving?'

He sighed. 'Oh, Zoe. Don't read too much into it.'

'I'm not, I'm not, it just all seems a bit sudden.'

'You're making too much out of it, Zoe.'

Zoe looked out of the window. Was she? Nadia had never talked about moving back to Perth before, in fact she'd always gone on about how much she loved living out of the city. She thought again about how Nadia had looked at Louise, and about the gift she'd chosen, then shook her head.

'No, Lachlan, something's not right.'

They stopped at some traffic lights. Two little boys pedalled across the road on shiny bikes that were just that bit too big for them, their helmets slipping over their eyes.

'Babe, I know you're worried but maybe she's telling the truth,' said Lachlan. 'Maybe she just wants to be near her family...'

Zoe turned away so he wouldn't see the tears in her eyes. She wanted him to back her up, to tell her that her feelings were legitimate, that they mattered. 'Lachlan, sometimes I wonder if you—'

Lachlan drove off as the lights turned green. 'What?'

Zoe paused before she spoke. She knew that once she said it, she couldn't take it back. He'd react angrily, she knew, but anything would be better than this detachment, this distance. She took a deep breath then spoke softly. 'I just wonder if you're coping OK with all this—'

'What?' He turned towards her; his face was angry, but she saw hurt in his eyes.

Zoe looked at her lap, picked at a thread on her dress. 'Babe, it's just that ever since we got Louise, you've been—'

'I've been what?'

'Well, you know, distant, preoccupied...' Her voice was practically a whisper now. She wondered whether she shouldn't have said anything, but she couldn't stop now. 'It's like you don't notice me, or Louise.'

'Zoe, that's a ridiculous thing to say! I can't believe this. Don't... don't turn this on me because you're so paranoid and insecure!'

'I'm not being paranoid! Nadia misses Louise, I can see it, I can see it every time she looks at her. She's regretting it—'

'Too bad if she does. It's too late for her to regret it, she has no rights any more.' Lachlan spoke with finality, as if it was all so black and white.

'I know, but it's not just about the paperwork, is it? Just because there's an order in place, that doesn't necessarily break such a strong bond and stop her feeling like a mum.' Zoe's voice cracked. 'You just coast along like everything's fine. We did a big thing, Lachlan, doing this. We did something that very few people do and it's not necessarily straightforward...'

'Well, didn't I warn you that it wouldn't be easy? I tried to say it was too hard, too risky, but you were so convinced that you wanted a child.'

Tears were running down Zoe's face now. 'Oh, so you didn't want a child?'

'Shit, Zoe, don't twist my words.' Lachlan floored the accelerator as they turned a corner, the force pushing Zoe back in her seat.

'The baby! Jesus, Lachlan!'

He said nothing, but his face was scarlet.

'Should you even be driving? How much did you have to drink?'

'Leave it.'

'I'm just—'

'Shut up!' he shouted. Zoe shrank back in her seat as she saw the hatred in his face. The veins in his neck bulged and his hands gripped the steering wheel. She wished she could take it all back, rewind to this morning when it was just the three of them at home in front of their Christmas tree. Instead of bringing them closer together, she knew she'd just forced them further apart.

Chapter Thirteen

Lou was still grounded. After another awkward dinner – her dad had come home early so they could all eat a meal together (something Ross had obviously suggested) and had tried to engage Lou in conversation – she had escaped to her room. Her dad had forgotten to take her phone back off her tonight; she'd been allowed to take it when she walked Sandy in case of an emergency, so it was still in the pocket of her running pants. She'd tried calling Theo when she was out, but he hadn't answered. He must be at swimming practice; he represented the state. She'd left a message, and texted him, hoping he might check his phone in between laps or something, but he hadn't called back yet.

Lou sat on her bed. Her laptop was on the dining table; she was only allowed to use it where her parents could see what she was doing. Her iPad was somewhere in their room, confiscated until she could 'earn' it back, though they hadn't told her the currency. She made sure that her mobile was on silent, texted Theo again, then checked her emails and Facebook updates to try to work out what he'd been doing. Her parents didn't understand how important it was that she contact him: Theo loved her but if she couldn't see him or talk to him, he'd find someone else.

There were plenty of other girls from her school waiting to pounce on him.

Her parents were bickering downstairs. She turned on the radio; surely they couldn't complain about that? They probably wouldn't notice anyway. They were making a show, now, of being interested in her, but when had they ever noticed what she did? All they'd ever done was hover over her, trying to force themselves into every aspect of her life without ever really listening to her. If, as they'd said to Ross, they'd been worried about her for a year, why hadn't they said anything twelve months ago, when it might have made a difference? Why hadn't her dad come home early for dinner then? She knew why, because this whole year her mum and dad had been arguing behind their bedroom door and pretending to Lou that they were fine, when she knew that something was very wrong with her parents' relationship.

They were shouting now. Maybe they'd heard the radio after all and assumed that she couldn't hear them, that she was oblivious to their shitty marriage. As if. Lou bit the inside of her cheek, then turned up the volume, but she could still hear them. She stood up, opened her door, then slammed it shut. They stopped yelling, though she could still make out the sharp whispers that they spat at each other like shards of glass. Lou's eyes filled with tears. Didn't they get it? How could they expect her to be perfect if they couldn't hold themselves together? She sat on her bed and squeezed her fists and her eyes tight. *This* was why she did it, why right now all she wanted to do was to go out and get pissed or smoke a joint or take a pill or get a razorblade and cut her arms. Because anything felt better than being here, listening to them.

She opened her schoolbag and emptied it onto the floor, not caring if her books were damaged as they thudded to the ground, then found the novel she was meant to be reading for English. She lay on her bed and flicked through the pages, trying to work out where she was up to. She'd only just found her place when there was a knock at her door.

'Louise?'

'I'm doing my homework, Mum!' she shouted, quickly wiping her eyes.

'Can I come in?'

Lou rubbed her forehead. Why hadn't her mum wanted to come and talk to her when Lou was happy, when she was getting those A's that her parents had apparently been so proud of? Now they were both upset and suddenly her mum wanted to have a heart-to-heart. 'Not now, Mum, please.' Her voice cracked.

Her mum paused, then spoke quietly through the door. 'All right, love. Well, when you've finished, come and talk to me, OK?'

'OK, once I've finished this homework.'

Her mum's voice was thick. 'Can I get you anything? Some toast?'

Tears spilled from Lou's eyes. 'No.'

'How about a hot chocolate? I can put marshmallows on top.'

'No, thanks.'

'All right.'

Lou listened as her mum walked away. Then she saw the screen of her phone light up with a message. It was from Theo. She smiled; thank God. She spent the next hour exchanging messages with him, though she didn't tell him how she really felt, because he hated needy girls. He promised he'd wait for her, until she wasn't grounded any more. After they'd texted their goodbyes, Lou clutched the phone, desperate to see him.

She needed to go to the toilet. She couldn't avoid her mum; Lou knew she'd be waiting to have this talk she so wanted to have. Lou looked at herself in the mirror above her dressing table, her reflection framed by peeling stickers of fairies and rainbows. Her eye make-up was smudged and looked like drips of melted black wax on her cheeks. She opened the dressing-table drawer, took out some cotton wool and cleanser, and wiped it all off.

She opened her door and looked down the hallway. Her parents' bedroom door was ajar and light spilled out; her mum would be reading in bed, as she did every night. Her dad must be in the living room; Lou could hear the sounds of a documentary on TV. She took a deep breath, then knocked gently on her mum's door and pushed it open.

The blankets on the double bed were rumpled on her mum's side, but she wasn't there. A thick book, a novel, lay on her pillow, bookmarked about halfway through. Lou started to turn away, then frowned and stopped. Peeking out from underneath the book was the corner of a photograph. But all of their recent photos were on the computer; they never printed any out. And all the old photos were in albums. She glanced down the hallway. The only sound was that of the television show. She stepped into the room, closed the bedroom door behind her, then went to the bed, lifted up the book and picked up the photograph.

It was a baby photo. She'd never seen it before, but she knew it was of her. She couldn't tell how old she was in it – maybe one? She hadn't seen many photos of herself as a baby; her parents had never – as far as she could remember – sat with her and looked at pictures of them all in the hospital. In this photo, she was with her aunt; she was gazing down at the baby – Lou – in her arms. There was the hint of a smile on her aunt's face, but she looked sad. They were in front of the railing of some sort of bridge with a lake behind them, its surface still and milky blue. It almost looked as though they were in the sky, surrounded by clouds, but Lou could tell by the shimmer around their edges that the clouds were reflected images. She frowned; the setting looked familiar, but she couldn't place it.

She heard her dad's voice from the living room, and her mum's reply. Somehow she knew that she couldn't be found here, with this photo. She quickly replaced it on her mum's pillow, put the book back on top of it, then hurried out of the room. She walked down the hallway and into the living room, trying to act as if nothing was out of the ordinary. Her mum was on the couch, her legs bent up beneath her, resting her head in her hand. She looked tired; Lou wanted to run over and curl up next to her, but she stopped herself.

'Hi, Mum.'

Her mother looked up and smiled. 'Hi. Your dad's just putting the kettle on. Do you want a cup of tea?'

Lou shook her head. 'I've finished now. Did you still want to talk?'

'Oh.' Her mum frowned, then rubbed her eyes. 'It's OK. You must be worn out from all your schoolwork.

I just… I just wanted to tell you how much I love you. You're a good girl, Louise. You really are.'

As her mum gazed at her with a sad smile, Lou thought about the photo she had just seen. There was something about the look in her aunt's eyes that she couldn't put out of her mind.

–

'Lou! They'll be here soon, hurry up!'

Lou sighed. She was about to tell her mum that there was no rush, but thought better of it. After weeks of doing everything her parents told her to do, and staying out of trouble, things were starting to settle down: she was allowed to go out once on the weekend, as long as she was home by ten pm and didn't drink. She was also allowed an hour a day on her laptop in her room, and in another week they'd increase it to two hours. Now she closed her computer, then swung her legs off her bed and went into the kitchen.

'God, Mum, how much have you made?' The benchtop was cluttered with bowls and plates full of food – cheese and biscuits, chips, dip, two salads.

Her mother waved a distracted hand at her. 'Just help me, will you? Clear the table of all that stuff so we can put the food out. Dad's gone to get them, they'll be back any minute.'

'I don't know why you make such a fuss, they hardly eat anything anyway.'

'That's precisely *why* I make a fuss. Your grandma tries her best, but really, she's not up to cooking at all. I wish they'd get some help.'

Lou went to the table and gathered up all the newspapers. 'Where do you want these?'

'Oh, I don't know. Use your intelligence, Lou!'

Raising her eyebrows, Lou walked into the kitchen and dropped the papers into the recycling bin. She heard the front door open, and went out into the hallway, smiling.

'Louise!'

'Hi, Grandma!' Lou grinned, hugged her, and kissed the smooth, cool skin of her cheek. She turned to her grandad and spoke loudly into his left ear. 'Hi, Grandad, how are you?'

'Good, love, good.'

Lou stepped out of the way as he shuffled down the hallway, and her grandmother followed, one hand gripping her walking stick. Lou hated seeing her grandmother's swollen red knuckles, and her fingers bent from years of crippling rheumatoid arthritis. She walked behind them, then pulled out chairs for them both at the table and helped them sit down. She sat opposite them while her dad got them drinks – a beer for her grandad, a white wine for her grandma – and her mum fussed in the kitchen.

'How's school, love?'

'Great, thanks, Grandma.' Lou smiled. It wasn't true, of course, but she could hardly tell her that she was being teased for going to see a shrink, and that she was worried that she wasn't going to pass her final exams. Or that her boyfriend was losing interest in her.

'I always told your mum and dad that you'd turn out all right, even after—'

'Martin!' her grandmother said sharply.

Lou's mum hurried over with a bowl of chips and the platter of cheese and biscuits and held it out to the old man. ‘Cheese? I bought some of that lovely double cream brie that you like.’

Lou looked at her mum, then back to her grandfather. He was blushing, and her grandmother was scowling at him. Lou’s heart sped up, though she didn’t know why. She frowned, watching all the adults fumble for something to say. What was going on?

‘So…’ her dad said. ‘Martin, Rosemary. How are your drinks? It’s roast lamb for lunch. I hope you’re hungry!’

Then all the adults began to bustle and chatter at once, filling the gap so there was no room for questions.

–

After her dad dropped Martin and Rosemary home later that afternoon, Lou and her mum went for a walk with the dog. To her surprise, Lou enjoyed it. They talked easily, about places in the world they’d like to visit one day, as they walked along the clifftops, looking down at the spit snaking out into the river, the boats bobbing in the bay, and the Rottnest ferry sailing upriver. It was nice to talk about something other than Lou’s behaviour. This was how things had been between them before, when Lou was in her early teens, before everyone started fighting. She missed it.

They ate leftovers for dinner, picking at bread rolls and cold lamb. Later, Lou sat on the floor with her back against the couch and her laptop resting in between her stomach and her bent knees. Her mum was on the couch behind her, watching the news as well as keeping an eye on what Lou was doing on the internet. Her dad was on the smaller couch with his own laptop on his knees, typing work emails, she assumed.

When the cooking show they'd been watching ended, Lou's mum changed the channel to the seven o'clock news, as she did every night at this time. Lou wished she could go and watch TV in her own bedroom, but her set was still confiscated; it sat on an old single bed in one of the unused bedrooms.

The news droned on. Lou looked up at the television every so often without really watching or listening. But the next time she glanced up, she stopped suddenly. She was looking at the lake: the lake from the photograph.

The news reporter stood at a lookout. Behind him, a long, narrow railing stretched across the top of the concrete dam wall above milky blue water. On TV, there were no clouds in the sky, or reflected in the water, but Lou knew it was the same place and that she had been there. Something stirred, rippled, in the depths of her memory. It was impossible – she had only been a baby in the photograph – but as she looked at the television screen, she was sure she heard the cackle of a kookaburra, the echo of a cry, someone singing.

Lou blinked. The image was gone from the screen. Now it showed a car park; she could see the tourist map on a wooden board behind the reporter. '*The body of a man was found this morning in the Mundaring Weir*,' the reporter was saying. '*The man is believed to be in his thirties. Police are at the scene now. At this stage, his death is not being treated as suspicious, but police are appealing for anyone with information to come forward*.'

Lou sensed a change in the atmosphere in the room. She turned around; her mum was staring at Lou but smiled blankly when she caught Lou's eye. Lou glanced over at her dad; he was staring at her too, pale. She thought of the photo again. With that flicker of recognition, something in her had shifted; the air around her had stilled. And from the way her parents were carefully avoiding each other's eyes, Lou knew they had felt it too.

Chapter Fourteen

Zoe woke with a jolt, and lay in bed with her heart hammering. She tried to settle her breathing, frantically rewinding her memory to work out what had woken her. Had it just been a dream? It wasn't Louise who'd disturbed her, she was certain. She lay still, but her eyes flickered towards the clock on her bedside table: one am. She was sure she'd locked up the house before going to bed: she visualised herself locking the security screens, the front door, then latching the front door with the chain and bolting the patio doors. All the windows were locked. The only way someone could get in would be to smash a window, and that wasn't what she'd heard. She lay, her muscles tense, but all she could hear was her heart.

Then a car drove off outside, and she released the breath she'd been holding. That was all it had been, a car door opening and closing, one of the neighbours coming home from a night out. If Lachlan had been home, or even before Louise, she wouldn't have stirred, but when she was home alone with the baby, she always had one ear twitching. Though she craved being alone with Louise, when she didn't have to worry about anyone other than the two of them, the responsibility was huge. As she locked up each evening, she was plagued by anxious thoughts. What if something happened to her in the night? What if she fell and knocked herself out when she got up to go to the toilet, or what if she died in her sleep? What would happen to Louise?

The front gate creaked. Zoe jumped as uneven footsteps thudded onto the verandah. She sat up, clutching the blanket to her chest. Her phone was charging in the kitchen. The handle of the screen door rattled. She froze, even though every muscle in her body was tense and ready to run. *He can't get in, he can't get in*, she repeated to herself.

The door rattled again.

This time, animal instinct took over. Zoe threw back the blanket, scrabbled across to Lachlan's side of the bed and felt underneath it for the cricket bat he kept there in case of a situation like this. She jumped out of bed and held the bat in two hands, shaking. It was heavier than she remembered; she doubted she had the strength to swing it. Was it more dangerous to be holding a weapon? she wondered. What if the intruder wrenched it from her and used it against her, or Louise? But what if he had a knife, or a gun? Zoe blinked back her tears; she needed something to protect them both. She'd always thought that in such a situation she'd lie still, pretend to be asleep, and let the burglar take what he wanted. But that was before Louise. Hearing a scraping sound at the front door, she tightened her grip on the bat.

She switched on all the lights in the hallway and on the front porch, then walked backwards into the kitchen, keeping an eye on the front door. The scraping continued outside. 'My husband's calling the police!' she shouted, trying to deepen her voice. 'They're on their way!' She quickly put the bat down on the kitchen bench, grabbed her phone and dialled triple zero, then moved her finger over the button to connect the call.

'It's me!' a male voice shouted from outside.

Zoe stopped, her eyes wide, finger still trembling above the phone. 'Go away! The police are coming!'

'Zoe, it's me, sorry...'

'Lachlan?' She moved towards the front door.

'Yeah, the door's locked. Let me in.' His voice was slurred but unmistakable.

She lowered her voice so she didn't wake Louise. 'Of course the door's locked, it's one in the morning! What are you doing? You're meant to be at work.' Acid spilled into Zoe's throat and burned the back of her tongue. He wasn't due home until next week. What had happened?

'Open the door, Zoe...'

'Where's your key?' Although she knew it must be Lachlan, for some superstitious reason she felt she needed to test him, to be completely sure before she opened the door.

'I don't have a key to the screen door.' He sounded weary now.

'Yes you do, I put it on your key ring.'

Her adrenalin began to ebb away; of course it was him. She didn't know whether to cry with relief or anger. She rested the bat against the wall, and slid open the security chain, then turned the latch on the door handle and opened the door. Through the security screen, she saw that it was no spectre. It was Lachlan. He swayed slightly, like someone finding his land legs. His checked red shirt was stained with sweat under the arms and he reeked of smoke and stale alcohol.

Zoe opened the screen. Lachlan stumbled back as it swung outwards. Zoe shook her head, cold fear instantly replaced with the heat of anger. 'Get inside, now!' she hissed. 'Shit, Lachlan. What the hell's going on? I was about to call the police.'

He stepped inside, his work boots clomping on the wooden floor. 'Sorry.'

'Shh, the baby's asleep! It's one o'clock in the morning! Why didn't you call?'

'Can I see her?'

'What? No, you'll wake her!'

'I miss her...' His voice quavered.

Zoe pushed him out of her way, dragged his bag inside, then closed and locked the door. When she turned around, he was stumbling down the hallway, his arms hanging by his sides. His head lolled onto his chest. He veered to the left, steadied himself on the wall, then managed to pull out a chair from under the kitchen table and sat heavily on it. He put his elbows on the table and held his head in his hands.

Zoe bit her lip. She wanted to shout at him, but something about the way he looked frightened her. His moods had been getting worse in the past month. She'd wondered if it had anything to do with the fact that Nadia had moved back to Perth now. Nadia had been around a lot more, spending lots of time with Louise, but whenever Zoe had tried to bring it up with Lachlan, he'd either been completely uninterested, or incredibly agitated. Louise was four months old now, she was developing a beautiful little personality, and she needed her dad. Zoe had watched, helplessly, as Lachlan continued to withdraw from them both. In some ways, she wasn't surprised to see him home; she had no idea how he could cope with the pressures of work, the way he was. She walked quietly down the hallway. In the kitchen, she took the jug of cold water out of the fridge, and poured him a glass. She put it in front of him and touched his arm. He jumped and looked up at her, then back down at the table.

'Drink this,' she said softly.

Lachlan nodded. He reached for the glass and gulped down the water.

'What's going on?' she said, sitting down next to him.

'I'm sorry.'

Zoe's heart thumped. 'Why? What for?'

He shook his head.

Zoe gritted her teeth and spoke in a loud whisper. 'Lachlan! For God's sake! You're meant to be hundreds of kilometres away, and you turn up in the middle of the night, pissed, without telling me, and scare the shit out of me! What the hell is going on?' Her fists were clenched. 'You tell me right now.'

His palms were flat on the table, and he stared at the back of his hands. 'I quit.'

'You quit? Quit what? What do you mean?' While she knew exactly what he meant, she refused to accept what she was hearing.

'Work. I quit.'

'How can you have quit? Why?'

'I don't want to talk about it now.' His eyelids drooped.

Zoe stared at him. 'Lachlan, you can't just tell me you've quit and not tell me why!'

'It's what you wanted, isn't it? You're always complaining that I'm away too much, that I don't spend enough time with you and Louise. Well, now I can!' He stood up, scraping the legs of the wooden chair on the floor.

'Keep your voice down! Where are you going?'

'Bed...' He looked around as if he wasn't sure he could find the bedroom.

Zoe paused, then shook her head. 'Fine. If that's all you've got to say, why don't you just go to bed. No, actually, the state you're in, sleep on the couch.'

She braced herself for an angry response, but instead Lachlan's eyes filled with tears. He walked to the linen cupboard in the hallway, got a blanket, then went into the living room.

Part of Zoe wanted to go to him, but her anger was stronger than her concern. She bit her bottom lip and tried not to cry, knowing that if she did, she wouldn't stop. She heard the thud of his boots dropping on the floor, one after the other. How could he have quit? How could they survive without his job? They'd used all their savings on the lawyers and doctors for the surrogacy; they had nothing left. How were they going to pay the mortgage? The car repayments? Food? She closed her eyes and breathed deeply. Surely it was all a mistake. It must be the drink talking. They would sort it out in the morning, when he was sober. She got up and poured herself a glass of water.

There was no sound now from the living room. She peered in. Lachlan was lying on his back along the couch with his feet on the floor, fully dressed, mouth agape. She turned and walked away. Let him wake up with a stiff neck, stinking clothes and a raging hangover; let him realise how pissed he'd been. Let him come to *her* and apologise.

She turned out the light, checked the front door was locked and went back into her bedroom, certain that she wouldn't get any sleep tonight.

Chapter Fifteen

Nadia pulled over but didn't get out of the car. Instead, she stared at the entrance to the church on the corner of the street, wringing her hands. There were three cars parked in the spaces perpendicular to the side wall of the limestone building. The large wooden doors at the front were open, and there was a sandwich board on the pavement with a piece of white A4 paper taped to it. She couldn't make out the black writing from her car, but knew that she was in the right place. Last week, Nadia had sent the organiser, Tracey, a brief email explaining how she felt. Tracey had responded the same day saying that while Nadia's situation was 'unusual' for this group, she was very welcome to come along. Nadia had been so overcome to find someone who finally validated her feelings that she'd sent another, long message describing how she felt. Tracey had then insisted she come, saying she was sure that it would be helpful.

Nadia turned off the engine, then listened to the tick as it cooled down. She'd come here straight after dropping the children at school and it had taken her longer than she'd thought to drive to the northern suburbs through the morning traffic. There were five minutes until the meeting started at ten am: perfect timing. She didn't want to be there early enough to have to make small talk, nor to walk in late and have everyone look at her.

She glanced in the rear-view mirror and drew her finger along the edge of her lip to wipe away a tiny smear of lipstick, then tucked her hair behind her ears. Taking a deep breath, she grabbed her handbag from the passenger seat and got out of the car.

She hesitated for a moment at the entrance. In the middle of the wooden floor of the church hall was a circle of eight grey plastic chairs. Two were already occupied; the women, probably in their late fifties, sat with their backs to the door, murmuring to each other. In the opposite corner was a beige trundle table with a hot water urn, a jar of instant coffee, a cardboard box of tea bags and a plastic carton of milk. Next to the table stood an elderly woman with cropped grey hair and red-framed glasses, holding a blue clipboard close to her stout chest. Nadia walked towards her, looking at the floor rather than meeting the glances of the seated women. As she got closer to the table, she saw a stack of paper cups, and a saucer with a discarded, soggy tea bag.

The woman smiled. 'Nadia?'

'Yes, hi. Tracey?'

'Yes!' Tracey said warmly. 'Lovely to meet you. Now, I've made you a name tag.' She peeled a rectangular sticker off the sheet on her clipboard and handed it to Nadia, who took it by the corner and slapped it onto the left side of her chest.

'Thanks. And thanks for letting me come along today. I know it's not—'

Tracey waved her free hand in the air. 'You're very welcome. You and I are not that different.'

Nadia nodded. Another woman arrived and greeted Tracey. Grateful for the distraction, Nadia smiled briefly and made herself a cup of tea, then slowly walked towards the chairs and sat down, leaving an empty chair between herself and the three other women. When Tracey closed the heavy wooden doors, a hush fell over the room. There were only the five of them. Nadia had hoped that there'd be more so she might go unnoticed, but there was nothing she could do now. She had made the decision to come here; she needed to see it through.

Louise was six months old now. Nadia had read, in all the pamphlets from the surrogacy counseller, that it was normal to grieve for six months, but that after that, she should really be getting on with her life. But Nadia couldn't. Instead of things getting easier as she'd approached that six-month mark, things had been getting more and more difficult. She couldn't sleep, she couldn't concentrate, she couldn't enjoy anything, not even her own children because all she could think about, day and night, was Louise.

For the past month, Nadia had spent her evenings looking online for other surrogates to talk to. There were plenty of sensational stories, of course, magazine exclusives and tabloid headlines shouting about extreme cases when it had all gone wrong, but those seemed mainly about money. She was looking for the ordinary surrogates, the women like her. She wasn't sure if she was the exception or if people were lying to themselves, but those she did find in chat forums enthused about how wonderful the experience had been for them, and how they'd do it again. Maybe there were other women like her out there, women whose overwhelming feelings were of loss and regret, but like her, they were silent, lurking online late at night while their husbands and children slept, trying to find someone who shared their shameful, secret feelings. Feelings that didn't fit with the image of what surrogacy was supposed to be like.

Perhaps it was her own fault; perhaps she had let herself get too attached to Louise. Or maybe it was easier for women who did it for strangers, knowing they'd never see the child again, or for women who were paid – it was an act of trade, of a thing, not a person. She didn't believe it, though. Why didn't those women talk honestly? Where was the shame in saying that you loved the child that you'd carried, that handing her over was like wrenching out a chamber of your own heart? All she could find online was doublespeak, a language that turned her, Nadia, into a carrier, an incubator, a walking womb, sites where people described themselves as socially infertile, commissioning parents, intended parents, consumers and recipients, where they had gaybies and twiblings and compared notes on the cheapest country to buy an egg or embryo or hire a surrogate, the places with the most lax emigration laws. But what had happened to *her* in all this? Where was the recognition of her not as a carrier but as a mother, a person? And what about the Louises – the twiblings and gaybies? Who was looking out for them? While she was searching for someone who would admit to feeling the way she did, Nadia had found this group with its own doublespeak title: a 'relinquishing mothers' group'.

Tracey welcomed them, then looked at Nadia and smiled. 'And this week we have a new member, Nadia.'

Nadia's cheeks burned as everyone looked at her. She glanced at each of them in turn, and muttered, 'Hi.'

'Nadia, would you like to tell us a little bit about yourself?'

Nadia inhaled nervously, shifting in her seat. This was why she was here; she needed to be honest, at last. Her voice shook as she began to speak. 'Yes, hello, everyone. This is my first time here – well, anywhere really, apart from seeing a counsellor who wasn't much help. Anyway, my situation is a little different to everyone else's, so I hope it's OK that I'm here.' She cleared her throat, tears starting already. 'God, I promised I wouldn't cry. I'm here because I had a child, a baby girl, Louise. I had her for my sister – she couldn't have children so I offered to be a surrogate for her. It was my biological baby, and my sister's husband's sperm. And anyway, I did it. But now...' She paused. 'Well, now, I'm... I miss her. Louise. I'm sad. I can't stop thinking about her, and how part of me is missing, and what she'll think of me for giving her up.' She stopped, trying to compose herself, and bent down to pick up her tea.

'Thanks, Nadia. When you emailed me last week, we discussed how *our* situation,' Tracey swept her arm around to take in the other women, who were nodding and smiling sympathetically, 'is not that different. We are all mothers who have given up our children to other parents. Some of us had them taken by authorities, some of us thought we were acting voluntarily by handing over our babies after being told we couldn't give them a good enough life, but regardless, we all relinquished our children, and we are all grieving. You are very welcome here.'

Nadia nodded a little, smiled, and wiped her eyes with her fingers. She caught Tracey's eye and saw, for the first time, someone who understood what she'd been through, what she was *still* going through. Tracey was a generation older than her, and yet Nadia could see that her grief was still acute and she hadn't forgotten the child that she'd given up.

Chapter Sixteen

Zoe looked around the bathroom door and smiled. Lachlan had his back to her as he chattered away to Louise, who was sitting up in the bath. He crouched in front of the tub, lathering shampoo into Louise's fine blonde hair as they both laughed. There were puddles of water on the black-and-white floor tiles. It was good to see him relaxed and smiling.

Since that night, almost two months ago, when he'd come home after quitting, he had refused to talk about what had happened. All he'd say was that he'd had enough of working in the goldfields. She suspected he'd had an argument with someone, stormed off and was now too proud to apologise. Zoe knew she had to stop worrying so much about Lachlan; it was just the stress of trying to find a new job that had made him so distracted and preoccupied. Although, she reminded herself, he'd been preoccupied even before he quit. She shook off the thoughts. He'd be fine when he found another job; worrying about money was getting to them both. They'd used up everything they had; soon they wouldn't be able to make the mortgage and car repayments.

Just then, Louise looked up and smiled at Zoe, her dimples flashing. Zoe was filled with tenderness at how adorable she was, and laughed as Louise suddenly raised her chubby hands and began to splash the bath water, squealing with delight.

'Good splashing, Louise! Are you splashing your daddy?' Zoe said.

Lachlan turned around. 'Oh, hi. Can you get me a towel?'

'Sure,' Zoe said. When she returned, he was rinsing Louise's hair with water from a plastic cup. Zoe stood beside him and held the towel open, and he lifted Louise up and into her arms. Zoe wrapped her up and held her close for a moment, then kissed the tip of her nose before handing her back to Lachlan.

'You remember I'm going out tonight?' she said.

Lachlan frowned. 'Oh, that's tonight?'

'Yes. I did tell you—'

'It's fine, I just didn't remember. What time?'

'I'm meeting them at seven at the boat harbour. We're going to the brewery. You'll have to settle Louise yourself, but she should be fine with her bottle.'

He nodded, and carried Louise out of the bathroom and into her room. Zoe leaned over, drained the water from the bath, then folded up the bathmat and hung it over the edge of the tub.

She went into Louise's room to find Lachlan holding up a yellow all-in-one suit. 'Oh no, that one's a bit small,' she said. 'I should put that away with all the other stuff she's grown out of.' She had almost said *for the next baby*. That's what people did, wasn't it? They stored away the clothes that their first baby had grown out of, keeping them at the back of the wardrobe for the next one. 'Actually, it'll do for tonight. I haven't got any other pyjamas clean for her right now.'

'OK.' Lachlan lifted Louise up, spread the outfit out on her change mat, then put a nappy on her.

Zoe watched as he struggled to get her chubby arms into the suit. 'Here, I'll hold her so she can't wriggle—'

'I'm OK.'

Zoe leaned down and put her hands on Louise's hips. Lachlan swatted her arm away. 'I said it's fine! Stop hovering over me! I know how to dress her!'

She stepped back, mouth and eyes wide. The bony edge of her forearm ached where he had batted her away. She rubbed it with her other hand, then turned and walked out of the room without another word.

Back in the bathroom, she closed and locked the door, then sat on the edge of the bath, on the damp floor mat that she'd just hung there, and put her face in her hands. She didn't know what to think about Lachlan's edginess. He was so sensitive these days. Was Zoe being too critical? Didn't she feel the same way when Nadia tried to give her any advice on how to raise Louise? She tried to breathe deeply: she needed to pull herself together. She was overreacting. He hadn't meant anything by it, he just wasn't thinking. She knew how easy it was to react angrily; even she had almost shaken Louise one night when she wouldn't stop crying. Lachlan was right; she didn't need to hover over him all the time, he was perfectly capable of looking after his daughter. She took another deep breath, then stood up and turned on the shower.

–

Zoe walked down to the fishing harbour; it only took fifteen minutes and she needed the exercise to help her calm down. Lachlan hadn't said anything about what had happened, and neither had she. She was determined to enjoy this evening. It had been ages since she'd been out with friends; that part of her life had vanished when she had taken Louise home. At first, she hadn't wanted to go out: she hadn't trusted anyone to be left with her baby. Then later, it just seemed too hard, especially when Lachlan was away. But tonight, Zoe needed to see that life outside of her own world – a world that seemed to be closing in on her – was carrying on as usual.

And it was, down here in Fremantle. The fishing boats still bobbed in the harbour, their chains clanking and sails snapping in the wind. Warm light glowed from the restaurants and bars, illuminating the oily black water below the boardwalk. The air smelled of fish and vinegar and the pungency of decaying seaweed. Zoe inhaled deeply as a gust of wind blew over and around her, and she rubbed her arms, now sticky with the salt carried on the breeze. She smiled and her shoulders dropped.

As she walked past the bronze statues of fishermen hauling baskets of fish from the water, she imagined the time before the harbour was built, when this water was an estuary, thick with black carpets of mullet. She went in the back entrance of the restaurant, a converted warehouse, past the children's sandpit littered with discarded plastic spades and toy trucks, then pulled open the heavy glass door and walked inside. Standing on tiptoe, she looked around the vast room. To her left, young couples sat at long wooden tables sharing pizzas and drinking pints of beer, while on her right was an open kitchen and pizza oven in front of glass walls displaying the giant vats of the brewery. The space was filled with the aromas of food and the yeasty, living smell of hops and barley. As she pushed towards the bar, she heard someone call her name above the noise of the crowd. Emma, Sally and Kath were sitting in a booth, with a bottle of wine in a silver ice bucket, and four glasses.

Zoe squealed and hurried over. She hugged each of her friends.

'How are you?' they all seemed to say at once.

'I'm great!' Zoe manoeuvred herself in beside Sally, opposite Emma. 'It's great to see you all!' As she said it, tears welled up in her eyes. It *was* great to see her friends; she had missed them.

They'd all studied nursing together; then, over the years, they'd worked with each other in various hospitals. But in the last few years, they'd grown apart. They all had children; Kath's two girls were already at school, while Sally and Emma each had a son at kindy. When Kath's first child was born, Zoe was only just planning her wedding, but when Emma and Sally had fallen pregnant within months of each other, Zoe was dealing with the grief of another miscarriage. She had tried to be happy for them, but the feeling that had overwhelmed her was bitter jealousy. As their babies grew into toddlers together, her friends had moved into a different world, leaving Zoe behind.

They knew about the miscarriages and the surrogacy, but every time Zoe had tried to talk to one of them on the phone, their own children would be crying or screaming or chattering in the background and she could never really open up. After too many stilted conversations ending with promises to catch up that never eventuated, Zoe had stopped trying. Now, though, she understood how much energy a child saps from you, and how, when you finally get some time to yourself, you have no room for anyone else's problems. But tonight, she was part of the old group again, and she was going to forget about Lachlan.

Emma reached for the wine bottle and raised it towards Zoe, water from the ice bucket dripping onto the table. 'Drink?'

'Yes, please!' Zoe held out her glass for Emma to pour the wine. 'Cheers, ladies! Great to see you all!' She took a sip, sighed and smiled.

'So how's life as a mum treating you?' Emma said.

'Yeah, it's great! Well, busy, you know?'

They all nodded in agreement.

'How old is she now?' Sally said.

'She's six months. It's gone so quickly!'

'I can't believe we haven't had a proper catch-up in that long! Is she sleeping through the night yet?'

Zoe shrugged. 'Yeah, most of the time. She wakes up for a bottle sometimes, but that's OK.'

Sally shook her head and smiled. 'You're lucky. George didn't sleep through until he was eighteen months, it almost drove me crazy. He was just so attached to the breastfeeding, you know? When I eventually gave that up and he learned that he wasn't getting any milk, he started sleeping all night.' She clasped her hand over her mouth. 'Oh, sorry, that was silly of me...'

Zoe took a gulp of wine, hoping they wouldn't notice her cheeks flaring. 'It's fine. So, how's work going? Is there any gossip?'

'Oh, it's just the same as always, you know,' said Emma. 'Same old people, same old politics, not enough staff, crap rosters, too busy.'

'Have you thought about when you'll go back?' Kath said.

Zoe shook her head. 'I don't know yet. I just extended my maternity leave, so hopefully another six months, but we probably can't afford much more than that.'

Sally topped up everyone's glasses while she talked. 'I loved going back to work. Being at home all the time just wasn't for me, I needed some adult company. I'm a much better mum now I'm working.'

Zoe nodded, remembering the bustle of the wards, and the kids who still managed to laugh no matter how sick they were. She liked her job – *had* liked it. Now she loved being at home with Louise, though sometimes it felt like they were on borrowed time, especially since Lachlan had quit. She cleared her throat. 'Well, I might go back sooner than that, maybe just a few relief shifts or something, to see how it goes.'

'I suppose it's hard for you with Lachlan working away. Daycare is useless when you work shifts. What about your mum, would she help out?' Kath said.

'Yeah, she would.' Zoe went on lightly, 'But anyway, Lachlan's at home at the moment, looking for a job in Perth.'

'Really?' Emma frowned.

Zoe didn't meet her eye. 'Yeah, it was getting too much, being away from home all the time. I think having Louise made him realise what he was giving up, you know, and he just decided that he didn't want to do it any more.'

'Has he got another job lined up?'

'Not yet. He will, though, that won't be a problem, there are plenty of jobs out there. For now, he's just enjoying spending time with Louise.'

Sally sighed. 'Oh, that's lovely.'

Zoe smiled, and held her glass aloft. 'Well, cheers again, girls. It's great to see you all!'

She caught the eye of a waitress and ordered another bottle of wine. Lachlan could get up for Louise tonight and tomorrow morning; Zoe had done more than her fair share.

–

Zoe took off her heels and walked barefoot up the path to the front door. She tried the handle; it opened. She frowned. It was almost midnight; the door should be locked. She pushed it open slowly, screwing up her face as it creaked. She held her breath, but Louise didn't cry out. The hallway was dark. She placed her shoes down on their side; then, with one hand on the wall to steady herself, tiptoed towards the back of the house. The door to the living room was closed, but light shone from underneath it and she could hear the television. She smiled; Lachlan must have waited up for her.

She opened the door then closed it behind her. Lachlan was lying on the couch watching a celebrity reality show. She clambered into the space between his bent knees and the back of the couch.

'Did you wait up for me?' Zoe hadn't realised before how slurred her speech was.

Lachlan looked at her and raised his eyebrows. His eyes were red and half closed. 'No. I couldn't sleep.'

'Well, it's nice you're still up.' Zoe reclined on his hip.

'Did you have fun?' he said.

'Yeah, I did, actually. It was like... I don't know, it was just like before, somehow. It was nice to be with my old friends, catch up on all the gossip. What did you do?' Zoe glanced at the coffee table and saw four empty beer bottles, but at least half a dozen bottle caps. She frowned, then looked back at him.

'Oh, I just got some pizza, watched a movie.'

'Which one?'

'I don't know, something on the movie channel.'

'What was it about?'

He glared at her. 'I can't remember, Zoe. Does it matter?'

Zoe sat up straight. 'OK, no need to be like that!'

Lachlan looked back at the television while Zoe counted silently to herself. She'd had such a lovely night, she wasn't going to let him spoil it. 'You want some water?'

'No thanks.'

She climbed over him again and went into the kitchen, where she stood for a moment pressing at her eyes with her palms. She poured a glass of cold water from the fridge and took it back through to the living room; this time she perched on the arm of the sofa.

'The girls were talking about work. It sounds like nothing's changed. It made me, I don't know, miss it in a way. Well, I don't miss it, I love being at home with Louise, but it was nice to think about what I used to do.'

Lachlan nodded. 'You used to love it.'

'Well, maybe *love* is a bit strong.'

'Yeah, but you were good at what you did, and you trained for a long time.'

She shrugged. 'That's what you give up when you become a mum. And it'll go so quickly – before I know it Louise'll be in kindy. Work will still be there, there'll always be people getting sick.'

'Maybe you shouldn't wait that long.'

Zoe gulped down some water to give her time to think before she spoke, trying to keep her voice steady. 'We talked about it before Louise was born. We said I'd stay home.' Her heart was racing. She watched Lachlan's face.

He lowered his eyes. 'I know, but things have changed, and if you miss it—'

'I don't miss it that much! God, I was only saying that in some ways it'd be nice to be doing something else. It's not that I want to leave Louise with some stranger and go back to night shifts and being short-staffed and dealing with other people's sick kids.'

'Well, you wouldn't have to leave her with a stranger, would you? I'm here now.'

Zoe felt her throat tightening. 'But you won't be. You'll get another job soon. I can't say I'll come back to work and then stop again in a few weeks, when you get a job. I don't understand, what are you trying to say?'

'I'm not trying to say anything! It's just that we need to think about it as an option, especially if it's something you'd like to do. I think you'd enjoy it. And if I get a job, there's your mum to help, and Nadia's close by now.'

Zoe shook her head. 'Stop watching the damn TV, Lachlan, and look at me!'

He clenched his jaw, jabbed at the power button on the remote and sat up straight. 'Forget I said anything. Just don't assume that I'll get another job and that we can afford for neither of us to be working.'

'Well, you shouldn't have just quit your job, should you?' Zoe realised she was shouting, and lowered her voice again. 'Babe, I don't want to go to work, I want to stay at home with Louise. After everything we've been through, I don't want to hand her over to Mum or Nadia. You must understand that?'

He sighed. 'I know, Zoe. I know. It's just not always that easy.'

'What isn't, babe?' She put her hand on his arm. 'Talk to me.'

He shook his head. 'It's late, let's get to bed.'

Before she could say anything more, he stood up and walked out of the room. She had no choice but to follow him, dread in the pit of her stomach.

–

Zoe rubbed her hair with the towel, feeling nervous about the day ahead. A month had passed since Lachlan had brought up the subject of Zoe returning to her old job. She didn't want to go back to work, but she couldn't wait any more for him to find a job. He said he was looking, but the promised interview was always another week away. They had no savings left, they had bills to pay and a child to support. Zoe had no choice.

Her alarm had gone off at five; her first shift was an early one. But at least then she'd be home to spend time with Louise in the afternoon and put her to bed. Zoe's eyes filled with tears. She longed to be the one playing with Louise all day. She'd wanted to see her start to crawl, witness her first steps, hear her first words, help her develop and learn. Yes, Louise would be with Lachlan, but he didn't seem to understand the amount of stimulation a baby needed to thrive. He would just let her play on the floor while he read the paper. Zoe swallowed down the lump in her throat. She was being ridiculous; Louise would be at home, safe with her dad. Anyway, Lachlan would find a job soon; this would only be temporary.

Zoe checked the bathroom door was closed, then took off her pyjamas and stood back, staring at herself in the mirror. Of course she didn't look any different to how she had before she left work – she hadn't been pregnant. She had no stretch marks on her stomach, and her breasts were still full. She should look more tired, but Louise slept well now; the bottle filled her up. It was ironic to wish that she looked more like a mum given the way that most mothers feel about their bodies after having babies. But she didn't want any reason for people to notice that she hadn't given birth to Louise; she wanted to blend in. Zoe clenched her fists: she had to stop thinking like this. When she'd had the miscarriages, she had sworn she would never complain about anything if only she could have a child. And now she had a gorgeous little girl, and she was the luckiest woman in the world; she couldn't renegotiate the bargain she'd made with herself. She was only going back to work. Other mothers did it; so could she.

After showering, she raked around in the bottom drawer of the vanity and pulled out her hairdryer. She untangled the cord, then plugged it in next to the sink and switched it on the lowest setting so it didn't disturb Louise. After drying her hair, she unzipped her make-up bag and put on a bit of foundation and mascara. Maybe it wouldn't be so bad today. It was important to teach Louise that women had careers too, that there was more to Zoe than, well, being a mother.

In the bedroom, Zoe kept the light off while she moved around quietly. Her eyes adjusted quickly to the dim light. She put on her uniform, which she'd ironed last night, then kicked her towel into the corner of the room, next to Lachlan's t-shirt and boxers from yesterday. She resisted the urge to bundle them up and take them through to the laundry; that was Lachlan's job now. Once she'd put her lanyard with her ID badge around her neck, she looked in the mirrored door of the wardrobe and smiled. Now that she was dressed, she knew what to do. She wasn't a stay-at-home mum any more; she was a working mum. She should be – was – proud of that.

Out in the kitchen, she forced herself to swallow a few spoonfuls of cereal. She looked at the clock on the oven: she had to leave or she'd miss the bus. Closing her eyes, she forced herself to breathe slowly for a few moments, then tiptoed back down the hallway. She pushed open the door to the bedroom and whispered to Lachlan, 'I'm off now.'

'Hmm...' he mumbled without opening his eyes.

'Remember, Louise's swimming lesson is at ten. I've packed her bag already, she just has to have a swim nappy on underneath her bathers, and try and get her to have a nap before she goes.'

He opened his eyes. 'We'll be fine, OK?'

'I know.' Zoe's eyes began to prickle with tears again. 'I've got to go.'

'Come here' He beckoned her over and gave her a hug. 'Good luck today.'

'Thanks.' She sniffed and stepped away from him. 'Please, just call me if you need anything. If I don't answer my mobile then call the ward, they'll get me.'

'Zoe, we'll be fine. Go on, you'll be late.'

Zoe nodded. 'Bye.'

She held onto the door for a moment more, then nodded again and closed it. She stared at Louise's door, listening hopefully for a snuffle so she had an excuse to go in, but it was quiet. Anyway, it was best not to disturb her. Saying goodbye to her would be too much for Zoe this morning. She picked up her bag, purse and phone from the hallway table and stepped outside in the faint early morning light, then closed the front door quietly behind her.

Chapter Seventeen

Zoe opened her eyes as Lachlan crawled into bed beside her. She glanced at the alarm clock: it was after midnight. Zoe felt foggy, disorientated, woken from a warm dream that now floated away above her and dissipated. She'd gone to bed at nine with a book, and soon dropped off, but it was an uneasy sleep, interrupted by the sound of the television and, every so often, Lachlan getting up and opening the fridge.

Being back at work was tiring; she'd hoped it would rejuvenate her, but all it had done was add more pressure. She was worried about Lachlan – he wasn't coping very well with being at home all the time with Louise. He managed to keep on top of things, but that was about all. She'd had to bite her tongue many times when she came home to find the washing unhung, or the floor unswept. She reminded herself that she'd had days like that when she was at home with Louise, and had bridled at his comments about the house being untidy. And she knew that Lachlan's identity was entwined with being an engineer, not a stay-at-home dad. Maybe the distance that was growing between them was due to his feelings of shame as he saw his wife having to support the family. Women were always expected to put their professional identities aside for their families – why did it only seem to be a problem for men to accept this loss of their sense of self? But women, too, often defined themselves by their career; she'd done it herself, telling people, 'I'm a nurse, but I'm on maternity leave.' Zoe could rationalise their situation, but she knew that both she and Lachlan would be happier in their old roles.

The mattress shifted as Lachlan turned onto his side.

'You OK?' she whispered.

'Yep.' He yawned, hissing the exhaled air out between his teeth. Zoe screwed her eyes shut, irritation jangling through her. Why hadn't he come to bed earlier? She had to get up at five, then Louise was up from six. Why did he stay up all night watching stupid television shows? *Let it go*, she told herself. *Let it go*. If he was tired during the day, it was his problem. She forced herself to breathe slowly and deeply, beginning to relax again and drift into sleep.

Suddenly, Lachlan jolted up from the bed. 'No!' he shouted.

Zoe jumped and gasped, wrenched from a deep sleep. She turned over quickly to look at him. In the dark bedroom, the outline of his heaving body was grainy and indistinct. He sat upright with his arms in front of his face, as if shielding it. Zoe heard a buzzing in her ears, a high-pitched throbbing like the whirr of a film reel.

She put her hand on his arm; it was damp with sweat. 'Lachlan, what's wrong? You're OK, babe, you're OK. It must have been a bad dream.'

His breathing slowed, but then he moved his hands onto his face and started sobbing. Zoe pulled him towards her.

'Oh, Lachlan, what is it?'

'Just leave me alone.' His voice was thick; he sounded haunted.

Zoe switched on the lamp on her bedside table. Lachlan lay back down and turned away from her. He said nothing, though his back shook and every now and then he sniffed wetly. Zoe turned off the light again and moved over towards him, fitting her own body around the curve of his clammy back. She kept her arm around his chest until his shaking finally stopped and she was sure he was asleep.

–

When Zoe got home from work the next afternoon, she said nothing to Lachlan about the previous night, or about the dark shadows below his red-rimmed eyes, or the dishes piled up on the kitchen bench. She greeted him as usual, and hugged Louise, who at least was clean and happy and plump. Holding Louise on one hip, she picked up a mug from the kitchen table, tipped the cold coffee down the sink, then went to put it in the dishwasher, but it was still full of the clean dishes from when she'd put it on last night before bed. Zoe closed her eyes for a second, hoisted Louise further up on her hip and closed the dishwasher door with her foot.

'Lachlan?'

'Yeah?' he shouted above the noise of the television.

'I thought we could go out for an early dinner.'

'Really?'

Zoe walked into the living room. 'It'd be nice, don't you think?'

He frowned. 'It's a bit hard, with Louise. We could just get takeaway.'

The thought of spending another evening tidying up and tiptoeing around Lachlan while he stared at the television was too much. 'No, it'd be good to go out,' she said.

Lachlan sighed. 'OK.'

'Well, don't sound too excited about it.' Zoe spun around and walked through to the bedroom with Louise. She was trying, she really was.

They parked right outside the restaurant. Zoe closed the passenger door and stumbled as her heel wobbled on the cobblestoned street. She had put on her tight jeans, heels, and a sheer short-sleeved blouse. She had even squirted on some perfume, but all it had done was make Lachlan sneeze.

While Lachlan stood waiting, Zoe opened the back door and leaned in to unbuckle Louise from her capsule. 'Have you got the stroller?'

Lachlan sighed, then went to open the boot. 'There won't be any room in there.'

Zoe closed her eyes and made herself wait a few seconds before answering. 'Yes there will, and it's better than having her sitting on our lap the whole time.'

'They'll have high chairs.'

'Lachlan, would you please just get the stroller, or else take Louise and I'll get it?'

Zoe slammed the door shut, then kissed Louise's forehead and smiled brightly as she walked to the restaurant. She held the door open while Lachlan pulled the stroller up the steps. In front of them was a big pizza oven; even though it was only six o'clock, there was already a queue of people waiting to collect their takeaway. To one side were refrigerated glass cabinets filled with tiramisu and panna cotta and pastries and cakes, and in the next compartment, stainless-steel containers of gelato.

The restaurant was more than half full already, almost all families. Zoe looked at Louise, and at Lachlan, and smiled. Yes, it was hard work taking Louise out to dinner, and maybe they wouldn't be able to relax like they used to, but they were a family too, and this was what families did. She stood up taller as they followed a young dark-haired waiter to a table near the back of the room. Louise was waving her arms up and down and babbling, and Zoe knew people were admiring her.

As they reached their table, a waitress came straight over to them, bent down and smiled at Louise. 'She's beautiful. Do you want a high chair?'

'Please.'

Lachlan manoeuvred the stroller behind the table, shaking his head. 'So, why did we take the stroller?' he asked. Zoe ignored him.

The waitress came back with the high chair and two laminated menus. 'Can I get you some drinks?'

'A beer, please,' Lachlan said, scanning the drinks list. 'A pale ale.'

'And I'll have a glass of…' Zoe swiped her finger down the list of wines by the glass. 'The pinot, please.'

'Should we get a bottle?' Lachlan said.

Zoe frowned. 'Well, we have to drive, I can't have more than a glass. Just have a glass when you've finished your beer.'

'Nah.' Lachlan looked up at the waitress again. 'We'll take a bottle of the pinot.'

Zoe frowned at him, but he didn't look at her. When the waitress left, Zoe strapped Louise into the high chair.

She started to whimper, so Zoe put her car keys on the plastic tray in front of Louise; she picked them up straight away and began chewing on the metal.

Once the waitress had brought their drinks and they'd ordered food, Zoe and Lachlan sipped their wine and beer, looking at Louise rather than each other.

'So how are you finding being a house husband?' Zoe said brightly, smiling at Lachlan.

'Fine. It's fine.' He shrugged. 'And how are you finding it being back at work?'

He was trying, even if it did sound like he was reciting a phrase learned in a foreign language class. She leaned back in her chair. 'It's OK. I mean, I enjoy it mainly, when I'm there. It's hard, though, to leave Louise.' Noticing Lachlan stiffen, she added, 'But at least she's at home with you.'

Lachlan nodded, then took a gulp of beer.

'Any luck on the job front?' Zoe picked up a bread stick from the canister that the waitress had put in front of her. She snapped it in half and gave a piece to Louise.

'No. Not yet.'

'That's a shame. Is it just that they're not advertising, or is there nothing that you want?' Zoe dared to look up and meet Lachlan's eyes.

'I don't know. There's nothing that's right yet. I *am* looking, you know?'

'I know you are. It's OK, I'm not trying to say anything, we're fine for now. I was just…' Zoe sighed. 'Do you think there might be something else making it difficult?'

Lachlan frowned. 'No. Like what?'

Zoe's heart began to beat faster, but she had broached the topic, she couldn't stop now. 'It's just, well…' She leaned over the table towards him and spoke softly. 'Something's just not right, and I'm worried.'

'What are you talking about?' he said, sounding defensive.

Zoe sat back again. 'I don't know. It's just ever since… well, ever since Louise was born, something's changed in you.'

He shifted in his seat. 'We've all changed, Zoe – how could we not? It's not just been the usual "let's have a baby" and we're off. You've changed too.'

'I'm sure I have, babe. I'm just wondering if we need to go and talk about things with someone.' Zoe ran her finger round the base of her glass.

Lachlan was quiet. When Zoe looked up, his face was red, and he was blinking hard. 'I'm OK.' It was almost a whisper.

'Are you sure?' Zoe whispered back.

'Yes.'

She nodded and sighed. 'All right. But Lachlan – remember, I'm not the enemy, OK? I'm your wife, you can talk to me.'

Without looking at her, he picked up his beer and gulped it down.

'Let's just have a nice dinner then,' she said. 'Just the three of us.'

Zoe could see that he was trying. He relaxed a little as he drank a glass of wine, then another. When he was almost finished the third, she poured the rest of the bottle into her own glass. But he picked at his food and she knew his mind was somewhere else, not with them, and she couldn't help but wish that they'd stayed at home.

On Saturday morning, Zoe went into the kitchen, still in her nightshirt, and smiled brightly. 'What do you want to do today?'

Lachlan glanced up from the weekend papers spread over the table, then looked down at them again and sipped his coffee. He was wearing the shorts and singlet that he'd slept in. The newspaper rustled when he turned the page, and he flattened it with his hand as he shrugged.

Zoe persisted. 'I have the day off, I want to do something as a family. It'd be nice, wouldn't it? I feel like all we've been doing is working and getting through each day. Let's go and have some fun.'

'What do you want to do then?' he asked flatly.

'Anything! We could have a picnic in the park, go and visit someone, go to the swimming pool, the zoo…'

'Who would we go and visit?'

Zoe shook her head. 'Oh, I don't know! Anyone! Your mum and dad? My parents?'

'I spoke to Dad yesterday. Anyway, I can't really be bothered talking to them, I've got nothing new to say.'

Zoe closed her eyes briefly. 'Well, what else?'

Lachlan looked up, eyes flashing with irritation. 'Fine, we'll go to the zoo.'

'You don't have to say it like that.'

'Are you ready then?' His face set, he started shuffling the papers together.

Zoe stared at him, then held her nightshirt away from her body with her thumb and forefinger. 'Yes, sure, I'll go like this. Of course I'm not ready! Are you?'

'Yep. I've just got to change.'

'No, there's a lot more to do than that. We need to wake Louise from her nap, get her dressed, pack her bottle and some snacks, put the stroller in the car, get the sunscreen and hats…'

'We're not going into the bush, Zoe, it's only the zoo.'

Zoe's eyes stung with tears. Her shoulders slumped and she began to turn away, then she felt the anger surge through her. 'Don't be so bloody rude to me, Lachlan! You just sit there all day while I do everything. You don't think I'd like to read the paper, to sit and have a coffee?'

He glared at her. 'So why don't you? Louise is asleep. Just sit down and read the bloody paper.'

'Well, I can't, can I? Have you even noticed that already this morning I've tidied up the breakfast things, emptied the dishwasher, washed and hung out a load of washing, fed and changed Louise and put her down to sleep—'

'Fine!' Lachlan shouted, slamming his palm down on the table. 'Neither of us will read the paper.' He put his hands on the edge of the table and pushed his chair back, the legs scraping across the floor.

'Shh! For God's sake, you'll wake the baby.'

He shook his head at her, his jaw jutting. Zoe flinched. He'd never before looked at her with such contempt, and for a moment, she hated him too. She turned around and went back down the hallway to the bathroom, her hands shaking. So this was how it felt to watch your marriage unravel. She was trying to bring them all closer, but more and more she longed for the days when Lachlan used to work away. At least then they didn't fight, and she didn't cry every day. Involuntarily, she'd begun to imagine life without him, a future where it was just her and Louise, and it scared her to know how enticing it seemed. She cupped her hand over her mouth as if she could catch the unspoken thought before it could be sensed by Lachlan, or, worse, by Louise.

As she closed the bathroom door and turned on the shower, Zoe allowed herself to cry silently. Louise deserved better than this. She deserved the mum and dad who had wanted her so much, who had done everything in their power to have her, not parents torn apart by hostility. Louise had been conceived out of love, out of hope and good intentions, but was the very way in which she had entered the world the thing that would break up her family?

Zoe took off her nightclothes and old knickers then glanced at them discarded on the floor. She must look a fright. This breakdown in their marriage wasn't all Lachlan's fault; she'd stopped trying to make an effort for him too. She stepped into the shower and let the hot water scald her skin until her shoulders were pink. Then the water pressure fell and the trickle of water turned cold. Of all the times that Lachlan decided to help, it was when she was in the shower. He *knew* that turning on the kitchen tap shut off the hot water to the bathroom. Zoe banged her fist into the tiled wall.

'Lachlan!' she shouted, though she knew he wouldn't hear her. 'The water!'

She took some deep breaths. She had to get control of herself; she was falling to pieces. Was he really the problem, or was she? He wasn't the only man who never did the washing, and he *did* stay home all day with Louise. She turned off the water, still a cold trickle, then stepped out to get ready for the zoo.

–

A few weeks later, Zoe leaned her elbows on the desk in the treatment room, a small area off the corridor at the back of the ward, and cradled her head in her arms. She closed her eyes but that just made her feel more dizzy. The sounds around her were muffled. She could hear a baby crying from somewhere down the corridor, and a phone ringing, and a high-pitched pager going off, and some laughter, but all the sounds merged into one noise that faded and amplified in time with the pounding blows in her head.

She opened her eyes, stood up slowly, then staggered towards the medication cupboard above the sink. She unlocked it and found some paracetamol, then ran the tap and cupped her shaking hand under the lukewarm water. One of the tablets stuck to the base of her tongue and the bitter powder began to dissolve. She gagged, then leaned over the sink and retched, bringing up the one tablet she had managed to get down. Sweat dripped down her face. She wanted to lie on the floor and cry, but she still had hours left of her shift. She turned the cold tap on full to wash the tablet down the sink, and splashed her face with the tepid water.

'God, Zoe, are you OK?'

The voice behind her made her jump; she hadn't heard anyone come in.

Zoe grabbed a paper towel from the dispenser above the sink and blotted her face, hoping that her make-up hadn't run everywhere. She turned around and saw one of the other nurses, Mei, frowning at her.

'Yeah. No... just a migraine.'

'You look terrible.' Mei steered Zoe over to the examining couch and sat her down.

'I was just trying to take some painkillers.'

'Sit there, I'll get you some. Do you get a lot of migraines?'

Zoe shook her head. She used to get headaches, but nothing like this. Mei didn't know about the lupus; Zoe hadn't told many people at work. She had learned as a teenager that people treated you differently when they knew you had a chronic illness. Every headache or rash became a relapse. She knew that she needed to call her rheumatologist. This was probably just a migraine, but it could be something so much worse: her kidneys failing, the lupus attacking her brain. She couldn't afford to be sick, not now. Not with Lachlan out of work. Tears rolled down her cheeks. She hadn't felt well when she woke up this morning, but had thought it was just exhaustion. Lachlan had been so restless during the night, tossing and turning; he eventually got up and went to watch TV on the couch, but she still hadn't been able to sleep. She was so tired. Tired of not sleeping, tired of worrying, tired of feeling torn between Louise and work and Lachlan, tired of having to work as well as organise everything at home.

She shook her head. 'Sorry, I'll be OK in a minute.' But she couldn't stop crying.

Mei pulled a few tissues from the box on the counter and handed the wad to her. 'I think you need to go home.'

Zoe wiped her eyes. 'No, I'll be fine. It's just this damn headache.' But she had barely finished the sentence before the tears began to fall again. She hated for others to see her like this. She must look a mess. 'Sorry, I'm not usually… I'll be OK, seriously, just give me a few minutes.'

‘No,’ Mei said. ‘I’ll tell Liz, we’ll manage for the rest of the shift. You need to go home and lie down.’

Zoe thought of home, thought of closing the door of her bedroom and crawling under the blankets, and knew it was all she wanted to do. Relief soaked through her. ‘I just feel bad leaving you all to cover for me.’

‘Don’t be stupid. I’ll close this door behind me so you can make yourself look pretty, then just go, I’ll sort it out.’

Zoe looked up through her tears. ‘Are you sure?’

‘Yes! Stop arguing!’

Zoe nodded and sniffed. ‘OK, thanks.’

Mei left and closed the door behind her. Zoe reached into the pocket of her work pants and took out her mobile. Lachlan answered straight away; Zoe was so relieved to hear his voice.

‘I don’t feel well,’ she sobbed.

‘Oh no, what’s wrong?’ He sounded tense.

‘A migraine or something, I don’t know. I hope it’s nothing else. I… can you come and get me? I don’t want to get the bus home.’ The thought of standing out in public waiting for a bus, then sitting next to a stranger made Zoe want to weep anew.

‘Yes, of course.’

Zoe let out a sigh. ‘Thank you. When can you come?’

‘Are you ready to go now?’

‘Yes.’ Zoe knew her voice was as high as a child’s, but that was what she felt like. She wanted someone to look after *her* for a change. ‘I’m sorry, I know it’s almost time for Louise’s lunch, but—’

‘It’s fine. I’ll leave now, I’ll be about fifteen minutes. I’ll pick you up out the front?’

‘Yes, thanks, I’ll be there.’

Zoe put the phone back in her pocket. To get out of the building, she would have to walk past everyone: the patients and their parents, the other nurses, the doctors. She couldn't go out there like this. She closed her eyes and pressed her fingertips to her temples, as if she could squeeze the pain out of her head, and counted her breaths slowly until she began to feel calmer. Standing up, she washed her face again, then patted it dry and opened the door. She kept her head down as she grabbed her bag from the nurses' station, and didn't look up as she hurried out of the ward.

Outside, she sat on a bench at the front of the hospital, feeling the damp seeping into her pants. There were small puddles at the side of the road from the autumn showers. She breathed in, and leaned her head back to let the breeze cool her face. Her head still thumped, but the tightness around her temples was starting to slacken. She took her phone out of her pocket again and looked at the time: it had been ten minutes since she'd called Lachlan. He'd be here soon.

A horn beeped; Zoe looked up and saw their car in the ambulance bay. She smiled, then knew she was going to cry again. Was it relief? Or did she want to make sure that Lachlan knew she wasn't faking it and that she needed him to look after her?

Zoe dropped her phone in her bag, stood up and ran the few steps to the car. She opened the door, flung her bag in, then sat down and closed the door.

Lachlan glanced in the rear-view mirror, then drove out of the ambulance bay. 'You OK?' he asked, his forehead furrowed in concern.

Zoe nodded and burst into tears. 'I just feel horrible… Sorry, I shouldn't.' She wiped her eyes then turned around and looked into the empty baby seat. 'Where's Louise?'

Lachlan glanced at her. 'Nadia's got her.' He indicated right and leaned forward to peer over the steering wheel, beginning to edge the car out into the traffic.

Zoe froze. 'What? Why does Nadia have her? I only needed a lift, you could have brought her.' She paused, thinking. 'How did you have time? I only spoke to you ten minutes ago.'

'She was already with her,' he said casually.

'What do you mean?'

'Nadia dropped in this morning, offered to take her to the park.'

Zoe couldn't breathe. 'I didn't know that. You never told me…'

Lachlan frowned. 'You were at work. I didn't think there was anything to tell.'

Zoe had stopped crying now and was looking at him with dawning dread. 'Has this happened before?'

'What? Yes, a couple of times. It's no big deal.' He accelerated hard and turned right, then settled back in his seat as the traffic eased. 'Do you want to go somewhere for lunch?'

'Lunch? I… Lachlan, I'm really sick, I just want to go home.'

'I thought maybe it'd make you feel better, it'd be nice to have lunch out, without the baby.'

'I just want to go and get Louise,' Zoe said, her teeth gritted. He clearly didn't think there was an issue. Did he think that inviting her out to lunch would justify his actions?

'Jesus, Zoe, she's with Nadia, she's fine.'

'But she shouldn't be with Nadia, she should be with you. The only thing that's been keeping me going at work is knowing that she's with her father. I don't want Nadia looking after her!'

'She is with me! It's just a couple of hours – you're overreacting, babe.'

'God, Lachlan, you're so... self-absorbed recently. Can't you understand why I wouldn't want Nadia looking after our baby? Do I have to spell it out?'

Lachlan glared at her. Zoe stared back, challenging him to respond, then looked out the windscreen. 'Watch where you're going.'

'I'm—'

'Just look where you're bloody driving, Lachlan!'

He clenched his jaw and looked forward. 'You're being ridiculous, Zoe.'

Zoe sank down in her seat. She wanted to open the door and jump out of the car, get away from him. She was so tired and hated working, but when Lachlan had the opportunity to spend all his time with his daughter, he palmed her off to the last person in the world who should be looking after her. And why had he kept it a secret? What did he have to hide? What did they talk about while she was dealing with dying kids and their distraught parents? She could picture them, Lachlan and Nadia, having morning tea while their child, Louise, played at their feet. A picture of a happy family. Surely not? Was that what this was all about – Lachlan and Nadia? She dismissed it; she trusted Lachlan. And Nadia. Zoe hated this feeling; she knew it too well. *Was* she merely jealous, though? That implied some fault on her part; it was an ugly word for an ugly person. Zoe was just trying to protect her family. She wasn't the one keeping secrets.

She looked out of the window. What did she have to do before Lachlan woke up and saw how she was feeling? What kind of a state would she have to be in before he'd show her that he loved her, cared about her? She sniffed hard and wiped her eyes again, not sure that he cared about her at all.

She remembered reading once that a relationship was most likely to break down in the first year after having a baby. At the time she hadn't believed it, never imagining that having a new child could be anything but bliss. Yes, there would be hard situations, but surely having a child together would be the thing that brought you closer as a couple, that took your marriage to a deeper level? There was a baby who needed you both – wasn't that enough to keep you together? It was for her; why not for Lachlan?

He was driving in the direction of home now. Zoe stared straight ahead. 'I take it we're not going for lunch then?' She knew she was being unreasonable, but she wanted to provoke him, to force him to engage with her.

He drummed his fingers on the steering wheel and didn't look at her. 'No. You made it quite clear you didn't want to.'

Zoe's lower lip trembled. 'Well, if it's all right with you, I'm going straight to bed. I'm sure you can manage to feed Louise and get her down when Nadia brings her back.'

'Fine.'

Zoe pressed her lips together tightly and held her head in her left hand against the passenger window. She thought about Louise, and what she and Nadia were doing together right now. As they drove over the bridge to

Fremantle, she saw the huge ships packed full of sheep bleating in distress. She looked beyond them, to the fishing boats motoring out the neck of the Swan River into the Indian Ocean, and the ferry sailing to Rottnest Island, where there was space, air, room to breathe.

Chapter Eighteen

It was the fourth meeting that Nadia had attended. The relinquishing mothers group met on the second Thursday of the month, always at the same time – ten am – always in the same church hall. Nadia no longer felt like the new girl. She looked forward to the hour that she spent with Tracey and the other women, because with them, she didn't need to explain herself. They managed to put into words everything she was feeling.

Eddie didn't know she came here; no one did. He'd gone back to normal life: the meetings and emails and dinners and squash games and Saturday morning kids' sports, as if nothing had ever happened, as if the last four years since this whole surrogacy started were irrelevant. He rarely talked about Louise, and he never asked Nadia how she was doing. Eddie – and everyone else – just assumed that she had moved on. But that had been their deal, Nadia reminded herself. Just the pregnancy, then it was over. Then they'd get back to normal and no one else in the family would suffer. And she was trying her best to stick to that.

Tracey closed the wooden doors and Nadia settled back in her chair with her paper cup of tea. She drew her thin cardigan around herself – the weather was cooling as autumn edged towards winter – and smiled at the three women already seated; they smiled back. She knew very little about them, other than their regrets at having lost their children, yet she felt close to them, knowing that they all kept the same secrets from their family and friends.

'Good morning, ladies,' Tracey said. 'And how are we all today?'

Nadia smiled, mumbled 'good' along with the others, then Jill, one of the women in the group, began. She was trying to find her son; she'd only been sixteen when he was born. She'd been unmarried, unemployed, and poorly educated. Not good mother material at all, according to the nuns who persuaded her that her infant son would be better off with another family.

'I've got all the paperwork to start the search,' Jill said, 'but I can't bring myself to send it in.' She reached into her handbag and took out an envelope, addressed and stamped. 'It's in here, but I just can't seem to drop it in the postbox.'

'What are you scared of, Jill?' asked Tracey. Everyone in the room knew the answer.

'I'm scared that he won't want to see me. I'm scared he'll reject me, that he'll be angry at me. That he'll think I was too weak to fight for him, or that I didn't love him enough. And if I don't send it, then I can keep the fantasy in my head that when we meet, he'll run into my arms and we'll have a relationship. But if I send it, I risk losing all hope and being worse off than I am now.'

'But you cry for him every day, Jill, you told us last time,' Tracey said softly, leaning forwards in her chair. 'Can it get any worse than it is now?'

Jill blew her nose on a paper tissue while they continued the discussion. Nadia said nothing, but struggled to keep herself from breaking down too. It was impossible not to feel Jill's anguish; it was the same pain that Nadia felt.

When it was her turn, Nadia put her tea down on the floor, then updated them on the past month. 'I've been seeing more of Louise recently. So I'm glad we moved here, even though it's been tough on the kids starting a new school. They've been acting up a bit, especially Violet, my middle child. She's been so demanding of my time. I had hoped Eddie would be around more with us living closer to the city, but, well...' She broke off. 'Anyway. The good thing is that I've been able to spend more time with Louise. Lachlan – her dad – has been letting me take her out on my own while Zoe's at work, just for an hour here and there. I take her to the park, or for a walk, or we go to my house for a snack. It's been...' She thought about the times with Louise. How could she explain the feeling she had when she was with her? 'It's been wonderful,' she said. 'I can't describe it other than to say that it feels as if everything's right and it's exactly how it should be.'

'As if you fit together perfectly?' one of the women said.

Nadia nodded, thinking of the way Louise was once tucked up tight in her belly, a perfect fit. 'Yes. Exactly. That's why this is all so hard. I tell myself it's wrong, that she's not mine any more, but when I see her, it's as if she is one of my children.'

'That's because she is,' Jill said.

There were murmurs of agreement from the group and Nadia looked round at them all, nodding a little. She knew that they were encouraging her relationship with Louise, because in Nadia, they saw the chance that they never had. But she also knew that they were biased, that this was a group of women who hadn't been able to forget and move forward – the women who had got on with their lives, maybe the majority, were out there living happily. That was one of the reasons why she hadn't told Eddie that she'd been coming here; she knew what he'd say. He'd say that she was just prolonging her grief by talking about how hard it was and reliving the trauma through women who'd had no choice but to completely let go. Perhaps he was right. Was the relationship she had now with Louise enough? She saw her at least a couple of times a week. Lachlan seemed uninterested in Louise a lot of the time, only too happy for Nadia to spend time alone with her. But handing her back was like torture.

The others were looking at her, waiting for her to speak again. But there was no pressure; they all got lost in thoughts during these sessions. For everyone except for Nadia, their thoughts were the only place they could see their children. But she wasn't the same as them, Nadia reminded herself. She had gone into this voluntarily. She had known what she was signing up for before she was pregnant. Perhaps she'd been naive, but she'd become pregnant with the sole purpose of relinquishing the child. Not like Jill and Tracey and the others; their children had been taken from them against their will.

Nadia cleared her throat. 'Sorry. Sorry... I was miles away. You're right, Jill. Louise is my child, biologically. But I've got no one to blame, no one to be angry at apart from myself. You can all point at someone – the church, the state, your families – and say that they made you do it, that you had no choice. I know you say I'm the same as you – and I thank you for making me feel so welcome here – but I'm *not* the same as you, because I did this to myself.'

Tracey shook her head. 'No, Nadia, you're wrong. We all thought that we made the decision ourselves. None of our children...' She swept her arm around the room. 'None of our children were wrenched from us. We all thought we were doing the right thing. Just as you do now. You're thinking what we thought twenty years ago, that we made the decision voluntarily. But the fact that you're here says to me that you felt the same pressures that we did – pressure to do the right thing, pressure to conform, pressure to give in to everyone else's expectations, but in the process, that pressure means that the decision hasn't been made voluntarily at all.'

'I'd give anything to be in your position, Nadia,' Jill said, leaning forwards in her seat and looking right at her. 'You still see your child. And you still have options. Don't let anyone tell you that Louise doesn't belong with you. You're her mother.'

Nadia had tears rolling down her cheeks and her head felt like it was going to burst. She didn't want to hear this, and yet it was exactly what she needed to hear. She was vulnerable, she knew that, open to suggestion. But she desperately wanted to agree with them, to ask for their help and strength to stand up for her rights as a mother. Rights, she reminded herself grimly, that she had relinquished when she signed the papers over to Zoe, her little sister, a kind, generous, and desperately unlucky woman who was also a wonderful mother to Louise.

Chapter Nineteen

Zoe tucked her chin to her chest to brace herself against the wind as she stepped off the bus; the rain trickled down the back of her neck. She glanced up as the bus hissed away from the kerb, then watched for a break in the traffic as the cars rolled along the wet road, splashing through puddles slick with rainbows of oil. The air smelled tangily of electricity. The thunder had stopped, at least for now. She looked behind her, towards the harbour and the ocean, but the horizon was blurred and grey.

When she'd left for the hospital this morning, Lachlan and Louise were still asleep, as usual. Zoe hadn't told Lachlan that she was leaving work early to see her rheumatologist; she hadn't wanted to give him anything else to worry about, but her headaches had been worsening for weeks. If she was relapsing, if she couldn't work, then what would they do for money? She'd only been back at the hospital for four months, she had no sick leave, and there was still no sign of Lachlan finding a job.

As the large storm had rolled in mid-morning, she'd concentrated on keeping the children calm. The power had flickered off and on, and even though the hospital had back-up generators, the atmosphere in the ward had been tense and anxious when the sky darkened, lit up only by flashes of lightning. There had been power cuts across the city, and a fire on the train line. Hail was forecast, and no one had yet forgotten the storm two years ago when the stones had smashed windows and the stained glass of the university's bell tower, and left cars scarred with pockmarks.

Zoe had hurried across the hospital campus to the adult medical clinics for her noon appointment. She dreaded having to go home and tell Lachlan the bad news. She was the only person holding their family together, and if something happened to her, Lachlan – and Louise – would flounder. But when she was called through to see the doctor, the news wasn't all bad; yes, her blood pressure was up and her kidney function had deteriorated, but the specialist was optimistic that with a change to her medication, they could keep it under control. She'd walked out of the clinic smiling. Finally, something was going right.

There was only an hour left until the end of her shift. Zoe had started walking back towards the ward; then, on an impulse, she stopped, turned and hurried the other way, towards the bus stop, before anyone spotted her.

By the time the bus arrived back in Fremantle, the rain had started again. Zoe stepped off the bus into a gust of wind. She held out her arms to steady herself; maybe she should have called Lachlan to pick her up from the hospital. Too late now. She tucked her bag under her arm and braced herself against the wind and rain, thinking of the warm house, a hot bath, an hour to herself before Louise woke up. She smiled and ran the five hundred metres to her house.

For a moment, Zoe stood under the shelter of the verandah and looked out at the garden. The water poured down from the sky in sheets, and yet here she was perfectly dry. It was like standing behind a waterfall. The water bounced off the paving slabs on the path and pooled on the patchy grass, then ran off onto the road in streams.

She bent down and took off her shoes. The leather was soaked through and her socks were sodden. She peeled them off too and propped her shoes against the wall near the front door. As she squeezed her ponytail, water poured out as if she had been submerged in the ocean. She opened the door, quickly stepped into the hallway then closed the door behind her. Once inside, she struggled out of her uniform, which stuck to her like a cold, wet shower curtain. When she was down to her bra and knickers, she tiptoed down the hallway. With the rain battering down on the tin roof, the sound of the storm inside the house was as loud as outside. She paused at Louise's closed door, but couldn't hear any cries; she was amazed that Louise could sleep through this.

As she neared the living room, she heard the tune of the games console. 'Lachlan?' she whispered loudly. 'It's just me.'

There was no answer. Zoe poked her head in the doorway. The television screen was glowing with the title page of a game, and the long grey cord of the controller snaked across the room to the couch. From this angle, Zoe could only see the crown of Lachlan's head above the arm of the couch. He wasn't moving. Then he let out a gasping snore, snuffled and panted, and went quiet again. He was fast asleep.

'Lachlan,' Zoe said more loudly. But he still didn't move. Zoe frowned. What if it was Louise crying from her room in this storm, how would he hear her? She stepped into the room. 'Wake up. It's me!'

She walked closer. He was lying on his side with his neck at an acute angle, and from the corner of his slightly open mouth a thin trail of saliva led to a damp patch on the green cushion. His right arm was draped across his body, just above where the controller lay on the floor. Zoe's eyes widened and her heart began to hammer. Had he collapsed, had a fit or a heart attack?

Then she noticed that there were five beer bottles next to the controller. She looked again. One was lying on its side, the other four were upright. All were empty.

'Lachlan!' She shook his shoulder. 'Wake up!'

He groaned and opened his eyes. His face was red and his dark hair stuck to his forehead. He raised his eyebrows and peered at her, clearly disorientated.

'It's the middle of the day,' said Zoe. 'What are you doing?'

He blinked, then wiped at his mouth and sat up, frowning. 'What time is it?'

'It's almost two. I'm home early. What are you doing?' she repeated.

His voice was slow and slurred. 'Just having a nap. What's wrong?'

Zoe was incredulous. What did he mean? What was wrong that meant she was home early; or what was wrong with what she saw in front of her; or what was wrong with him, with their marriage, with their entire life?

She held her hands in the air. 'What's wrong? I come home at lunchtime and you're passed out on the couch in a filthy house—'

'Give it a rest! I'm not passed out!'

'You're drunk.'

Lachlan groaned. 'Oh, here we go again.'

'*Here we go again?*' Zoe pointed to the bottles on the floor. 'You've been drinking? While you're meant to be looking after our daughter?'

'I was just having a nap!'

'Lachlan, I walked into the house, through an unlocked door, and had to shake you to wake you up. Why the hell are you drinking in the middle of the day?'

Lachlan sat up, then stood, a little unsteady. 'Don't start this again.'

She stared up at him, furious. 'Don't start? Here I am, going to work every day, and I come home to this? You're playing computer games and drinking when you're meant to be looking after Louise! Has she been with Nadia again, is that it? While you sit on your arse and do nothing? Do you know where I've just been? I've been to the doctor because I've been sick but I was too scared to tell you because you're so preoccupied and depressed and I didn't want to worry you, but look at you! I'm sorry, but I… I can't do this any more.' She shook her head and ended with a cry.

Lachlan flinched a little at her words, but then stepped to the side as if to walk around her. Zoe moved in front of him. He was *not* getting to walk away from this one. She had meant it when she said she couldn't do this any more. 'No, Lachlan, don't you dare run off again. You need to tell me what's going on. I've had enough!'

As Zoe watched, his face changed. His jaw clenched and his eyes narrowed, and he spat his words at her, 'You've had enough?' He shook his head in disgust. 'Get out of my way.'

Zoe's hands began to shake but she didn't move. 'No, I'm not letting you walk away from me,' she said firmly. 'You need to deal with this.'

'Move!' His face was livid and the sinew in his neck was taut beneath the black and grey stubble.

'No!'

He stepped towards Zoe, and before she could react, raised his arms and pushed her chest with full force. She screamed and lost her balance, arms flailing. She crashed hard onto her back, landing on one of Louise's wooden blocks that littered the floor. The sharp corner of the cube dug into her flank, and her upper back rolled onto the wooden floorboards. It happened so quickly, yet every movement seemed to occur in slow motion. Her head thumped on the floor and she heard herself cry out again. Lachlan loomed above her. He stared at her, with stunned horror on his face, then looked down at his hands as if they belonged to someone else, as if there was a stain on them that only he could see. Zoe rolled onto her side and covered her head with her arms, waiting for the next blow.

She lay still, waiting, frozen. She sensed Lachlan step over her, then heard him run down the hallway. Above the noise of the rain, the front door slammed.

When it was obvious that he wasn't coming back, Zoe began to wail, lying on the floor among the toys and the beer bottles, bedraggled in her wet underwear. She lay where she'd fallen, her breath heaving with sobs, listening for the door. While she was terrified of what Lachlan might do if he came back, a huge part of her wanted him to open the front door and come in and kiss her and say he was sorry.

But even when she had cried herself out, he still hadn't returned. The rain was slowing now, just a patter on the roof, and she heard Louise squeal and laugh from her bedroom. Zoe eased herself up to sitting, and rubbed her back, which already felt stiff and bruised. Suddenly frightened again, she got to her feet, ran down the hallway and locked the front door. She quickly dressed in dry clothes and went to pick up Louise.

She gave Louise some milk and plain biscuits, then sat her on the living room floor with her toys. After switching on a kids' TV show, Zoe hurried into the bedroom and took a sports bag out from under the bed. She put a few clothes into the bag, then went into the bathroom and packed up her toiletries.

In Louise's room, Zoe packed some baby clothes. She picked up Louise's favourite pink rabbit, and her tears started to fall again. She wiped them away and tried to concentrate on what she needed, chanting the list of things in her head to block out any other thoughts. *Bottles, formula, nappies, cream, bottles, formula, nappies, cream.*

When the bag was packed, Zoe sat on the edge of the armchair in Louise's room. Lachlan had been gone for over an hour now. Where was he? What would he do when he came home and found them gone?

Zoe walked out into the hallway and put the bag down next to the front door. She paused, then opened the door and peered out. Rainwater dripped through the rusted holes in the gutter. Zoe almost expected – hoped – to see Lachlan sitting on the verandah in the wrought-iron chair, waiting for her, racked with regret. She looked up and down the street, in case he was walking back through the spattering rain with his head bowed and his hands in his pockets. She imagined him finding her loading Louise into the car, and collapsing at her feet, begging for her forgiveness. Biting her lip, she looked again: there was no one in the street. The occasional car splashed past, lights blurred by the wet air. Zoe slumped against the doorframe. Was he sad? Worried? Or was he still angry, full of loathing? She thought again of the enraged look in his eyes, the contemptuous sneer when he pushed past her. He wasn't even man enough to stick around and apologise. For all he knew, she was still lying hurt or unconscious on the floor, while Louise cried in her room. He deserved this.

Zoe went back inside and scooped up Louise, who had crawled over to the couch and pulled herself onto her feet. Zoe turned off the television but didn't tidy anything else up. He could do that when he came back. If he came back. Zoe frowned; why was *she* going? He should be the one to go. She shook her head. She was so confused and couldn't trust herself to be strong enough if he walked through the door begging for forgiveness. The future – either with Lachlan, or without him – terrified her. But she knew that if he came back and she forgave him, and he hadn't changed, Louise would ultimately be the one who was harmed and Zoe couldn't live with herself if that happened. She knew he'd never physically hurt Louise, but it was as painful for a child to live amidst fear as it was to have her bones broken.

No, Zoe had to go. She had to protect Louise.

Chapter Twenty

Zoe let herself into her parents' house with her spare key. They were both at work; her mum would be back from the university at around four, she guessed, and Martin after five sometime. Zoe kept the doors locked, and her phone by her side so she could call for help if Lachlan turned up; she tried to distract herself by playing with Louise, to show her that everything was normal. She froze when a car pulled up outside, then breathed out as she heard her mum's heels approaching the door.

The door opened, and Zoe stood up as Rosemary walked along the hallway to the living area. 'Mum,' she said, her voice immediately breaking.

Rosemary shrieked, then put her hand to her chest. 'Zoe. You scared me!'

'Sorry, I thought you'd have seen my car out on the street.'

Rosemary took off her damp jacket and hung it on a stool. 'It's raining again, I wasn't looking. Is everything OK? What's going on?'

Zoe took a deep breath, trying to stay calm, but then her chin began to quiver. 'I didn't know what else to do. Lachlan… he…' She burst into tears and covered her face with her hands, collapsing back down onto the couch.

Rosemary hurried over and sat next to her. 'What, Zoe? Lachlan what?'

Zoe dropped her hands away from her face. 'He... hit me.'

'What?' Rosemary's mouth opened in shock. 'He hit you? Are you OK? Jesus...'

'Well, he didn't really hit me, he pushed me and I fell. I came home... he was drinking. He's been so... oh, I don't know...' The sobs started again.

'Oh, darling.' Rosemary hugged her tight, and Zoe let herself be held. She had no energy left; she could no longer look after a baby *and* a grown man.

She felt her nose streaming and pulled away, then gave a sad giggle. 'Sorry. I've messed up again.'

'Don't be stupid. You've never messed anything up. This isn't your fault. Tell me what happened.'

Zoe described the day's events, and then told her mother about the past few months, about the way Lachlan had been acting with her, and with Louise. 'But maybe it's not all his fault, Mum. I pushed him into this surrogacy thing, he was never as keen as I was—'

'Stop it! For Christ's sake, he's an adult. You sound like some stupid woman blaming herself for her husband's violence. Next you'll be saying you deserved it.' Rosemary's mouth was pinched and her eyes blazed. 'What about the police? Have you called them?'

'No! I don't want to do that.'

'But—'

'No, Mum, please. Honestly, I don't want to involve them, it'll just make it harder for us all – for Louise. I'm sure it was just a one-off, and he didn't really hit me, it was more of a push...'

Rosemary raised her eyebrows. 'I'm going to call Martin to come home straight away, just in case.'

'Oh, Mum, he won't cause any trouble. Really, it wasn't that bad.'

'Well, you'll stay here, of course, until we work out what to do. Have you got your stuff?'

Zoe shrugged. 'Just a few things, enough for now.'

'Right. Stay there, I'll be right back.'

Zoe nodded, then looked down at Louise, who was playing with Zoe's purse on the floor. When Louise noticed Zoe, she grinned, crawled towards her and held her arms out. Zoe picked her up, then held her close and nuzzled her face into Louise's fine blonde hair. Poor Louise. She'd been divided and shared around from the time her life was just an idea, a hope. She had seen her parents begin to drift apart, and now violently tear away from each other, with Louise caught in the seething channels in the middle. This all needed to end.

–

Nadia sat on the edge of her dad's and Rosemary's bed with Louise nestled in the crook of her arm as she tried to get her to nap. She could hear Zoe crying in the living room, and Rosemary trying to soothe her. When Rosemary had called her and told her what had happened, that Lachlan had hit Zoe, she had raced over to her parents' place. She had known something like this would happen: she had seen Lachlan's drinking – they all had – and felt the tension between him and Zoe, how desperately her sister was trying to cling on to her marriage. Why the hell had Zoe let things get this bad? Nadia didn't believe that this – the violence – had come out of nowhere. What else had Louise been exposed to? What had her life been like, living with parents who were falling to pieces?

The dummy moved rhythmically as Louise's breathing got slower and slower and her eyelids closed. When Nadia had tried to put her in her cot before, Louise had screamed to be held; obviously Zoe rocked her to sleep. It made sense now: Louise felt unsafe. Well, she was safe now. All she'd known was a life of anxiety and fear, of being pulled this way and that. That was not the life for a child. She needed stability.

Louise's mouth went slack and the dummy dropped out. This should be how she always felt – peaceful. Nadia knew that Zoe loved Louise, of course she did. But so did she, Nadia. When it came down to it, she had the connection with Louise, the biological investment in her, that Zoe could never have. Lachlan was her true father, but he had given up any rights he once had today when he made the decision to expose his daughter to domestic violence. Zoe, technically, was Louise's stepmother. This was a child's life they were talking about, not a toy. Louise was an individual who would grow into a young woman, a mother herself some day. Nadia sat up straighter and arched her back, then stood up and put Louise gently down into the travel cot. This time, she didn't wake.

Nadia walked back through to the kitchen, her hands trembling. Zoe was still sobbing on the couch, barely able to talk for sniffling. Nadia wanted to go over to her and shake her, tell her to grow up, to pull herself together, for Louise's sake. Instead she took her mobile phone out of her pocket. The kids were at Eddie's mum's; this was no place for them, not today. She walked through the living room, past Rosemary and Zoe, and opened the patio doors. She walked over the deck, onto the wet lawn and into a corner of the garden, under the thick, bare branches of the flame tree. As she turned to face the back fence, she remembered the last time she and Zoe had sat here, after her dad's sixtieth, when the tree was covered with crimson-tipped flowers. So much had happened since then. She dialled.

'Eddie, it's me.'

'Hi. What's happening? Are you still at your dad's?'

'Yeah. Zoe's in a state. I only just managed to get Louise settled. I don't even think she's called the police. Eddie, I can't believe she'd let him get away with this…' Nadia's voice broke.

'Oh, Nadia, it'll be OK. You don't need to be so upset…'

Nadia heard the concern in his voice. She took a deep breath. 'Eddie, I don't know how to say this.'

'What?'

'I can't do it.'

'What do you mean?' he said cautiously.

'Louise. I can't let her grow up with a father who's violent, an alcoholic. I just can't, Eddie, not when we can give her so much more.'

He was silent.

'Did you hear me? I can't do it any more. I can't sit and watch Louise's life being ruined.'

'Shit. Nadia…'

'When will you be home? What will I do?'

'What will you do? Nothing! Don't do anything! God, Nadia. It's too late. I warned you about this, I knew it'd be too hard on you.' His voice was full of concern.

Nadia stared up into the sky. A sense of calm came over her, a lulling in her body that she hadn't felt since she'd become pregnant with Louise. This was the right thing to do, the only thing to do.

'Nadia. Everyone's had a scare – just let the dust settle, OK? We don't know the whole story yet. I'll leave work now, I'll come straight over. But remember, Louise is their child, not ours. It's been settled in the courts.'

Nadia sighed. 'Well, come as quickly as you can. You'll understand when you see Zoe. She's in no fit state to look after Louise right now.'

'Come on, love, give her a break. She's just walked out on Lachlan after he hit her, she's allowed to be upset.'

'I know. But, Eddie, I'm just thinking of Louise. Even if I'm just her aunt, I can't sit by and watch her life get ruined.'

'All right, I understand, but everything will be OK. Louise will be fine. Zoe's a good mum, with or without Lachlan.'

Nadia hung up. That was the one thing – the only thing – that stopped her from acting immediately. If she had given her child to a stranger and this had happened, she wouldn't care how hurt the intended mother might be; she would never leave her flesh and blood in such a dangerous situation. No question, she'd call child protection, she'd call her lawyer, and she'd get her child back. But she didn't know if she could really rip Louise out of Zoe's arms, because she remembered too well, as vividly as if it was yesterday, what that had felt like. Could she do that to her sister?

–

Zoe clasped one hand over her mouth; with the other, she gripped the edge of the open door. Nadia was standing under the flame tree, drops of rain dripping from its branches. She was facing away from the house, scuffing her gold ballet flat back and forth on the ground, talking on her phone.

Zoe hadn't noticed Nadia go outside; she had thought she was still in the bedroom with Louise. Her mum had gone to put the kettle on; Zoe had intended to go out onto the deck to gulp down some fresh air and cool her face, hot and swollen from crying. As she approached the door, she saw Nadia. Zoe paused at the door, and then the high, tense pitch of Nadia's voice carried over the garden towards her.

I can't sit by and watch her life get ruined.

Zoe had frozen, her heart pounding. But Nadia hadn't said much else, just ended the call, and now she was looking at the ground, deep in thought.

Zoe gripped the door tighter. Nadia must have been talking about her, Zoe, surely? She was worried about Lachlan, about what he'd done. She couldn't be talking about anything – anyone – else. Or could she? Did she mean Louise?

She saw Nadia wipe her eyes and turn. Zoe quickly let go of the doorframe, and stepped back before Nadia could see her.

–

Nadia was waiting at the front door when Eddie arrived. She opened the door and fell into his arms, clutching him tight. He held her, then gently moved away from her, still holding her shoulders as he looked into her face. 'Are you OK?'

Nadia nodded. 'I just can't believe it.'

'Any news?'

She shook her head. 'Nothing since I spoke to you. He hasn't been in touch, but she's too scared to go back to the house.'

'Has anyone called him?'

'No. She said he was drunk. I don't think it's a good idea.'

'I'll go and look for him.'

'No, don't.' Nadia knew what Eddie would do if he found Lachlan.

'If he dares to show up here, I'll—'

'Eddie. Not now.' Nadia took his hand and pulled him inside, grateful to have him with her. She was ashamed to think she had ever complained about her marriage or doubted Eddie. Whatever he was, he wasn't violent, and he wasn't a drunk. He treated her well, he loved her and he was a wonderful father.

Zoe began crying again when she saw Eddie. He hugged her, then greeted Rosemary. Martin, who had just got home too, stood up and shook Eddie's hand. His face was pale, his jaw set. Nadia knew Louise would be safe here. There was no way her dad would let Lachlan get anywhere near her.

They made yet more tea, then sat around the dining table. Zoe's face was blotchy, and her hands trembled. Louise was awake again, now in a high chair, eating a biscuit and banging a spoon on the tray. Nadia could feel the stress pulsing through Louise's body as easily as if they were one being. She watched Zoe, so caught up in herself that she didn't even see what this was doing to Louise. Nadia took the baby out of the high chair and held her on her lap.

'Why don't you come and stay with us, Zoe? It'll be nicer for Louise, to have her cousins around.' She hated even saying the word cousins; Charlotte and Violet were her sisters, Harry her brother.

Zoe looked up, frowning. 'No, there's more room here. If that's OK, Mum?'

Rosemary nodded. 'Yes, of course it is. As long as you want.'

Nadia frowned at Rosemary. 'But you and Dad will be working during the day. It'll be safer for Louise to be at our place. I'm at home all day, then there are two of us. Just in case he comes looking for Zoe.'

'He won't,' Zoe said. 'Anyway, it's not like he's done it before, it was just—'

'Don't you dare start making excuses for him!' Nadia snapped.

'I'm not, I'm not...' Zoe shrank back in her chair. 'It's just, I don't think he's going to come looking for me.'

'You don't know what he'll do,' Eddie said. 'Are you sure he hasn't done this before?'

'Of course not!'

'Shh, it's all right, Zoe,' Rosemary said, glaring at Eddie.

Zoe widened her eyes as she looked at her mum. 'I just want to stay here.'

'Of course,' Martin said. 'Have you got everything you need? Do you want me and Eddie to go to the house and pick up some things?'

Zoe shook her head. 'I've got some stuff, enough for a day or two anyway.'

'I've got heaps of baby things at our place – when I was unpacking I found boxes full of them,' said Nadia. 'I've got old sleeping bags for Louise, some toys and clothes. We could go home and get some, bring them back.'

'That's a good idea,' Martin said.

'We've got to get home soon for the kids anyway,' Nadia went on. 'Why don't we take Louise, give you some time to calm down? Then we'll get her fed and bathed with our kids – they'll love that – before bringing her back. Or she could stay the night with us.' She glanced at Eddie, saw the warning in his eyes.

'No,' Zoe said quickly. 'I want to be with Louise.'

'Of course you do, darling,' Rosemary said. 'Why don't you go with them, get what you need from Nadia's place, then come back? I'll make up the spare room, and Dad'll go to the shops and get something nice for our tea.'

Zoe looked around at everyone, and her eyes stopped on Louise, still sitting on Nadia's lap. Then she looked down at the table and nodded. 'OK.'

Nadia saw how detached Zoe was. She had given up all control, and was instead floating through this, swayed by everyone around her. That was the problem: she waited for others to make decisions for her instead of standing up for herself and Louise. Zoe should have made Lachlan get a job instead of allowing him to sit around all day drinking, and she should have left him at the first sign of trouble. Instead, she'd let it get to this point, and now she was drifting around, unanchored, while everyone else had to take charge and pick up the pieces. Louise needed someone to be a parent to her, to make sacrifices to keep her safe. Zoe simply wasn't up to it.

But even as she thought it, Nadia felt sick. Could she do it? Could she take Louise?

She stood up and hoisted Louise onto her hip. 'Come on, we'll feed her at our place, then get you back in time to put her to bed.'

–

Zoe watched helplessly as Harry, Charlotte and Violet bombarded Louise with squeals and cuddles, and Nadia clattered around the kitchen. This was the last place she wanted to be. She didn't really want to be at her mum's either; she wished she was at home, putting Louise to sleep in her own bed. But she stopped herself from thinking about that – she wouldn't let herself cry again, not in front of Nadia.

'Zoe, while I do this, do you want to have a look through the box of old baby clothes?' Nadia said. 'There's not a huge amount there, I threw out anything that was a bit grubby, but I'm sure there are some things that'll be useful. There should be a few bottles and toys too.'

'Sure.' Zoe didn't want anything from Nadia, but the quicker she grabbed some things to keep her sister happy, the sooner they could leave.

Nadia wiped her hands on a tea towel, then led Zoe through to their study at the back of the house. There was a desk underneath a window overlooking the garden, with purple flowers of native hibiscus tapping against the pane. The ceiling was decorated with geometrical plasterwork, with a glass art-deco light fitting hanging from the centre. While stacks of unopened packing boxes still blocked the large bookshelf that stretched along one wall, Nadia had managed to find time to hang her university certificates from the picture rails – her undergraduate psychology degree and her master's certificate.

'We haven't got round to unpacking these yet…' Nadia dragged the boxes around until she found one labelled *Baby things.* 'Have a look through this. I'll just get the kids' dinner on. Take your time, we'll feed Louise.'

'Thanks,' Zoe said, and smiled, though she had no intention of taking her time. Once Nadia had left, Zoe kneeled on the floor and ripped the tape off the box, then folded back the cardboard flaps. She quickly pulled out the clothes, and took a few things that looked like they'd fit Louise. She didn't need much. Zoe didn't plan on being away from home for long. Lachlan could move out, then she would change the locks. The tears welled up again. She didn't want to think about this being the end of her marriage. She still couldn't quite believe what had happened earlier today, and she didn't know if she could give up on her relationship with Lachlan because of one act of drunken violence. Closing her eyes for a moment, she wondered what he was doing now: where he was, what he was thinking, why he hadn't come looking for her.

She had a small pile of clothes, two bottles, a pink beanie hat and a sleeping bag. That was enough. From the kitchen, she heard the clang of metal – a spoon tapping on the side of a pan. She gathered the little collection of things and stood up. She used her foot to push the box back against the bookcase, but it was askew and jammed at an angle between the other boxes. Sighing, she put down the pile of baby items and crouched down. She straightened the box, then pushed it into the tight space.

As she stood up again, something caught her eye. In the bookcase, just above head height, was another, smaller box, resting on top of a row of books. It looked like it was made of cardboard covered in a pale turquoise fabric. A small metallic square frame on the visible end held a white label, and it was this that had registered with Zoe. On the piece of white card was written, in black marker pen, *Louise*.

Zoe froze, staring at the box. It was probably nothing, just the documents from the surrogacy process. But then she remembered the black binder that Nadia had filed everything in, the folder she had dragged out whenever they met to discuss anything legal or medical, and dread began to spread through her. The box looked expensive, something intended for keeping special things. Mementoes. Memories.

Zoe glanced back towards the hallway. She could hear Nadia and Eddie cajoling the kids into eating, chairs scraping, the TV going. She stepped towards the door and closed it gently. She could still see the hallway through the panels of fluted glass, so she'd have some warning if anyone was coming.

Noting the exact position of the box so she knew where to replace it, she stood on tiptoe and took it down gently, feeling things inside it shift. She sat on the floor, leaning against the door, and looked more closely at the box. It looked new. The fabric was clean, the corners still sharp. It was a little larger than A4 size, with a snug-fitting lid. She glanced over her shoulder again, then curled her fingers round the lip of the lid and took it off.

Realising she was holding her breath, Zoe exhaled slowly, then let her eyes focus on the contents. She saw the long strips of the ultrasound images, pieces of printed paper folded in half, some greeting cards, and the edges of photos. On top of the pile was a photo of Louise. One that Zoe had never seen before.

She recognised the park where it had been taken: in the background she could see the boat ramp and the river, even a black swan in the distance. It was near here, near Nadia's house. Louise was nestled into the black rubber seat of the swing with the strap across her belly, little hands gripping the chains. She was grinning, showing her two top teeth and her two bottom teeth, and her head was tilted back, looking at the sky. She was mid-swing, strands of her fine blonde hair blowing in the wind. Louise was central in the picture, but Lachlan was behind her. He too was smiling, and must have been pushing her. Nadia had taken this picture.

Zoe's mouth was dry. She riffled through the box. There were dozens of pictures of Louise. A few of them Zoe had given Nadia, but so many more were recent pictures, pictures that Zoe had never seen before.

Frantic now, Zoe tipped the box upside down on the floor. There was a copy of Louise's original birth certificate, the one with Nadia and Eddie's names on it. There were newspaper and magazine cuttings, articles about surrogacy; Zoe had seen many of them herself. There were printouts from the internet, sensational stories about surrogacies that had gone wrong. Zoe looked over her shoulder again, then turned back to the paper she was holding. She noticed the date on the printout: three weeks ago.

The paper began to shake in her hands. There was another printout from three weeks ago, several pages stapled together; it was the surrogacy legislation. Zoe had studied this legislation so many times in the past too, but not for months now. She turned the pages quickly. One sentence was highlighted in bright pink: *The court may make an order discharging a parentage order if it is satisfied that there is an exceptional reason why the parentage order should be discharged.*

Zoe stared at it in confusion. Why had Nadia highlighted this particular provision of the legislation? And why had she done it three weeks ago – not before Louise was born and not today, after finding out about Lachlan? What was an 'exceptional reason'? Zoe's heart thumped in her ears as she realised that Lachlan had just given Nadia exactly what she wanted – her justification for getting Louise back. And by running to her mother's house, and telling her family what Lachlan had done, Zoe had played right into her hands.

Domestic violence.

Alcohol abuse.

These would be textbook 'exceptional reasons'.

Even as she held the evidence in her hands, Zoe still couldn't believe that Nadia would do this to her. Not her sister. But then she thought of all the other things that, together, were now so clear: secret photos she'd never seen; Nadia's phone conversation with Eddie today; the way she held Louise and gazed at her; the expensive bracelet… Would she really do this?

Zoe heard laughter from the kitchen. She wiped her eyes then rapidly stuffed everything back in the box, making sure that the photo of Louise and Lachlan was placed on top. She quickly put the box back into the bookshelf, grabbed the pile of baby things, and opened the door.

She kept a smile fixed on her face as she walked along the hall and stood in the kitchen doorway. The four children were seated around the table, Louise in a high chair. Louise was the only one with blue eyes, but otherwise they all looked similar, like siblings. Nadia and Eddie pottered around them, pouring glasses of water, wiping up spills, helping cut up food. Louise looked like part of the family already.

Zoe wouldn't let herself cry again; that was what Nadia wanted. Louise *wasn't* part of Nadia and Eddie's family: she was Zoe's child. Louise belonged to her, and no one was going to take her away.

She walked casually into the room, though she was certain that Nadia and Eddie could see the confusion and fear seeping out of her.

'Did you find what you needed?' Eddie asked.

Zoe tried to keep her voice even. 'Yes, I did. If it's all right with you, we'll get going now.' She walked towards Louise.

'Are you sure you don't want to stay overnight, save you the drive back?' Nadia said.

Zoe paused in the midst of unbuckling Louise from the high chair and stared at Nadia. They locked eyes. Zoe wasn't going to be the one who looked away first; as they stared at each other, she saw a flicker in Nadia's eyes, as though her sister had realised that Zoe knew what was going on. Nadia looked away first.

'No,' Zoe said, feeling more in control. 'I need to get Louise back and settled. It's late, past her bedtime. She's had too much excitement for one day. Tonight, she needs her mum.' She picked up Louise. 'Don't you, sweetheart? You just need your mummy.' She looked at Eddie. 'If you're too busy right now, I can get a taxi.'

Eddie frowned, then stood up suddenly. 'No, no, I can take you.'

'But—' Nadia started to say something, then stopped when Eddie looked at her, nodding so slightly that Zoe was sure she wasn't meant to see.

At that moment she knew her suspicions were right. She had to take Louise, and she had to go.

–

Zoe smiled brightly during breakfast the next morning, avoiding her parents' anxious glances. While her mum and Martin got ready for work, she rinsed out Louise's bowl. She glanced at the clock on the microwave; it was after seven. She had booked the ferry and accommodation last night, secretly, when they got back from Nadia's.

She ran a cloth under the tap, wiped soggy cereal from Louise's hands and face, then unstrapped her from the high chair and sat her on the floor. She wondered if Lachlan was thinking about her. No, he was probably at home, fast asleep, sure that she and Louise would be back soon. She wasn't going to cling to him any more, and she wasn't going to let Nadia take control either. Zoe stretched out her fingers, looking at her thin, freckled hands and bitten fingernails, the skin around them torn, then rolled her wrists to get all the tension out. She looked down at Louise, who was staring, hypnotised, at the television; she'd probably learned to love it from all her hours with her father. Zoe shook her head and bit the inside of her cheek. Leaving the living room door open, she went quickly to the spare room. She could hear her mother's hairdryer whirring from the bathroom. She collected her dirty clothes from yesterday and balled them up in her bag, then picked up her phone and glanced at the screen. There was a text message.

Zoe's stomach lurched as she opened the message. It was from Lachlan, sent ten minutes ago. *I'm sorry. Where are you? Come home.*

Zoe sat on the edge of the bed and stared at it, knowing that he'd be staring at his phone too, waiting for her to reply. She threw the phone down on the bed. Who the hell did he think he was? She looked at the message again: seven words, that's all he'd written. Was that all their marriage, their family, was worth to him? Did he think he could do whatever he wanted, then send a message the next day and everything would be OK? He'd probably only just noticed she was gone. Had he stayed out all night, and just stumbled in, pissed, or feeling sorry for himself after spending the night on someone else's floor, with the excuse that he was drunk and didn't know what he was doing? He should have called last night, come over and begged on the doorstep, told her he couldn't live without her. But no, he'd gone to bed, and then sent a seven-word message. It wasn't very hard to find her, here at her parents'; he hadn't really tried, had he? Well, see him try now.

Zoe shoved her phone in her bag and zipped it closed. Then she opened it again, tore a page out of her notebook and wrote a quick note, just so her parents wouldn't worry. Unlike Lachlan, she thought about the consequences of her actions.

She heard a thump from the living room, then Louise began to cry. Zoe took a deep breath and fixed the smile back on her face, then went to pick her up. In three hours, she and Louise would be on the ferry to Rottnest Island.

Chapter Twenty-One

Lou and her parents sat in their usual chairs in Ross's office. They had been coming here for months now, and even though things had definitely been better at home, it seemed to Lou that they were just covering the same old stuff every week. Sometimes she saw Ross alone, and that was easier. She dreaded these family sessions; not because she found it any more difficult, as she knew very well by now how to play the game, but because she hated seeing her parents get upset. When her mum cried, or her dad squirmed and clenched his fists and talked so slowly and quietly that she knew he was only just holding it together, Lou wanted to scream at them: *I'm the child, you're the grown-ups! You're meant to be in control here*. She supposed that Ross thought it was helpful for her to see that her parents were just people too, that they had emotions and flaws, but she needed to believe that they knew what they were doing; she needed them to hold the boundaries of her life firm so that she knew exactly where she belonged.

'How have things been?' Ross said, smiling and settling back into his chair.

'Lou has been doing much better at school, haven't you?'

Lou glared at her mum, hating the sickly-sweet voice and the hopeful smile. 'I suppose so,' she said. She had been getting better grades, it was true, even if it was mainly to keep her parents off her back. She was also sensible enough to know that this was her final year at school. In two months she'd be done with it, and she needed to get into university. While she told her parents that she didn't care about it, she did. She wasn't ready to work: what would she do? No job she could find would pay enough to get an apartment of her own, or even a room in a share house, and that would mean she was stuck at home. She wanted to leave Perth, study somewhere far away from here, maybe Melbourne or Sydney, like Charlotte, Violet and Harry had done.

They were all still looking at her, waiting. 'My exams are next month, so I've been studying a lot,' she said reluctantly.

'And are you finding that you're able to concentrate all right on your studies?' Ross asked.

She shrugged and nodded.

'We're very proud of Lou, and how she's turned things around in the past few months.'

Lou looked at her dad from the corner of her eye; he too was smiling at her. Why didn't he tell her that when they were at home, instead of flicking through his emails constantly? She wondered why they came here when it was clear that all three of them were just putting on an act – but for whose benefit, she wasn't sure.

Ross put the palms of his hands together as if he was praying. 'Well, it certainly seems as if things are improving. Slowly but surely!'

Lou raised her eyebrows. He looked pleased with himself, as if it was his doing.

Her mum cleared her throat. 'We have something we – well, Lou – wants to ask you. After her exams… well, it's year twelve, and it's schoolies, you know, she's graduating from high school and going off to university. Well, hopefully. Anyway, Lou's friends from school are going to Rottnest for a few nights. We're just a bit anxious about letting her go, you know, after all the trouble she's been in before.' She laughed. 'We've all been there, I'm not naive enough to think they'll be sitting around playing Scrabble!' Then she spoke more quietly. 'There'll be alcohol.'

'I won't be drinking, Mum. As you've told me a hundred times, I'm still under age.'

'Well, Lou, I know the pub will be strict with ID, but that won't apply in the houses.'

'The police check on all the parties, so I won't be able to drink.' Lou looked at her mum with her eyebrows raised and her hands held open, but they both knew that everyone would be drinking, including her. That was what you did when you finished school. But this was the game, the dance they needed to go through, otherwise they'd never let her go.

Still smiling, her mum turned back to Ross. 'You can understand that we're a little unsure. It *is* true that Lou has been trying really hard since she was arrested, since we started coming here. She's done all the right things, and she hasn't been using alcohol or drugs, or self-harming.'

'Is that true, Lou?' Ross tilted his head to the side. Lou knew that he was trying to get her to be honest: she had admitted to him that in those early weeks, while her friends abandoned her and her parents argued in shrill whispers, she'd cut herself a few times. She'd been careful, doing it on her thighs and her stomach, where her parents wouldn't see, but she'd been honest with Ross when she'd said she wasn't trying to seriously hurt herself. It was just what she had needed to do to relieve the tension, to *feel* something. He also knew that she wasn't doing it any more, that she hadn't for ages now.

'Yes, it's true.'

'Can you understand why your parents would be anxious about you going away, unsupervised, to a place where we all know it will get pretty wild?' He smiled again, and nodded at everyone in the room.

'Yes, of course.'

'Talk to them, not me.' Ross waved his hand towards her parents.

Lou hated this, the way he used his touchy-feely counselling tricks. Just because he forced her to talk to them in this room didn't mean he was magically transforming their family. She pursed her lips and sighed loudly, then swivelled her body round.

'Yes, Mum and Dad, I can understand why you're worried. You're scared that I'll get into trouble again, or that I might come to some harm. But *I'm* worried about the fact that I'm about to turn eighteen, that I'll be going off to uni in a couple of months – if I get in – and you won't trust me to go away for three days with the friends I've known my whole life. If you can't trust me now, what's going to happen when I leave home soon?'

Her mum frowned, and looked at Ross, then her dad, who sat forward. 'Lou, we do trust you. Your mother and I are worried, but it's because we love you very much.' His voice broke; Lou shifted in her chair and started wiggling her toes inside her school shoes, but he managed to compose himself. 'As you know, we said we'd discuss it here because we think it's also important to involve Ross in the decision.' He looked at Ross.

'Well, it's not my decision to make, I'm afraid. This is something that you as a family need to decide.'

Lou pressed her lips together to stop herself from smiling.

'But I will say,' Ross continued, 'that Lou's behaviour has been quite stable for the past few months, and she has a point about trust. It seems that she is asking you to let her prove to you how much she's changed.'

Lou watched her parents as they looked at each other. Her mother was biting her lip, her dad scratching his chin. She knew that they wanted to go and talk about it between themselves in private. Well, this was about communication, wasn't it? After all, it was *her* life they were making a decision about. 'Well?' she asked.

Her mum sighed, then nodded a little. 'OK.'

'Yes!' Lou shouted, grinning. She jumped out of her chair and went over to hug her parents. They both laughed and hugged her back.

'But,' her dad said in a stern voice, 'between now and then you must study hard, and if there's any concerning behaviour before then, the trip's off, OK?'

Her mum added, 'And I need you to tell me where you're staying, who you're staying with, and you must have your mobile phone on all the time, and be contactable. Otherwise I will come over there and collect you myself, understand?'

'Yes, Mum!'

Her dad grinned and leaned towards her, speaking in a stage whisper. 'And what could be worse than your mother arriving on Rotto in the middle of schoolies?'

Lou grinned back. Finally, she had something to look forward to.

–

Lou jostled at the exit with everyone else as they waited to alight from the ferry. There was a cheer from the crowd of teenagers when the door opened and they all poured out, down the ramp onto the jetty. Lou still felt queasy from the big swell on the trip over; she took a deep breath, and stretched her arms up. She straightened up and took off her hoodie, then tied it around her waist. The sun was warm now she was out of the sea breeze, and her nausea started to settle.

She looked around at the other kids on the jetty. Many she knew, but school leavers from all over Perth were here this weekend. Most of the kids from her school had grown up spending summer holidays on Rotto, either in rented villas or staying on their parents' boats, moored in one of the bays. Lou had only been here twice before: once on a primary school excursion, and another time on Astrid's dad's boat when Astrid's older brother was doing the Rotto swim. Her parents had never brought her here, though; they had always preferred to go south, to a house they rented every summer in Eagle Bay. It wasn't that Lou hadn't loved it there; she had – swimming among rays and schools of fish in the clear water of the sheltered bay, fishing with her grandad, cycling through the bush with the other kids. But Rottnest had always been there across the ocean, unreachable, teasing her with glimpses of the white lighthouse.

Now she *was* here, standing on the island. Exams were finished, school was over forever, and she had three nights of freedom, away from her parents, to relax and have fun with her friends. She couldn't wait.

She and Astrid chatted while their bikes were unloaded from the ferry. They waited until the police dogs had sniffed them for drugs, then pushed their bicycles along the jetty towards the visitor centre. They had booked a three-bedroom villa with four other girls from school. Two of them – Melissa and Claire – had already turned eighteen, so they had to collect the key. It had already been decided that Lou and Astrid would share one bedroom, Melissa and Claire the second, and Julietta and Heather the third. Theo and Ben were staying in the same bay with friends from their own school.

The two girls came out of the office, grinning. 'Got the keys!' Claire said. 'Let's go!'

They all jumped onto their bikes, fastened their helmets in case the police were watching, then set off. Lou soon found her balance and pedalled hard, listening to the crunch of the sand under the tyres and the flap of her thongs against her heels as she rode out of Thomson Bay, along the edge of the salt lakes, then up the hill until Geordie Bay was spread out below them. They found their villa, propped their bikes against the wall of the small courtyard, and ran inside to claim their beds.

Their bags had already been delivered. Lou threw hers on the single bed nearest the window in one of the tiny bedrooms. The walls were whitewashed brick, and thin blue curtains hung at the window. Between the two beds was a small table, and on the far wall was a set of wooden shelves.

Lou opened her backpack and took out the cooler bag that her mum had packed for her and went through to the living area. The polished cork floor was already coated in a film of fine sand. She put the bag on the kitchen table, then rummaged around in it: a box of muesli bars, three apples, a bottle of lemon cordial, a bag of chips, a block of cheese, crackers, and a plastic bottle of multivitamin tablets. Lou smiled as she opened the vitamins. Chewing on one, she hurried back to the bedroom where Astrid was looking through her own bag.

'Beach?' Lou said.

Astrid smiled. 'Definitely! Everyone's meeting there at twelve.' She turned back to her bag. 'I'm just trying to find my bikini...'

'I'll go put mine on now.'

In the bathroom, Lou changed into her bikini then stood as far back from the mirror as she could in the tiny room. She had to stand on tiptoe to see herself. She turned from side to side. There were still some scabs on her stomach, just above her hipbones. She tied her sarong around her waist to hide them. She'd lie on her stomach on the beach.

Astrid knocked on the door. 'Hurry up!'

'Coming!' Lou checked the mirror again, then opened the door and ran back through to the bedroom. She unfolded a beach bag, packed her towel, hat and sunscreen, put on her sunglasses and hurried after Astrid.

–

The afternoon was beautiful: the sun shone, the sea was calm, the breeze was little more than a whisper. Throughout the day, more and more teenagers arrived on the beach, squealing and shrieking as they hugged and kissed their friends. Lou could see that even in this idyllic setting the usual rules applied: there were cliques to which you either belonged or didn't. Even without knowing them she could work out which groups people belonged to by their swimwear, sunglasses, hairstyles.

Melissa came back from a swim, water dripping off her goose-bumped skin. 'God, the water's cold.' She shook the sand off her towel and wrapped it around herself. 'Some guys out there are pissed already. They're trying to snorkel, but they're going to get themselves in trouble.'

'Who are they?' Astrid asked, looking up from her magazine.

Melissa shrugged. 'No one we know. Hey, I'm going back to have a shower and get ready for tonight. We're heading to the pub soon.' She waved her hand towards Claire.

'So unfair,' Lou said. 'Do you reckon we could sneak in?'

'No chance,' Astrid said. 'Have you seen how many cops are around? And they've got extra bouncers on all weekend to check ID.'

Lou sighed and sat up. A breeze blew in off the water and she shivered. 'It's getting chilly now. Why can't schoolies be during February or something? Should we get something to eat?'

Julietta rolled onto her side, moving into the shrinking patch of afternoon sun. 'The boys are having a barbie at their place. I said we'd bring some sausages or something. Shall we go to the store and get some?'

'Sounds good.' Lou looked at Claire. 'Before you guys go to the pub, can you go to the bottle shop for us?'

'Yeah, if you hurry.'

Lou grinned. 'Yes! Let's go now. It's going to be a great night!' She sat up, brushed the sand off her elbows and gathered up her things.

–

And she *was* having a great night. Lou drank bottles of lime-flavoured vodka mixers with her friends, while they laughed and celebrated being out of school forever. Music blared from portable speakers, and teenagers from the neighbouring villas trickled into the party. Every so often someone would get a call from a friend in another part of the island to warn them that the police were patrolling, and they'd all rush inside and turn the music down so they didn't get done for under-age drinking.

As she tossed back her head and laughed, Lou watched Theo talking to his friends and saw that he was watching her too. She smiled a little at him, knowing that this weekend, they'd get back together. It wasn't really his fault that he'd had to move on from her: Lou had been under lock and key for so long, she couldn't expect him to wait for her forever. But this weekend there was no one hovering around keeping an eye on her; for the first time in as long as she could remember, *she* was in control. This was what it felt like to be an adult.

–

Lou was having trouble keeping track of the conversation. She'd lost count of how many bottles she'd drunk. It was dark now, and the villa they were in – a different one to earlier – was crammed with people dancing. Her thongs stuck to the tacky floor as she elbowed her way through the crowd to the verandah to get some fresh air. Outside, about half a dozen people were leaning on the railing, or sitting on the floor, smoking. Someone was passing a joint around; the sweet smell of marijuana was thick in the night air.

Lou stumbled over someone's leg then found a space in the corner of the verandah. She sat down and rested her head on her bent knees as the world around her spun. She swallowed the saliva pooling beneath her tongue, then clasped her hand over her mouth as she gagged. She struggled to her feet and ran back through the crowd then down the wooden steps at the front of the villa. Her guts began to heave; she took her hand off her mouth and braced herself against a tree as she retched. When it was over, she wiped away the tears running from her eyes, then checked the front of her dress for vomit, but all she could see was a damp patch from where she'd spilled her drink earlier.

Her eyes had adjusted to the darkness. She was about ten metres away from the light spilling out of the villa, but it felt much further. The music and voices behind her sounded distant, drowned by the hissing and gentle crashing of the waves on the sand. The ocean breeze brought snatches of laughter from the boats lit up on their moorings in the bay. She walked away from the pool of vomit, towards the water, then collapsed on the sand. Her mouth tasted foul, of sour bile and sweet, sugary alcopops; she wished she was at home in her own bed. She stretched her arms out behind her and tipped back her head until she was looking up at the sky. The stars were brighter here, away from the lights of the city, but they were blurred and moving in small circles. Lou groaned as she started to feel dizzy again, then tipped her head forward. The wind blew; she blinked as sand as fine as dust scratched her eyes. She inhaled deeply, then gagged. The air, rather than being fresh, smelled rotten. She tried to breathe through her mouth but the taste of decay stuck to her tongue. Putting the top of her dress over her mouth and nose to act as a filter, she looked to either side of her, but it was too dark to see what might be the source of the smell. She remembered the dugites, long dark-brown snakes, that she'd seen curled up earlier on the beach, resting in the shade of the rock overhangs, and then the tiger sharks and great whites swimming around the island. Her heart racing, she stood up quickly and ran back towards the party.

She found Theo and tapped him on the shoulder. His eyes were glazed, threaded with thin red lines. He smiled, a lazy, cocky smile. 'Hey,' he slurred. 'I wondered when you'd come and say hello. Been ignoring me?'

Lou raised her eyebrows. 'Hardly. I think you've been avoiding me…'

He leaned towards her, the tang of Red Bull on his breath. She hoped she didn't smell of vomit. 'Stay there,' she said, leaning forward and kissing him on the lips. 'I need to get a drink, I'll be right back.' He winked at her.

Lou went to look for a bottle of vodka. At this time of night there was always one belonging to someone who was too pissed to remember to hide it. She headed to the small kitchen, then noticed that everyone was going the opposite way, out of the villa. She paused, looking around.

Theo grabbed her hand. 'Come on,' he said. 'There's a dead whale at Stark Bay. Apparently there's heaps of sharks eating it. Let's go!'

'Where? I—'

'Come on, it's not far. Grab your bike.'

'But—' Lou didn't know why she was protesting. Of course she'd go. Everyone was going, Theo was going. 'Wait for me, don't go without me.'

She ran back to her villa, only a few houses away, and grabbed her bike from outside. Astrid's was gone already; the villa was empty. Smiling, Lou found the key under the rock near the front door, then grabbed the bottle of vodka that they'd hidden under a bed for tomorrow night, and shoved it in her bag. She pedalled back to the party where Theo was waiting for her.

-

Lou didn't have lights on her bike, but the tourist bus didn't go this late, and there were no other cars on the island, so she just concentrated on following the noises of the cyclists in front of her. Now that her eyes had readjusted to the dark, she relaxed. This was a beautiful way to see the island, even if the putrid smell was getting stronger as they cycled west. 'Wait, Theo,' she laughed as she tried to pedal up a steep hill. 'Wait for me!'

He stopped and put one foot on the ground. The others kept going. Lou jumped off her bike, giggling, and pushed it up the hill towards him. As she neared him, he smiled again and took her hand, then led her to the edge of the road. She smiled as she stumbled. 'What are you doing?'

'I don't know, what are *you* doing?' he mumbled. He pulled her further back from the road, then put his arms around her waist. 'I missed you.' He began to kiss her, and she kissed him back. Her lips were dry, and stung as his kisses became more insistent. Her mouth was parched; she needed a drink.

'Wait,' she whispered, and took the bottle of vodka from her bag. She unscrewed it and took a swig, then coughed as it burned her throat and the back of her nose. She passed it to Theo and he drank some too, then kissed her again. The alcohol hit her bloodstream and warmed her body as Theo's hands seemed to be all over her at once: down the back of her dress; under her skirt; tangled in her hair. Her head jerked back as his fingers stuck in the knots. She groaned. They dropped to the ground. She heard the whirr of wheels as someone cycled up the hill past them, but she wasn't embarrassed; she felt brave, daring. It made it better, more exciting. Her fingers fumbled with the drawstring on Theo's board shorts; at that moment, she knew what was going to happen. She ignored the anxiety in her stomach. As he slipped the straps of her dress off her shoulders, she scolded herself for being so prudish. She was an adult now. She had left school, she would soon leave home, and here was the ideal place to leave her childhood behind.

–

Afterwards, they lay on their backs on the sandy ground and looked at the stars. They talked, they laughed, and they drank the vodka. Lou couldn't stop smiling. It was as if the past few months hadn't happened. She and Theo were perfect together, and as they talked about their dreams and plans for the future, she never wanted the night to end. She saw a shooting star, then the sky spinning, and she laughed. Her skin felt hot and she couldn't really understand what Theo was saying any more as his voice got louder and softer, louder and softer, but she knew that she felt wonderful. She picked up the vodka bottle again and frowned as she realised it was almost empty. But then she felt cold, and her arms and legs began to shiver, then shake, and her teeth chattered, and Theo was telling her to get up but he didn't understand that her limbs were too heavy and she couldn't move them, but she was so cold, and everything was going round and round, but then she felt the hot trickle of urine scalding her freezing legs, and she couldn't understand what Theo was saying to her, and then someone was screaming and lifting her, and then it all went dark.

Chapter Twenty-Two

Nadia dropped the girls and Harry at school. She smiled briefly at the other mums, but didn't engage in conversation, instead hurrying back through the school grounds and out the gate to her car. She got inside and closed the door, then leaned back in her seat, trying to breathe slowly. She didn't know what to do. She didn't want to go home; she couldn't think there among all the clutter and mess.

A car horn beeped. Nadia jumped and looked up. A four-wheel drive had pulled up next to her, and the driver was leaning over, seatbelt straining, waving at Nadia through the open passenger window. Nadia lowered her own window.

'Are you going?' the woman shouted.

Nadia stared at her. 'I'm—'

'You're in the drop-off area, can you move?'

Nadia nodded and mumbled an apology, then quickly put on her seatbelt and turned the key in the ignition. Her hands shook; her mouth was dry. She pulled out, and the other car reversed up the street, then swooped into her space.

Nadia drove a few metres to the junction with the highway, then began to cry. She wished she'd parked further up the street, away from the drop-off zone, and walked; then she'd never have had to encounter that awful woman. And why had *she* apologised? She'd done nothing wrong. She'd had enough of everyone telling her what to do, of giving every part of herself to other people.

The road in front of her was clear. She flicked the indicator right, in the direction of home, then changed her mind and flicked it left instead. She turned onto the highway, and drove past the old flourmill, its giant red dingo logo towering over her. She turned right over the Fremantle traffic bridge, then right again towards the town centre, went past the prison and kept going. She drove for half an hour, then turned around and drove back, this time alongside the water, heading towards the beaches of North Fremantle.

The wind rocked the car as she pulled into the beach car park. Nearby was an old kiosk with faded ice-cream adverts and a closed grey metal shutter on the front. The dark green shrubs on the dunes were buffeted by gusts of wind, and the ocean was churning, white waves breaking on the beach then tumbling back out. Past the breakers the water was teal, the sky an electric grey; on the horizon was the silhouette of a container ship.

Nadia pushed the car door open against the wind, pressed the fob button to lock the car, then ran along the path and up the stairs into the shelter of the new cafe above the surf club.

A waitress with a tattoo of a dove on her wrist led her to one end of a long wooden table. The glass doors to the balcony were closed and streaked with raindrops. Nadia sat on a green wooden chair, ordered a flat white and a slice of lemon and poppy-seed cake and stared out of the window.

She had felt so detached from the world over the past few months. The only person who made her feel alive now was Louise, but those moments of joy were tangled up with heartbreak whenever she said goodbye to her. The only people who understood were the women of the relinquishing mothers' group. These women – Tracey, Jill, the others – they all had regrets; every single one of them said that if they could turn back the clock they would do anything to hold onto their children, no matter how hard it would be. Because life without their children was harder. It was because of them that after their last meeting Nadia had pored over the legislation to see if there was anything she could do. But, then, she had quickly realised that there was no way to challenge the parentage order: without an *exceptional* reason, there was no way to get Louise back.

But now things had changed.

When Rosemary had called yesterday and told her that Zoe had disappeared that morning with Louise, Nadia had screamed and sobbed in Eddie's arms. He'd held her and told her not to worry, that they'd come back soon, but he didn't understand. He never had. It wasn't just the physical connection of pregnancy that he had missed out on; Eddie had avoided anything to do with the surrogacy. He'd done the things he had to – the legal and counselling sessions – but he hadn't gone with her to the antenatal appointments, or the scans. He must have known how difficult it would be for her to see the baby on the screen while Zoe and Lachlan hugged and cried and wanted the ultrasound photos for their damn baby book, but he had taken the easy way out, detached himself from the pregnancy, and from Louise. He'd detached himself from

Nadia, too. He had no right now to tell her that her feelings weren't legitimate.

On the phone, Rosemary had told her to calm down, that Zoe had left a note saying not to worry and that she just needed some time to think. Afterwards, Nadia had called Zoe's mobile again and again, but it was switched off. She *did* trust Zoe to keep Louise safe, physically, in the short term at least; she knew Zoe loved Louise as if she was her own. But she couldn't trust Lachlan. Not after what he'd done. He was unstable, he could be dangerous. And Nadia was sure Zoe would go back to him: she'd seen how she defended him, even while her bruises were still forming. On the other hand, if Zoe didn't go back to him, Louise would then be raised by a single mother, who would have to work shifts to earn a pittance, who had a chronic illness and could end up in hospital, sick or disabled, at any time. The thought that had kept Nadia wide awake all night was the fear that Zoe might never come back, and that Nadia might never see Louise again.

When they'd all gone through the counselling before starting the surrogacy, the four of them had discussed hypothetical situations: what would happen if the scan showed the baby had Down syndrome or was born with another disability? What would happen if Zoe and Lachlan split up? They'd all laughed; it had seemed so unlikely. Hypothetically, they'd said that Louise would remain in the shared custody of her parents, Lachlan and Zoe. But they hadn't just split up; Lachlan was disturbed, violent. And in Nadia's eyes, that meant all bets were off. She would not have her daughter – and Louise *was* her daughter – put at risk, physically or emotionally. Louise needed stability, a family who could provide for her best interests. The way things were, Louise's best interests were not being met with Zoe – either with or without Lachlan. What kind of mother packs up a baby already traumatised from domestic violence, and takes her away from her family?

The coffee and cake arrived. She sipped slowly and picked at her cake. She needed to sit here for a while longer, among normal people going about their everyday lives. She imagined what she would say to someone else in her situation. An alcoholic, unemployed and unstable father, and an ill, erratic mother who disappeared with a traumatised baby. Nadia shook her head. She knew what she had to do. She had to detach herself from the fact that Zoe was her family. She had no choice: this was no longer about them; it was all about Louise.

Chapter Twenty-Three

Zoe sat on a plastic chair on the balcony with a glass of red wine. She'd had a bottle delivered from the island store along with the other groceries that she'd need for a few days. Sparrows darted and danced in the dusk air, catching insects. Rottnest was quiet, now, in midwinter. During the day, a few tourists puffed up the hills as they cycled against the blustery winds, but by late afternoon most had boarded the ferry back to the mainland. Every so often Zoe heard the distant squeals of children hurtling down a path on their bikes, and the clatter of bottles being emptied into a recycling bin.

Zoe had spent the last twenty-four hours locked in the villa with Louise, only venturing out onto the balcony for some fresh air. She didn't really think Nadia could find her, but she worried that she'd attract attention as an out-of-season visitor if she went into the village, especially struggling alone with Louise. Right now she needed time to think. She had called work yesterday from the ferry and told them there was a family emergency, so at least they wouldn't be looking for her. She reminded herself again that she hadn't done anything wrong. Louise was her daughter; Zoe had the paperwork to prove it, a birth certificate with her name on it, but for some reason she still expected the police to track her down and take Louise away.

The breeze was picking up again, throwing cold spray over her from the surface of the roiling ocean. Zoe shivered and pulled her thin cardigan tighter around her. She should have brought more warm clothes. Another gust of wind blew straight off the water, carrying the scent of the sea and rotting seaweed from the beach. White gulls coasted on the winds, looking for scraps of food. What was she going to do now? Zoe thought numbly. She needed to eat something. She needed to get Louise some long pants and some socks. She shook her head. She wasn't talking about what she was going to do in the next few minutes and hours. The real question was: what was she going to do about Nadia? About Lachlan? About Louise?

Zoe stood up, went inside and refilled her glass of wine, then opened a bag of chips. She picked up her phone and took everything back outside. The seat was cold and damp. Out over the bay, grey rain clouds were gathering. She'd switched off her phone yesterday, when she arrived, and had kept it off. Now she closed her eyes and took a deep breath, then held down the power button. She knew her parents would be worried; she should send her mother a text at least. Nadia would be frantic. Zoe tensed as she thought again about her sister, the way she'd been plotting behind her back to get Louise. Who did she think she was? For how long did she expect Zoe to bow down to her? The surrogacy was done, legal – how dare Nadia scheme to ruin everyone's lives? She had no right.

The home screen of her phone lit up. It was blank – no messages. Zoe bit her lip, then gulped a couple of mouthfuls of her wine. She slammed the glass down, and it clanged on the frosted-glass table. She wished it had cracked, smashed, cut her. She held up the phone in case it wasn't getting any reception, but four bars were displayed. Her parents weren't even worried; the note was obviously enough for them. She didn't want to be found, but she wanted them to try. She wanted Lachlan to be terrified, begging her to come back. She wanted her parents to be distraught, to demand to know what was going on, so she could tell them that Nadia wanted Louise, and for them to take her side and put *her* first. And she wanted to make Nadia feel as helpless as she did.

Zoe wiped her nose on the sleeve of her cardigan. Then her phone beeped twice – a message coming through. It beeped again. And again. And again. Zoe smiled in relief. They *were* looking for her, they did care. She looked down at the screen: she had voicemail, and text messages. From Nadia, Lachlan, her parents. She breathed out, feeling less alone.

She sipped her wine as she read and listened to them all. She deleted Nadia's message immediately, but texted her mum to let her know that she and Louise were fine and that she'd be in touch. That would be enough to reassure them, for now.

Then she listened to Lachlan's short message again. He was sorry. He needed to see them. As Zoe listened to it over and over, she tried to picture him. He was crying, or had been recently: his voice was thick and nasal, and his throat sounded raw, gruff. Then again, he could just be hungover. She felt some satisfaction at the thought of him feeling wretched, experiencing a little bit of what she had felt when he'd left her lying on the floor – was it only two days ago? They said that people needed to hit rock bottom before they would change; maybe this was what he needed to realise he had to do something. He needed to know what he might lose – no, what he *had* lost. She put the phone down on the table and switched it off again. Had he already lost them?

The tip of Zoe's nose was icy cold now as the drizzle started to creep off the ocean towards her. She felt an itch on her ankle and swiped at the mosquito that had already flown away. She would go back inside, make herself some food, and have an early night. She couldn't think clearly now; she would start again tomorrow.

–

Over the next few days, Zoe tried to convince herself that she and Louise were on holiday, but they spent most of the time huddled in front of the gas fire in their unit, while the wind battered the windows and rattled the walls, and rain streaked down the glass. Occasionally, when there was a break in the weather, they ventured out to walk along the deserted shore of the bay, stepping between the mounds of washed-up bluebottle jellyfish, watching crabs scurrying along the beach and burying themselves in the sand. Zoe smiled brightly as she pointed things out to Louise, but she couldn't quell her agitation. Everything seemed more frightening now that she was on her own. She had isolated herself deliberately, but when darkness fell on the island, all her fears emerged from the shadows, and she knew that by cutting herself off from Nadia, she'd also cut off any information or support; the lack of control over what was happening back in Perth now seemed more treacherous than being there and facing Nadia.

Louise had been unsettled since they arrived, fussing every time Zoe tried to put her down, refusing to eat, waking in the night crying until Zoe took her into her own bed where they slept fitfully together under the musty blankets. As Zoe gazed into Louise's tired eyes when they both lay awake, she saw the trust that Louise had put in her, and it made her want to give all this up, to go back to Perth and admit that she had failed. But, now she was here, she didn't know how she could go back without looking like a fool.

–

Zoe woke up to the first bright day in almost a week. She opened the balcony door and looked out over Geordie Bay, smiling at the sight of the sun shining down on the ocean. The white sand was littered with seaweed and driftwood washed up during the last few days of storms.

Louise hadn't woken last night, but had stayed in her cot all night. Zoe had slept better too, and knew that she had to start making some plans for the future – hers and Louise's. Louise was babbling in her cot; Zoe went in to her room. 'Good morning, darling!' She picked her up and unzipped her sleeping bag. 'Let's get your breakfast, then we'll go for a walk and get some fresh air.'

When they had eaten and dressed, Zoe scribbled a list of things she needed to buy from the general store. She'd called the visitor centre yesterday and booked the unit for another week, but knew that her hiding here, on Rottnest, couldn't last. As each day passed she knew that it brought her a day closer to having to return home. Zoe shuddered at the thought of everything she'd have to face. Not yet. She wasn't ready.

She had let her mobile phone battery go flat; every time she'd switched it on there were too many messages from her parents and Lachlan, and she couldn't deal with them right now, not until she'd worked out what she was going to do. Because when she thought of home, of Nadia and Lachlan, Zoe was reminded that while in this moment, out here, she was in control, across the water she had only the weakest grasp on her life, a life that could be ripped away from her in an instant. This paradise was just a mirage, a trick she was playing on herself, a dream that would slip away as soon as the tides changed.

She sighed, then strapped the baby carrier to her chest and fastened Louise into it. She needed to keep active, not allow herself to think too much. They would walk the two kilometres to the main village at Thomson Bay. She would go to the store and organise a delivery of groceries, then take Louise to the playground and jetty, maybe even have lunch in the garden of the pub if the weather held.

As they walked, Zoe saw a quokka. She stopped and pointed it out to Louise, who squealed. They watched as it sat on its hind legs, then hopped across their path and disappeared behind some bins. Zoe looked up at the sky, smiling as the sun warmed her face and neck. Why couldn't life stay like this?

She bought a banana muffin and a takeaway coffee from the bakery, and walked down to the playground. She unstrapped Louise and sat her on the grass, then tore off a piece of the muffin and gave it to her. They sat together, licking crumbs from their fingers, looking out at the harbour. A ferry was coming in, a speck on the water that slowly grew bigger.

Zoe pushed Louise on the swing, tickling her toes every time she neared, making her shriek with delight. These were the moments that Zoe wanted to remember, the moments when they were together, happy. She wanted to breathe Louise in, inhale her joy and her trust. Her eyes filled with tears. She slowed the swing, unfastened the safety chain and held Louise to her, trying not to sob with the sudden terror of losing her. She squeezed her eyes shut, then crouched down and gathered up their things. She needed to keep busy. With the baby carrier fastened to her chest again, she set off for a walk before lunch. It was better to keep moving.

She trudged along the sandy paths, avoiding quokka droppings and swooping gulls, heading away from the beach towards the interior of the island. She passed the old settlement buildings, and soon she was walking on an expanse of patchy grass, still damp from the rains. She stopped in the shade of a melaleuca tree, the scent of tea-tree wafting around her, and rubbed at her bare arms. Perhaps she'd been a bit optimistic to wear just a t-shirt; it was cool out of the sun.

As she looked around, she realised she'd been here before. As children, she and Nadia had run around the clearing here, playing with some other kids they'd met. She remembered chasing after Nadia, her legs and chest burning; older and taller, Nadia always managed to dart away just before Zoe caught her. Then, as the sun went down, they had all lain on their backs on the grass, looking up at the sky, telling ghost stories. They were near the cemetery. The boys had told stories of the hundreds of Aboriginal prisoners who were beaten or starved to death in their damp prison cells, cells that were now four-star accommodation for tourists. Zoe had moved closer to Nadia as the boys described how the terrified men had been dragged in chains onto tiny boats, knowing they were doomed, and sent away from the mainland to the island that was home to the spirits of the dead. That night, back in their room at the beach villa, Nadia had shone a torch under her chin, casting eerie shadows, and told Zoe that if she listened carefully, she'd be able to hear the prisoners' moans as they shivered in thin blankets, the very blankets they'd been buried in, facing east so they could see the sun rising over their homes. Zoe had had nightmares for months, seeing those desperate and ragged ghosts rising from the ground like the ocean mist, gazing back towards the fires lit by their women on the mainland, then sinking again into their cramped, cold graves until the next night.

Now she shuddered, rubbed her arms again and looked around. She laughed aloud, hoping to banish the fear creeping under her skin. Just then she heard a mournful call: *may-aw, may-aw*. She jumped, unsure what she'd heard, then turned and saw a shimmering peacock bobbing through the pine trees.

'Let's keep moving, Louise,' she said brightly, scolding herself for being so jittery.

She hurried back along the path towards the settlement. Emerging into the carefree streets, she saw that the ferry was docked at the jetty. She watched the passengers – a few families, a group of backpackers – stumble off, swaying slightly when they put their feet on solid ground, as she had done just over a week ago.

Then she froze. It didn't matter that she couldn't see his face clearly from this distance; she didn't need to. It was Lachlan. Here, on Rottnest.

Zoe couldn't move, torn between running towards him and hurrying away. She put her arms around Louise and held her tighter. Her heart was pounding. What was he doing here? What should she do? She moved into the shadow of a building so she could watch him. Maybe she was wrong; maybe it was just someone who looked like Lachlan. But as the man came closer, there was no mistaking him. He was unshaven, thinner than he'd been only last week, and his face looked ashen. He walked with his chin tucked into his chest, his hands in the pockets of his faded jeans. His black t-shirt was creased and he had a sports bag slung over his shoulder. Zoe stared at him, at the man who looked so unlike the husband – strong, kind, capable – she knew. So much had passed between them. But she didn't feel frightened of him, not any more. As she watched him trudge up the hill, she knew with an utter certainty that she couldn't live without him. She hadn't made a conscious decision, but her body had taken over; she looked down at her feet as they walked of their own volition towards the visitor centre, where she knew their paths would meet.

Within a minute, she and Lachlan were standing a metre apart, just a little too far to touch. She stared at him and he met her eyes.

'Hi.' His voice shook. 'How are you?'

'Good. You?'

He nodded, then looked down at Louise, who had fallen asleep. Her back was to him, and Zoe still had her arms tightly around the baby carrier.

'How's my girl?'

Zoe felt her eyes fill with tears again. 'She's good. She's... perfect.'

Lachlan looked at the ground, but she could see his face reddening.

'How did you find me?'

He glanced up, gave a half-smile. 'Credit-card statements – the ferry, the store.'

'Wouldn't make a great criminal, would I?' She smiled sadly.

'You always were too honest, Zoe.'

'What are you doing here?'

He sighed, then hoisted his bag higher on his shoulder. 'I... I had to see you. You wouldn't answer my calls. Your mum said you had been in touch but then your phone's been off. I was worried.'

'How are they?'

'Your parents?' He shrugged. 'I went over, tried to talk to them, but Martin... well...'

Zoe felt a surge of warmth at the thought of her parents being protective. 'What do you expect? They know what happened.'

Lachlan blinked a few times, then looked at his feet again. 'Zoe, about that...'

She knew he wanted her to say that it was OK, that she understood, that she'd forgiven him, but none of that was true. She waited, said nothing.

'Zoe, I... I'm sorry.' His voice cracked. 'I don't know what happened, I've just been so...'

'So *what*, Lachlan? What's going on? Ever since Louise was born, you've—'

'No, it's nothing to do with her, it's not that at all.'

'That's what you keep saying, it's nothing to do with her, that you love her and me, and yet you've been absolutely horrible. You've been irritable and angry, and drinking all the time, and… violent. *Something*'s been going on!'

'You're right. We need to talk.' He looked around. 'Jesus, Zoe, this week has been horrible, just horrible, the worst week of my life. I miss you, and Louise. I… I need you…'

Zoe took a step towards him and held out her hands in exasperation. Louise jerked awake as the baby carrier moved. She let out a whimper; Zoe stroked Louise's head as she spoke. 'Lachlan, do you understand what you've done? Do you? You've played right into Nadia's hands. Do you know what I saw when I went to her house? She has this whole secret box, photos I've never seen – with *you* in them, I might add. And she's highlighted information about how to get the courts to cancel the parentage order! I heard her talking on the phone to Eddie, saying that she couldn't let Louise grow up in our house, because of what you did, Lachlan! She wants Louise, and you've given her exactly what she needs to get her. You never believed me when I said she was having regrets, but I was right!'

'I know. That's why I'm here,' he said grimly.

Zoe stared at him, her anger turning instantly into fear. She had expected him to tell her she was being ridiculous. 'What?' She thought about the photos of Nadia and Lachlan and felt the blood drain from her face. 'Oh my God. Is that what this is about? Are you and Nadia… ?' She couldn't finish the sentence.

He shook his head. 'No, don't be stupid, God no…'

She looked around her. 'I need to sit down.'

Lachlan stepped forward and put his hand gently on her arm. She looked into his eyes, silently begging him to fix everything, although she knew he couldn't. 'Come on.' He gestured with his head to a bench outside the visitor centre. He led her over and they both sat down.

'Lachlan. What do you know?' She unstrapped Louise, who was now awake. When Louise saw Lachlan, she grinned and squealed, bobbing up and down in delight. Zoe hesitated, then held Louise out towards her father.

Lachlan took Louise, and held her close to him, kissing her face over and over. Louise rested her head into Lachlan's chest; he ran a finger under his eyes before he spoke. 'There was a letter. Yesterday, from Nadia and Eddie's lawyer. Addressed to us both. It said that "in light of recent developments", they're applying to the family court to discharge the parenting order. I called Nadia straight away, and Eddie answered. He said she wouldn't talk to me. She's made up her mind. But he told me that… well, she's saying that she's worried about Louise's safety.'

No, no, no, Zoe thought. She realised that she had been clinging to a hope that she was mistaken about Nadia's intentions, in spite of what she had heard and seen. But a lawyer's letter? Court? Was this really happening? She held her trembling hand up to her mouth. 'My God.'

'I tried to call you, but your phone has been off. I had to come.'

'She can't…' Zoe whispered.

'She can, Zoe. I've already called our lawyer. He said Nadia has every right to try. It's unusual, he hasn't seen it before, but the law says that if there's an exceptional reason—'

'What, like domestic violence?' Zoe spat the words at him. '*That's* the reason. Because *you* have turned into a drunk, and *you* were comatose when you were meant to be looking after our daughter, who we have put every ounce of ourselves into – the stress, the money, the fear – everything we've gone through, and you just fuck it up!'

'Zoe—'

'No!' she shouted. Louise squirmed in Lachlan's lap. Zoe reached over and took her back, then stood up and pointed at Lachlan. 'This is all your fault. You need to go, you need to get out of our house, or else I'll lose her!' Zoe's heart was pounding, and she knew what she said was true. Even if she could forgive Lachlan, she could never be with him, because then Nadia would have what she needed to take Louise.

Lachlan was crying now too, oblivious to the glances of two teenage boys walking past. 'I'm sorry. I'm so, so sorry. I haven't had a drink since that day – I mean it. But I'd never, never hurt—'

Zoe closed her eyes, and he broke off. She believed him, that was the sad thing. Maybe that made her one of those women, a woman who told herself that he'd never do it again and went back for more, but listening to him now she believed what he was saying, and the knowledge that her marriage was over was worse than any physical pain she could imagine. 'But you *did* hurt us, Lachlan. You already have. It's too late.'

–

Zoe poured herself a glass of wine. She started to take a second wine glass out of the cupboard, then hesitated and glanced at Lachlan. He was sitting on the couch holding

Louise, humming a lullaby as she gazed at him with her eyes half closed. Zoe drank a mouthful of the wine, then poured the rest down the sink and filled the kettle instead.

They hadn't said much as they walked back to the unit. How she'd longed for Lachlan to take her hand, put his arm around her, but instead they had walked with a space between them full of things unsaid.

The groceries had been delivered while she was out. The butter, milk and eggs had been put in the fridge; now Zoe busied herself with unpacking everything else. 'I was just going to make some pasta, with bacon and veggies. That OK?'

Lachlan looked up, nodded and smiled. She almost wept. She had missed this, missed him so much. She had missed being part of a couple, having someone – Lachlan – to keep her company, to share everything with, the good and bad. And yet there was still that distance in him, and Zoe couldn't work out if it was manners, respect, or that same something that had changed when Louise was born.

'Should I put her to bed?' he whispered.

Zoe shook her head. 'Just hold her a bit longer, until she's sound asleep. She's missed you.'

She saw his Adam's apple rise and fall as he swallowed. He settled back into the cushions and resumed his quiet singing. Was this really the same man who had shouted at her and pushed her, who had ignored and neglected Louise? Could it have just been the drink, the pressure of being a stay-at-home dad, the shame of sending his wife out to pay the mortgage? She had never made him feel that she resented going to work. Or had she? Zoe shook her head; there she went again, blaming herself. She needed to stop making excuses for him. The anxiety returned as she thought about money, work, about the unpaid leave she was taking. When she looked at Lachlan, she knew that she had to face reality sometime. But when she looked at Louise, she wanted to claim just one more day with her, one more moment. Before it all fell apart.

She made two cups of tea and took one over to Lachlan. She put it down at his feet and paused for a moment to look at Louise. Zoe's hands started to tremble and she wanted to clutch onto them both, her family. How could this be happening? What if she refused to go back, refused to accept what Nadia was doing? But if she didn't go back, what could she do? She couldn't stay here forever. What kind of mother would that make her? Not one that would be allowed to keep Louise, of that she was sure.

'You could try putting her down now,' she said. 'I moved her cot into my room so you can have her room tonight.'

'I can get somewhere else…'

Zoe shook her head, and her voice broke. 'We can't afford it. Not if…'

Lachlan nodded, then slowly stood up. Louise didn't stir. Zoe walked towards the bedroom to hold the door open for him.

–

They ate dinner like a couple on their first date, skirting around the important issues. He told her the meal was great; she knew it was nothing special. She told him how Louise could stand on her own now, and would be walking soon, and he acted amazed. When they'd finished eating, he stood up quickly and cleared the dishes. She picked up the salt and pepper, their glasses of water, and followed him into the small kitchen. He put the plug in the sink and started to run the water.

Zoe put her hand on his arm. 'Leave it.'

'I'll just—'

'We need to talk.'

They stared at each other for a moment, and Zoe felt a pull so strong that she swayed on her feet. It was physically painful to look at him and not be able to touch him. She had an urgent need, a hunger in her guts, to connect to him again, to join together. As they stared at each other, she knew he felt it too. She leaned towards him, and that was all it took.

Lachlan leaned forward too and they grabbed onto each other. She pressed herself against him, breathing in the scent of him, then held up her face so that he could kiss her. Her hands were under his t-shirt; his hands were on the back of her neck and his lips were on her throat, and she pressed her groin against his, wrapping one leg around him so that every part of her was touching him. As her face and body burned with desire and hatred and sorrow, she began to cry, for she knew that she was betraying herself, betraying Louise, and that this was the end for them all.

Afterwards, she picked up her jeans and underwear and ran to the bathroom. She didn't make a sound but her body heaved with silent sobs and she clenched her fists, digging her nails into her palms, trying to draw blood, to leave four little crescent-moon scars etched into the life line and love line and head line, so that she'd see them every time she looked at her hands, a reminder of her weakness, of her stupidity in following her heart when, to have any chance of keeping Louise, she needed to ignore it.

–

Zoe sat on the end of the jetty with her feet dangling over the edge. Louise was fast asleep in her arms, wrapped in a blanket. The ferry – with Lachlan on it – was long gone, but she could see the twinkling red and green channel markers, and some white boat lights in the distant ocean: probably day trippers sailing home after a long day moored in a bay, fishermen maybe. She had passed a man still fishing off the jetty as she walked out here, but the white plastic bucket next to his reels and jigs was empty. It was dark now, but her eyes had adjusted to the gloom. She looked down into the black water, watching the colours of the rainbow dancing on a patch of slick oil below her, and the bloated corpse of a blowfish floating by. When they used to go fishing in the Swan River together, Lachlan had told her never to throw the dead blowfish back in the water, to always throw them in the bin. It could kill a dog, he used to say. Just a lick; that's all it would take.

The past forty-eight hours no longer seemed real, and Zoe almost wondered if she had dreamed them. Had it all been her imagination, a trick of the light, an echo of his voice? But she knew they had happened because she could still smell him, taste him, and she knew that she could never be with him again. It was Lachlan, or Louise.

After the passion of the sex on that first night, it was like nothing had changed. He was trying – she could see every cell of him straining with the effort to act normal – but he was still so disconnected, distant. When she touched him, he flinched. When he touched her, she remembered those big hands shoving her, remembered his furious face looming over her as she lay crying on the floor in her rain-soaked underwear. The second night, when they had sat on the balcony while Louise slept inside the villa, he had tried to kiss her again, but this time she had pulled away.

'Why won't you talk to me?' she said. 'We can't just go back to the way things were. You need to open up, tell me what's been going on.'

'I'm sorry, I said I'm sorry...'

'You're still so far away, Lachlan, it's like you're not here.' She took both of his hands in hers. 'Please, talk to me...'

He closed his eyes, shook his head, and let the tears spill out. It almost broke her heart.

'Please,' she whispered, begging him to give her a reason, an excuse to be with him.

'I can't.'

She pulled back, rubbed her hands over her face. She looked at him and knew what she had to do. 'Lachlan. You're dragging us both down, and I can't keep all of us afloat if you won't help me. I need to do what's best for Louise. Please, just go, just leave.'

'But—'

She stood up. 'There's a ferry in the morning. Sleep in the spare room tonight, then go before Louise and I wake.'

She had desperately wanted him to argue, to fight for her, but he had wiped away his tears and nodded. 'I'll move out of the house as soon as I get back.'

And with that, the space between them had become impossible to bridge any more. In the morning, she had heard him zip up his bag and close the door behind him.

Out here now, on the jetty, the breeze smelled of salt, of fuel, of decay. She could see the lights of Perth far across the water. She thought back to the ghost stories. They weren't just stories, though. Those men had been real. Their women, back on the mainland, had lit fires on the shores to tell their husbands, their sons, that they were thinking of them. They sang to the whales that travelled up and down this stretch of water, begging them to bring their men home. Zoe's eyes filled with tears, and she took a swig of the beer she'd brought with her. Was there a light over there for her? For Louise? She closed her eyes and listened hard: to the water lapping against the jetty, the tink tink of sails against the masts of the sailing boats, the hush of the waves. Was someone singing her home, begging her to bring back Louise?

Louise was happy with her, Zoe had no doubt of that. But it wasn't real, this place, this life. Zoe had hoped that all Louise needed was her, but knew now that she – alone – wasn't enough; Louise needed more than just Zoe's desperate love. She had to take Louise home.

No matter what happened, it was time to go back.

Chapter Twenty-Four

Nadia hung up the phone and stared at it for a moment. She looked around her living room: the vacuum hose snaking across the floor, the basket overflowing with unfolded washing, the unpacked grocery bags. It was as though she was in someone else's house; she barely recognised it. None of this, the domestic drudgery, mattered. Finally, Zoe and Louise were coming back, and Nadia could move again, stop treading water.

She dialled Eddie's number. He answered straight away.

'They're coming back,' she said.

'When?'

'Later. Dad just called me – he got a message that they'll be back this evening.'

'Wow.' She heard the scratch of his hand on his stubble. 'Where's she been?'

'Rottnest, apparently.'

'What's she going to do about Lachlan?'

'I don't know. She didn't say anything, just sent a bloody text message. This is typical of her, to disappear then just come back again with no explanation. What will I do, Eddie? Will I go over there?'

'No, Nadia, not right now, give her a chance to settle back in.'

'But I want to see Louise...' Nadia began to cry. God, she'd missed her daughter. She'd tried to distract herself by focusing on what she could control: the court process. Instead of admitting to the despair she had felt at not knowing where Louise was, she had stayed up all night poring over legal documents, past cases, stories on the internet. But now, knowing that Louise would be back in only a few hours, she let herself feel it again, all the fear and grief.

'Don't – don't cry,' Eddie said.

'Can you leave work early today and pick up the kids from school? I want to go over to Zoe's place, wait there until they come back.'

'No, don't—'

'I'll ask Rosemary then!' Nadia snapped. 'If you can't tear yourself away from work to help me.'

Eddie groaned. 'You know that's not what I mean. The kids have been upset enough, let's just keep their routine for now. It's going to be a tough time for them.'

'What do you mean? They're only upset because they miss Louise. And that's exactly why I need to go to Zoe's: I need to see Louise and check she's OK so I can tell the kids their sister is all right!'

'Nadia, please,' he said quietly.

Her chin trembled. 'What? Please what?'

'Don't bring the kids into this.'

'I'm not bringing them into anything! They're in it already, they always have been. Louise is their sister, they're missing a sibling! Zoe can't just do what she wants!'

Eddie sighed. 'OK. Look, I'm behind you. I support whatever you want to do about Louise.'

Nadia's face burned. 'Whatever *I* want to do? So you don't want to do this? You don't think we should be trying to get our baby back, protecting her? Jesus, Eddie! We're about to go through the courts and you don't even think we should be doing it? Don't you think the psychologists and psychiatrists and judge will pick up on that? You're going to ruin it! You won't even come home to help me when they're on their way back – my daughter!' Tears spilled out of her eyes.

'Fine, I'll pick up the kids.' He sounded defeated.

She wanted to hurl the phone across the room. 'Don't worry about it. If you're going to be like that, I'll sort something else out. I'll see you later.'

Before he could answer, Nadia ended the call, then threw the phone down on the couch next to her. She clenched her fists and screamed out loud, then grabbed her hair in her hands. Why was this so hard? All she asked for was some support from her husband instead of this passivity. He'd been like this from the beginning: patronising, humouring her as if they were talking about a pet, not a child. The truth was that he'd never supported her in this; he was always the one cautioning her, warning her. He was setting her up to fail, so he could say, *I told you so. I told you that you wouldn't be able to do this.*

She wondered if he was right.

–

Nadia picked the children up from school as usual, gave them some fruit and popcorn for afternoon tea, then chopped up the vegetables for dinner while they watched some television. Then she sat down with the girls and helped them with their homework while Harry played with his games console. Afterwards, she folded the washing and put it in neat piles, then began cooking the kids' risotto. Eddie was wrong: the kids weren't suffering. She was still here for them, doing everything she had always done.

When she heard Eddie's car pull into the driveway at six, she took the lamb chops – already marinated with rosemary, chilli and garlic – from the fridge. She'd made the salad too; it was in the fridge covered in cling wrap. The kids were bathed and only needed to brush their teeth after their story. As Eddie opened the front door, Nadia was gathering up her keys and phone. She passed him in the hallway.

'I'll be back in an hour,' she said, without looking at him.

'Where are you going?'

'The kids just need a story. We can quickly barbecue the meat when I get back. It's all ready, there's nothing left to do.'

He put his hand on her arm, then spoke softly. 'Nadia, I'm sorry about earlier, it's just—'

She shook him off. 'Don't. I'll be back soon.'

It took less than fifteen minutes to drive to Zoe and Lachlan's house. Nadia parked the car on the street, a few houses away from theirs, and switched off the engine. She drummed her fingers on the steering wheel, then leaned over to rummage through her handbag on the passenger seat. She checked her phone, but there were no messages or missed calls. She hadn't expected any, but she'd thought that maybe Eddie would have wished her luck, or at least let her know he was thinking of her. After taking a deep breath to calm her nerves, Nadia unplugged her seatbelt and put her hand on the door handle.

Headlights from an oncoming car blazed through the twilight. She shielded her eyes with her left hand as the car slowed, then stopped on the opposite side of the road, and a light on top of it switched on. It was a taxi. Nadia froze, her heart racing. With her right hand still gripping the door handle, she slouched down in her seat.

Zoe stepped out of the cab with Louise on her hip. Nadia shook her head at her sister's stupidity: there were no baby capsules in taxis. That was typical of Zoe, another example Nadia would document for the court. Why hadn't Zoe organised someone to pick them up?

Nadia watched the taxi driver get out of the car, open the boot and lift out a bag. He slammed the boot closed. Zoe struggled across the road, carrying the bag in one hand and a handbag over her shoulder, while Louise squirmed in the other arm. Still Nadia didn't move. She watched her sister put down the bag, open the gate and push the bag through with one foot. She couldn't see any more from where she sat, but she could hear Louise's cries, muffled from inside the car. Nadia closed her eyes and tried to mentally send a message to Louise, to tell her that she was coming to get her, she was trying. That sound, the cry that she had first heard in the delivery room, was her siren song, and she was helpless to resist. She opened the car door and stepped out, then pushed it closed quietly behind her.

She walked stealthily towards Zoe's house. Was Lachlan in there? Their car was parked outside, but it looked cold, abandoned. At the next-door neighbours' gate, Nadia stopped. She could see Zoe standing at the front door, her back to the street; Louise was still crying. Nadia put one hand out and held onto the fence to stop herself from running to Louise, snatching her away. Zoe was rummaging in her handbag, for her keys presumably. Without moving her feet, Nadia leaned forward, trying to close the space between her and her child.

Then Zoe drew out her keys, and hoisted Louise higher on her shoulder. She patted the baby's back and swayed her body from side to side. Nadia could see that she was hushing or singing in Louise's ears, softly, gently. Louise stopped crying. As Nadia watched, Zoe unlocked the door and stepped inside, then let it slam closed behind her. She heard Zoe call out, 'Hello?', and then nothing more. Nadia's legs began to shake, and she let go of the fence and staggered back to her car.

–

Zoe had waited two more days before leaving the island. As he'd promised, Lachlan hadn't contacted her, and while she was relieved, she was also disappointed. But she knew that he was showing her in his own way that he was decent, that she could trust him. So she had trusted that he'd also seen their lawyer. Now Zoe had to do her part and bring Louise home.

This morning, she had sent a text message to Lachlan and her parents to say that she would be home that evening; then she'd packed up and caught the last ferry off the island. When they arrived at the O'Connor Ferry Landing in Fremantle, she'd staggered off the boat with Louise and looked around, but there was no one waiting for her. She'd collected her bags, then she and Louise had caught a taxi home.

After paying the driver, Zoe struggled up the path with Louise and the luggage. At the door, she held out her hand and let it hover for a moment just in front of the door handle. She wondered if she should knock. A part of her hoped Lachlan would be there, but she knew he wouldn't be. She began searching in her handbag for her keys, but Louise started to squirm, then to cry.

'Hold on, Louise.' She tried to lift the baby up on her hip, but Louise's cries got louder. Zoe's eyes filled with tears too – Louise had been dragged around so much. 'Oh darling, Mummy's sorry.' She took out her keys, then put both arms around Louise, patting her back and swaying from side to side, murmuring into her ear. Louise rested her cheek on Zoe's shoulder and her cries quietened, then stopped. Zoe waited until they were both calm, then unlocked the door and stepped into the house.

'Hello?'

There was no answer, of course. She dropped her keys on the hall table near the door, put down the bags, and went down the hall with Louise still in her arms. The floorboards were streaked with swipes of soapy water, and she could smell furniture polish. In a vase on the kitchen table was a bunch of flowers, still wrapped in the florist's foil. She opened the fridge: there was fresh milk, cheese, butter and eggs, a tub of her favourite pâté, and a foil tray of lasagne from the local butcher. She closed the door again and opened the cupboard: three new jars of baby food, formula, a bottle of red wine. Zoe closed her eyes, filled with tenderness for Lachlan, but then she reminded herself what he'd done, and what she stood to lose.

She busied herself with feeding, bathing and settling Louise. When the baby was snug and fast asleep in her own bed, Zoe finally sat down at the kitchen table. The house felt far emptier than it ever had when Lachlan was away working. Her chin quivered for a moment, but she'd had enough of crying. She got up again, put the oven on to heat the lasagne, and opened the bottle of wine. As she sipped a glass, she pulled the small envelope out of the bunch of flowers on the table; she looked at it for a few moments, then opened it quickly. It held a small card, with a picture of a heart on the front, and Lachlan's handwriting inside.

> *I love you. Meet me tomorrow, 10 am, C.Y. O'Connor Beach. Please.*

Chapter Twenty-Five

Zoe turned the car off the main road. The safety barriers next to the railway line were raised, but she slowed the car anyway and looked both ways before accelerating across the metal grid, her body shuddering as the tyres bumped over the tracks. The image of a train hurtling towards her flashed before her eyes and she immediately thought of Lachlan. She pushed away thoughts that she didn't want to acknowledge, then sped up and turned right.

There were a few empty cars in the parking area, including Lachlan's mum's car; he was here already. Zoe stopped the car, got out and then, with Louise on her hip, hurried past the wooden gazebo shading gas barbecues, and along the path through the green lawn towards the beach. She couldn't see it from here, just the ocean over the crest of the dunes, and the dark outline of Rottnest on the horizon. To her left, the red cranes of the ports stretched up into the blue sky, towering over the buildings like monstrous megafauna. But to her right, she saw nothing but the Indian Ocean, flat and still. She started up the slope to the top of the dune, her feet slipping in the loose sand. On either side of the track, a wire fence held back clumps of spinifex. Louise wriggled; Zoe shifted her into her other arm. Over the crest of the dune, the long beach swept out to her right. In the distance, a dog ran through the shallows, its bark faint but joyous, and ahead of it walked someone in a large floppy hat and billowing shirt. But Zoe couldn't see Lachlan. She frowned, scanning the edges of the dune. Now she saw him, a small figure, sitting alone against the steep slope of the dune, arms hugging his knees. She could just make out the red stripe on his pale grey baseball cap.

She walked quickly down the track onto the beach. Her feet sank into the sand; she kicked off her thongs, left them at the fence post and started out towards Lachlan. She was faster barefoot, but then she stood on something sharp; her leg buckled. The broken edge of an opaque milky cuttlebone poked up through the sand. She stared at it for a moment, thinking of the times she and Lachlan had gone jigging for squid, and how she had loved to watch him at home pulling out the translucent quill and spattering the sink with black ink. How he had changed; how they both had. She picked it up. The wind blew and she squeezed her eyes closed and shielded Louise's face with her body.

As she neared Lachlan, she saw that he was staring out to sea. She knew what he was looking at. They'd been here before, and sat together in this very spot. In front of him, a rusted chunk of orange metal rose from the edge of the water like the jagged tail of a whale. Beside it, the tide sucked and bubbled over the submerged outline of another, rectangular piece of metal, all that was left of a ship. The rest of the wreck was below the sand, covered up by more than a hundred years of relentless shifting sands and tides. But that wasn't what he was looking at. About thirty metres offshore, a bronze statue rose from the ocean. A man on his horse, his head turned back, looking north towards Fremantle Harbour. The horse's neck was long and stretched as it whinnied into the air with a frenzied look on its face, frozen in time as it would have looked a hundred years ago as it heard the gunshot, felt the jolt and the warm blood spattering over it, and felt its rider slump down in the saddle as he dropped his gun into the ocean. Zoe and Lachlan had sat here before and watched the tide rise; watched the horse and man being slowly swallowed by the ocean.

Why had Lachlan chosen this place? She slowed down as she approached him, not wanting to startle him. He didn't look up, but continued to stare out to sea. She sat down next to him, crossed her legs and propped Louise up in the space in front of her. She reached out her hand, slowly, until it rested on Lachlan's arm, still hugging his knees.

'He took his teeth out, you know.'

Zoe frowned. 'What?'

Lachlan nodded his head towards the statue. 'Before he did it. He left his daughter at home, picked up his gun, rode his horse out here into the water, then took out his teeth and put them in his pocket before he shot himself.'

Zoe closed her eyes. 'Lachlan,' she whispered.

'I always thought you'd have to be in a rage, you know, out of control to do something so… final, but it's not always like that, is it?'

'Lachlan, babe. You're scaring me.' She leaned into him and laid her head against his shoulder. Louise pulled herself to her feet and batted her hands against Zoe's chest.

He let out a laugh. 'Don't worry. I can't take my teeth out.'

'Jesus!' She sat back from him. 'You think it's funny?'

He laughed, then sobbed. He put his head on his knees and cried, while Zoe tried not to cry too. What should she do? She reached her right arm around his shoulders and pulled him towards her, her eyes wide.

He looked at her, and then at Louise. 'I'm so sorry, Zoe. So sorry, I don't know what's got into me, I can't believe I've been such a dickhead. The time on Rottnest, it made me realise how much I've got to lose. And leaving the two of you there while I got on that ferry by myself, the empty house… I just can't. I can't be on my own. I need you both. But what can we do? I've messed up, so much—'

Zoe was unsure of what to say. 'It's OK, please, stop…'

'I can't believe I did it. I can't believe I hurt you.'

She couldn't stop her own tears now. 'You've got to talk to me! I don't understand what's going on! Is it Louise? Is it me?'

He shook his head. 'No, I've been telling you that for ages, it's not you.'

'What then? Is this one of those "It's not you, it's me" things? Just tell me, Lachie. I can't do this any more. I don't know what's going on, and there's so much else to worry about with Nadia, I just need to know what's happening with you so I can try to fix everything. Why are you here? Why did you want to meet me? I thought we'd decided what to do when we were on Rottnest!'

He shrugged. Zoe took deep breaths, stroked Louise's head while she played with the sand. She had to pull back; she knew that if she kept on at him, he'd retreat again. She waited.

Eventually he spoke again, quietly, his voice ragged. 'I've been coming here a lot, while you were away, just to think. You know they sang to make him crazy?'

'Who did, Lachlan?' she whispered. 'Who sang?'

'The Noongars, the Aborigines. When he built Freo harbour, they cursed him.'

'What does this have to do with anything?' Zoe knew she was screeching but she couldn't help it. 'You're scaring me.'

'Sometimes I wonder if I'm cursed, you know. I feel like I've been going crazy. Maybe I have.' He turned his head to the left, caught her eye. 'I need to tell you about something.'

'What? Go on.'

'After… when I got back from Rottnest, I went to the doctor.'

She exhaled. Thank God. 'Good. What did he say?'

Lachlan continued as if he hadn't heard her. 'I went to the doctor because I haven't been well. I haven't been able to describe it. I've been… it's like I'm not here any more. I keep having bad dreams, I feel so bloody angry about little things, and in other ways I'm… disconnected. The doctor asked me when it started. And I know exactly when it started.'

Zoe waited. She knew too. When Louise was born.

'The day Louise came, you remember I was up at work.'

'Of course.'

'There was an accident that day. A young bloke. Killed.' His voice caught, the words stuck in the space between his private thoughts and speech. 'I was there. It was at the pit.'

Zoe saw the tiny drops of sweat starting on his brow, trickling down from below his cap, and on his upper lip. His hands trembled and she felt his muscles tense beneath the arm she still held around him.

'It was hot out there, so bloody hot. There were flies buzzing around my face, big blowflies, filthy things. I swatted one away, wiped my face. It came away red, dirty from the dust. I was sick of it, wished I was home with you, getting ready for Louise. I didn't want to be there. I wasn't concentrating, you see. I was supervising, meant to be overseeing it all. It was bright, even with my sunnies on, the sun was bouncing between the sky and the desert, and I was so bloody sick of it. It just gets you, under your chin, the palms of your hands, in the spaces between your cheek and your sunnies. I was standing there looking down into the pit, thinking of you, the baby, how hot it was. The trucks looked like toys, driving down around the edges of the mine, scooping up the ground then struggling back up again. It all seemed to be under control. I turned around to go back to the office, into the air-con.'

Lachlan stopped, looked up to the sky, and a tear dropped down from beneath his sunglasses. He took a deep breath then breathed out slowly. Zoe could feel his body trembling.

'Go on,' she whispered.

'Now, when I think back to it, I'm sure I heard him shouting. I can hear him now, at night, in my sleep. He's screaming out, "Stop!" Sometimes he calls my name, but I know it would have been impossible to hear him above the roar of the engines, the din of all the machinery. But something made me turn around, maybe it *was* him.' Lachlan rubbed his face with both hands, groaned. His foot tapped up and down, up and down on the sand. 'It didn't make sense. You've seen the trucks, haven't you?'

She nodded her head. She had, when she'd visited Kalgoorlie with Lachlan.

He continued. 'The wheels, they're as tall as two men, three maybe. They're like something from another planet. That's what it's like up there, it's like being on the moon. When I think back, it's like a movie. People were shouting, waving at the truck driver. The truck stopped. It was full of ore. Do you know how heavy that is?'

'No,' she said quietly.

'This stuff is what the core of the earth is made of; you can't imagine how much it weighs. Then everything seemed to go into slow motion. It was silent, except for the thud of my boots as I ran across the hard, baked dirt. Boom boom, boom boom, like horses thundering around a racetrack. But it was more than sound: I could *feel* the shock waves from my steps, the clunk of the gears of the truck as it tried to reverse. Then it was just my breath, panting, louder than anything else around me, then my voice yelling, screaming.'

He looked at her now, his face white. 'Zoe, it was like that scene in *The Wizard of Oz* when the house lands on the wicked witch and all you can see is the stripy stocking and witch's shoe. All I could see was his work boot. The sole of it was caked in red mud.' He stopped, eyes wide.

'Oh, Lach—'

He spoke rapidly. 'It was just all wrong, it didn't make sense. His foot was at the wrong angle, and all I saw was his tiny boot and this massive tyre. I kept running but it was like I was on a treadmill and I wasn't getting any closer even though I ran and ran and ran, it was always out of reach, but of course it was all just too late.'

'Oh, God, I'm so sorry…' Zoe wiped her own tears away. Lachlan's face was as pale as the pearly cuttlebone on the sand next to them.

'Then it was like someone flicked a switch and everything went back to normal. The sounds were deafening, everyone was shouting, you could hear the terror, even the machines seemed to scream, people were running everywhere, dropping things on the ground and sprinting as if somehow they could do something. The driver had climbed down and was just staring at him. I yelled at him to move the truck, get it off him, but he was frozen to the spot. Someone else must have moved it, but…' Lachlan broke off, staring out to the statue in the ocean.

Zoe picked up Louise and cuddled her close with one arm, her other hand over her own mouth, trying to imagine what he must have seen, but unable to imagine it at all.

Lachlan's voice was hard now. 'I was useless. Do you want to know what I did? I turned around and threw my guts up into the dirt. I moved my feet out of the way so I wouldn't get any vomit on them.' He turned to look at her, his eyes bloodshot and dark with pain. 'I was worried about puking on my own boots when that was all that was left of him. What kind of a person does that make me?'

'Darling, you—'

He held his hand up, almost shouting now. 'I was meant to be in charge. Every time I close my eyes, I see the boot: the ridges of the rubber sole, how worn down it was around the toes, the clumps of red dirt, the fraying laces. And when I sleep, I see blood dripping down it, pouring down and pooling beneath it because the ground is so dry that it won't soak anything up.'

'Why didn't you tell me?' she pleaded, but Zoe knew why: she'd been so preoccupied with Louise and Nadia that she hadn't asked. Hadn't given him a chance to talk. The space, the time.

He shook his head.

'Oh, Lachlan.' She moved onto her knees and leaned towards him, still holding Louise. She embraced him, feeling his body heave.

'I'm so sorry,' she murmured.

'I'm so sorry I hurt you, you must know that. I love you and Louise.'

'Shh, that's all that matters. We'll get through this. We're all that matters. Thank you for telling me.'

'I should have told you before, but I just couldn't...' He sniffed, wiped his nose with the back of his shaking hand and pulled back.

'It's OK, everything's going to be OK now. You, me and Louise, we'll get through this.'

'But I've ruined it all. You were right: you're better off without me. We can't risk losing Louise, and I'm the reason Nadia's trying to get Louise back, because of what I did.' He clenched his fist and slammed it into the sand beside him. 'It's all my fault!'

Zoe let go of him. All her doubts, all her fear, flew out of her mind, out with the easterly wind over the water towards Rottnest, then further out over the Indian Ocean until the memory of them was merely a whisper.

'Look at me, Lachlan, look at me.' She gently put her hand on his face and turned it towards her. 'Don't even think about that. We will not lose her. You are her father.

Louise belongs with us, and if Nadia wants to try and challenge that, then let her.'

Zoe looked down at the baby, her eyes squinting in the sun. Lachlan was Louise's father, biologically and emotionally. And Zoe was Louise's mother, not genetically, but in every other sense of the word.

She looked out again over the water, lapping around the statue, slowly rising over the man and his horse as the tide came in.

'No more running, Lachlan. No more running. This has to end.'

Chapter Twenty-Six

Zoe cleaned Louise's face with a baby wipe before unclipping her car restraints. 'Shit! There's soggy biscuit all over this top already.' She looked through the car to Lachlan, sitting in the driver's seat. 'I told you not to give her anything else to eat once I'd changed her. This was a new top.'

'It doesn't matter,' he said. 'You took about five changes of clothes anyway!'

She glared at him. 'Very funny. I don't need this right now.' Her hands shook as she lifted Louise out, holding her away from her own blouse. 'Get me another top from the nappy bag. I really wanted her to wear this one…'

'Well, she can still wear it, Zoe! I don't think they're going to say we're not fit parents just because she has a smudge of biscuit on her top. They're not interested in that!'

'We don't know what they're interested in.' Zoe went around to the other side of the car and laid Louise down on the seat, where she struggled to get her undressed. 'We don't know what Nadia's been saying to them.'

Lachlan was behind her now; he held a change of clothes over her shoulder. Zoe snatched it from him, dressed Louise again, then handed her to him. 'Hold her while I get all this cleaned up.'

Louise began to cry and fuss in Lachlan's grip, holding her arms out towards Zoe. Zoe closed her eyes for a moment, trying to compose herself. Louise was picking up on their tension, and she hadn't had her nap this morning. Today of all days, Zoe needed to stay composed, and keep everyone else calm. Everything that happened in the assessment today was admissible in court. Her future with Louise depended on a stranger's scrutiny of her family on this particular morning, in an artificial setting where she and Lachlan knew they were being watched. What if Louise was clingy, or cried all the time? What if Lachlan couldn't cope with the stress and unravelled, became upset or angry?

He put his hand on her shoulder. 'Come on,' he said.

Zoe opened her eyes, and put her own hand on top of his. 'I'm scared, Lachlan.'

'Me too.'

Zoe turned around and took Louise from him. He locked the car, then hugged her, with Louise between them. Hand in hand, they walked into the building.

–

At exactly ten am, a woman came out into the waiting room and smiled at them. She held a clipboard under one arm. Her face was unlined, but her long hair, tied back in a low ponytail, was ash grey. 'Mr and Mrs McAllister?'

'Yes, good morning…' Zoe stood up, balanced Louise on her left hip, smiled and held out her right hand.

'I'm Diana,' the woman said, shaking Zoe's hand. She turned to Lachlan, also standing, and shook his hand too. 'I'll be chatting with you all today.' She beamed at Louise. 'And this must be the little lady. Hello!'

'Say hello to the nice lady, Louise!' Zoe said in a high-pitched voice, although of course Louise couldn't speak yet. What was she doing, putting on an act for this woman? She had to stop doubting herself. She *was* a good mum, Lachlan *was* a good dad, so why couldn't she just be confident that they were good enough? Perhaps because simply being good enough wouldn't do; this was about being better than Nadia.

They followed Diana down a corridor lined with paintings of beach scenes and into a small room. One wall was made up of a large mirror, with a small wooden table underneath it. A two-way mirror, Zoe knew. There were two pale blue couches against the other walls, and a bright patchwork rug on the floor. On it was a white plastic tub full of toys. In the corner, up above the door, was a small black video camera. Zoe breathed slowly, then lowered herself onto one of the couches, clutching Louise on her lap. Lachlan sat next to her and wiped his palms on his beige chinos. She glanced at him, trying to communicate a reassurance that she didn't feel herself. The court knew about his problems: his diagnosis, his drinking. She needed him to show Diana that he could be calm under pressure – and this assessment was probably the biggest pressure imaginable. If he could get through this, Zoe was sure she could depend on him to cope with anything. She knew he hadn't slept last night; neither of them had. She also knew that he blamed himself, not just for the accident but for everything that had happened since, and that if they lost Louise, he'd never forgive himself. Never.

Since Lachlan had been getting help, Zoe had seen only a little improvement in him. She knew how hard he was trying, but he still thrashed around in his sleep, and Zoe still sensed the irritability just below his skin, and his deep, deep sadness and guilt. She had told him over and over again that she understood now what he had been going through, why he had acted the way he had, but they both knew that if they lost Louise, she would never forgive him either.

Diana sat opposite them on the other couch and put her clipboard down next to her. She looked at each of them in turn and smiled again. 'Thank you so much for coming in today.'

'Pleasure,' Lachlan said automatically. Zoe glanced at him.

'I'm a family consultant, approved by the court to work with families going through the court process, particularly when there are custody disputes. I understand that your situation is slightly different to the usual families we work with, but the principles will be the same. My job here is to get to know you and Louise, and make an assessment of the main issues. What we want to keep in mind is that the court will always act in the best interests of the child. As you know, the judge has asked for a family report, so I need to remind you that I will be providing the court with a written account of our time together. That means that this session isn't confidential, as you might be used to.' Diana looked at Lachlan as she said this. Zoe saw his face redden, and her heart sped up. She shifted ever so slightly towards him so he could feel her support.

He cleared his throat. 'That's fine. We understand.'

Louise writhed in Zoe's arms; she set her down on the floor, but Louise immediately cried and tried to pull herself back up. *Don't do this now, Louise*, Zoe begged silently. *Please be happy and show them how settled and confident you are. Just like you are at home.* She reached for a doll from the toybox, then lifted Louise back up onto her lap.

'For today, I just want us all to have a talk,' said Diana. 'Please try to relax and just do whatever you'd normally do with Louise. I know how hard this will be for you. Please don't feel that I'm here to judge you.'

Zoe nodded. But judging her was exactly what Diana was here to do, what the court would do too, and it was exactly what Nadia had already done.

–

Nadia stood at the back door watching the children jumping on the trampoline, dead leaves and windblown twigs catapulting into the air with each bounce. She turned around and went back into the kitchen.

'Eddie?' she shouted. 'What are you doing? They'll be here soon.'

'Coming!' He came out in bare feet, wearing jeans and a faded grey t-shirt.

Nadia frowned. 'Are you ready?'

'It's only your parents,' he said.

The doorbell rang. She shook her head. 'Please, put something nicer on.'

She walked to the front door, smoothed down her hair, then opened the door wide with a big smile on her face. 'Hi, Rosemary! Hi, Dad! Come in!'

Martin leaned forward to kiss her cheek; Rosemary nodded curtly, not meeting Nadia's eyes.

In the kitchen, Nadia opened a bottle of riesling and poured two glasses, then handed a beer to her dad. Eddie returned, still wearing his jeans but in a red polo shirt and with some thongs on his feet at least, and greeted his in-laws. Nadia smiled at him, then went to the back door. 'Kids!' she shouted. 'Grandma and Grandad are here. Come and say hello!'

'Leave them, I'll go out there,' Rosemary said, joining her at the door.

'No, sit down and enjoy your drink!'

Rosemary shook her head. 'It's fine. I like to see my grandchildren.'

Nadia nodded. 'They love to see you too.'

She had invited her dad and Rosemary over today to try to clear the air; she knew how upset they were about the custody case. No matter how many times Rosemary had told Nadia that she was just as much her daughter as Zoe was, she had never treated them equally. Now, she was clearly choosing sides. Nadia didn't blame her; she knew how strong the pull of shared genes was. But she hated to think that she was the cause of the coldness she could feel between her parents.

Martin came over and stood beside her. They both watched Rosemary totter down to the back of the garden holding her glass of wine aloft.

'How are things with you, Dad?'

'Yeah, fine. And you?'

Nadia let out a small sigh. 'Same. Busy.'

'Have you seen your sister?'

She looked up at him, frowning. Martin looked out over the garden, not meeting her eye. 'No. She won't see me. I've emailed her, but she didn't even respond. The only time she let me see Louise was when we did the parenting assessment last week. It's not up to me any more.

We'll just have to see what happens when we go to court in a few weeks.'

He shook his head, slowly.

Her cheeks burned. 'What?'

He said nothing. Rosemary walked back towards them with a smile fixed on her face. 'They don't need me out there.'

Nadia nodded. 'Let's go in and sit down.'

Eddie was cutting a round of brie in half as they returned to the kitchen. He put it on a plate, then gestured to them to sit at the table.

Rosemary, Martin and Nadia sat with straight backs. Nadia took a deep breath. 'Eddie, Dad was just asking me about Zoe and Louise. I was just about to tell him what our lawyer said.' Eddie's hand, holding the plate of cheese, hovered for a moment, then he put it down gently and went to the pantry for a box of crackers.

'What's that?' Rosemary said with raised eyebrows.

Nadia sipped her wine. 'Well, when I told the lawyer that Lachlan has moved back in, he said that was a very interesting development. Those were the words he used, weren't they, Eddie?'

Eddie sat down. 'Yes.'

Nadia continued, trying to keep her voice steady. 'Well, he said that with Lachlan's history of violence, mental illness, and now the fact that Zoe has allowed him back into the house, that could be the exceptional circumstance that we need to make sure Louise is safe.'

'Of course she's safe,' Rosemary said, putting down her glass, her face red. 'I told you about Lachlan's diagnosis because I wanted you to understand what's been happening to him, why he did what he did, not so you could use it against him.'

'But it doesn't matter why, does it?' Nadia insisted. 'It's even more worrying to me that he has a mental illness, it means he might not be able to control himself. The fact is that there has been domestic violence in that house, and Zoe has made a decision to return to it.'

'I don't know that it's that simple, darling,' Martin said.

'Dad, maybe she did the right thing when she left him. She shouldn't have disappeared like that, but at least she was trying to protect Louise. But now, she's just showing such bad judgement. I'm not the one making the decision here, it's up to the judge; the courts are impartial and they'll decide what's best for Louise.'

Eddie put his hand on Nadia's shoulder. 'Nadia's just worried that nothing has changed and that Louise is back in the same position she was before. We all saw Zoe that night, how distraught she was.'

'This is not about that night.' Rosemary looked into the corner of the room, blinking furiously.

'What do you mean?' Nadia forced herself to smile. 'Of course this is about that night.'

'Nadia, I don't want this to come between us all, but Zoe told me that you were already trying to find a way to get Louise back even before that happened. I don't understand you. You have everything.' Rosemary swept her hand around the room. 'You have three kids out there, beautiful children, and Zoe has nothing except Louise.'

'And Lachlan,' Eddie said.

Nadia looked at him, trying to thank him with her eyes.

Rosemary glared at him, then at Nadia. 'It seems to me that you were always planning this. When Zoe disappeared you said she was irresponsible and erratic. When she left Lachlan you said she wasn't capable of being a single mother because she has an illness – a stable illness, mind you – or because Louise would have to go into daycare. That wasn't good enough for you, although it's good enough for thousands of other kids in this country! And now that she's trying to get her marriage with Louise's *father* back together you're moving the goalposts again! What would you be happy with? He's stopped drinking, he's in treatment – he's on medication, he sees a counsellor. I've seen him with Louise, he's a great father—'

Nadia snorted. 'I don't think so.'

Rosemary ignored her. 'And Zoe is a wonderful mother. She's all Louise has ever known, and to rip them apart would be awful for everyone, never mind that poor little child at the centre of this. You're trying to take her from her mother! Who is this about, Nadia? We raised you better than this. This is not about the best interests of Louise at all, it's about the best interests of you!'

'Rosemary...' Martin took his wife's hand.

She pulled away, then stood up quickly. 'Excuse me. I'm just going to the bathroom.'

Nadia nodded, not trusting herself to speak. How could she explain it to them? She could see how this must look to people on the outside. But her stepmother was wrong: Nadia didn't have three children, she had four. And one thing she'd learned from the sessions with the other relinquishing mothers was that you can't replace the child you've lost, given up. Just because you have other children doesn't mean there isn't a huge chasm where the one you gave up should be. Louise was made up of half of *her*; to know that she had given her to someone else was heartbreaking. How could she express that?

'Rosemary's worried about Zoe,' Martin said softly. 'And you too.'

Nadia looked down. 'I'm not a monster, Dad. I'm worried about Zoe too. I'm sorry, I just...' She wiped away a tear as Eddie put his arm around her shoulders. 'I just can't explain how I feel, other than to say that I don't have a choice.'

Martin nodded, sighed, and they all sat in silence for a few moments. They heard Rosemary coming back down the hallway. When she came in, her face was red, her mascara a little smudged. She sat down at the table; as she reached for her drink, Nadia put her hand over her stepmother's. Rosemary froze, then sighed, but didn't move her hand.

For the next hour, they all made small talk while they picked at the food and finished their drinks, then Martin and Rosemary left, saying they had things to do. When they had gone, Nadia had a blinding headache. She asked Eddie to order some pizza for the children, then, leaving them to it, she ran herself a scalding hot bath.

Chapter Twenty-Seven

Lou's parents hadn't said a word to her since they had arrived home. Her dad's jaw had been clenched as the doctors at the hospital explained that she'd been flown off Rottnest by the emergency helicopter with alcohol poisoning after being found half-naked in the bush. Her mum had just stared at her as if she didn't even know her. When they got home, her dad had looked at her with shame burning off him. Lou had said she was sorry, over and over, told them that she couldn't feel any worse, but he'd shaken his head, tears in his eyes, and walked away. Lou's throat felt raw from where the emergency staff had intubated her to make sure she could breathe, her muscles ached and she still felt nauseous.

Lou had lain on her bed for what felt like hours, wishing her mum would come and knock softly on her door, maybe bring her some sweet tea and hot buttery toast as she used to when Lou was sick, but no one came. Eventually, she had stopped crying, her eyes stinging, her head thumping. Now, she realised she was hungry. She lay curled on her side under the blankets, until she heard the TV in the living room go off. After a few more minutes, she slowly opened the door of her room and stepped into the hallway, hoping her parents would now be in bed so she could get some food. But no: they were talking quietly in the kitchen. She heard the grating noise of someone unscrewing the biscuit jar and the bubbling of the kettle; she crept forward, hoping the floorboards wouldn't creak, and strained to hear their conversation, which had a well-worn air of words often repeated.

'I thought she was getting better, and now this happens!' said her mum. 'What have we done wrong?'

'We haven't done anything wrong, we've done our best. It's not our fault, love.'

'We should have told her! Maybe if we'd told her from the start… Ross said, you know, that kids pick up when something's not right. The research says it's better to tell them early, but—'

'There's no point thinking like that now, though. We didn't. We did what we thought was right.'

A teaspoon clinked against a cup. 'We did what was right for *us*, not for Louise. Were we really thinking of her? I wasn't! I was thinking of myself, delaying the day when she'd look at me and know the truth! Jesus, how can we tell her now? I can't help but think sometimes that we should never have done this, any of it! We've been thinking of ourselves from the very beginning—'

'Don't be stupid. Then we wouldn't have Louise.'

'But what have we done to her? She's a mess.' Her mum's sobs were muffled; Lou imagined her dad holding her to his chest.

'Stop it, love, it'll be OK. It's not the end of the world. She's not the first kid to get drunk.'

'Drunk?' Her mum's voice was loud again. 'This wasn't just being drunk! She was airlifted by an emergency helicopter and ended up in intensive care—'

'It was just a precaution.'

'I don't care! No one else's daughter was on the bloody news as an example of what's so terrible about teenagers! No one else's child ended up gravely ill in hospital – she could have been raped, for all we know! Or choked on her own vomit, died from hypothermia. Don't you see?' Her mum paused for breath, then spoke more quietly. 'There's something wrong with her, with us, with our family… I thought she was getting better, I don't know what else I can do!'

'We'll tell her, then.'

'But what if she rejects us – me? I don't want to lose her.'

'We won't, darling.'

'But she's so fragile, I don't know if she can cope with it.'

'You heard what Ross said, it might help, in the long run.'

'I know…'

Lou's heart was racing, the familiar buzz of fear in her ears. She didn't want to hear any more. She went back into her room and closed the door. She wanted to scream, to kick the door and punch the walls and bang her head on the floor and gouge at her eyes. What the hell was going on? She'd had enough of everyone: her parents for all the lying and hypocrisy; Theo for not looking after her; her so-called friends, who hadn't bothered to interrupt their holiday to make sure she was OK. Her parents had just confirmed exactly what she'd always thought: that she was a big disappointment to them, a mess. Lou felt the pressure building inside her, but knew she had to hold it together. If she fell to pieces, her parents would drag her back to hospital and have her locked up.

But she couldn't go on like this. They were keeping something from her. She had always known that there was something wrong with her family; it was a feeling that she'd been pushing away for as long as she could remember. Now, she needed to find the answer.

–

Lou didn't have to wait long for her opportunity. The following weekend, on Saturday, her parents were getting ready to take her grandparents out for lunch. Lou had been surprised that it had only taken a day or two for her parents to thaw and start talking to her again. She suspected they'd called Ross for advice, or were feeling guilty for hiding this secret from her. The secret that she needed to uncover.

'You sure you don't want to come, Lou?' Her dad put a coffee capsule in the machine, then reached up into a cupboard to hunt for his travel mug. 'We'll go up to the Boat Harbour, have lunch on the water there.'

Lou finished her mouthful of cereal and dropped her spoon into the bowl. 'No thanks.'

He put his travel mug under the spout and switched on the machine. 'It'll be fun…' He smiled, raising his eyebrows.

Lou laughed. 'You wish you could stay here too?'

He sighed. 'Oh yes. But then your mother would kill me.'

'I'm going to sort out all my school things, see what I can throw out now I've finished.'

'Ah, so you'd rather tidy than come for a lovely lunch with your family. That says a lot.' He winked.

Her mum came into the kitchen. 'All right, time to go.' She walked over to Lou and kissed the top of her head. 'You're sure you'll be OK?'

'Yes, Mum!'

Lou saw the hesitation in her mother's eyes, the battle between trusting her and the fear that she shouldn't, before she smiled and nodded. 'OK. We won't be more than a couple of hours.'

Her dad took the car keys from the table. 'Let's go.'

'Have fun!' Lou waggled her fingers. Her dad rolled his eyes, and then they left.

Lou listened to the car drive off. She waited another five minutes to make sure they weren't going to come back for something they'd forgotten, then she went to the front door and put on the chain. If they came back to find it locked, she'd say that she'd heard a noise outside and been frightened. She took a deep breath. Did she really want to go looking? Part of her didn't: what if she found something terrible? Then she could never go back. But it was already too late; there had always been a secret floating in the whispers around her. It was already between them all, and inside her, and she needed to know the truth. It was something to do with that photograph of her as a baby with her aunt.

Lou hesitated at the door to her parents' room, then gently pushed it open. The bed was unmade, and her mother's clothes were strewn across the rumpled blankets. Two pairs of her mum's shoes were discarded on the floor; Lou stepped around them, careful not to move anything. She picked up the novel on her mum's bedside table and flicked through it, but there was no photo tucked inside, just dog-eared pages. She kneeled down and looked under the bed; there was a single thong of her father's, and a couple of socks, but nothing else. She stood up again, then walked to the built-in wardrobe and slid open the mirrored doors. The rails were stuffed with her dad's business shirts and her mum's dresses. There was a set of shelves at one end of the wardrobe. The lower shelves were filled with shoes and bags; the upper shelves were where her parents used to hide the birthday and Christmas presents. Lou peered up at the top shelf. She could see the brim of a straw hat, and the shimmering grey of a silk scarf. She stretched up and felt around the edge of the shelf with her hand. There, under the soft fabric, she felt something angular.

Her heart began to race. She dropped her arm and stood for a moment, clenching and unclenching her fists. It could be anything, she told herself, another shoebox. She walked over to the armchair in the corner of the room, noted its position exactly, then dragged it across to the wardrobe. She stepped up onto it, holding her hands out for balance as her feet sank into the soft seat cushion. Looking at the shelf, she could now see that the scarf was draped over the edge of something slightly larger than a shoebox. She slid the scarf aside. On the shelf was a box covered in turquoise fabric, its corners a little frayed and grubby. She'd never seen it before. On one end of the box was a small silver frame with a cardboard label. The black writing had faded, but it was still easily legible: *Louise*. She lifted the box out and sat down on the chair; then, before she could change her mind, she opened the lid.

The photograph was on top, of her aunt holding the baby. It was possible that it was Harry, Charlotte or Violet, and not herself at all; Lou had noted how similar the four of them looked in their baby photos. But she was certain that her first instinct was right and the baby was her. Anyway, the box had her name on it.

There were more pictures: one of Lou with her aunt and mum together, photos from a Christmas at her grandparents' place when she was a tiny baby – probably her first Christmas. Nothing unusual. She picked up some dark strips of photographic paper with white pixelated images: ultrasound scans. She smiled. In some she had no idea what she was looking at, but in others she could see the outline of a face – it must be her own – in the womb. She'd never seen these before; they were amazing.

She put the scans down on the floor and kept looking through the box. Below the photos was a clear A4 plastic sleeve stuffed with papers. Lou slipped her hand inside and drew out the bundle. There was a birth certificate, folded into thirds. She'd seen her birth certificate plenty of times, she was sure of it. She had needed it when she applied for a passport for a school trip to New Zealand. She unfolded it anyway, then held her breath as she realised there were two, folded together. With trembling hands, she held the documents side by side. Both had her name on them. On one, in the spaces for the parents' names, was written 'Nadia Jane Boyd' and 'Edward George Boyd'. On the other, the names were 'Zoe Mary McAllister' and 'Lachlan William McAllister'.

Lou stared in disbelief. How could she have two different birth certificates? And what were her aunt and uncle's names doing on them? Lou rummaged frantically through the papers, no longer caring about keeping them in order as the whole messy truth was finally displayed before her. One letter from the plastic sleeve was headed

'The Family Court of Western Australia'. Lou held it in both hands to try to keep it still as she read; then she let it fall.

She finally understood.

Chapter Twenty-Eight

It seemed wrong to Zoe that Louise's future was about to be decided and yet she wasn't here; she was with a babysitter. Everyone else was here at the family court. When they'd been here for the parentage order, less than a year ago, the whole family had chatted and joked outside before they went in. But not today.

Zoe was sitting at the table on the right of the court-room, in between Lachlan and their lawyer, Ravi. They had first been to see Ravi to draw up the surrogacy contracts; back then, everything had seemed so straight-forward. When Nadia had instigated proceedings to take back Louise, Ravi had told Zoe and Lachlan that he had never heard of such a case in Perth before, and had certainly never dealt with one, but that he – and the court – would treat it like any other custody case, that the issues were the same. This morning when he'd reassured them outside the court he'd seemed confident, but now he shuffled his papers and fidgeted. Zoe said nothing, unsure if the microphones on the table in front of them were turned on or recording.

Nadia and Eddie's lawyer was an older man, stocky, with receding grey hair. He sat in the nearest seat at a table on the other side of the court, a mirror image of their own. Zoe's view was partially blocked, but she could see that

Nadia was next to him, and Eddie was at the end. Zoe felt strangely calm now that the day had arrived. There was nothing else she could do, and a sense of inevitability had taken over. It was surreal; she had never imagined that she and Nadia would be fighting over anything in a court, never mind a baby. She thought of her parents sitting behind them in the public gallery watching the two of them – children they had brought up together as sisters – tear the family apart. She didn't want to turn around and see which side of the room they were sitting on. The middle, probably.

How would things be after today? Zoe had spent nights thinking about what would happen if Nadia won and took Louise home with her. She had sat on the floor of Louise's room, watching her sleep, listening to her little breaths puff in and out of her open mouth, knowing that if Nadia won, she would have to forgive her, for Louise's sake. It was no different to a custody dispute in a divorce. There was always acrimony between separating spouses, but eventually they worked things out and a new order was found. That was the story Zoe liked to tell herself anyway, that she would be mature and responsible; but recalling the terror that had periodically gripped her over the last few weeks, she wasn't sure she would survive if she had to hand Louise over. She thought about how she had acted these past few weeks, refusing to let Nadia see Louise at all. Had she done the wrong thing? She did it for the right reasons, she knew – it would be too confusing for Louise to have two women trying to be her mother. But did it *look* wrong? Would it count against her?

A hush came over the room as the judge swept in, an older woman wearing black robes, red-framed glasses and a short wig. There was a scuffle of feet as everyone stood. Zoe took a deep breath, put her hands on the table in front of her and pushed herself up. The judge nodded slightly, then took her seat and looked out over the room as everyone else sat down too. Zoe's heart pounded and she placed her hands flat on the table. Lachlan put his hand on her knee, and she could tell by the way he gripped it that he too was hanging on for dear life. Louise was waiting for them to come and take her home. What if they couldn't? What if Zoe could never call herself Louise's mum again? She felt sick. She wanted to stand up and run over to Nadia, get down on her knees and beg her, *Please, please, don't do this to me, to Louise*. That was the one thing that she hadn't tried, and now she wished she had. Though she doubted that it would change anything. She thought, not for the first time, that maybe she should have just accepted that she couldn't have children, that there was a reason for it. Perhaps this was her punishment for trying to interfere with the natural order of things.

Her curse to bear.

–

Nadia turned her body slightly away from the centre of the courtroom and clasped Eddie's hands. She needed to see the judge's face as she spoke, but didn't want to catch Zoe's eyes. She couldn't believe that they were all sitting here. This morning, as she had dressed in her grey skirt suit, then kissed the children goodbye when her friend came to take them to school, she had almost picked up the phone and called the whole thing off. As the court date had approached, the little doubts that she'd been pushing away had grown stronger. It wasn't that she doubted that she wanted Louise, not at all. But Rosemary's accusations had stuck with her. Was this really the right thing for Louise, or the right thing for *her*? Nadia missed Louise terribly, but she also knew that she and Zoe were as stubborn as each other. And as Zoe had continued to refuse to let her see Louise, so Nadia in turn had hardened in her resolve. If only Zoe had been more reasonable, maybe she *would* have changed her mind this morning. She might even have gone along with the myth that Lachlan was getting better now he was in treatment, but for that, she needed to see Louise for herself, and Zoe wouldn't allow that, and wouldn't even talk to her or attend mediation. Zoe had forced her to go through with this. What other choice did Nadia have? To have absolutely no contact with her biological child? To never be allowed to go to Louise's birthday parties or spend Christmas with her? How was that fair?

Eddie was looking past her at the other table, where Zoe and Lachlan sat. She squeezed his hands slightly; he raised his eyebrows at her, then smiled. She knew he had doubts, many more than she had. She didn't blame him: Louise wasn't his baby, after all. He and Lachlan were – or had been – mates, and she knew Eddie felt bad about depriving him of the right to be a father. But what about Louise's right to be happy and safe and secure? And what about Nadia's rights, as Louise's biological mother? She thought back to the last time they'd been here in court, of the papers she'd signed then, giving up her rights as a mother. But she knew now that this was far more complicated than words on a document, an order in a court; her primal need to protect her child was far more powerful.

The judge took off her glasses and held them in one hand as she looked out over the courtroom and introduced herself and the case. She slid some papers across her bench in a long row, then put her glasses back on and began to read from them.

–

The judge had finished her introduction. Zoe had listened to her summary of their lives, the turmoil of the past four years, the assessments, the surrogacy approval, the artificial insemination, the pregnancy, the birth, and how it had all started to go wrong. Zoe knew that it had gone wrong long before the night Lachlan pushed her. The psychological assessments during the surrogacy approval process had said they were all mature, resilient, aware of the risks. But she knew how easy it would have been for Nadia to lie – to Eddie, the psychologist, and herself. After all, Zoe was guilty of that too, lying to herself about her feelings towards Lachlan, and telling him that she didn't blame him for them all sitting here today, when really she knew that a big part of her did.

The judge held up some papers. 'I have received a report from Mr McAllister's treating psychiatrist, Dr Simon Lorenzo, in which he details his diagnosis of post-traumatic stress disorder; major depressive disorder, in remission; and alcohol abuse, also in remission. He has helpfully outlined Mr McAllister's ongoing symptoms of low mood, irritability, nightmares and anxiety. One of the applicants' main concerns is Louise's safety, particularly with regard to Mr McAllister's history of domestic violence and ongoing mental health issues.' Zoe sensed Lachlan tensing, retreating into himself.

'Against this, I also have a number of character and employment references demonstrating his previously unblemished history. In addition, his psychiatrist reports that since seeking help, Mr McAllister has been compliant with all recommended treatment and Dr Lorenzo does not feel that he is a risk to either himself or others. He feels that this episode of domestic violence was likely to have been an isolated incident in response to extreme stress and intoxication.'

Zoe glanced at Lachlan; he was looking down at his hands, blinking hard. She thought back to their conversation on the beach, as they watched the water slowly rise over the statue of C.Y. O'Connor and his horse. Lachlan had kept so much hidden from her over the past year; she wondered what he had told his psychiatrist.

'However, in considering the best interests of the child, Louise, mental illness and a violent history in a parent does have to be taken into account. Furthermore, the applicants claim that Mrs McAllister is unable to provide the appropriate environment for the child. They refer to Mrs McAllister absconding with Louise and refusing to tell anyone where she was, as well as her medical illness, systemic lupus erythematosus.' The judge stumbled over the words, then looked at Zoe, an apologetic expression on her face.

'There does not seem to be any evidence that Louise was at risk when Mrs McAllister disappeared with her, and she did inform her parents that they were safe. In the context of the domestic violence, I can accept the respondent's explanation that she was frightened and trying to keep her child safe. However, I share the applicants' concern that this was a rash action that could be distressing for a child, to take her suddenly from her home environment and family. The situation became further confused when she allowed her husband – from whom she was apparently fleeing – to stay with them, and soon afterwards allowed him to return to the family home.

'Regarding her illness, I have here reports from Mrs McAllister's rheumatology specialist, Dr Ian Shelley, detailing her long medical history and treatment. He notes that her condition is currently stable, but that her illness is one that can flare up. However, he does note that her illness, while being the primary reason for her infertility and need to use a surrogate and egg donor, is not currently causing any disability that would affect her ability to parent Louise effectively.'

Zoe exhaled, then reached out and gently touched Lachlan's shoulder. He was motionless, and she knew that he was bracing himself. She willed him, through her touch, to come back to her, to the present. They had to face this together.

–

As she listened to the judge's words, Nadia couldn't work out whose side she was on. On one hand, she agreed with all Nadia's concerns, but then she seemed to override them with whatever nonsense Zoe had fed the court. And of course Zoe and Lachlan's doctors would write favourable reports: they had to support their patients. They had only heard one side of the story. Was this bias allowed?

'Turning to the reports from the family consultant…' The judge slid another document over in front of her. 'This is where the difficulty arises, because both families have a very warm and engaging manner with Louise, and either set of parents would provide a loving home for her.'

Nadia looked at Eddie, panic in her eyes. The judge was wrong: Lachlan was mentally ill, violent. He couldn't provide a loving home for Louise.

The judge went on: 'I note that despite our family consultant's best attempts to find a solution through mediation, Mrs McAllister refused to attend, saying that she did not want to find a middle ground but rather wanted full custody of Louise.'

Nadia let out a big breath: that had to count against Zoe.

'This case is particularly complex given the surrogacy arrangement, the fact that a legal parentage order is in place, and the fact that Louise has a biological parent in each of the two families seeking custody. Overall, the family court must decide what is in the best interests of Louise's welfare. That is two-fold: the opportunity for Louise to have a meaningful relationship with both biological parents, and the need to protect her from any physical or psychological harm.

'Turning to the first issue. Louise's biological mother, Mrs Boyd, and biological father, Mr McAllister, have been unable to come to an agreement about custody. The reports indicate that Louise's primary attachment is to Mrs McAllister. I do also take into account that the Boyds have three older children, who are biological half-siblings of Louise. It is in her interests to have an ongoing relationship with as many biological relations as possible.'

Nadia let herself smile just a little, though she couldn't take her eyes off the judge.

'Now to the second issue: this need to protect her from harm has been the trigger for the Boyd family to seek the overturning of the parentage order and the return of Louise to their legal custody. The issue of abuse is pertinent, as exposing a child to domestic violence is something that the family court takes extremely seriously. I do also have concerns about Mrs McAllister's refusal to allow Louise to see the Boyds, though I take the view that Louise is *not* at significant risk of abuse or neglect in her current living situation.

'In taking all these factors into account, I have thought long and hard about how to proceed. Louise's life has been complex to date, but it appears that the McAllisters are reaching stability now. Mr McAllister is no longer drinking, is on medication and is undergoing therapy, and otherwise has been of exemplary character, and I don't believe that it would be in the best interests of Louise to upset her life further by discharging the parentage order and taking her away from either her father or the woman she sees as her mother.'

Nadia opened her mouth as if to protest, but said nothing. She didn't look over to the other table, although she could sense the jubilation. She grasped Eddie's hand.

'However,' the judge continued, 'I do feel that Louise should be able to maintain a meaningful relationship with her biological mother and her biological half-siblings. Where reasonably practicable, Louise should spend every second weekend and half of her holiday periods with the Boyds. Also, the McAllisters and the Boyds have equal, shared parental responsibility for significant long-term decisions relating to Louise's life. There must be a genuine effort on both sides to reach a consensus on areas of dispute.'

Nadia felt Eddie's grip on her hand tighten, but wasn't sure if it was a gesture of support or of warning. This must be what it feels like for divorced fathers, she thought, to be told they were an equal parent and yet only to be allowed to see their children every couple of weeks, until they slipped further and further out of their childen's lives. Every second weekend, what kind of relationship was that? She wanted Louise to be part of her family. Her eyes began to sting. She'd made everything worse. Before all this, she could see Louise as much as she wanted – at least a few times a week. Louise knew her, smiled and held out her arms to her. Now, Zoe would probably only let her see Louise on the days written in the court orders, no more. Her relationship with Louise would be framed by strict boundaries, instead of spontaneous moments. She turned towards Eddie and leaned into him.

He held her and murmured in her ear, 'Nadia, this is good. We still get to see her. We're still a part of her life.'

Nadia shook her head in his embrace. It wasn't good at all.

–

Zoe almost collapsed with relief when the judge said that Louise would remain with her and Lachlan, even if it meant that Nadia and Eddie had access visits. She grabbed Lachlan's hand, then looked over her shoulder for her mum. Rosemary grinned and gave her the thumbs-up. Zoe turned towards Lachlan; he looked back at her, his eyes damp. She smiled, trying to tell him that everything was OK now.

Then she looked over at the other table, where her sister was embracing Eddie. She tried to imagine how Nadia was feeling. Zoe had thought that she wouldn't care how Nadia was, that she never wanted to see her again, but as she considered the judge's words, she accepted that this was the best thing for Louise. In some ways, it was what Zoe had imagined it would be like from the beginning: being Louise's mum but sharing the delight of watching Louise grow into a young woman with Nadia, who had done such an amazing and selfless thing. It was a pity that they'd had to go to court to enforce that.

Over the past few weeks, Zoe hadn't been able to bear the thought of Nadia having any time alone with Louise. Now, though, she felt secure that Louise would always see Zoe as her mum, and would always come home to her and Lachlan. She thought about what Louise would be doing now, at home. She'd be getting hungry for her lunch, missing her mum and dad. Zoe looked back at the judge and smiled at her; the judge smiled back.

They all stood up as the judge left the court, and then the room filled with noise: laughter, crying, chatter. Lachlan's and Eddie's parents were there too, shaking hands and patting each other on the back.

As the judge left the court, Zoe put her arms around Lachlan's neck and they held each other. 'I can't believe it, Lach. I can't believe it!' She could feel his body shaking, but hers was too. She pulled back and looked at him. 'It's all going to be OK, babe!'

He nodded, then wiped away his own tears and grinned. 'Thank God.'

Rosemary and Martin appeared beside them and hugged them both. 'I'm so glad it's over,' Rosemary said.

Martin nodded. 'We all are.' He smiled at Zoe, then at Lachlan, then glanced to his left. 'Excuse me, I'll be back in a minute.'

'I'll come with you,' Rosemary said, and Zoe watched as they walked over to Nadia and Eddie.

'What should we do?' Zoe said quietly. 'Should we go over too?'

Lachlan sighed. 'Yes, we should.' He took her hand. 'Come on.'

She didn't move. 'What will I say, though? Maybe it's not the right time, it'll be too hard for her.'

He shook his head and started to lead her gently towards her sister. 'Come on. We're going to have to do it sometime. Let's get it over with, for Louise's sake.'

Zoe took a deep breath and nodded. Her elation was gone now, replaced with the same feeling she'd had when she first took Louise from Nadia's arms in the hospital: guilt.

–

Nadia hugged her dad tightly and sobbed as he stroked her hair. 'I'm sorry, darling,' he whispered. 'But Louise is so lucky that you both love her so much.'

'But it's not enough, Dad!' Nadia knew she was being selfish, pathetic, but she couldn't help it, and right now she didn't care.

Rosemary put her arm around Nadia's shoulders. 'We'll make it work, Nadia, as a family. We're all in this together, we all love Louise.'

'You heard what the judge said,' Martin added. 'Louise can stay weekends with you and the kids, and the holidays, and you'll still see her at all the usual family times!'

'Zoe won't let me, Dad.' Nadia looked up at him through her tears.

'Yes, I will.'

Nadia froze and then turned to look at Zoe, who was standing just behind her, holding Lachlan's hand. Had she come to gloat?

'Nadia, I know how you feel, I'm sorry you—'

Nadia narrowed her eyes. 'You don't know how I feel at all.'

Zoe shook her head. 'You're wrong. I know you don't believe this, but I feel the same way about Louise as you do.'

'You don't know what it's like to carry a child, give birth to her, and then hand her over!'

Zoe bit her lip, then glanced at Lachlan before talking softly to Nadia. 'You're right, I don't. I never will. But I can't keep living my life with this terror that you're going to snatch her away from me, this feeling that I'm indebted to you and that I'm on borrowed time with Louise. I've been with her since the day – the moment – she was born, I *am* her mother.' She began to cry. 'I've missed you, Nadia, and Louise has too. This is going to be hard for everyone, but we'll work it all out.'

'It's easy for you to say that, because she's with you!'

'She's always been with us,' Lachlan said, stepping forward. 'We're all she knows.'

Nadia glared at Lachlan. 'Just because you're all she knows doesn't mean it's right.'

'Nadia,' Martin said. 'Come on, now isn't the time. It's done, finished. This is about Louise. She needs all of us.'

Nadia let out a sob and covered her face with her hands. She felt someone touch her shoulder; when she managed to catch her breath again she opened her eyes. It was Zoe, crying too. Nadia knew her father was right, that this was about the child that they all so desperately loved and wanted, but that didn't stop her from feeling as if a part of her body had been wrenched out from inside her. But she didn't pull away from Zoe, just let her hand rest on her shoulder for a moment, until Zoe gently removed it and took a step back. She stood beside Lachlan as he held his hand out towards Eddie. The men shook hands, silent, and then Zoe and Lachlan walked away with their arms around each other.

–

Later that afternoon, Nadia was lying on her bed, staring at the ceiling, when the doorbell rang. She thought about pretending she wasn't home, but Eddie's footsteps were already clomping along the hallway. She sat up, trying to compose herself. She heard voices murmuring; a moment later her dad appeared in the doorway of the bedroom.

'You OK?' he said quietly.

She shrugged. 'I just want to forget about this morning.'

Eddie put his head in the door. 'I'm going to take the kids down to the river for a play, OK?'

Martin turned and clasped his shoulder. 'Thanks, Eddie. Nadia, I'll help get them ready, then I'll wait out the back for you.'

Nadia nodded. She listened to the thumps and squeals as the kids got their shoes on, then the front door closed. After this morning, all she wanted to do was hide away, but she knew her dad meant well, so she forced herself to get up off the bed and walk outside.

The garden felt strangely quiet to Nadia, as though all the noises were coming from very far away. The birds chattered, whistled and cooed; a bus hissed by on the road; a lawnmower droned, sounding as natural as the pitter-patter of the gum leaves landing on the tin roof and the bees humming around the daisy bush. But none of these sounds was able to impinge on her sense of detachment.

Martin stood facing the back fence, twisting the grapevine tendrils through the gaps in the wood. As Nadia approached, he turned, then smiled at her sadly.

She looked at the ground. 'Do you want something to drink?'

He gestured to the bench. 'No. Let's sit down.'

They sat on opposite ends of the garden bench, looking at the sagging net of the trampoline. 'What is it, Dad?' she asked.

'How are you, really?'

She put out an entreating hand. 'Not now. Please.'

'Don't keep it all inside, Nadia. I've seen what this has been doing to you, your marriage, to your kids.'

'The kids are fine.'

'You're lucky. They're good kids,' he said.

Nadia rubbed her face. 'I know, OK! I know I have three great children, I'm sick of everyone telling me that! You want to know how I am? Sometimes I wish I had never agreed to do this, any of it. I wish I had just left things the way they were.'

'You don't mean that.'

'I do. I was happy. I'm not now.'

He put his hand on her arm. 'But think about Louise. She's perfect. If you hadn't been a surrogate, she wouldn't exist.'

'But then everyone would be happy.'

'Not Zoe. You know, Nadia, sometimes we have to sacrifice ourselves, our own needs, for our children.' Martin leaned back and looked up at the sky.

'Like my mum?' Nadia whispered, glancing at him. The few times over the years she had tried to talk to her dad about Hilary, he had looked away, his eyes haunted as they were now, and changed the subject. And so she had stopped asking.

When he spoke again, the grief caught in his throat and made his voice rasp. 'I should have talked to you about this a long time ago.'

'It's all in the past, it doesn't matter.' She knew it did, though.

'It does. All this, you know, with Louise, it's made me realise how much it *does* matter.'

Nadia waited for him to go on, frightened that if she said anything, he'd stop.

Martin spoke quietly. 'Your mum, you were all she thought about. Even before you were born, she put you above everyone: me, herself… By the time I found out, it was just too late, the cancer was too advanced. More treatment wasn't going to make any difference to her.'

Nadia couldn't help herself. 'I just wish I hadn't had to grow up without a mum.'

Martin put his hands flat on his knees. Nadia saw the tremor in his splayed fingers. 'No one can ever replace her, I know that, but I always tried, and Rosemary did her best…'

'I know that, Dad.'

His voice had softened now. 'I never wanted to tell you this, but I think it's important for you to know. Your mother knew she had cancer. She didn't tell anyone, not even me. She left it too late, too bloody late, until there was nothing they could do.'

'What?' Nadia felt sick.

'I remember the day she told me. You were a few weeks old, three weeks maybe. You were screaming, she was trying to breastfeed you, but you wouldn't feed from one side and the other side was empty. She just started sobbing, begging you to drink her milk. I took you from her, but she wouldn't stop crying. She took my hand and put it on her chest, and told me to feel.' He closed his eyes. 'I didn't know what she was talking about, and then she put her hand on top of mine and pressed my fingers onto it. A lump. It was big, craggy, hard, and then she lifted her shirt and I saw that the skin above it was puckered and dimpled. She said nothing, just looked at me, but we both knew what it meant. I tried to reassure us both, said that it was probably just the breastfeeding, an infection or something…'

Martin cleared his throat and paused. Nadia waited.

He went on, his voice almost a whisper. 'When she had fallen pregnant, she had been sore, you know, in her breasts, and one day in the shower, she had felt the lump, like a piece of gravel under her skin. She ignored it, but it got bigger. Her mum – your grandma – had died from breast cancer. Your mum wasn't stupid. She knew.'

Nadia could barely breathe for the dread building in her. *Stop, Dad*, she wanted to say. *Don't tell me.*

'She didn't tell anyone. She thought that if she did, she'd have to choose between the pregnancy – you – and her own life. She thought she'd have you first, and then get treatment. From the moment she knew she was pregnant, you were real to her, and she would do anything to make sure that you… that you were born, no matter what it meant for her.'

Nadia visualised the photograph of her mother holding her as an infant. The smile on her face, the joy, the relief. How she wished she could remember her touch, her voice. She took a deep breath. 'Dad…'

He held up his hand. 'Let me finish. I drove her to the emergency department that day. By now, we were both frantic. She'd held onto this fear for the best part of a year all by herself, locked it away in a little compartment inside herself and wouldn't let it out until you were safe. All I could think about as we waited for the surgeon to arrive, and when they told us that they needed to start the tests that day, was how scared she must have been the whole time. She should have told me. I was so angry that she hadn't told me, hadn't let me share her fear or do something about it.'

Nadia's whole body shook as she thought about her father as a young man, himself a new dad, how he must have felt that day. What would he have done if he'd known about the cancer earlier? Would he have forced Hilary to seek help, to save herself over their unborn child? What was more important? A wife, a marriage, or the potential of another, different love, of a child in whom you will live on?

Martin pursed his lips and exhaled. 'Anyway. We tried then. But it was too late. She had the lot: surgery, radiotherapy, chemotherapy. She was so bloody sick from the treatment that she couldn't even hold you. So she decided enough was enough. The doctors were honest – they said the treatment might give her a bit more time, but no cure.

She decided that spending every second she could with you, laughing and happy, was better than having a few more months but not being able to enjoy them.'

Nadia shook her head. 'Oh, Dad. I don't know what to say. I… I didn't know. I'm sorry…'

Martin turned towards her and clutched her hands. 'No, no, don't ever say sorry. Don't ever apologise. You were just a baby, tiny, you didn't have any say in this. I was furious with her when she died, for leaving me alone, but I know now that she knew I wouldn't be alone. She made her decision, and as much as I wish she was here, I know that in you, she is. Every day. All I want is for you to be happy, to enjoy every moment of being a mother. Don't tear yourself apart. I can't tell you what to do about Louise, but just think about what you want for her and *all* your kids. I know you love her; Zoe does too. We all do. Just don't waste a moment with them, moments that your mother would have given anything for. It doesn't matter how Louise got here. She's been loved from the instant she was even thought about, as were you.'

Nadia nodded, then leaned into him. She was full of pity for her father, and shame for the way she had acted. He was right, she needed to cherish everything that she did have. And she had a lot. They were both silent, thinking of the woman who was gone, and yet was everywhere around them.

Chapter Twenty-Nine

Zoe and Lachlan drove east on the highway out of Fremantle, passing the massive road trains rolling down the hills towards Perth, their containers caked with blood-red dust from the desert. Zoe gripped the door handle as the car shook with the roar of a truck that passed too close to them. She swallowed, glanced at Lachlan, then looked forward again. They turned off the highway and soon they were climbing up into the hills, along a winding road surrounded by thick bush. A flock of black Carnaby's cockatoos flew over them, screeching.

As soon as the court case had ended last month, Nadia and Eddie had packed up and moved back to the hills. Their tenants had moved out and their house was lying empty, so they'd given up their rental in Perth straight away. Zoe had been relieved in a way that there would be some distance between Louise and Nadia, but sad, too, for her sister, that she was retreating back to the country.

'I wonder why they wanted to meet us at the weir,' Zoe said. 'Do you believe that she really wants us to all have an amicable picnic together?'

Lachlan shrugged. 'They can't even have unpacked yet; maybe Nadia's embarrassed about the state of the house. Or maybe she's honestly trying to make amends, patch things up again between us all. In a way I'm looking forward to it. It'll be nice for us to see the girls and Harry again too, I've missed them.'

'Yeah, me too, they're growing so quickly. Although it can't be good for her kids, all this moving around. I wonder if she'll move them back to their old school?'

'Who knows?' Lachlan said.

Zoe leaned back in her seat, looking out of the window. 'I was always envious of Nadia living up here. It's so… peaceful. Imagine if we lived somewhere like this, Lach, with Louise. Far away from everyone, just us…'

'In the height of summer?' He looked over at her and smiled.

Zoe frowned, looking at the thick bushland all around them. 'Bushfires?'

He nodded, slowing down to turn a tight corner. Zoe imagined the crackling and snapping of the dry branches as the fire took hold, the oils from the gum trees hissing and spitting as they started to smoke and then explode. She shuddered. 'Do you think Louise will have missed us?'

Lachlan reached over and put his hand on her knee. 'Of course! Zoe, you've got to stop thinking of Nadia as a threat; there's nothing else she can do to us now. We'll get used to it. It's just like Louise is going for a sleepover with her cousins, that's all.'

She sighed, and turned around to look at the empty baby seat. 'I know.'

They drove for another ten minutes, largely in silence. Zoe looked down at the green fields in the valley below where a few horses grazed, and then she saw the glint of the lake through the trees ahead. Minutes later, they pulled into the car park. They were at the top of the weir, and she gazed down at the water, twenty metres below. The air was still, quiet except for the chirps of cicadas and the occasional call of a duck. There was one other car there, a four-wheel drive with empty bicycle racks on the back. Nadia's car wasn't here yet; she was probably savouring every minute she could before she had to hand Louise back. Zoe couldn't help but feel nervous.

'The picnic area's on the other side,' Zoe said.

Lachlan nodded, and they got out of the car and locked it. They walked in silence up the short flight of steps to a paved lookout. Zoe leaned on the fence and looked down. The water barely moved, except for the odd ruffle when a whisper of a breeze skimmed over the surface and blurred the sharp reflection of the clouds above.

Zoe felt a flutter of anxiety as she slowly followed Lachlan onto the narrow path that formed the top of the concrete dam wall. She looked down on either side of her. The dam level below them was low, with puffs of algae in the milky green water. Zoe staggered, feeling her head swim with vertigo.

She made herself look straight ahead, to the other side of the dam, where blackened wooden railway sleepers twisted their way up the steep grassy slope, the only remnant of the days when people would catch the steam train here from the city to swim on hot summer days. You couldn't swim here any more; it was drinking water, at the start of its journey through the Golden Pipeline, across the desert to the goldfields.

'Lachlan, wait for me!' she shouted, noticing how far ahead he was. Her voice echoed in the still air, and she recalled the childhood stories of the spirits trapped in the shells, chanting. There was something here, a memory in the air, a voice trapped in the valley, echoing between the cliffs. She walked faster, but not so fast that she risked stumbling, catapulting over the wire fence, her limbs flailing, looking up at the clouds and down at the clouds with no sense of whether she was falling or flying.

–

As expected, there was no sign of Nadia, Eddie or the kids at the picnic area either. Zoe paced around the paving stones below the formal lawns and old rose gardens.

Lachlan took her hand and squeezed it. 'We're early, Zoe, don't worry.'

'I'm not.' But she was. *What if she doesn't show up?* she thought. *What if she's taken her?*

Zoe looked back across the weir, but she couldn't see the road clearly. She put her bag down at the bottom of the steps and sat down below the handsome bust of C.Y. O'Connor looking out over the lake. Lachlan sat next to her. She knew they were both thinking of the last time they'd seen a statue of this man, that day on the beach when they had watched the dark figure slowly submerging as the tide came in, waves lapping over the body of his horse, moving up towards his face. This was where it had begun, O'Connor's dream; the beach was where it had ended. They sang, Lachlan had said that day on the beach. The Noongars had sung to make him crazy, to curse him for destroying their sacred waters, the estuary that fed them, when he built Fremantle harbour. She had dismissed it then as just a legend. But here, she could almost believe it.

'You OK?' she asked, seeing the haunted look in Lachlan's eyes.

Lachlan nodded, gazing out. 'It's so sad that he spent his life working on such an amazing thing but he never saw it, you know? He never saw that first drop of water drip into the pipe and trickle all the way, through the scorching desert, to pour out into the driest place you can imagine, frontier country. He never lived to see that what he did made such a difference to everyone who lived there, to the entire country. We couldn't have mined without it, and that's the money that built this entire state. All he knew was blame, anger.'

Zoe took Lachlan's hand and stroked it. 'No one ever knows the effect on the future of the things we do now; we just have to do what we think is right at the time. And that doesn't get forgotten. And it's no different to what happens now: people protest about mining in the Kimberley, farmers complain about gas being drilled on their land. There's always opposition to change.'

'But the anger wasn't directed at a company, or at a government, it was all thrown at him. They singled him out.' Lachlan's voice broke and he looked at her, his eyes damp. 'He was trying; he was just doing his job, he did everything he could, and still it wasn't good enough.'

Zoe saw the tear trickle down his face and knew that, like that first drop of rainwater that had entered the pipeline, it had to roll through the dust, colour to ochre as it washed clean the memories from the desert. She reached up and wiped his cheek gently.

'You *are* good enough, Lachlan.'

-

Nadia stood on the path atop the dam wall, Louise in her arms, and looked down at the lake. The kids had run on ahead, with Eddie hurrying along behind them carrying the esky for the picnic. She wanted everything to slow down. It had been wonderful having Louise stay with them overnight, with the other kids. It really felt as though she was part of their family, back in the house where the kids had grown up. But Louise had been unsettled all night, waking, crying, fussing to be held. Then this morning, when Nadia had explained again to the children that Zoe and Lachlan were meeting them to take Louise back to their house, *they* had cried. Nadia longed for one more minute with Louise; their time together was so short that it seemed as if all she could do was count it down until the moment when she had to hand her over again. And thinking about that felt as bad at it had on the day when Louise was born.

'Eddie!' she shouted. 'Wait!' Her cry echoed around her and she gripped Louise a little tighter.

He stopped and looked back. 'What?'

She beckoned to him. He dropped the esky then walked back towards her. 'What is it?' He turned around and shouted, 'Kids, be careful!'

Nadia reached into her handbag for her camera. 'Can you take a picture, of Louise and me?'

'Here?'

She nodded, glancing over her shoulder at the lake behind her, then handed the camera to him before Louise could grab it.

Eddie took a few steps back from her then held the camera to his eye. 'OK, ready?'

Nadia glanced up at him. She didn't want to smile at the camera; instead she looked back down at her daughter, into eyes that were her own. *I see you*, she thought, *and*

I know you know I see you. She began to hum softly to Louise, as they gazed at each other. A tear dripped onto Louise's face. Nadia wiped it away quickly, then looked up at Eddie. 'Did you get it?'

'The photo? Yes.' He frowned and put his arm around her shoulders, hugging her and Louise. 'Are you OK?'

She nodded.

'You sure?'

No! she wanted to scream, loud enough that it would bounce off the walls of the canyon and be screamed here for ever more. *No, I'm not sure at all.*

But instead she nodded again, knowing that she had to let Louise go.

Chapter Thirty

By the time her parents returned from lunch at the boat harbour, Lou had stopped crying. She had examined everything in the box over and over again until she had absolutely no doubt. Everything made sense now. She had thrown herself down on her parents' bed and sobbed, pummelled her fists into the mattress, gripped her hair in her hands and pulled, but then she had stopped. She hadn't gone further, hadn't reached for something sharp, because she knew now that she hadn't been imagining things. The whispers, the loaded glances, the disconnection in her home. She – Lou – wasn't the problem. The problem had existed long before she was even born.

Lou had taken the box through to the kitchen, and arranged the documents and photos on the table in neat piles. Then she had gone to her bedroom and lay on her bed listening to music until she heard the car pull up outside. She was calm as she stood up and walked out of her room to meet her parents.

'Lou!' her mum shouted through the door as she tried to open it against the security chain. 'Lou!'

'Coming!' Lou walked slowly to the door. She still had time to gather up the contents of the box, close it and put it back in her parents' wardrobe, and keep from them a powerful secret – that she *knew*. Her parents were no longer in control. She clenched her fists again. How dare they? They had no right to lie to her about how she came into the world, about how she was passed backwards and forwards like a toy. Or, if she was to use the language she had just read, *commissioned* and *relinquished*.

She stood with her hand on the chain, the door slightly ajar. It took all her self-control not to slam it in her mother's face; instead she closed it softly, slid off the security chain, then swung it open.

'Thank God we're home,' her mum said, walking straight past her. 'I'm exhausted.' Her dad followed, and closed the door behind him. Lou walked behind them into the kitchen.

'What's— Oh!' Her mum clasped her hand over her mouth as she stared at the open box on the table, the pile of photographs and court documents.

Lou's dad stopped too. 'Oh, Lou,' he said.

'When were you going to tell me?' Lou said quietly.

Her parents looked at each other, their faces pale, trying to communicate with their eyes, ask the other what to do, what to say.

Her dad cleared his throat, took a step back towards Lou, put his hand on her shoulder then steered her into the kitchen. 'Sit down.'

Her mum was breathing quickly, and her hands shook as she sat on a dining chair, still clutching the car keys.

Lou let herself be guided to the table. She sat opposite her mum, with her dad on her right-hand side. None of them looked down at the documents. They didn't need to; they all knew what was written there.

Lou's mum reached for her hands, but she pulled them away. 'Is this true?' she asked.

Her mum nodded, her face pale. 'Louise, we wanted to tell you before, but you've been going through so much lately and we thought it would be too much for you right now, when you've been so upset—'

Lou raised her hands in front of her in exasperation. Didn't they understand that she was the way she was because of *them*? Because of their lies? 'Upset? Seeing as you've dragged me to counsellors and therapists, I think it's fair to say that the way I've been feeling is a bit more than *upset*! But it all makes perfect sense now, don't you see? You're the reason I'm like this, why I'm your problem child. I always knew there was something!' She paused to take a breath.

'Lou, please...'

She looked at her mother's bloodshot eyes, her smeared mascara. She knew now, looking into that face, that this was why she felt so alone, because this woman was nothing to her. There had always been something blocking the relationship between them, she had thought, but now she knew it was the opposite – it was a *lack* of something. How could she have missed it? They looked nothing alike. Who *was* this woman who called herself her mother?

Lou snorted with laughter, though she wanted to cry. 'Now I know why Grandma always used to say to me, "You're your father's daughter": she was trying to tell me! No one ever said I was my mother's daughter, did they? Because I never was. I was my aunt's daughter.' She turned to her dad. 'How could you keep this from me?'

He looked up. 'You heard your mum, Louise. We did what we thought was best for you. We were always going to tell you, but it didn't seem like the right time...'

'Did *Ross* know about this? Is that why we always had to have secret sessions, why I wasn't allowed to know what you were whispering about in his room? It all makes sense now, all the questions he asked me about my childhood. He was trying to see what I knew! Did you put him up to it? Did he come running to you afterwards and reassure you that I knew nothing?'

'No, of course not. He didn't tell us anything about your sessions. Those sessions were for *you*, to help you!'

Lou pointed her finger at her dad. 'I'll tell you how you could have helped me – by being honest with me! By telling me this years ago, not waiting until I found out! You... you lied to me!'

'We didn't lie...' Her mum stood up and moved around the table towards her.

'Yes, you did! You lied to me every day by calling yourself my mother!'

Zoe froze, then retreated back to her side of the table. She nodded a few times, and spoke quietly. 'I'm sorry. Louise, I'm sorry we didn't tell you. But it doesn't change anything.'

Lou shook her head. 'Of course it does! This is my life. This changes everything!'

'Lou...'

She swiped away her dad's hand and swivelled in her chair to face him. 'Don't! You were in on this too! You all were!' She stood up, her chair scraping on the floor, and pushed past him towards the kitchen door. She stopped there and turned around to face them. 'This is *my* life, I'm not your little project!'

Lou expected them to stand up and run to her, to grab her and stop her from leaving, but they stared at her, stunned. Zoe's face was deathly pale and she looked like she was going to pass out; Lachlan didn't move except for the rapid pulsing of a vein in his temple. Lou hesitated for a moment, giving them one more chance, then shook her head at them and ran to her room.

She kept her door closed all day, all evening. She ignored her mother's pleas for her to come out and eat something, and let the scrambled eggs that her mother left outside her room go cold. She felt that old familiar numbness, but now at least she knew why she felt that way. There was a part of her missing. Her aunt – no, her mother – had given her away. She had been traded, a commodity to be commissioned and relinquished. Lou had also seen, in the box, letters to and from the lawyers, showing that Nadia and Eddie had tried to fight for her, to get her back, while Zoe and Lachlan did everything they could to keep her. Who could she blame for this: Nadia, who had given her away then fought – and failed – to get her back? Or Zoe, who had been her mum since the start, but had lied to her all these years? The court order had said that Nadia and Eddie should be involved in her life, and that Lou should have spent every second weekend with them, getting to know them and Charlotte, Violet and Harry, but that had never happened. Her aunt and uncle and cousins had lived overseas, and then in Sydney, for years, sometimes coming home for Christmas, but more often not. Why had Nadia given up on her so easily, after all that?

They were all as bad as each other: Nadia, Zoe, Eddie, Lachlan. They had all kept this from her. Had they thought about *her* when they sat in a lawyer's office and wrote her life story into a contract?

She took her school dictionary from her bookshelf and flicked through the pages. Relinquish – such an awful word. *To voluntarily cease to keep, or claim. To give up.* And that's why she should have been told. Because *she* was the one who was given up, given up on, the one whom someone – her own mother – ceased to keep. There was someone else waiting to claim her, to keep her, someone who didn't want to give her up, but that didn't matter to Lou as much as the fact that her mother – her real mother – had let her go.

–

The next morning, she walked into the kitchen. Her parents looked as if they hadn't slept – their eyes were red and puffy, with dark shadows. Lou could feel the air of defeat surrounding them both. She watched them for a moment until they suddenly realised she was there. Her mum stood and rushed towards her. 'Lou—'

'Don't.' Lou held up her hand. 'I need to see Nadia, I want to talk to her myself.'

There were no protests. 'OK, darling,' her mum said. 'I'll call her.'

Lou nodded, looking at the floor, and watched as a tear splashed on the tile next to her toe. She turned around and walked out again.

–

Lou hadn't slept, even for a moment. She knew this for certain because she had watched the digital clock next to her bed change, minute by minute, until she heard the clunk of the pipes that meant her dad had turned on the shower. She waited ten minutes until she knew he'd be finished, then went into her bathroom and showered too. If she was honest, she didn't really want to go any more, but she had to. She'd made such a fuss about it, caused so much hurt, and now everything had been arranged. Zoe was scared, Lou could tell from her desperate hugs, as if she was clutching onto Lou to stop herself from falling. She turned away to hide her tears, but Lou could see traces of them on her face.

Once she had dressed, Lou went through to the kitchen. Her dad was already there, wearing jeans and a checked shirt, freshly shaved. He was sitting at the table, eating toast spread with marmalade. There was a crumb at the corner of his mouth, shining orange in the light from the pendants hanging above the table. Lou wanted to reach over and flick the crumb away. Instead she smiled a little, then pointed to the corner of her own mouth. Her dad quickly wiped his face.

'All gone?' he asked.

She nodded. 'All gone.'

'Did you sleep OK?'

'Yeah, not bad.'

'Can I get you some breakfast?'

'I'll do it.' She walked to the pantry and scanned the plastic tubs filled with different cereals, then chose the muesli. The last thing she wanted to do was eat, but if she didn't he'd know how uncertain she was about doing this. What did she really think would happen? She wanted some answers. But to what questions? What could she ask that wouldn't make her sound selfish? 'How could you do this to me?' That would make it sound like her mum and dad were terrible parents, and Lou knew that really they weren't. She needed to find where she belonged amongst all this confusion, but she was frightened of pulling too far away from her parents in case she stretched their relationship so far that it broke.

'Is Mum coming?'

He sighed. 'No, I don't think so. She – we – thought it might be better to give you the space to do this without worrying about her feelings.'

'Is she OK?'

'Yes, darling, she's fine. Don't worry about her, or me. We're grown-ups, we know today is important for you, and we knew it would happen one day.'

Lou took the yoghurt from the fridge and added two dollops to her bowl, then sat down opposite her dad. Without looking up, he lifted the business section out of the paper and slid the rest over to her, then raised his eyes a little and smiled at her. Lou grinned, then looked down at the table to hide her sudden tears. She stirred her muesli, then brought the spoon to her mouth. She felt sick. Would it have been better not to know? If she hadn't broken in to her mum's work all those months ago, this would never have happened. She had been so stupid; she should have said no to Theo when he asked her to get the drugs. And where was he now? Funny how quickly people deserted you when things got tough. She wished she could go back to that day and, instead of telling him to pull into the car park of the practice, make him take her home. Then she would never have found out. But even as she thought it, Lou knew she didn't really mean it. She had to go through with today, because even if she'd never uncovered the truth, this secret had always been there, drifting around the house, and ever so softly slipping between them. The only way to bring them close together again, to make herself whole, was to clear those spaces by finding out the truth.

–

They arrived too soon. Lou wasn't ready. They had driven without speaking; she hadn't even complained that her dad had listened to an AM talkback show, because she knew that neither of them really cared what it was as long as it filled the silence in the car. She had thought it would take longer, thought that each moment would stretch out and she'd have plenty of time to work out what she was going to say. But the city was already behind them and they were climbing over the scarp, high into the hills.

Nadia had moved back to Western Australia just over a year ago. Lou hadn't been to visit her aunt at all, but she knew that Zoe had. Lou had overheard her parents whispering about it, about how Nadia had moved into a run-down old house in the same street that she'd lived before, when Lou was a baby, and that Eddie had stayed in Sydney. Lou also realised that it was when Nadia moved back that the fights between her parents had started. And when she herself had started to unravel.

The car shuddered as they drove up the long dirt driveway. The single-storey house ahead of them was made of timber, surrounded by native bush. Gum trees towered over the roof, cluttering the gutters with clumps of leaves. A wooden deck surrounded the house, with a faded red hammock swaying between two of the supporting posts. Cerise blooms of bougainvillea clambered over the fences, and puffs of yellow wattle flowers littered the few steps up to the house. The deck was dulled with dust.

Her dad switched off the engine, and the car ticked while Lou sat motionless in the passenger seat. 'Here we are.'

She nodded, then undid her seatbelt. Her dad did the same and got out of the car, then came round to her side and opened the door for her. She took a deep breath, swung out her legs and stood up.

He hugged her as they stood beside the car, looking at the house. 'I'll come up with you, then I'll go for a drive,' he said. 'I won't be long, I'll just give you some time to yourselves to talk. Call me if you need me back sooner.'

Lou tried to smile at him. 'Thanks, Dad.'

'I love you.'

'Me too.'

Her foot slipped a little as they trudged up towards the house. Just as they started to climb the wooden steps, the front door opened. Nadia was dressed in dark blue jeans as worn and soft as her face, looking far older than Lou remembered; but then again, it had been years since she'd seen her. Her fair hair was tied back in a ponytail with wispy grey hairs around her temples, and she held onto the door as if she might fall without its support. Lou stopped moving, unsure what to do: shake her hand, kiss her politely on the cheek, or run to her. She looked up at her dad, who put his arm around her and walked with her a step closer. As she looked back into her aunt's eyes, she saw Nadia's chin begin to twitch, and she no longer had a choice. She ran up the steps into her embrace.

-

Lou sat on the edge of the dining chair and looked around. A potbelly stove was in the centre of the space and the smell of years of woodsmoke lingered in the room. There was no television. In one corner of the room were two wicker couches on either side of a wooden coffee table. Beside one of the couches was a tall bookcase, the old-fashioned type with locked glass doors at the top. It was crammed with books, horizontal stacks piled on top of the vertical rows. Two frayed rugs covered the floor-boards: one under the coffee table, one under the dining table where Lou now sat. Nadia fussed behind her in the kitchen, which was small, with wooden cupboards. Utensils, blackened around the edges, dangled from a row of hooks above the old oven.

Nadia walked over and put two mismatched side plates down on the dining table, then returned with a white teapot and two mugs. 'I made a cake,' she said. 'I didn't know if you'd be hungry. Do you like tea? I did buy some lemonade, if you'd prefer. I didn't know what you liked...' She smiled sadly.

'Tea is good, thanks.' Lou squirmed in her seat.

Nadia was back in the kitchen now. 'I hope it tastes OK, the cake. I just iced it but I think it was still a bit warm so I'm praying it hasn't run too much. Hopefully it still tastes nice, anyway. It's lemon. From the garden. I always have so many lemons and limes and I don't know what to do with them all. When your cousins...' She paused. 'When Harry and the girls were little, I used to make them homemade lemonade. But now... it's not the same on my own. But I like the quiet, you know. Your uncle Eddie, he needs to be in the city for work. That's why he stayed in Sydney, he'll visit when he can...' She looked out the window.

Lou nodded. 'I'm sure the icing will be fine.'

Nadia brought the cake over on a plate, then sat down opposite Lou. 'Would you like some?'

'Please.' The last thing she wanted was cake, but she could see how hard Nadia was trying.

Lou watched her cut a big slice. She knew she wouldn't be able to eat it; her mouth was dry. She watched Nadia's hand as she gripped the knife, then looked down at her own, searching for similarities, shared imperfections. The way Nadia frowned as she tried to lift the slice of cake onto the small plate without dropping crumbs was the way she herself frowned. How could she not have noticed it before? Because her parents had kept her away from Nadia so she couldn't work out the truth. As her anger resurfaced, although she was no longer sure who she should be furious at, Lou twirled her ankle then tapped her foot, her ballet flat wiggling. How dare they all keep this from her?

'Here.' Nadia slid the plate towards Lou, then cut herself a slice. 'I'm glad you're here.'

'Me too.'

'Do you remember our old house?' Nadia said suddenly.

'No,' mumbled Lou.

'No. You wouldn't. It was close to here.' Nadia gazed at Lou with sad eyes. 'Louise. I never wanted it to be like this, you know?'

Lou shrugged. 'It's not your fault. Mum never wanted me to see you.'

Nadia shook her head slowly, then took a small piece of cake from her plate with her fingers and stared at it. 'It was hard. Hard for us all.' She suddenly raised her head. 'I've got something for you.'

Nadia stood up again, disappeared briefly down the hallway, then came back with a while muslin bag, tied with a ribbon at the top. 'Here,' she said, then sat down again.

Lou looked at the bag, then untied the ribbon and looked inside. There was a solid silver chain-link bracelet, laden with charms. Lou frowned, and looked up at Nadia.

'On your first Christmas, I don't know if you still have it, but I gave you a present, a bracelet with a charm on it.'

Lou nodded, her eyes filling with tears. 'Yes, it's always been in my mum's – Zoe's – jewellery box. It's too small for me now, though.'

Nadia smiled. 'It would be. You were so tiny then, I got the smallest bracelet I could. I bought you a new charm every Christmas; there are another sixteen here. I was worried I'd lose them so I put them all on a new bracelet for you. I should have sent them to your mum and dad every year, but...' Her voice trailed off.

Lou's eyes filled with tears as she handled the heavy, cool charms. A teddy bear, a horse, a little house with a door that opened. She spoke in a hoarse whisper as Nadia helped her fasten the bracelet around her wrist. 'Did Mum tell you not to contact me?'

Nadia's voice cracked. 'No, no. This wasn't your mum's fault. She tried to keep me involved, sent me pictures and videos of you, said I could come and visit you. It was my fault.'

Lou spoke loudly now. 'Don't defend her. She should have told me. I heard her, she told Dad that she wished they'd never done it, that they'd never had me.'

'Oh, Louise.' Nadia leaned over the table and put her hand on Lou's. 'She didn't mean that. I'm absolutely certain she didn't mean that. This... situation has been so hard on us all. There are so many things I regret – and I'm sure your mum feels the same – but you are not one of them! We could have done so many things differently, not been so naive. I... I thought I could just detach myself from you, think of you as my niece, myself as a babysitter. But as soon as I was pregnant, that was it. I just couldn't stop myself thinking of you as anything but my child. The day I had to hand you over...' She sat back again, held her hands palm to palm, then shook her head. 'That was the most devastating moment of my life. Letting you go.'

Lou looked up to the ceiling and tried to blink back her tears. 'Then why? Why did you? I hear you say that but all I know is that you just shut yourself off from me. I saw the court order – you had the chance to see me, for us to have some kind of relationship – the court said we could spend weekends and holidays together, I could have known you, known Charlotte and Violet and Harry instead of having no one.' She looked back at Nadia, into eyes fringed by fair lashes like her own. 'But you didn't. You gave me up again and I don't understand why!'

'I didn't want to!'

'But you did! You ran off to Singapore and never came back! You had me, then you let me go, then you had me again and then you did it all over again! No wonder Mum and Dad hate you! You shouldn't have done this to me, to us!' Lou stood up and gripped the edge of the table, still looking at Nadia. 'You have no idea, do you, no idea what you did to me.'

'Oh, Louise, you were just a baby...'

Lou gritted her teeth. Did she really not understand? 'I don't even know why I came here!'

'Louise—'

Lou's face was streaming with tears now. 'Did you think that we could just pick up where we left off?'

'I didn't… You were the one who wanted to see me! I would never have barged in and expected anything from you, I would never have disrupted your life like that if you—' Nadia's face was full of panic, and Lou could see how desperate she was to explain, but Lou *didn't* understand.

'So it's my fault?'

Nadia stood up and came round towards her. 'No, no, of course not, that's not—'

'Don't come near me!' Lou screamed. She could barely breathe; her chest was tight and she felt the familiar tingle around her mouth and in her fingers that told her she needed to get away, to calm down. Nadia's face loomed, distorted, and the space around it blurred. All Lou could hear now was the sound of her own blood whooshing in her ears, and the air whistling into her lungs and rushing out again too quickly. The room began to spin. She staggered backwards a few steps, then turned around and wrenched open the front door. She had to get out of here, away from the lies and the self-pity. She heard Nadia shouting, 'Louise! Come back! Where are you going?'

Lou jumped down from the deck; without thinking about what she was doing, she ran down the driveway, avoiding the fallen branches and tree roots that jutted into her path. Nadia was still calling behind her, but Lou wasn't listening any more. She squeezed her eyes shut for a moment, trying to clear the tears that continued to pour out. At the end of the driveway she turned right, away from the direction her dad had driven them from the city.

Where had he gone? They had all passed her around like a doll, a toy, pushed her and pulled her, and they were still doing it, even now. Lou kept running, though her calves and hamstrings burned on the steep road. Her flat shoes flapped and threatened to slip off as she ran. When she reached the top of the hill, she turned a corner and saw a clearing in the bush ahead of her. She stopped, gasping for breath.

She knew where she was. It was the place from the photo. Mundaring Weir. The dam where the body on the news was found, floating in the still, calm water.

Trying to catch her breath, she began walking towards the lookout on the hairpin bend ahead of her, listening to the loose dirt grinding under her shoes, the cries of the birds around her, and the vast, watery silence ahead. She reached the lookout and leaned on the railing. Below her, the water was still, and it stretched out across and along the valley. The massive concrete wall of the dam seemed much bigger than in the images she'd seen. The water level was low; the sheer wall, stained with water levels from years before, dropped away into the lake. Lou thought about that man, the one whose body was found here, wondered what he was thinking before he fell. Or jumped. She looked along the length of the dam wall, the round white building in the centre, and the flimsy fence on either side.

She turned and walked quickly away from the lookout, down some steps and onto the path that formed the top of the wall, the same path that she'd been on with Nadia in the photo. Where was the exact spot that it had been taken? It seemed important to find it. She kept moving, looking around for something she recognised. She had stared at the photo for so long that it was etched in her mind, impossible to forget.

'Louise!' The cry echoed around her in the still air. The birdsong paused as her own name repeated and faded in the vast hollow of the dam. Now she felt it again. The memory of being here.

'Louise!'

Lou looked back. Nadia was running along the path towards her, and behind Nadia was Lachlan. Nadia must have called him as she ran after Lou.

'Go away!' she yelled. 'Just leave me alone!'

'Come back. Please, Louise, just stop, stay right there!'

Lou covered her face with her hands and screamed. Why did they do this to her? What did Nadia care? She hadn't cared enough before, she had just disappeared with her other kids, her other family, and forgotten about her. And her dad, he was no better. Lying to her, along with the woman who called herself Mum, who hadn't even bothered to come out here with them and stand up to Nadia and fight for her daughter. She'd had it, with all of them. With her friends. With Ross and counselling. This wasn't her fault. *They* had done this to her. They all said that everything they had done had been for her, for Lou. But that wasn't how it had started. At the beginning, she was just an idea, a whisper of an imagined person. A dream. When did *her* story even begin? Her story began not at her birth, not even at her conception, but before that, at a moment of grief, at the agony of loss. And what was ever in it for Nadia? People didn't do things out of altruism, not really. People were selfish, Lou knew that. Nothing they ever did was completely about someone else, never mind an unborn child: that was just something people told themselves so they wouldn't have to admit their real reasons. Even saints did things because, ultimately, they wanted to end up in heaven. Nadia did it to prove something, to gain something. To be a martyr.

Lou felt the sun beating down on her shoulders, burning her skin, but she didn't move. Were there other children like her, children who had been relinquished? Children believing the myths that their parents had told them, stories trotted out so often that they became true? The whole lot of them – Zoe, Lachlan, Nadia, Eddie – had tricked themselves, tricked her, because it made it that bit easier. The truth, the truth that it was *never* about her, was brushed aside, like tucking back a hair that tickles your eye, until eventually you do it by sheer habit alone. Well, Lou had had enough of their lies.

She could no longer hear Nadia and her dad shouting, just her own sobs as she gripped the metal fence and thought about how it would feel to just fall down, down, down…

Chapter Thirty-One

Zoe watched her nieces and nephew run up the steps and across the lawn towards where she and Lachlan were waiting. Grinning, she stood up and opened her arms out wide to give them a hug. 'Hi! It's so good to see you all! Have you been having fun with Louise?'

As Charlotte told her about the tree house that Eddie had been building for them, Zoe kept glancing at the path, watching Nadia and Eddie slowly walking towards them, both focused on Louise in Nadia's arms. Zoe's stomach was in knots. She and Nadia had barely spoken since that day at the court, except to make arrangements for this visit. How could they ever renew their relationship after everything that had happened? But she knew that for this to work, for Louise to have a sense of a normal life, they had to try. She never wanted Louise to think that she was the cause of the breakdown of her family, or to hear them fighting over her like a toy. Louise was a child; they were adults. It was up to them to make this work.

As Nadia and Eddie came closer, Zoe saw that Nadia was crying. She bit her lip. Couldn't Nadia hold it together? The time for crying was over; they had to move on, for everyone's sake.

Zoe walked towards them, leaving Lachlan playing with the children. Seeing her, Eddie nodded and smiled, then walked past her, leaving the two sisters facing each other, about a metre apart. They were at the top of the hill, in the shade of the mature trees, surrounded by rose bushes. Nadia glanced up at Zoe, then looked back to Louise. Zoe felt as she had on the day Louise was born: she wanted to grab her and run away, but she also knew that Nadia needed time. But how much time? It had been decided, Zoe was Louise's mother in every sense of the word, except for the one link that could never be broken. And that was the link that kept Zoe tiptoeing around her sister, because she knew Nadia wasn't just a surrogate. She was Louise's mother too.

Zoe cleared her throat. 'How has she been?'

Nadia smiled sadly. 'Good as gold.' She blinked away some tears then looked up. 'She missed you.'

Zoe wanted to smile in relief but stopped herself. She took a step closer, and Louise began to squirm in Nadia's arms. Just as she had done that day in the hospital when Louise was born, Nadia closed her eyes and held the baby out in front of her, and Zoe lifted Louise into her own arms. She held her child close to her and breathed in the scent of unfamiliar shampoo, and the body that seemed to have grown so much in only one night.

'You OK?' she said quietly to Nadia.

'It was hard, harder than I thought. Hard for Louise, for the big kids...' Nadia gazed at the three older children, who were chasing each other around the picnic benches and barbecues.

Zoe looked over at them too. 'They seem happy.'

'They are. They were. I didn't sleep last night.' Nadia looked at Zoe. 'I thought I had what I wanted, Louise asleep in the house with all of us, waking up with us, and it is, it is what I want, but I think somewhere along the way I forgot that it isn't about me. It's about Louise. It's not fair on her, this confusion.'

Zoe frowned, her heart hammering.

Nadia wiped her eyes, looking drawn and defeated. 'Eddie was offered a job in the Singapore office. We weren't going to go – of course. It's too far from Louise. But we spoke this morning. He's going to take it. We're all going to go.'

Zoe's eyes widened. Did she want to take Louise with her to Singapore? 'What? What do you mean?'

'I'll talk to my lawyer again, explain it all, and get them to change the family court orders. She's your child, yours and Lachlan's. I'll still be her aunt, but we'll be gone for at least a couple of years. It'll be good for us, for the kids, to get away.'

'I don't understand. Nadia, you don't have to—'

Nadia held up her hand and looked Zoe in the eye. 'I'll be an aunt to her. No more.'

Zoe nodded, not sure whether to thank Nadia or pity her. She glanced at Lachlan, saw him watching them, and she wanted to grin, to run to him with Louise. But she also saw her sister, standing across from her, her world shattered. She took a step forward and hugged Nadia with her free arm, Louise between them, then turned and walked over to Lachlan and Eddie. She could tell from his sombre face that Eddie understood that Nadia had told her. His hand trembled when he reached out to give Louise a goodbye hug.

Zoe took Lachlan's hand and squeezed it. 'Let's go,' she whispered. 'We won't stay for the picnic.' They said goodbye to Charlotte, Violet and Harry, then Zoe looked back at Nadia one last time. She was staring up at the sky with wide, wild eyes, with her hand over her mouth; she looked broken. Just then, a kookaburra cackled, a sad, mocking laugh. Zoe resisted the urge to run to Nadia; she picked up Louise's bag, then walked back along the dam wall, listening to the echoes of their footsteps.

Chapter Thirty-Two

'Lou. Please.'

It was her dad, speaking slowly, softly, but with a note of terror in his voice that Lou had never heard before. She didn't turn; her fingers had frozen around the metal railing as she looked down. This hadn't been her intention, this wasn't how it was meant to turn out. She wanted them to leave her alone; with every step her dad and Nadia took towards her, she felt herself leaning closer to the rails. They were forcing her into this. She just wanted them to go. They were making it worse, not better.

'Louise. Come here. Please.' His voice broke into a sob.

Lou shook her head, left to right, left to right, again and again. 'Just leave me, Dad, please.'

'I can't.'

Her hands shook, and she gripped tighter to steady them. Her knuckles ached. She saw the green moss on the concrete wall below her, the smooth curve of it, and her stomach lurched.

'Louise.' It was Nadia this time. Lou turned her head. Her dad had let Nadia step in front of him, though she could tell by the way he leaned forward that he was ready to sprint, to leap. Lou had started something that she couldn't stop. It wasn't meant to be like this.

'Please, come here, come away from there,' Nadia said.

Lou felt the light touch of Nadia's hand on her shoulder. Nadia did no more, just left her hand there. Lou wanted to shove her away, to scream at her to leave her alone, but the touch felt so familiar, so right, and as she stood there sobbing, a warmth passed through her upper arm, her forearm, to her fingers; finally, as her tears subsided, Lou's grip relaxed and her hand fell. Nadia moved a step closer and put her arm around Lou's shoulders. Lou started to shake as Nadia led her back along the path, towards her dad. As they neared him, he held his arms open, and Lou felt Nadia's arm fall away. She took a step forward, leaned into him and held on tight.

She thought of her mum – Zoe – at home, how she'd be sitting at the kitchen with her shoulders hunched, staring at a cold cup of tea, trying to face once again the fear that she would lose her. Their dog would be lying at her feet, his head resting on his front paws. Lou wished she was at home with her now, sitting at that table with them, sipping on a hot drink.

Lou breathed deeply and turned around in her dad's arms. Nadia was watching her, ashen. They didn't say anything; they didn't need to. They gazed at each other, and Lou saw herself mirrored in Nadia's eyes.

At that moment, there, at the weir, in the silence, she heard it: the echo of a memory.

I see you, and I know you know I see you.

–

Lou opened the front door and slowly walked inside, her legs scarcely able to take her weight. She heard a chair scrape across the floor, and when she reached the threshold of the kitchen, her mum was standing, one hand on the back of the chair, the other open, pressed against her chest. She wore faded jeans and a white t-shirt, and her feet were bare. Her dark hair was loose, wavy. Her cheeks were blotchy, and her eyes were puffy, with no make-up. She and Lou looked at each other, silent.

Lou's dad came up behind her, and she saw her mum's eyes flicker towards him for a moment, communicating without words.

'We're home,' he said.

Zoe nodded, looking back at Lou. 'Louise. Are you OK?'

Lou's cheeks began to burn. She managed to nod, then her chin quivered and she ran into her mother's arms, to the space just in front of her heart, where they fitted together perfectly.

Chapter Thirty-Three

Over the weeks and months after Nadia and Eddie moved to Singapore, Zoe tried to re-create stability for Louise. She made sure Lachlan was taking his medication and attending his therapy appointments. He wasn't completely better, but he was getting there. She often had to bring him back when he stared off into the distance, his face haunted; she held him when he woke from nightmares, sobbing and sweating; she had to stop herself reacting when he flinched at her touch or his rage spilled out at her. But she could also see him, her husband and Louise's father, slowly returning, and so she held tightly onto the frayed edges of him and their life together. He started looking for another job, and that was enough for Zoe, for now.

One morning, as she stood outside the front door putting Louise in her pram so the three of them could walk to the shops, the postman's van pulled up. He flung open his door and jumped out, then hurried towards the gate. Zoe met him there, scribbled her signature on the electronic pad, and took the parcel he handed her. She frowned; she wasn't expecting anything. It was addressed to *The McAllister family.* She recognised the handwriting, and looked at the postmark: it had been sent from Singapore.

Her hands began to shake and she ran back inside, pushing the pram just inside the door. 'Lachlan!'

'Coming!'

She ran into the bedroom, where he was sitting on the bed tying the shoelaces of his sneakers. 'Lachlan, look!'

'What is it?'

'I don't know. It's from Nadia.'

She watched his face whiten. 'Well, open it.'

Zoe nodded, then sat down next to him, her mouth dry. The rectangular parcel was wrapped in a few layers of thick brown paper. She put a finger under one of the seams and ripped it. She peeled off the paper until she saw the colour turquoise. She stopped, realising what it was. 'It's the box,' she whispered. 'The box I told you about.'

Lachlan frowned. Zoe tore off the rest of the paper. The turquoise box was more battered than the last time she'd seen it, and the lid was secured by an elastic band. Tucked under the band was a folded piece of thick cream-coloured writing paper. Zoe lifted up the elastic band and removed the paper, then unfolded it.

These belong to you x

She glanced at Lachlan, who took the note from her and read it. Zoe pulled the elastic band off the box, and then removed the lid. On the very top was a photograph of Louise with Nadia. Louise was smiling; Nadia was gazing at her sadly. Zoe's heart pounded. She knew exactly when it had been taken: she could see the lake in the background, the milky water reflecting the blue sky and the clouds. She held it, trembling, towards Lachlan. 'She must have taken this before she told us, that day. When she was walking over to give Louise back to us.'

He nodded, and Zoe saw the tears in his eyes. She riffled through the box, through the photos and scans she'd seen that day in Nadia's house. She wiped her eyes with the back of her hand, not wanting to damage any of these precious mementoes with her tears. She saw again Nadia's face in that photo, and thought about what she'd done for Zoe and Lachlan, for Louise, and about how it must have felt to let her go. She leaned into Lachlan and he held her to him. 'Do you think she kept copies of these, Lachlan? I hate to think of her left with nothing.'

'I don't know,' he mumbled, his voice thick. 'But she doesn't need these to remember, Zoe. She hasn't been left with nothing.'

'I should have called her. I've just let her move away, and now I feel like I've lost my sister. It should be me sending *her* photos of Louise.' Zoe sniffed. 'I should call her. Should I call her?'

Lachlan sighed. 'Not now. There's plenty of time. Come on.' He stood up. 'Let's look at this later. Louise is waiting for us.'

Zoe hesitated, then left the box on their bed and followed him to the front door. He was right. The photos and documents could wait. Louise was waiting for them.

Acknowledgements

Let Her Go would not have become the book it is today without the support of my publisher, Vanessa Radnidge, and my agent Benython Oldfield, who both encouraged me to develop a vague idea into the novel that it is now.

Thank you to the entire team at Hachette Australia, particularly Matt Richell, Maric Isaacson, Fiona Hazard, Anna Hayward, Karen Ward and Clara Finlay, and to the rest of the staff of Zeitgeist Media Group, especially Sharon Galant. I feel very fortunate to work alongside such talented, enthusiastic and lovely people.

For reading early drafts and providing honest (and sometimes blunt!) feedback, thanks to Vicky Dawes, David Thornby and Rebecca Freeborn.

I'm lucky enough to be part of a writing group of very talented West Australian women writers who looked over some chapters with critical and experienced eyes; thanks to Natasha Lester, Annabel Smith, Amanda Curtin, Sara Foster and Emma Chapman.

Thank you to those who helped me to research the world of infertility and surrogacy: Anne Wigham, who talked me through the complicated surrogacy procedures and processes; Julia Barker, who helped me with the legal research; and the women who were brave and kind enough to share their stories with me.

And finally, thank you to Will, Isobel, Isla and Olivia, and to my family, both near and far.